Loose Lips

Loose Lips

Teresa McClain-Watson

sepia

★BET BOOKS

BET Publications, LLC

SEPIA BOOKS are published by

BET Publications, LLC
c/o BET BOOKS
One BET Plaza
1900 W Place NE
Washington, DC 20018-1211

All Kensington Titles, Imprints, and Distributed Lines are available at
special quantity discounts for bulk purchases for sales promotions,
premiums, fund-raising, and educational or institutional use. Special
book excerpts or customized printings can also be created to fit specific
needs. For details, write or phone the office of the Kensington special
sales manager: Kensington Publishing Corp., 850 Third Avenue, New
York, NY 10022, attn: Special Sales Department, Phone: 1-800-221-
2647.

BET Books is a trademark of Black Entertainment Television, Inc.
SEPIA and the SEPIA logo are trademarks of BET Books and the BET
BOOKS logo is a registered trademark.

ISBN 0-7394-3476-4

First Printing: May 2003

Printed in the United States of America

*To my husband, Johnny,
my knight in shining armor*

ACKNOWLEDGMENTS

I owe a debt of gratitude to a vast number of people who helped me along the way. To name but a few: Fred McClain Sr. for believing that anything is possible; Steven Murray for giving me my first writing job; Minnie Hogan for her dedicated service to mankind; Marilyn Enos Upthegrove, Deborah Lee, and Betty Gainous, friends for life; Annie Ruth Brookins and Annette White for their great encouragement; Dolphus "Buddy" Jordan for never allowing my supply of paper to run short; Glenda Howard-King, my editor; Frank Weimann, my agent; and a host of family, friends, and well-wishers.

NOT MY TYPE

He was a hero in the community, a sixties activist turned successful businessman who knew how to keep a low profile. My editor wanted me to interview him for inclusion in our newspaper's "Where Are They Now?" series. A good assignment, I thought, because I respected the brother too. That is, until, in the middle of our interview, he leaned back in the executive chair in his spacious office, an office that overlooked a sweeping view of the Atlantic Ocean, and tried to hit on me.

"I've never met a reporter quite like you," he said, and I was thinking it was a compliment, given the probing questions I had just asked him. But then he added: "You fine, girl, you know that?"

At first I just stared at him. The brother had been top-rate professional throughout our time together, reaffirming in my mind why he deserved his hero status. His sudden lapse into a petty flirt surprised me. "I don't know what you mean," I decided to say.

"Come on, Josie Ross. You know exactly what I mean. You're fine. You got it going on. Baby got back, you hear me? You're the finest-looking sister I've ever seen."

I shook my head. I couldn't play the game even if it was the only game in town. "You expect me to believe that?" I asked him.

He hesitated, as if annoyed that I would even deign to question his wild assertion. "Yes, I expect you to believe it. It's the truth."

"You're telling me that you've never laid eyes on a woman finer than me?"

He smiled. "That's what I'm talking about."

"I'm the finest one?"

"The undisputed finest. In my humble opinion."

"Either you're lying or you don't get out much. Now which is it?"

His smile disappeared. Just like that. And that, of course, marked the end of our interview. But tough. I wasn't wasting my time on his or anybody else's bullshit. These guys know what they're doing. Lay a few lines on her. Loosen her up. Get her in bed. That was their game and I wasn't playing it. Pure and simple. I used to watch my mother in action. After my father died when I was twelve years old, she played the game. Thought she was good at it too. Thought she wasn't being played because she wanted it just as bad as the guy. Until the guy left. Then she'd cry all night long on my little shoulders, cry and curse life and get angry with me because I didn't have the answers either. Then she'd spend all day nursing her broken heart, vowing never again to let love make a fool out of her. Until the next love of her life showed up. Then the game was on again. And I saw my sisters in action, year after year, falling into deep depressions and wanting to kill themselves because some man wouldn't act right. Please. Who needed all of that drama? I could do bad by myself.

I believed all of this, however, before I met Ben. Judge Benjamin Braddock. Unlike the community hero who tried to hit on me, or all of those losers who dropped in and out of my mother's life, Ben Braddock was a different kind of man. He changed my entire views about love and happiness and he showed me how the good life was more than just avoiding bad experiences. And it was all good, for a while. But then the bullshit came. And it came like rain and muddied up everything I thought was so clear and easy to see, until nothing was clear and nothing, not even Ben, was what it seemed.

It all went down a little over three months ago. I lived in Jacksonville, Florida, in a condo in Baymeadows, and I woke up that morning expecting a normal day. Finish my story on the death penalty. Work on new assignments. Meet my best friend, Scotty, for dinner. A regular, ordinary day. It turned out, however, to be everything but.

I woke up to a quiet home, a big, somber town-house-style condominium with a large living room, kitchen, and fireplace downstairs, and a big bedroom with bath upstairs where, Scotty was always quick to point out, there had yet to be a man in that bed or showering in that bath. But I always took his little offhand remarks in stride. I didn't play that hit-and-run shit, that was the deal. Nobody was getting any wham-bams off of me. I saw what that scene did to my mother and my sisters, how their entire lives became unbearable because love went south. I wasn't going out like that.

So my work was the center of my existence. And as I stepped into the shower on the morning of my fateful meeting with Ben, it remained front and center in my life. I had no idea that my ironclad worldview on life and love and work and games was about to crumble.

I stood in my shower, the warm water careening down and relaxing every muscle of my body. When I caught myself falling asleep standing up, I jerked my head back, waking myself up, and got out.

I stood in front of my bathroom mirror and stared. I was twenty-eight years old but had been told countless times that I looked younger. Something about my eyes, they'd say. They were pear-shaped hazel eyes, more green than gray, but stood out strikingly bright against my brown skin. I was slender in appearance—slender shoulders, slender arms—but I had just enough hips and backside and boobs to elevate my shape from that straight-up-and-down look to a sister who just might have it going on.

Not that I felt as if I did. I didn't. I was nothing special, in my view, just a hardworking girl who decided long ago to speak the truth regardless of the consequences. My hairstyle consisted of neat, long braids most of the time, I favored African dress styles, and I was undoubtedly obnoxious in the way I played my music loud and drove my car fast and spoke my mind freely, maybe too freely. But guys seemed turned on by me, almost to the point of obsession, and not a day would go by when I wasn't approached by some man who just knew beyond a shadow of a doubt that I was the woman for him.

"God told me you gonna be my wife," one man said, coming up to me.

"He did?" I asked. "Well, He forgot to tell me."

"I'm not asking for a long-term commitment," another guy said to me. "I just want you to be the mother of my child."

"I'll be the mother all right," I said, "but it ain't gonna be of your child."

"You sooo good looking," yet another man said, "you make ugly pretty!"

I looked at him. "But you don't," I said.

It all bordered on insanity and I just couldn't take it seriously. How could the brothers think for a second that a self-respecting, smart sister was going to fall for that hokeydoke? Not this sister anyway. They were the fool of the fools if they thought I was going to fall for that game.

After showering I dressed quickly, and by nine-fifteen was in my car—a flame-red Mustang Sports Coupe—and was driving across the Fuller Warren Bridge, heading for downtown Jacksonville. I had moved to Jacksonville from my home state of Alabama four years ago, and the only reason I relocated at all was that the *Gazette* offered me a job worth traveling for. Back then my only knowledge of the town was that the Jaguars played there and it was the corporate headquarters of the big Winn Dixie supermarket chain. It turned out to be a nice little bustling metropolis after all, populated by a million-plus people, with museums and coffee shops, libraries and art galleries galore. It was also a port town surrounded by water and beautiful bridges, like the sloping Buckman or the more hectic Fuller Warren, and each side of town seemed like a town unto itself: Arlington, the Beaches, San Marco, Baymeadows. Everybody converged, however, in traffic, where distinctiveness was less precise, where the flow of cars was as fickle as the town itself, where traffic was either so scarce the roads looked ghostly, or bumper to bumper.

It was bumper to bumper when I hit the road, but that didn't stop me from being the epitome of the irresponsible driver. I was checking out my makeup in the rearview, constantly fluffing my braids, drinking my homegrown cappuccino, and changing CDs from Lauryn Hill—sister girl was cool but I was tired of her—to Janet Jackson, still my ace boon coon. She was singing her *Nasty* CD and I was moving and grooving to the sound of the acoustics with no regard whatsoever for those in surrounding cars who were rubbernecking just to look at me, causing me to really lay it on thick then: bouncing my shoulders and nodding my head and singing loudly with Janet J about those nasty boys too.

But my loud music and hyperactivity weren't in vain because, by the time I arrived at work, I was pumped and ready for whatever the day might bring. The famed *Gazette* building was three miles north of Alltel Stadium where the Jaguars played, and it was located on the west end of Forsyth Street. It was a brown and yellow ten-story building in desperate need of a paint job. In its glory days of old it was heralded as the premier newspaper in northeast Florida, with a wall of Pulitzers and Rodgers and Allendales to prove it. Now it was just a liberal rag in competition with the *Daily News,* a conservative rag, and both papers together couldn't hold a candle to the *Florida Times-Union,* the new leader in town. But I always felt alive when I saw the old building. The *Gazette* men and women were warriors, fighting for civil rights when it wasn't popular to do so, and women's rights when it wasn't cool. And even with the turning tide, where so-called compassionate conservatism hijacked liberal values and made a mockery of them, the *Gazette* still stood liberal and proud because somebody had to buck the tide. And since I was well known for bucking too, it seemed to be the perfect fit.

I parked my car in the half-empty lot on the side of the building and hurried toward the steps, my briefcase and hobo bag slinging as if they were empty, my high heels stepping as if I had no time to waste.

I was wearing a pantsuit made out of African kitenge cloth, and it consisted of a long shirtdress over a pair of matching flair-legged pants, coming down to the top tip of my newest pair of Anne Klein's bow slide shoes. My coworkers, especially my African-American colleagues, found my taste in clothing odd and often could not hide their displeasure. "You dress too ethnic for me," one sister came out and told me. "I'm not dressing for you," I told her. Another sister pulled me aside to remind me that I was a professional journalist, not some African scrub woman, and should dress as such. "All those bamarams you be wearing make us look bad, girl," she said as she pulled and tugged on the tight skirt of her tight suit that barely fit her tight ass. But all of that pulling and tugging didn't make her check out her own appearance, she was too busy complaining about mine. "We have arrived," she said. "We want to blend in like everybody else. But how can we blend at all when you keep walking in here like you're Mrs. Kunta Kinte?"

I'd been called worse, let me tell you, so I ignored the sister. There were only twelve African-Americans working for the entire organization and I was the youngest and the most vocal, so I guess I kept the rest of them embarrassed and off balance. Not that my white colleagues took to me either. They didn't. While the blacks were complaining that I was too "ethnic" and wanted me to tone it down, the whites complained that I was too radical and needed to tone it down. So I was mainly a group of one, running alone, working alone, deciding that I wasn't going to let some uptight females bother me. I was Josie Ross, nothing more, nothing less, and they could take me or leave me. They could kiss my ass, okay? But I was cool about it. They had the right to talk their talk, even if they didn't know what the hell they were complaining about.

I shrugged off the thought of all that negative stuff and walked up the steep steps that led to the *Gazette*'s front entrance. The flags that hung full staff in front of the old building were flapping briskly in the wind, and the *Gazette*'s logo—a pair of watchful eyes hovering above a painted Jacksonville skyline—and its motto—WHERE THE RIGHTS OF CITIZENS DARE TO BE HEARD—sat atop the building like a warning. *All right, Josephine,* it seemed to say. *Don't let the bullshit alley you're about to enter disturb you. This isn't about you. This is about the citizens. Your readers. The voiceless.*

I often referred to the inside of the *Gazette* as bullshit alley because there was always mess going on. First I had to pass Leroy, the front-desk security guard. He could always be counted on to jog over to the elevator where I stood and compliment me endlessly on what he perceived to be my enormous beauty. I'd tell him thank you and then ignore him, because he annoyed the hell out of me, but he never, not ever, seemed to care how I felt.

"It's a crime to look that good," he said. "And that pantsuit you're wearing. Uh-uh-uh. It's so different. So African. I bet you won't find an outfit like that on them picnic tables at Kmart's."

I pressed the elevator button eagerly, as if my repetitive pressing could hasten the opening of the doors. I liked Leroy okay and I understood that he was just trying to front, but I always knew that one day I would have to shine on his behind if he didn't ease up. But there was something pathetic about him, the way he stood there with his wide ears and sad eyes, praising my life as if he hated his own, not having a clue that my gold didn't glitter either, so I would usually cut him some slack and ignore his irritating comments.

But I just wasn't in the ignoring mood that morning. The *Gazette*'s logo was still my warning, but I wasn't heeding it. "Like, what is your problem?" I asked him and finally stopped pressing the elevator button.

His smile lingered longer, as if he didn't even hear me, and then it suddenly disappeared. "My problem?"

"Yes! You know I don't like it when you come at me like this, but you don't care. You do it every morning."

He seemed immediately defensive, as if he was finally being found out. "Do what?" he asked. "What I do every morning? I was just giving you a compliment."

"You were just hitting on me, Leroy."

"What? Hittin' on you? You crazy."

"I'm crazy?"

"Yeah, you crazy. I was just giving you a compliment. You too good for a compliment now?"

He was getting loud in his defensiveness, so I decided to pursue it no further. "Forget it," I said.

"You don't tell me what to forget," he snapped. "Forget you!"

The elevator doors finally opened and I hurried inside. Leroy continued to stand there, his anger still rising within, his body tense and unable to stay still. As the elevator doors began to close, our eyes eventually met, and I knew then that he was angry all right, but he was also disappointed. I was his ideal woman, some meek little innocent neophyte who, in his eyes, couldn't harm a flea. Now he knew better. He knew, like my mother always said, that I was hell on two legs. Watch out, in other words.

My escape from Leroy's mess was short-lived, however, because as soon as the elevator doors opened on the third floor and I walked down the narrow hall that led to the newsroom, I had to contend with more of the same.

First there was Mike Cooper. Coop, as we called him. He sat near the entranceway and you couldn't walk into the newsroom without passing his desk. He was a sports reporter who was famous for overly praising athletes, no matter what their vice. He was well liked and admired around the office because he was chummy with half of the Jaguars and many other big-name athletes across the country. I, however, was no member of his admiration society. To me he was just a middle-aged party boy who drank too much and tried too hard to be a player.

"Do my eyes deceive me," he said as I walked in, "or did the most beautiful girl in the world just walk into this place?"

"Can it, Coop," I said as I walked on by. He laughed out loud.

Then there was Lester, the fashion editor, or fashion police, as we called him. Many thought of him as a little mousy, bookwormish man, maybe even a homosexual, but I knew better than that. Boyfriend was a womanizing freak, who got his jollies in the fetish scene, who wouldn't be caught dead with a human being but give him a shoe or an undergarment and brother man was good to go. He was leaving the newsroom as I was coming in, and he made it a point to press his stubby little fingers to the hem of my dress sleeve and feel my material. "Kitenge," he said. "Nice." And then he smiled his reptilian smile and slithered away.

Eddie Harris was less obvious than most, who didn't go for that complimenting routine at all, but was more slick with his game. He spoke only curtly to me, I spoke back, but as soon as I walked away from his desk he would begin his routine of lustful looking, as if he could undress me with his eyes. I usually ignored him too. But not that morning. I turned back toward him, quickly, catching him in his stare, his eyes so lust-filled they looked drowsy.

"You need to cut that shit out," I said to him.

"Cut what out? What are you talking about?"

"Stare at your wife," I said. "Not at me." Then I turned and headed for my desk.

"You know you like it," he said in a low voice, but I heard him.

"Yo mama like it," I replied without looking back.

Others in the newsroom looked my way, and I could see on their faces that, to them, I was the one out of line. Eddie was just being Eddie, after all, their looks of disgust seemed to say, and everybody knew how Eddie could be. What was my problem?

I dropped my briefcase and hobo bag to the floor and sat down at my desk. It was always my fault, no matter what. Guys could hit on me, make catcalls at me, and I was supposed to just sit back and take it. And when I didn't feel like taking it anymore, then I was the bitch, I was the drama queen, I was out of line. So I gave up. I threw my hands in the air and gave the fuck up. I was never able to please people, even when I tried my damndest, so I completely stopped trying.

My desk was in the middle of the large newsroom, and the newsroom itself was a wide-open space filled with rows and rows of desks topped off with computers and ringing phones. The long, beige-colored walls were lined with numerous award plaques, citations, stand-out newspaper clippings, and framed pictures of old white guys with fat jowls and forced smiles, known by us as the Geritol gents, but known by everybody else as the founders. The columnists had the choice workstations, because they were the ones with the following, and the ace reporters, who usually handled the police beat or city hall, wrote their own tickets too. I mainly handled special assignments, although I'd been known to handle every beat imaginable, depending on what the bosses wanted.

But the least among us were the Bullshit Brigade, a group of five female reporters who thought they were the bomb but were nothing more than pompous instigators, and I gave them their name when I realized what they were up to. There were Cathy, Monica, and Staci, three white women who thought the sun rose and set just because they graced the land, and Andrea and Helen, two sisters who didn't think the sun rose and set because of them, but knew it did.

Helen was the ringleader. Helen McCoy. She sat three desks in front of mine and would lord it over the newsroom as if she were actually in charge of something. Like me, she was African-American, never married, and full of opinions. But she was one sister I couldn't stand.

When I first started working for the *Gazette* she tried to get me to join her posse. I thought she was cool back then so I went out a few times with the crew and partied with them. But then I started paying attention. And it didn't take long for me to see that they were some of the most conceited females I'd ever met. Life was a game for them and it was all about how good you looked and how much money you had and how they could manipulate and use you to their advantage. And they were petty as hell. They'd laugh at overweight people, point fingers at gays, and ridicule the unattractive. When I started turning down their invitations, because I wasn't even trying to live my life like that, I became the outcast, the sister with an attitude, the turncoat. So Helen and I locked horns on almost everything soon after, and she made it her business to constantly try to push my buttons.

She was in her late thirties, short and shapely, with banana-colored skin and thick red lips that she always had to suck just before she got ready to speak as if the queen mum herself were about to make her opinion known. And when she spoke I wanted to crawl under a table. She knew everything there was to know about everything and was so wrong most of the time that it astounded me. But she didn't care about facts. Oh no. Facts were of little consequence to a know-it-all like her. And her partners helped to keep the delusion going, treating the sister as if she were in the same league intellectually with Maya Angelou, Toni Morrison, and Condoleezza Rice!

She also thought she was God's gift to men, which astounded me even more. Not that she was ugly, but she certainly wasn't in the gift category. She had blond-colored weaved hair down her back, for instance, and when she walked she would jerk her head so hard that her hair often flew around violently, whipping people in the eye and face and upside their heads. She thought it was cute. "It's just a hair whip," she'd tell the offended party. "Good gracious!"

Well, one day sister girl tried that hair whip on me, and then she tried to cock an attitude because I didn't like it. But before she could move a step away from my desk, it was *my* attitude that was cocked. I grabbed that hair, whipped her around, and snatched out a sizable track of weave. She looked at my hair-filled hand, figured out the connection, and then touched the brand-new bald spot on her head. And without saying another word, she ran from the newsroom in tears. She didn't return to work for days after that. But hey. I didn't feel bad at all. I wasn't whipping my hair in her face. And it for damn sure was the first and last time she whipped hers in mine.

But what I mainly disliked about Helen McCoy was her nosiness. Sister girl gossiped about everybody every single day, often telling so many contradictory lies on people that I wondered how she could keep a straight face most of the time. When I arrived in the newsroom, for instance, she, Andrea, Cathy, and Monica were huddled at her desk gossiping. She looked up when I walked in and then started whispering about me. I held my hand up the way teenagers do to disrespect somebody, gave her that "what-*ever*" look just to let her know that I knew what she was up to, but then I went on about my business. Girlfriend wasn't going to worry me that day. But before I could barely place my hobo bag in my desk drawer and turn on my computer, she already had coaxed Cathy into coming over to my desk to bother me. And then she and the others, like a pack of wolves, followed Cathy.

"May I ask you a question, Josie?" Cathy asked. I hesitated, because I knew in the end it was going to be foolishness, and then I looked up. Cathy was about my age, had a tall, thin body, a wide face, and short, blond hair. She wasn't much of a reporter, most of her work was puff pieces inside the Lifestyle section, but when she wasn't around Helen and the gang, she was almost bearable.

"What's up?" I said to her as I slid a disk into my A-drive.

"Men like you," she said. I looked at Helen, who was, by now, standing beside Cathy. She rolled her eyes and sucked her teeth. Then I looked at Cathy. I wasn't sure if she had just asked a question or was rendering an opinion, so I didn't respond.

"It's about Curtis," she said.

It was always about Curtis. "What about him?" I asked.

"He's changed so much, Josie. When we first got married it was great. He treated me like I was his princess. But everything's changed. First he wanted us to buy this ridiculous sports car. I didn't want us to, we can't afford it really, but I didn't argue with him. Now he doesn't want, you know, regular sex anymore."

I looked around at the male reporters who sat near my desk. All of them pretended to be busy, all seemingly reading something, but I knew they were all ears.

"What kind of sex does he want if not regular sex?" I asked.

Helen sucked her lips, which warned everybody that she was about to speak, and then she said, "He wants her to get his freak on!" and snapped her fingers. Her partners thought it was so funny. I thought it was juvenile.

"He wants to do me from the back," Cathy said.

"Okay," I said.

"And from the armpit. And the elbow. And the neck. And from under my feet."

A frown came on my face as even imagining those positions was impossible. And Cathy was absolutely stricken with the fear that she would actually have to fulfill her husband's barbaric wishes. I decided to disabuse her of that notion immediately. "You shouldn't have to do anything you don't want to do," I told her. "A marriage isn't about what the husband wants all the time. The wife is an equal partner. She got a say-so too. And if you don't want to sit on his face or let him ride you like you're some damn pony, then you shouldn't have to."

"But he said he'll leave me if I don't do it."

"Then let him leave!"

"But I can't just let him leave, Josie. I love him."

"Then ride, baby, ride. But if it's not what you want, then to hell with it. You have feelings too."

Helen's long, narrow face betrayed her disgust with me as she pulled Cathy by the sleeve. "Come on, Cat," she said. It was obvious that she and the others had given her the exact opposite advice. Cathy thanked me, more out of common courtesy than heartfelt appreciation, and she and her posse went back to their huddle to decide what next to do about her problem. "She's got all this advice," I heard Helen tell her. "At least you've got a husband. Where's hers?"

I laughed out loud. "In the same place as yours!" I yelled to the never-been-married Helen. She frowned. But before she could zap me back, or even attempt to, the barely discernible Hispanic accent of our city editor could be heard over the intercom. "Josie Ross!" he yelled.

"Yes, sir!" I yelled back with a smile, and hurried to his office.

Mel Sanchez was a stern, no-nonsense man who chain-smoked cigars and complained endlessly about the sorry state of journalism in today's society. The twenty-four-hour cable news networks drove him nuts. And the tabloids? Forget about it. They didn't practice journalism, but sadism, in his view. Although he was born and raised in the Bronx, New York, the son of a German mother and Puerto Rican father, he was most proud of his Puerto Rican heritage, even to where he would lay the accent on thick when anybody had any doubts about his true ethnicity. He was a man in his late fifties, with brownish gray hair that shagged down to his neck, watery green eyes, a kind but aged face, and a body thin and frail from too much attention to his work and too little to himself. Although most of the reporters found Mel's almost revivalistic liberalism a liability to the paper, I found him refreshing. Here was a man, I thought, who knew what he believed in and didn't give a damn if others disagreed. And since I was usually in lockstep with him on almost every issue, his style was my inspiration.

"Sit down, JR," he said, and I quickly obliged. If he wasn't calling me JR, which I didn't like at all, he was calling me Josie Ross, which I wasn't too crazy about either because Mel had a knack for making my first and last name come together as if they were one name. Like EddieMae. Florajean. JosieRoss. But Mel didn't seem to mind that I didn't like the way he pronounced my name. He thought he was being cute, maybe even clever. But he was just being Mel.

He leaned down from his six-two frame and sat on the edge of his desk. He took off his glasses and rubbed the bridge of his nose. He was tired, as usual, from too many fifteen-hour days, and simple matters, like giving an assignment, seemed exhausting.

"What's up, Chief?" I finally asked and crossed my legs. He looked at me, from my crossed legs, up to my chest, and then our eyes met. He smiled.

"You look pretty today."

"Thanks. But I know that's not why you called me into your office."

He folded his arms. "And how do you know that?"

"Come on, Mel."

"I liked your article on the death penalty."

"Then why did you return it?"

"Because, like most everything you write, it's too judgmental."

"You didn't agree with it?"

"I agree with every word you wrote. But that's not the point. You were supposed to be writing a balanced story on Florida's death penalty, not an opinion piece."

"It was the truth, Mel. How can anybody be in favor of the death penalty even with all this new DNA information? Information, I'll remind you, that's turning once condemned men out of prison left and right. And the fact that minorities are incredibly overrepresented means something too."

"Okay, okay," he said and threw up his hands. "Just tighten it up a little and I'll run it. I didn't bring you in here for a sermon. I've got an assignment."

"Good," I said. "I only hope it's something juicy, because another 'Where Are They Now?' story isn't my idea of a load of fun, know what I'm saying?"

"Ben Braddock's office has agreed to an interview."

I couldn't respond immediately because I didn't get it. I hadn't heard anything newsworthy concerning Judge Benjamin Braddock. "Why?" I finally asked Mel. "What has he done?"

"Mr. Lawrence Dinkle, our great managing editor, thought it would be a neat idea if we were to include him in our 'Rising Black Professional Class' series."

"Wait a minute here. Let me get this straight. You want me to interview Benjamin Braddock, Judge Benjamin Braddock, for our series on great African-Americans?"

"Right."

"Why would we want to include that pompous idiot? What interesting thing has he ever done?"

"Dinkle feels he represents a segment of the black upper class that is too often overlooked."

"You mean the Uncle Toms?"

Mel almost smiled. "Why do you do this to me, JR? Why can't I give you an assignment the way I do everybody else and you just kindly take it and go on and do your job? Why does everything have to be a battle for you?"

"But why would we want to include a guy like that? He doesn't represent black people."

"Larry Dinkle thinks he does."

"Then Larry Dinkle's a damn fool."

"He has also pointed out to me that Judge Braddock happens to be a close, personal friend of Marshall London, the publisher of this paper, so whether we like it or not, Braddock will be included."

"So that's the deal. Politics as usual. And here I was thinking we were only profiling courageous blacks, those sisters and brothers who overcame racism and sexism and all the other *isms* to represent the race with dignity and class. Now you want to throw that self-righteous, right-wing Ben Braddock in the pile. He doesn't deserve it, Mel. Just because he's powerful and has friends in high places doesn't make him worthy."

"Have you ever met the man, JR?"

"What does that have to do with it?"

"Just answer my question."

"I don't need to meet him. I know his views. I read the papers."

Mel sighed and shook his head. "You're a lost cause, you know that? The *Florida Trailblazers* magazine just named Braddock citizen of the year. The American Bar Association named Braddock one of the best judges in the country. Over fifty organizations across this state have bestowed awards on him for his contributions to the judicial process. Yet you, Miss Josie Ross, don't feel he's worthy. Just go interview the man, all right?"

"But have you read some of his views, Mel?"

"Yes, I've read 'em. Is he a liberal-minded individual? No, he's not. But that doesn't make him any less formidable than all the other profiles we did."

"But why do I have to interview him, Mel? Why not Eddie Harris? He's into that black Republican bullshit. I'm not."

"You don't have to be into it. All you have to do is interview the man. He's agreed to sit down with one of our reporters after morning recess, which is around ten, ten-thirty. Which means you need to get going."

"But he's a right-wing, ultraconservative nutcase!"

"He's not ultra anything and he's no nuttier than you and me and our left-wing, bleeding-heart liberal rhetoric. Now get over there, Josie Ross, and do your job."

"I'm serious, Mel. I can't deal with guys like Braddock."

"Well, that's just terrific. A tough broad like you can't deal with the big, bad man."

"That's not what I mean. I mean why does it have to be me?"

"Because you're a left-wing, bleeding-heart liberal and he's, well, not. You won't let him b.s. his way through the interview. You'll keep him on the ropes. Don't badger the man, however. But be firm as I'm sure you will be. Dinkle said we need his opinion for the series. So get his general opinion about the black upper crust and move on. That's all. You're a very ambitious reporter, Josie Ross. Your dream is to make the big time. Interviewing him just may help launch your career."

Mel smiled. I looked at him angrily. How could interviewing a joker like Ben Braddock help anybody's career? He was a sellout in my community, a brother who made it to the top of his profession and then no longer understood the black experience in America. There was no need for affirmative action, according to Judge Braddock, because there was not now nor ever was any institutionalized racism or discrimination or any other injustice. The problems in our community were figments of our imagination, let His Honor tell it. And Mel was right. He was perhaps one of the most highly regarded black men in the entire state. But Florida was a Bible Belt state filled with Bible Belt Dixiecrats galore. And in their eyes he was sweet as honey. In mine, however, he was sweet all right. Bittersweet.

SOMETHING ABOUT BEN

The Duval County Courthouse was located on the east end of Bay Street, about ten blocks from the *Gazette* building. I decided to walk. It was a chilly morning in downtown Jacksonville as the wind blew across the Saint Johns River and rammed into the shoreline, creating a cool breeze that penetrated the inland and pounced against my brown face. This was my kind of weather, cool and comfortable, the remnants of a winter that never really materialized, and now, here in February, was nearing the end of its run after only a handful of really cold, churn-up-the-heater days.

The downtown traffic was just as brisk, as the late arrivals honked horns and outmaneuvered one another to get the few remaining parking spots, and then hurried into their tax offices or banks or insurance companies to begin their daily routines. I hurried up Forsyth, past the back side of the Haydon Burns Public Library, the front side of the Florida Theater, where *Get Happy*, one of those traveling black gospel plays Scotty loved to attend, was on the marquee, turned right on Market Street, and then stepped onto Bay, the street that housed the courthouse, the Police Memorial Building, the old Jacksonville Shipyard, and other well-known landmarks in town. Other than a few construction workers whistling at me, causing me to give them the finger, and a stray dog that suddenly appeared out of nowhere and nearly caused me to run for my life, it was an uneventful walk.

The courthouse stood like a tall stone monument within a hundred yards of the river's edge and I arrived with my notebook and pen tucked inside my hobo bag and my enthusiasm buried even deeper. Mel knew how I was. He knew I didn't take kindly to rigid ideologues like Braddock. But it wasn't like he cared.

I went by the judge's chamber first but was told by his secretary, some tall, thin sister in those old-fashioned Cat Woman glasses, that he was still in court. So I went to the courtroom. And there he was. Benjamin Braddock. Sitting on the bench like a large swan. The courtroom was less than a third full but I sat in the dead-last row anyway. This was my first person-to-person contact with the judge and the back was close enough for me.

It was a murder case. The defense and prosecution attorneys were arguing, outside the presence of the jury, over the admission of evidence. The defense attorney was Mark Hathaway, a nice-looking brother who tried to hit on me every time he saw me, somebody I found insulting and brutish but the black community loved and trumpeted as their very own Johnnie Cochran. His argument for inadmissibility was melodramatic as usual with all of the conspiracy theories he was famous for, while the prosecutor, some stiff named Deutsch, was bumbling as usual, giving too many nonlegal reasons for a very legal problem. And there was Braddock, sitting there in what I could only describe as a blank stare, looking at the attorneys as if they were from another planet, sizing them up as if he knew their arguments verbatim.

Hathaway concluded his arguments for inadmissibility by making convoluted statements about the Fourth Amendment and his client's right not to be the victim of an illegal search and seizure. His client, a large brother in a suit and tie, sat quietly while Hathaway did his thing. That "client" looked like a thug if you asked me, but Hathaway had tried his best to clean him up. It didn't work, in my opinion.

But it was Judge Braddock's opinion Hathaway was after. That was why, after giving his seemingly well-rehearsed arguments, he then asked the judge if he had any questions. Braddock continued to look at Hathaway and then he leaned forward.

"How old are you?" he asked him.

Hathaway seemed baffled by the question, but did not hesitate to respond. "Forty-six, sir," he said.

"Do you have children?"

"Excuse me?"

Braddock refused to repeat himself.

"Yes, sir, but I don't see—"

"Girls included?"

"Nothing but."

"How many?"

"With all due respect, Judge Braddock, I don't see the..."
Hathaway started to battle Braddock, but then he wisely decided
against it. "Three, sir," he said.

"Three girls. Well. Cindy Kaufmann, you remember her, don't
you?"

"Yes, Your Honor, she's the mother of one of the victims."

"She's the mother of Marcy Kaufmann. Marcy was her only girl.
Her only child in fact. But of course that's not relevant to you, is it?"

"Not during this suppression hearing, no, sir."

"You remember Ray and Maureen Logan?"

Hathaway actually looked to the prosecution for relief but he was
wasting his time there. Deutsch and his cronies loved Judge
Braddock. He was a prosecutor's judge, a man who never met a defendant he liked, even if the guy was possibly innocent. But that's
how those rigid folks were. Guilty until proven innocent even if it
was an impossibility.

Hathaway, quickly realizing that he had to play the game Braddock's way or no way, acquiesced once more and responded skepti-
cally that yes, he knew Ray and Maureen too.

"They had two daughters," Braddock said. "One daughter, her
name escapes me but I believe she's a student over at Edward Waters
College, and Penelope. Penelope, as I'm sure you are well aware, was
found in the same trunk with Marcy. Two girls who never knew each
other in life shared a trunk in death together. The trunk of your
client's car. A car he happened to be driving in search of a dumping
ground when an officer of the law decided that he had run a stop
sign, which is illegal, mind you, and pulled him over.

"Now you come in here and say we should forget the fact that
two human beings, two beautiful girls not unlike your own daughters, were found butchered in that car trunk because the officer probably had no call to stop your client, let alone search his trunk. Your
client, you now say, was the victim of racial profiling. Stopped because he was driving while black: DWB. And I, as a black man, am

supposed to applaud that assertion because no black man could ever run a stop sign, God forbid, and therefore the evidence seized on the scene was an illegal search and seizure because of the prevailing illegal act of the officer. Maybe it was, maybe it wasn't. But you haven't proven to me that it was. You haven't proven to me that he was stopped in violation of his Fourth Amendment rights either. Just saying it's so doesn't make it so, Mr. Hathaway.

"The proof I have, then, overwhelmingly supports that the exclusionary rule is not applicable in this case. I can't believe we're even here discussing this nonsense. I am of the opinion that this entire morning has been a total waste of time and we should start locking up some of you frivolous lawyers who grapple for straws to get a name for yourselves, who come before this august body talking all of this foolishness about your poor clients and how they're the victims of these grand police conspiracies, taking the spotlight off of them and their heinous crimes and putting it on somebody else. Well, the other judges in this building may be driven by your distractions, but I'm not. Two innocent young women are dead. That is and will always be the issue for me, Mr. Hathaway."

The courtroom went silent as the judge completed his tirade and leaned back. I leaned back too. The brother was deep. And serious as a heart attack. But I'd never heard such a load of crap before in my life.

His office was on the second floor, two doors down from a broom closet. A fitting location, I thought. I knocked on the door and, when no response was forthcoming, quickly walked in.

His secretary was absent, her large, hollow desk seemingly metaphorically in tune with Braddock the man. The door to his inner sanctum was closed and I hesitated before knocking. I looked down at my kitenge pantsuit and fluffed my braids. Looking good was important in a situation like this. I look good, he gets relaxed. While he's relaxed I ask him explicit questions about his crazy views, which causes him to get defensive because he didn't take me for that kind of girl. He gets defensive and then I've got a hellava story about how the great Judge Braddock couldn't even keep his cool.

I knocked very lightly on the door that led to his private chamber and then peered inside. And there was Ben Braddock, walking back and forth behind his desk like some wounded animal, moving in one

direction and then reversing course harshly, quickly, his every movement appearing to make him more agitated, his thoughts seemingly
buried deep inside as if he were wrestling with himself.

He was an odd sight, to say the least, but I didn't delay. I walked
into the office and closed the door firmly, certain that the sound of
the door slamming would make him aware of my presence and he'd
slow his behind down. But he didn't even skip a stride. He was too
wrapped up in his own little world. A bomb could have exploded
and he would have missed it. I shook my head. Not only were his
views crazy as hell, but so was he. I wasn't getting any breaks.

"Judge Braddock?" I finally asked. *Judge Sellout* was more in
tune with what I wanted to ask, however. But, to my surprise, those
words alone stopped him on a dime and he looked at me. The inten-
sity in his face as he turned my way, a face that seemed spooked, not
by my presence, but by demons far more menacing than I could ever
be, caused me to shudder.

"Yes?" he asked, his face frowned and irritated. "What is it?"
And for the first time in my entire life, I didn't know what to say.

"Well?" he said. "What do you want?"

I still couldn't speak. His eyes did it, his bright brown, oval-
shaped eyes that seemed to penetrate mine; eyes that didn't seem to
embody the views of the man, because they were too soft, too caring,
too damn sexy! His body did it too, a body that was tall and muscular, solid to the bone, as if he'd been an athlete all his life and was
determined to keep working it in his middle age. This was *Ben Braddock?* This was *Judge Sellout?* His pictures didn't look like this in
the newspaper. He didn't look like this when I saw him in the courtroom. I was in the far back of the courtroom when I saw him, but
damn. I thought he was some unimpressive old fart, not this gorgeous, tortured hunk of creature who just had to look my way and
all of my big talk and bravado were instantaneously shot to hell.

"If you're here for a court appearance you're in the wrong place,"
he said. "Are you here for a court appearance?"

Still no words would leave my lips.

"Miss? Did you hear me? Are you here for a court appearance?"
I still couldn't speak.

"Now look," he finally said. "Either tell me what you want or get
out of my office, and I mean now."

What? The way he spoke to me, using that same condescending

tone he used on Mark Hathaway, woke me out of my trancelike stare and I suddenly had a lot to say. "I'll be glad to get out," I said. "But I'm from the *Gazette* and they want me to interview your crazy ass. But hey, if you would rather not, that's cool with me too."

He looked at me more intensely when I spoke, his expressive eyes looking over my body and then my face as if I were an object on display, and the longer he looked at me the less irritated his expression became. So much so, in fact, that he suddenly appeared not irritated at all, but embarrassed. He even began backing up, as if there were some trapdoor behind him that he could use to flee the scene, but then he reversed his course once again and walked up to his desk. "You're late," he said harshly.

"You just got out of court," I said. "You're late."

Again he looked at me, my clothes first and then my face, for what seemed like an incredibly long few seconds, and then he motioned for me to sit down.

I sat down in the chair in front of his desk and pulled out my writing pad. He began shuffling some papers on his desk and closing folders as if he was so absentminded that he had forgotten I was even there, but I didn't sweat it. He was the one on a tight schedule, not I.

When I saw him in court I saw him from a distance, and all I could detect was that he was an older, big, bulky man who, beyond a mustache, had no distinguishing characteristics. But up close and personal painted an entirely different picture. He was no longer wearing his large, black robe, and although he was still a big man, he was more muscular than bulky. He was tall too, easily six feet, with deep brown skin, those unforgettable light brown eyes, and a wavy crop of grayish black hair that was trimmed almost-to-the-skull low. His jaw was square and his forehead smoothed down into thin eyebrows, a small, straight nose, and a thick mustache. When he talked his mustache lifted up, lines appeared on the side of his eyes, and dimples appeared like sudden indentations on his cheeks. I knew his age to be forty-eight from earlier press reports, but if he wasn't so damn ill-tempered and quick to frown and show his agitation, he easily could have passed for a younger man.

I was high-strung by the time I sat down, my awe of him now completely over, and was ready for the fireworks to begin. But when he finished his almost compulsive paper shuffling and walked from behind his desk to the chair beside me, he was cool, moving slow, the demons that had him like a raging bull now calming him. As he sat in the chair beside me, I crossed my legs. And checked him out. He was extremely well dressed, in a dark blue Italian suit tailored to perfection against his muscular body, a pair of wing-tip Ferragamos, and I knew his cologne when I sniffed it. It was that same old Brut by Faberge we used to buy our daddy every Christmas. Some brothers wouldn't wear a pair of underwear unless it had some magical, expensive brand name stitched on. But at least Braddock seemed to draw a line somewhere. He had on his nine-hundred-dollar suit, but he used the same cologne my wonderful but poor-as-dirt daddy used to splash on. That was saying something.

So this odd judge I had on my hands smelled good and looked good. He was so gorgeous, in fact, that it stunned me. I found myself unable to look into those eyes of his for any extended period, and when he sat down beside me I actually could feel my heartbeat quicken. It was crazy even to think that I could be attracted to a man with his kind of off-the-chain, right-wing views, so I decided to get down to business. And I came out swinging.

"Judge Braddock," I asked, "why does the black community regard you as a sellout?"

He looked at me as if he could not believe I would ask such a question. "Why do they what?" he asked.

"Why does the black community regard you as a sellout, an Uncle Tom, an Oreo?"

A noticeable frown overtook the once calm expression on his face. "What's your name?" he asked me.

"My name?"

He did not repeat himself. He just continued to stare at me as if he were confounded by me; as if he didn't have a clue why I would be so hostile.

"Josie Ross," I said. "My name is Josie Ross."

"Good morning, Josephine." He said this and waited for my reply.

"Josie. Not Josephine. Josie. Good morning."

He hesitated. I was a bitch and he couldn't stand it. "How long have you been with the *Gazette*?" he asked me.

I smiled. It was an old trick he was trying to pull and I knew it like the back of my hand. He was trying to lure me into his world, where the interview was suddenly not about him, but me. But I wasn't going out like that. And especially not with a brother like him. "The *Gazette* informed you that they were sending a reporter to interview you. Correct?"

Again, he didn't answer. So I answered for him. "Yes, they did," I said. "I, therefore, do not see where my length of employment has anything to do with this. You agreed to be interviewed. That's the point. So let's cut the crap, okay, and get this over with, if you don't mind? And if you do mind, well, that sounds like a personal problem to me."

His facial expression didn't turn angry as was normally the case when somebody told you off, but instead he took on a depressed, almost morose look, as if I wasn't saying anything he hadn't heard before. "I'm not in lockstep," he said.

I looked at him. "Excuse me?"

"That's probably why they view me as a sellout—and I'm using your word here."

"Oh," I said, remembering my original question. "So you dismiss the concerns of the African-American community as merely a difference of opinion, Judge? You're not in lockstep all right. You're not in lockstep with the modern world, wouldn't you agree?"

He hesitated. "Yes," he said.

His response almost threw me. I fully expected a more combative answer. "How does it make you feel to be so out of tune with your own race? That must be a lonely place to be, or do you surround yourself with like-minded folk who ease your confusion?"

He actually smiled, revealing sparkling white teeth, but his smile wasn't a lingering one, but short and abrupt, like he knew an enemy when he saw one. "I think I've answered that question," he said.

"But with respect, Judge Braddock, that question goes to the heart of why I'm here. One aspect of our series will deal with the sellouts, if you'll excuse my French. We want to know why it is that when some brothers and sisters make it to the top of their profession they somehow feel a need to distance themselves from the concerns of their less-fortunate brethren. They've been Democrats all their lives, now they're Republicans. They themselves relied on affirmative action to get into the university of their choice but now it's a giveaway for the untalented. That's partly what this series is about. We just want to know why."

"How old are you?" he asked.

"What does that have to do—"

"Will you please knock it off?" He said this so gruffly that I was, at first, startled. "What are you, twenty-two, twenty-three?"

I sat erect. "I'm twenty-eight."

"I see. Just old enough to know it all. I'm a third-generation Republican, young lady, for your information. I graduated at the top of my class at Florida. But perhaps you're right. Perhaps it was affirmative action that got me into Florida in the first place and Harvard Law later on, but I doubt it since I refused to answer the race question on my application for admission. If you believe that those set-aside programs are the way to go, then that's your business. You have every right in this world to believe that. But I'll be damned if you're going to abridge my right to disagree with you. Liberal Democrats aren't the only ones with rights, Josephine. Now if you want to ask me some substantive questions on my background and experience, even on my views, do so. If not, if all you want is some sensational us-versus-them story, then have a nice day."

I almost smiled. My mother always said I would one day meet a man who was going to "shat my mouth" once and for all. But a brother like Ben Braddock with that honor? I didn't think so.

"In court this morning you dismissed racial profiling as a joke. Why?"

"I didn't dismiss it."

"Then you acknowledge that it exists?"

"Of course it exists."

"Then why did you refuse to even entertain the possibility that the defendant was stopped simply because he was a black man?"

"Relevancy."

"Meaning?"

"It was irrelevant."

"Irrelevant? How can you say that? It was totally relevant. But for the fact that he was a black man, that cop wouldn't have thought about stopping that automobile."

"And a murderer would have been free to murder again."

"But it's a question of civil rights, Judge Braddock. That's why they say it's better that ten guilty men go free than one innocent man be imprisoned."

He looked at me with a curious frown, and for some strange, crazy second, my heart fluttered. "They say a lot of things," he said, "that I don't agree with."

"But everybody agrees with it, Judge. It's the bedrock of our judicial system."

"Setting guilty men free isn't the bedrock of anything. Who told you that nonsense?"

I sighed. "It's not the point that guilty men are set free, but that innocent men are not wrongfully convicted."

"Hogwash!" he said and stood up quickly. "One hasn't anything to do with the other. It's nonsense, Josephine." And then he pointed at me. "Stop believing nonsense!"

He walked to a small coffee stand against the wall and prepared to pour himself a cup of coffee. I wanted to battle him back but I didn't know what to say. Something was wrong with me. I didn't feel like myself around him. I was more subdued than normal, less feisty, and whenever he looked at me, whenever his light brown eyes looked into my hazel eyes, my heart would actually quiver. It was unbelievable. A man like that, with such archaic views that just listening to him sickened me, was turning me on. Talk about off the chain!

"Would you like a cup of coffee?" he asked as he poured himself one. I didn't respond. For some reason I couldn't. He turned and looked at me. I don't know what he saw exactly, but whatever it was it immediately softened him. He poured another cup of coffee, walked up to me with both cups, and handed me one.

"Thanks," I said and quickly took a sip. He stood over me a few moments longer, his hand in his pocket, his stomach tight but slightly visible over his belt, and I could feel his stare above me. Then just when it seemed unbearable and I might actually drop the cup of coffee from raw nerves alone, he walked to his desk and leaned against it.

"The beautiful thing about America," he said, "is that we all have a right to disagree."

I didn't say anything. I just sipped more coffee. He was staring at me again as if there was some mystery about me that he just couldn't figure out, and no matter how hard I tried to relax, I was uncomfortable as hell. And remarkably I couldn't think of a single interesting question to ask him. And it had to be a clever question, not some *how do you like being a judge?* crap, but one that would prove to him that I knew what I was doing too. But the harder I tried to think of something, the more frustrated I became. *Me, Josie Ross, not knowing what to say? If Scotty were here he would have a coronary.*

"How do you like being a judge?" I asked finally, giving up.

He sipped his coffee before answering. "I like it fine," he said.

"You don't find it scary?"

He frowned. "Why would I find it scary?"

"You have the power of life and death in your hands. I would think it would be terrifying."

He didn't say anything, he just began looking at me again, staring at me again, until the telephone on his desk rang. He had to turn slightly away from me to answer it. While he talked on the phone I wondered if there was any possibility that his heart could be fluttering like mine. Was my sudden intrusion in his life causing him to be as off balance as I was? But then I smiled. There was something too smooth about Ben Braddock, too steeped in life experience, that the idea of him falling for somebody like me, somebody too young, too loud, and too liberal for his refined taste, was too ridiculous to even think about.

He hung up the telephone and turned my way. At first he seemed taken aback by me, as if something about my look was perplexing the hell out of him, but then his facial expression shifted once more and he settled back down.

"It's a job that I have to do," he finally said, answering a question I had forgotten I had asked. "Fear doesn't enter into it."

"Even if you're wrong?"

"Fear doesn't enter into it. I do my job."

"It's always rewarding then?"

He hesitated. "Not always," he said. Then he stood up. "But I'm afraid I'm going to have to cut this short. That telephone call just made my docket a little more expansive than had earlier been the case."

"Oh," I said and stood up too. I handed him the coffee cup. He placed it on his desk and then extended his hand to me.

"It was nice meeting you, Josephine," he said.

I placed my hand in his. And just the touch of his hand gave me an indescribably warm feeling, a feeling so foreign to me that it made me giddy. "It's nice meeting you too," I said, smiling broadly.

We held each other's hand longer that we should have, which was strange too, and when I went to remove mine from his I could feel a hesitation in his release. I looked into his eyes. What could this mean? But as quickly as I looked at him, he just as quickly loosened his grip and allowed my little hand to slide along his big hand until the tips of our fingers separated into thin air.

But what was really weird was that I was disappointed that the interview, an interview I would have paid dearly to get out of, was ending. I decided to think of something. I just didn't want it to end.

"Could I get a little background information before I go?" I asked him. "If you don't mind?"

He did mind, I could tell by the reluctance in his response, but he agreed anyway.

"Are you originally from Jacksonville, sir?"

"I'm from Key West."

"Ah. The isle of writers. And bones, of course."

He smiled very slightly, but it was obvious he wanted me to get on with it.

"Are you married?" I felt embarrassed when I asked it, because it seemed rushed and beyond the normal line of questioning, but for some reason I was dying to know.

He seemed to hesitate in responding, which only heightened my curiosity. "No," he said.

"You've never married?"

"I was married for eighteen years."

"Eighteen years? That's a long time."

"Yes."

"It just didn't work out?" It was a question that went beyond the pale, way beyond, but my journalistic training taught me to ask all questions and leave it up to the person being interviewed to answer or not.

"My wife was very ill during the entire time of our marriage. She died."

It sounded so heartbreaking. "I'm so sorry," I said. He would not say anything. "And you guys didn't have any children?"

"She couldn't. She was too ill."

Eighteen years of marriage filled with sickness and despair. My heart went out to Benjamin Braddock. But that didn't stop his impatience.

"Is there anything else?" he asked.

By now I was too intrigued with his story not to find out more. "You never remarried?"

He hesitated on this. "No," he finally said.

"Why not?" I asked. *A good-looking, successful brother like you,* I wanted to add.

He looked at me curiously. "I just never did," he said.

"But it's been how long since your wife died?"

"It's been ten years since my wife died, but is there anything else?"

His insolence started annoying me and my mouth, as usual, took over. "What is your problem?" I asked him.

"Excuse me?"

"I was just asking you a few questions, which, incidentally, is why I'm here, and you're acting as if I'm annoying you."

"You were prying into my personal life."

"I was not prying."

"You were prying."

"I was not prying and I don't appreciate you telling me that I was!"

He seemed surprised by my response, as if he wasn't accustomed to being talked to just any kind of way, and he stared at me before responding. "Whatever you were doing," he finally said, his voice lower, measured, "it wasn't relevant to why you came. I haven't remarried and that's the end of that. All right?"

What a jerk, I thought. And to think I was actually falling for his snooty behind. So I got down and dirty too. "Most African-Americans find your views highly offensive, do you realize that?"

"I told you already that I know how I am perceived in the black community."

"But I don't think you do, Judge. To them you're worse than the Klan. Just a common, everyday Uncle Tom who got to be a house nigger. You don't believe in affirmative action. You don't believe in discrimination. You don't believe in racial profiling. You don't believe in reparations. What do you believe in, Judge Braddock?"

He stared at me, as if he had misjudged me badly. But his look wasn't driven by anger. He seemed saddened, almost painfully disappointed.

"Have a nice day, Josephine," he said softly, without smiling, and then walked slowly behind his desk. I just stood there. It all seemed like a blizzard to me where feelings that I didn't think I had were coming to the surface and penetrating everything I thought I believed in. I was so not me! Just the idea that I could find a guy with views like his attractive was remarkable, and the way I had to grapple for words around him didn't make sense. I looked at him. Who was this guy that he would have me so off balance? I wasn't used to this.

He eventually looked up at me, probably because I was just standing there like an idiot, and when he looked into my eyes, a happy, terrible, sinking feeling came over me.

"Is there anything else?" he asked in that condescending tone of his, and his voice alone brought me back to earth.

"Nope," I said confidently. "Nothing at all." And then I turned and left his office.

Although I was pleased that I didn't let the likes of him get the best of me, I was also disappointed by some of the things I said to him. And the look that came over his face when I called him a common, everyday Uncle Tom bothered me. That much I understood. What I didn't understand, however, was why.

Mel looked up from the article I had written and smiled. He was in his office, his legs propped up on his desk, his half-moon glasses perched on his nose. "You're nuts, you know that?"

"I was just telling the truth," I said. I was standing in front of his desk, unusually anxious for his approval.

"*Justice in White, Black, and Oreo?*"

"Yes, Oreo," I said. "Black on the outside, white on the inside."

"I know what it means, Josie Ross. But what a hellava title. Couldn't you have been a little kinder? Ben Braddock is a popular figure around town. You've got the man sounding like some right-wing infidel."

"If the shoe fits."

Mel shook his head. "Yeah, yeah," he said. "You're the slash-and-burn queen and this will live up to your reputation immensely." Then he removed his glasses and looked at me. "You don't even attempt to hide your bias, do you, kid?"

"What's that supposed to mean?"

"You hate the guy and every word on this page makes it clear. You loathe him."

His comment puzzled me. I had a lot of crazy feelings toward Benjamin Braddock, feelings I didn't understand myself. But hate wasn't one of them. "Is it accepted, Mel?" I asked. All I wanted was to be done with that assignment and move on with my life. And that damn Benjamin Braddock, who had the gall to knock me off balance for a hot minute, would be nothing more than a bad aftertaste in my mouth.

Mel put on his glasses and looked over my article again. "Yeah," he said and looked at me.

I relaxed. "Thanks."

"Besides," he added, "that bastard deserves a raking-over. I can't stand him either. But you know the conservatives in this town love the guy, he's their poster boy, so don't be surprised if this article inflames their ire."

"So what are you telling me? You aren't going to print it?"

"Like hell I'm not. It'll be the lead for the Metro section in tomorrow's paper, darlin', don't you worry. Those right wingers have the *Daily News* in their pockets. They ain't getting the *Gazette* too!"

And Mel and I actually high-fived. At least he was on my side.

CHANCES ARE

Scotty was late, as usual, coming into the restaurant nearly half an hour after the time we said we'd meet. He seemed his usual frazzled self too: tossing his scarf around his neck as he hurried in, telling the maître d' without breaking his stride that he didn't need assistance because his dinner companion had already arrived, moving toward my table like a man on a mission, and then plopping down in the chair in front of me, his long, perfectly smooth hands resting on the table as if I were his manicurist.

"Girrl," he said as only he could, "I know you mad at me, I know you are, but I have a perfectly legitimate reason for being late this time."

I looked at Scotty. He was a character all right, with an almost fixed whimsical expression on his face, a high-yellar pale complexion, and large brown eyes. But what was most intriguing about Scotty was his hair. It was thick, halfway down his back, and all his. He wore it in one long Indian plait most of the time, but sometimes, like now, he let it all hang out. "And what is your excuse this time?" I asked him.

"FYI: Bruce."

"Not again, Scotty."

"Don't 'not again' me. Yes, again. But not to worry. It's different this time."

"It always is."

"He's different. I mean it. His name is Bruce, child, he's got to be different. And it was so cute how we met. I was coming out of my art gallery, you know, figuring I was gonna have my behind on time for a change. So I lock my little door and turn to go to my car. And tell me if the finest Negro in J-ville didn't walk right past me. Yes, he did. Well, naturally I gave him a look, of course I gave him a look. Hell, I nearly broke my neck looking, okay? And, Josie, he looked back. Yes, he did. So I smiled. And he smiled. And we talked. And to make a long story short, he gave me his number, girl!"

His smile was so broad that I couldn't help but smile too. But I couldn't smile long. Scotty was notorious for getting all excited about some scrub who in the end never, ever acts right. I looked down into my glass of sherry. "How old is he?" I asked.

I looked at him as he leaned back, his enthusiasm immediately deflated. "I knew you wasn't gonna be happy for me."

"How old is he?"

"What does age have to do with it? He's an adult, that's all that matters."

"Another young one."

"He's not that young. He'll be twenty-three in two months."

"And you're forty. It's the same story, Scotty. He'll let you wine and dine him and buy him fabulous clothes and he'll even move in with you if he's really hard up. But as soon as you say no—no more money, no more clothes, that's the end of that fairy tale."

"Maybe I won't say no. You ever thought about that, Miss Dupree?"

"You'll say no. You always eventually reclaim your self-respect."

He rolled his large eyes at me and crossed his legs. "I hate you," he said halfheartedly.

"Sure, buddy," I said.

"You could have pretended to be happy for me."

"I would be happy for you, Scotty, if I didn't know your history. And let's face it, you ain't got no good track record. You always pick the worst possible person for you. Some young hunk. Why would he want you, Scotty? Think about it. You're good looking and you have a fantastic personality, but you're old as rubber. I'm sorry, but to a young dude it's true. It's not love he's after. It's your money. Your art gallery. Your generosity, Scotty. Face facts."

He wouldn't look at me. He folded his arms and looked at the walls, the other guests, the shoes on the people walking by. It was hopeless. I was wasting my breath. "What do you want to drink?" I said to quickly change the subject.

He smiled and removed his scarf. "G and T sounds good to me."

I motioned for the waiter and placed Scotty's order for him. He then looked around at the restaurant, which was a large room filled almost to capacity with quiet-speaking patrons conversing over the soft sound of Baroque music. I'd known Scotty Culpepper for four years, seeing him for the first time at his art gallery where he was showcasing some unique African batik-cloth paintings, and from the moment we met he began sharing his love stories with me. He was thirty-six then and in love with a nineteen-year-old. This was the one, he told me, he was certain. Of course he wasn't the one, just like all the others before and since weren't, but Scotty kept trying. Now he was forty and less circumspect. He would tell me about his various affairs, he can't hold water, but when I disapproved he'd change the subject and act as if his every thought were on our conversation rather than the newest version of the love of his life.

"Diamond's is loaded tonight," he said.

"You're telling me. I'm glad I called ahead."

Scotty hesitated. Then he looked at me. "A guy came by the gallery today who wanted your phone number."

"What guy?"

"A friend of mine."

"And I know you didn't oblige him."

"Of course I didn't. Why should I waste my time settin' you up? I tried that before. Remember?"

"Do I ever. There was Jake and then Paul and oh, let's not forget Dirk."

"You didn't give Dirk a chance."

"He looked like a cross between Coolio and Snoop Doggy Dogg, Scotty."

"It's Snoop Dogg. He dropped Doggy a long time ago, girl, where you been?"

"What-*ever*, okay?"

"Dirk was a good man, Josie."

"He was a thug."

"He was not a thug. He was a good guy. And you really hurt his feelings. His teeth reminded you of a character out of a James Bond movie? I know you didn't go there, girl."

"He told you that?"

"Yes, he told me!"

I smiled. "Well, they did."

"Okay, keep laughing," Scotty said seriously. "When your behind ends up an old maid, don't come running to me."

I sighed. Scotty was a man who believed in love and was terrified that I didn't. "I didn't like Dirk. All right? He was full of shit."

"Of course he was. Just like every man you've ever dated. They're all full of shit. You've got all the sense, they got all the shit. Life without love is cold as ice, Josie, I'm telling you."

"That's the difference between you and me. I refuse to let love make a fool out of me. You couldn't care less."

"Of course I care. But you have to play the game to get the victory, sweetheart. I lose a lot, I admit that. But at least I get back in there. But you? You don't even know what it feels like to be in love. A dude tries to get close to you and you book. Every time. You're practically a virgin at twenty-eight years old, Josie. That should tell you something."

"I am not practically a virgin."

"You're right. I do apologize. So tell me again, when was the last time you got laid, Miss Thang?"

"None of your business."

"Three years ago, that's when! Three years ago, girl! With Hank. Remember Hank? Wasn't nothing wrong with him."

"How can you say that?"

"There wasn't. He was a good catch if you would have given him half a chance. But he makes one little mistake and you dump him."

"A *little* mistake, Scotty? Well, I guess you're right. I guess sleeping with half of the city is a *little* mistake. I mean, he didn't sleep with everybody, right?"

"You're not your mama, Josie, okay? You grew up watching all those guys break her heart, over and over again, and now you've got to protect yours. But it doesn't work that way. You ain't her. You're practically a virgin just like I said and that should tell you something, just like I said."

"It tells me something all right," I said. "It tells me that I'm nobody's fool. It tells me that precious few men on the face of this earth can claim to have been with me. I'm proud of that. Hell yeah, I'm practically a virgin. I'm not letting some guy get me to fall for his behind and then he decides that I'm not his type or he's not ready for a commitment. Bump that crap. I can do bad by myself."

Scotty shook his head. "Life without love is cold as ice."

"My life isn't without love."

"Sure, buddy."

I glanced at Scotty. "You love me," I said.

"That's not what I mean."

"But you do love me. Don't you, Scotty?"

He looked at me as if I were some pathetic puppy. "Yes, I love you. Okay? Somebody's got to!"

I laughed out loud and Scotty smiled and hunched his shoulders. And we both decided, just like that, to leave that love talk alone.

I opened the menu to browse. "I guess we need to decide what we're going to eat," I said.

"Oh. My. God." Scotty said this very slowly, sounding out each word as if it were a separate sentence, and I looked up. Scotty had a hand on his chest and was looking toward the restaurant's entrance-way.

"What?" I asked, and then turned to look too. And Scotty wasn't kidding. Oh. My. God. Judge Benjamin Braddock was standing at the entranceway, waiting to be seated. My heart dropped.

"It's that actor," Scotty said. "You know, the guy who was in that movie with Ice Cube?"

"What movie with Ice Cube?"

"You know him! His name is right on the tip of my tongue. He was in that movie with Jackie Chan. In *Rush Hour!*"

"Oh." Then I was dumbstruck. "You think he looks like *Chris Tucker,* Scotty?"

"That's the one! My goodness. Chris Tucker is in the house!"

He was wearing his same dark blue suit and stood tall in Diamond's, like a man of distinction by any barometer. He threw me off my game earlier, even to where I almost fell for his odd man routine. But I was determined to get even. That was why I tore him up in my article. And when it appeared in tomorrow's paper, I was going to rejoice. I was a bumbling idiot when he saw me, showing the kind of deference to him that a man with his views wasn't worthy of. But when tomorrow came and he read my article, it was going to be I, not he, who would get the last laugh.

I turned back around. "That is not Chris Tucker," I said, shocked that Scotty would even think that it was.

"He sure looks like him to me. His eyes may not be as big as Chris's, and he'll need to lose the mustache, and he's a little older than Chris."

"A *little* older, Scotty?"

"Okay a lot older. But damn it, damn *it!* That is a fine-looking specimen there! Now I wouldn't have a problem with a man that age who looks like that. But with my luck they never look like that. So I settle for the younger generation, yes, I do, shoot me if you want, and I say to hell with the geriatrics! But if Chris is interested, hey, we can talk."

I frowned. "I told you he's not Chris Tucker, Scotty."

"Okay! He ain't Chris Tucker! But he's still good looking. Hell, good looking? He's gorgeous!"

I didn't bother to look at him again. I knew he was gorgeous and sexy and every other euphemism possible. But he was also crazy as all get out and rigid as hell and arrogant to the core. Forget him, I thought, and continued to peruse the menu.

"I feel like pasta tonight," I said.

"You look like pasta tonight," Scotty said, "with those braids of yours and those she-woman clothes you love to wear."

"I dress in the traditional garb of the motherland. Now if you can't deal with that, then to hell with you."

Scotty stared at me in his regular deadpan, humorous way, and I couldn't help but smile. "Yes, ma'am, Mother Nature. Excuse me for breathing on your hallowed land." And then he looked over at the entranceway and smiled. "Now if I was a betting man, I'd bet Chris was coming right toward our table."

"Oh no," I said without turning around to see.

"What you mean oh no? Oh yes. Come, Chris, please come."

"Let me handle this, Scotty."

"Handle what?"

"Just follow my lead."

"Follow what lead? What you talking about, girl?"

"Hello, Josephine." The decidedly strong voice of Benjamin Braddock was heard just above our heads, and Scotty and I both looked up. And we both smiled.

"Judge Braddock, how are you?" I said.

"I didn't mean to disturb your dinner."

"Oh, no, sir, you're not disturbing anything, not at all. I mean we were going to eat, that's true, but it's not like we're eating. Yet, I mean. As in not now." I looked at Scotty. I could tell he wanted to laugh.

"You come to Diamond's often?" Braddock asked.

It was a simple question but my nervous behind had to think about the answer. "No, sir," I finally said. "I mean, I've been here before. It's just that I've not been here often. I've been here a lot, I mean, but not like every day."

He nodded. By now Scotty was smiling for real. He'd never seen me so unnerved. I felt so idiotic, in fact, that I decided to sip my sherry and shut the hell up.

Braddock stood there, and then he looked at Scotty.

"Oh, I'm sorry," I said. "This is Scotty Culpepper, Judge. My best friend."

"Hello, Scotty," Braddock said and extended his hand.

"Judge, hello," Scotty said and shook his hand.

"You look vaguely familiar," Braddock said. "Have we met before?"

"Oh, no, sir. I mean yes, sir. I mean no, sir." Scotty said this and looked at me, as if to remind me that following my lead might not be a good idea. Then he looked at Braddock and got serious. "What I mean to say is no, we've never met before. Not to my knowledge anyway, because, honey, let me tell you, if we would have met it would have been on, you hear me?"

Scotty was just being his normal, outrageous self, and normally I ate it up. But for some reason I didn't want him clowning around Braddock. For some reason I was embarrassed by his display. But Braddock wasn't. He merely chuckled at Scotty as if his flirtatiousness didn't bother him at all. Then he looked at me. His bright brown eyes trailed down from my face to my chest, and then back up again. Only they came back up with that lustful, drowsy look. "I'd better move on," he said. "Nice seeing you, Josephine."

"You too."

"Why don't you join us, Chris?" Scotty asked.

"Excuse me?"

"Why don't you join us, Judge?"

"Thank you, but no. I don't wish to interrupt."

"Interrupt what? We ain't doing nothing."

"Thanks anyway, Scotty," Braddock said, "but I'll go on to my table." He looked at me after saying this. That sinking feeling that I felt in his office returned. "Good evening," he said. And then he gave me the once-over once again, and walked away.

Scotty and I both stared at him as he moved in an almost slow-motion, lumbering gait to a booth across the room. Then he sat down, slipped on his reading glasses, and picked up the menu.

We looked at each other. "Damn, Josie," Scotty said.

"What?"

"Where you get a brother like that from?"

"Where did I get him? What's that supposed to mean? That's Benjamin Braddock, Scotty."

He looked at me as if I were speaking French.

"Judge Benjamin *Sellout* Braddock?"

He was still confused.

"He's a right-wing, in-your-face, ultraconservative nutcase who doesn't believe in anything that we believe in. He makes Jerry Falwell look liberal."

"You mean he's like a Republican?" Scotty had a way of cutting to the chase.

"Well, yeah."

"And you don't believe a black man can be a Republican?"

"That's not what I'm saying."

"Girl, you need to quit, you hear me? That brother is a walking hunk of sex appeal and you're worrying about his *political affiliation?* You gonna be an old maid, Josie, I'm telling you. He's a Republican. And? Like that's some crime. Child, please. But I'll tell you what: if you don't want him I will gladly take him off your hands. And when I finish with him he wouldn't care what party he belonged to just as long as he belonged to me!"

He said this and shook his shoulders. I smiled and shook my head. The waiter arrived with Scotty's gin and tonic and we made a toast to friendship. I sipped my sherry and while Scotty requested from the waiter a description of practically everything on the menu, I took another peep at my new adversary the judge. He sat in his booth alone, his broad shoulders straight, his reading glasses limply in his hand, as he stared at the animated comradery of a family at a nearby table.

Scotty and I left Diamond's early, as soon as we had finished eating. Braddock was still there, eating his supper quietly, and he did not look up as we walked out.

We stood in the parking lot at Diamond's. I kissed Scotty on the lips and urged him to take my advice and forget about Bruce, the young man he had met earlier. He said that he would, although he and I both knew that he couldn't get home fast enough to give the dude a call, and then he plopped down in his little silver and blue Mazda Miata and drove away waving.

I drove away too, up Old Saint Augustine Road to San Jose, heading toward Baymeadows. The traffic was bad for a weeknight and I ended up stuck in the middle of a bumper-to-bumper slowdown as police cleared a wreck near Sunbeam Road. I leaned back against my headrest and tried to stay calm by listening to Tracy Chapman.

But I couldn't get Ben Braddock off my mind. Now there was a truly stuck-up brother if ever there was one, who never seemed to have a kind thing to say about the less fortunate in our society, who probably ate alone in restaurants because nobody was willing to put up with his crazy behind.

But I couldn't stop feeling bad that he was eating alone like that. And the way he stared at that happy family, probably thinking about his dead wife and the children he never had. I mean the brother had been widowed for ten years, yet he refused to disgrace his wife's memory by hitching his wagon to some fly-by-night female who'd be up to no good anyway. Now that's decent. He could probably have any woman he wanted in a town beaming with beauties, but he chose to be alone. In my idealistic little mind where character matters still, that was saying something.

But then again, I thought, maybe it wasn't saying a damn thing. Maybe I was reading too much into too little information. He was alone tonight, yes, but that didn't mean he was alone every night. Maybe he got stood up. He could be engaged for all I knew. And just because he was decent enough to walk up to my table and speak—especially after the rather combative interview I had had with him—didn't erase the fact that he harbored the kind of views I despised.

And that was when it hit me. I wasn't sitting in the thick of a traffic jam worrying about Ben Braddock because he ate alone. I had written a scathing rebuke of him, a devastating piece that would appear front and center in tomorrow's paper. And it wasn't based on facts, but was a personal rebuke based on my own need to be in control of everything around me. I had called him everything but a child of God. Him—the man who came up and spoke to me tonight and didn't, like so many other high and mighties, disrespect Scotty's differentness. Yet I disrespected his.

Therefore, and without giving it more thought, I turned around, drove up San Jose until it merged with Hendricks, crossed the Main Street Bridge, and headed straight for the *Jacksonville Gazette.*

"Are you insane?" Mel asked as he stepped onto the elevator. I had just stepped off and was explaining to him my need to review my story on the judge. So I stepped back on.

"I just need to change a few words, that's all."

"It's ten o'clock at night, JR."

"I know what time it is, Mel. I just need to take a look at the story."

"No way, Jose. It's in the can."

"But it's not ready yet."

"It's ready." He looked at me sidelong, his green eyes as unfamiliar with this side of me as I was myself. "What's with you? You know I'm not about to pull that story now."

I sighed and leaned against the elevator wall. Mel, seeing my out-of-character frustration, pressed the hold button and the elevator came to a screeching halt. "You okay, kid?" he asked.

I told him that I was, although every outward sign said differently.

"What? Did those conservative bastards threaten you or something?"

"No, Mel."

"Because if they did they got Mel Sanchez to answer to!"

"Nobody threatened me. I was just concerned about the story."

"Concerned how? It's a good story."

"It's a biased story. You said so yourself."

"And?"

"And? How can you print it if you know this?"

"Because that's all you write and I love you so I let you write it."

I looked at Mel. "You love me? What is that supposed to mean?"

"They're just words, Josie Ross. I'm just kiddin' around. What?"

"But what you're telling me," I said, "is that you don't really care what I write."

"Baloney. That's not what I'm saying at all. I care. You know I care. But you ain't never been a fair and balanced reporter, now, that's a fact. But it works for you, our readers expect it from you, it ain't no big deal."

I shook my head. "No big deal? I'm a lousy reporter, but that's fine, because in the immortal words of my boss, 'it ain't no big deal.'"

"Let's just put it this way: you ain't gonna win no Pulitzer. You're a woman with courage of conviction, that's why I let you get away with a thousand times more crap than anybody else. You write from the heart. If something is wrong, you say it's wrong. Guys like Ben Braddock are a cancer that's plaguing the criminal justice system and you expose that cancer and help to root it out. Journalism needs the fair and balanced reporters, they're what it's about. But we need you too."

"But I was wrong, Mel. The Braddock story may have some inaccuracies."

"I'm sorry to hear that, I really am. Especially at this late hour. But stop sweatin' it, kid. Inaccuracies never stopped you before."

I looked at Mel hard. He wasn't kidding either. Inaccuracies never stopped me before, he said, and he said it as if I should be proud of my problem. I'm an unfair, unbalanced, inaccurate reporter. But that's fine, that's perfectly all right because I believe in my unfair, unbalanced, inaccurate reports.

I pressed the elevator button and stepped off on the first floor. Mel asked if I wanted to have a drink with him at the café across the street, but I didn't respond. I couldn't.

At work the next day it was congratulations all around, with even Helen McCoy, who never seemed interested in my work before, giving her approval. "That oreo cookie became an M&M when you finished with him!" she said and laughed.

Cathy, who totally ignored my advice and patched up her differences with her husband, Curtis, joined in. "I used to wonder why they called you the slash-and-burn queen. Now I see why. You don't be playing."

I sat at my desk and smiled and nodded and said my routine thank-yous, but inwardly I was devastated. I thought about Judge Braddock, who was probably just sitting down, his coffee in front of him, as he opened the paper to the Metro section. And there was the headline: JUSTICE IN BLACK, WHITE, AND OREO.

It was a harsh article, with no balance, no discussion of Braddock's character and competence and concerns, but an unforgiving lambasting of his views. My ambition had something to do with it, because I still wrote every story as if it could be picked up by the wires and carried in papers across the country and then the big boys would come knocking, but that was only partly it. The main reason was get-even time. I threw down on Braddock to prove to myself that nobody, and especially no hotshot brother like him, would ever get the best of me. That article was nothing more than a vehicle for me to sprout my liberal views and to create a caricature of Ben Braddock the man. It was so obvious to me, and so irrelevant to my colleagues, that I began to feel ill. And before any other reporters could congratulate me with their phony accolades, I left.

I went to Scotty's art gallery. It was a chic establishment in San Marco, where all things chic abound, and Scotty's place, called the Culpepper Gallery, stood near the corner of Bell Front Road sandwiched between a sidewalk café and a novelty shop.

I parked behind his Miata and stepped out. It was another cool day, with the breeze blowing briskly, and I hurried across the sidewalk to his gallery's front door. There were a few customers inside, looking at some mud-cloth paintings and postcards, and Scotty's employee, Fran Merritt, a tall, good-looking sister with an overhyped desire to please, was behind the counter.

"Hey, Josie," she said. "I like that outfit, girl."

I looked down. I was wearing a pantsuit made of light blue and white Masai material, with a matching blue and white cap. "Thanks," I said. "Scotty here?"

"He's in the back."

"Who's in the back?" Scotty said this as he walked up the short corridor from the back of his shop. It always amazed me how serious he looked at work. Suit, tie, glasses, all business. But for his long ponytail, he looked like a common, everyday businessman. And he did not allow anything, or anybody, to get in the way of his service to his customers.

"You were in the back," Fran said as he came behind the counter with her.

He picked up the telephone that was lying, off the hook, on the counter. His large eyes were staring at me, but it was obvious that his mind was on the telephone conversation he was about to engage in. "I checked again," he said into the phone. "I can have it by Wednesday evening at the earliest. Absolutely. Yes. Completely authenticated and hand-delivered. Of course, sir. We can accommodate that too. But it'll have to be at a twenty-percent markdown, that's the best I can do. I understand. But I'm afraid it'll have to be twenty. Certainly I'll hold."

He removed the phone from his ear and leaned over the counter. "Come here," he said. I leaned over the counter toward him and he kissed me on the lips. "You look like a hell-bent little kid with that silly cap on," he said.

I shook my head. "I can always depend on you to cheer me up."

"Whatever works for you, baby."

I looked at Fran. She had an enormous crush on Scotty, the kind that kept the sister up nights, we believed, and every time he showed me the least affection, she simmered.

"You okay, Fran?" I asked simply because I couldn't believe how ridiculous she was. Scotty looked at her. But then he was once again distracted by the person on the other end of the phone.

"Yes, I'm here," he said into the phone. "Okay, good. Twenty agreed. And we guarantee delivery by Wednesday. Thanks, Ed. Bye."

He hung up. "Yes!" he said and smiled.

"We got him?" Fran asked.

"We got him."

"Oh, Scotty," she said and hugged him. "That's wonderful."

He allowed her hug and then removed himself from her grasp. "As for you, Miss Thang," he said to me, "come with me."

We walked out of the gallery to the café next door, where tables lined the sidewalk and were only half full given the midmorning hour. San Marco was Jacksonville's version of Greenwich Village, the part of town where the artists hung out, and the traffic drove slowly along redbrick-lined streets seemingly in tune with the easiness of the area.

Scotty ordered two lattes and stared at me. "Okay," he said, "what ails you?"

I folded my arms and shook my head. "Nothing."

"Nothing?"

"Nothing." And then I smiled. "I see Fran's still in love."

"Isn't she crazy? She would be the last female on earth that I would cross over for, okay? And I tell her so too. But the poor thing just won't believe me."

"That's what you get for sleeping with her," I said and looked away from him.

"Are you ever going to forget that I slept with Fran?"

"No."

"One time, Josie. I did it one time."

"But why would you sleep with her of all people?"

"I told you why. It just happened."

"But Fran?"

"Now look here, Miss To Do. You never liked her, that's your problem. But I damn well can and will sleep with whomever I wish to sleep with. Hell, I'm forty years old. And guess what? My mama's name is not Josephine but Mildred, and she's been six feet under for well over twenty years. So I guess that rules you out, don't you think?"

I suddenly felt emotional, as if I could actually start crying, so I got up to leave. Scotty grabbed me by the wrist. "Sit down, Josie."

"I gotta go."

"Just sit down."

I hesitated, but then I sat back down.

"What is it with you?" he asked.

"Me? You're the one jumping down my throat."

The waitress returned with our lattes. I began sipping mine but Scotty didn't budge. "I read your article this morning on our friend the judge."

I looked at him. He recognized my problem without my having to say a word. "And?" I said.

"And it was vintage Josie Ross. You call 'em like you see 'em. But I sure wouldn't wanna be an enemy of yours."

"You think I was too hard on him, don't you?"

"No. But you do."

"A little, yes."

Scotty smiled. "So it's true."

"What's true?"

"You're in love, girl."

I dismissed his suggestion out of hand. "Don't be ludicrous. Me? In love with *him*? Please."

"I picked up on it at Diamond's last night but I wasn't sure. Now I'm positive."

"That's crazy, Scotty. He's the last man on earth I would be in love with."

"Then why the long face and the sorrow over being too hard on him? You never cared about being too hard on anybody else. What's so special about him?"

"It's not him. I just didn't think I wrote a balanced story, that's all."

"You never write a balanced story."

"Scotty! How can you say that? I'm a journalist. How can I be a journalist if I'm not fair and balanced?"

"You're fair and balanced on stories that you don't care about. But if politics are involved or some issue you believe in, forget it, girl."

I leaned back in my chair and sighed. Was I wrong to be idealistic? To believe in something?

"You just need to cool it, that's all," Scotty said.

"Cool it?"

"Yes, cool it. So what, you wrote a tough article on a nice guy. What else is new?"

"I just don't feel right. I don't know what's wrong with me."

"You don't feel like yourself, do you?"

"No, I don't."

"You're constantly annoyed and irritated, aren't you?"

"Yes."

"You think about Benjamin Braddock every chance you get, don't you?"

"Yes," I said before I realized I was saying it, and Scotty smiled.

"That's not what I meant and you know it."

"You're falling in love, Josephine. Don't fight the feeling. There's nothing weird or strange about falling in love."

"I'm not falling in anything."

"It's a beautiful thing."

"I'm not in love, okay?"

"Face it, girl. You always telling me to face facts. Benjamin

Braddock is the only man who has been able to knock you around a little. You ain't so tough around him. You don't talk as loud, you ain't as proud, when he hits the scene. But why? Think about it, Josie. There's something about him, that's why. He's different. He turns you on."

"You don't know what you're talking about, Scotty, okay? That right-wing hard-ass does not turn me on in the least."

Scotty folded his arms. "All right."

"He doesn't."

"I hear you."

"It's the truth."

"Did I say it wasn't? I said all right."

I sighed. "All right then," I said. "Well, I guess I'd better get back to work."

"I guess you'd better."

I stood up. "See ya later, alligator."

"After while, crocodile."

I tried to smile, but I couldn't. So I just left.

Macy Gray's graveled voice was loud and I was almost in dreamland when I first heard the doorbell. I was on my lounger, a half-empty glass of sherry beside me, the book that I was trying to read lying limply on my chest. I looked over the fireplace at the clock on the wall. It was a quarter past eleven at night.

The bell rang again and again before I was able to orient myself enough to get up and answer it. Macy was singing "I Try" as I opened the door and saw Mel Sanchez standing there.

He smiled and tried to move with the rhythm of the beat. "Sounds good," he said. "Who is it?"

I yawned. "Macy Gray," I said.

"Who?"

"It's late, Mel."

"I know. All right. Can I come in at least?"

I wanted to tell him no, but I didn't. I stepped aside and allowed him in. I quickly moved to turn off my music. Mel dropping by unannounced wasn't new, but what was new was the lateness of the hour. He never dropped by later than eight, eight-thirty. Never. Something was up.

He appeared tired, as usual, as he walked around surveying my home. He liked my decorative flair, and my taste in art was excellent, he said.

"No thanks to me," I said as I sat down on my sofa. "Scotty selected every piece of art in here. Every single piece. He doesn't even ask me. He just brings them over and goes from there."

"He's good."

"You should go to his gallery and check it out. You'll be impressed."

"Me? At an art gallery? Come on."

I smiled. Mel was a lot of things, but a connoisseur of fine things he was not. He therefore cut his tour of my home short and sat down beside me on my sofa.

"Maybe you can come to my place someday and decorate it."

"I don't think so, Mel."

"Why not? I can use your expertise."

"I don't have any expertise. I just like what I like."

"And I like you, so that should be the perfect fit."

An awkward pause came between us as we both seemed uncomfortable with his last remark. But when he wouldn't go on, when he just sat there and continued his looking-around routine, I decided to move him along a little. "I know you didn't come all the way to Baymeadows to recruit me as your interior designer."

"Point taken," he said and leaned forward. "You remember Wade Shepard, don't you?"

I thought about this. "I don't think so."

"He was that mildly retarded kid accused of killing three of his family members about four years ago, around the same time you first started working for us."

"Oh yeah. The one who supposedly wrote that college-level confession that was later thrown out?"

"But he was convicted anyway, yes."

"What about him?"

"The *Gazette* has learned that Mr. Wade Shepard has been exonerated by DNA."

"Get outta here! Are you serious?"

"I'm very serious. The guy whom our very own Judge Oreo sentenced to death for a triple murder he apparently never committed has been exonerated, Josie Ross. He's innocent."

My heart dropped. The kid didn't do it. And Braddock was the judge? Braddock again! "My God, Mel," I said. "This is fantastic news."

"I've been in touch with one of his attorneys. They're expecting the conviction to be vacated. Of course the prosecutor's office is going ballistic. DNA or no DNA, they're still convinced the kid is guilty."

"Those guys. They make me sick with that. Can they ever admit they're wrong?"

"Never. But it may not matter in the long run."

"And Braddock was the presiding judge?"

"Yep. He's the one who laid down the sentence of death."

I swallowed hard. "What's been his reaction?"

Mel hesitated. "That's where you come in."

"Me?"

"Braddock has agreed to an interview tomorrow."

"With me? He's agreed to be interviewed by me?"

"He has agreed to an interview with the *Gazette*. He didn't ask, nor did we tell, which reporter we were going to send."

"I wrote that 'Justice in Black, White, and Oreo' article, remember? He's not going to tell me anything."

"Oh, yes, he will. He knows you're a journalist first. He'll probably be steaming mad and bark out quotes he never thought he'd use. First your scathing article on him, and now this. I think he'll have a lot to say."

I looked at Mel and nodded. It seemed useless. It seemed as if Benjamin Braddock and I were just destined to keep tripping into each other.

IF THE FALL DON'T KILL YA

He was sitting in a wing chair beside the window when I walked in. His feet were flat to the floor, his head was leaning against the back of the chair, and his eyes appeared closed. His hands were clenching the arms of the chair as if those arms were some kind of security blanket, and he looked exhausted.

"Judge Braddock?" I said as I walked in. He did not acknowledge my presence. He just sat there, his suit coat off, his expensive shoes sparkling against the light from the window, so I inhaled, stood erect, and continued to walk and talk. "Your secretary wasn't at her desk so I came on in."

He still did not respond. "The *Gazette* sent me over to get your reaction to the Shepard situation."

"Sit down, Josephine," he said without moving, or even glancing in my direction. I sighed, finding him just too odd, and sat down in a chair opposite his. It was then that I realized his eyes weren't closed at all, but were staring downward, at the floor, at what I could only determine was a tiny dirt spot in the carpet.

I pulled my notepad from my bag and crossed my legs. "As you know, Judge Braddock, Wade Shepard's DNA does not match any of the blood at the scene where those murders took place, nor did his DNA match the blood found on the victims." He continued to stare at the carpet. I kept wondering why, I even looked down there myself a time or two; then I decided to bump it. He was just crazy, that was why he was staring at the carpet.

"This is a startling revelation," I said, "considering that the prosecution's entire case rested on that blood evidence. Now it's been proven that the young man could not have done what he was convicted of. You sentenced an innocent man to death, Judge Braddock. How does that make you feel?"

It was only then that he looked at me. And I thought I could handle it. But when those bright brown eyes of his looked at me, that quivering feeling returned and I once again felt out of sorts. I was casually dressed in a pair of jeans, a Fubu jersey, and tennis shoes. My goal was to downplay our get-together as much as possible. Our last meeting had me on the ropes, I felt, trying too hard to please and ending up looking like some lapdog. I was determined not to let that happen again. But it was happening already.

"I'm sorry," he said, "what did you say?"

"I was talking about the Shepard case."

"Ah, yes, the Shepard case. There's a problem with the blood evidence."

"I know."

He looked at me. "Yes, you would, wouldn't you?" Then he hesitated, his eyes staring unblinkingly into mine. "How old did you say you were?" he asked.

"Excuse me?"

"How old did you say you were?"

"What does that have to do with the Shepard case?"

"Did I say it had something to do with the Shepard case?"

I should have told him none of his damn business, that's how old I am, but I couldn't. His eyes were the problem. They were soft eyes, filled with warmth, and it became impossible for me to look into those eyes and be my regular, combative self. "I'm twenty-eight," I said.

He nodded, as if I had just confirmed something he had originally thought, and then he rose quickly and headed for his desk. I shook my head. What was with this guy?

He began shuffling around papers on his desk, looking for some particular papers, I supposed, and my presence in his office seemed to have been forgotten. I stood up. "Judge?" I said. But he didn't respond. I walked toward his desk. "Excuse me, Judge?" He looked up. "I need to know your reaction."

"My reaction?"

"Yes. To the Shepard case."

"I sentenced him to death, Josephine," he said harshly. "What do you think is my reaction?"

His anger seemed to have come from out of nowhere and, once again, I felt as if I was being caught off guard. "The prosecution, that is, the prosecutors are saying he's still guilty regardless of the DNA evidence. What do you say?" I asked.

"Thank God for DNA."

"But how could you . . . What did you say?" I asked.

He looked at me. "Thank God for DNA."

"Then you're not upset?"

He frowned. "Do you listen to yourself sometimes? Why would I be upset, Josephine?"

"You were wrong. You sentenced the wrong man to die."

"I very well may have."

"And?"

"And what?" he asked, but I didn't know what to say. I had had a lot to say before I saw Braddock; now I was at a loss.

Braddock, for his part, didn't seem overly concerned about my lack of competence. He began rifling through more papers on his desk, pretty much ignoring me.

"Is that all you've got to say?" I finally blurted out.

He looked at one paper in particular as if he were reading it. "Yes," he said.

I sighed and flipped closed my notepad. It was no use. He was too preoccupied to participate in some interview with me.

"I've got a trial this afternoon," he said as if he could sense my surrender. "What about dinner?" He said this and looked up again, his handsome face intense, as if my reaction, more than my response, was what he was curious about.

But I didn't know how to react. "What about it?" I asked him.

He didn't respond, which I should have expected. It was obvious he was asking me out without asking me out, which always annoyed me. But Braddock was different. If any other man had asked me for a date with all of this alluding-to-without-coming-out-and-saying-it foolishness, I would have told him to take a hike. But Braddock? "Dinner's fine," I said.

"Okay," he said as if he was relieved, although he still seemed preoccupied. "Just write your address down and leave it on my desk.

I'll pick you up at seven." He didn't even look at me again. He just grabbed the stack of papers he had apparently been searching for, and then walked out of his office.

Nothing fit. Not my kitenge suits, not my damask suits, not even my damn dashikis. I went through ten outfits, all perfectly fine yesterday, but now they were either too tight or too loose or just too something.

I lay across my bed and closed my eyes. Who was this Benjamin Braddock anyway? Just some dude. Why should I break my neck for him? He asked me out when I was in a pair of jeans, for crying out loud, why should he care what I wear? But I cared. And that was the problem. I actually wanted this man, this crazy, insensitive, always preoccupied man to like me tonight. And it was an urgent feeling too, as if this was going to be my one big chance to see what all the fuss was about.

When I told Scotty about my sudden dinner plans, he shouted hallelujah on the phone. For some reason he liked Braddock. And then he started giving me pointers.

"Get to the hairdresser without delay," he told me. "Go to the Hair Queens over on Dunn and ask for Jermaine. He'll hook you up, girl. And for God's sake kill the African tonight. No more of that motherland stuff. Wear you one of those pretty little tight dresses of yours, a pair of the highest heels you've got, and step on out, girl. And I mean work it! You be looking good in them dresses, I'm telling you. And for heaven's sake, Josie, do not, I repeat, do not call the man Mr. Braddock or Judge Braddock like you did at Diamond's."

"What do you want me to call him?"

"Benjamin. Damn. Ben. His name. If he thinks you're intimidated by him he'll never respect you. Call him Ben. And if he don't like it, if he thinks he's all that and you like everybody else has got to bow down to him, then he can kiss your ass. Right?"

"Right," I said, although it was clear that I was the one who had already puckered up.

By six thirty-five I decided to give up my stubbornness and take Scotty's advice. At least part of it. I slipped into a red sequined dress that was so tight and so short that I felt like a bona fide hoochie. I took my braids and tossed them up and used a barrette to hold them in place. I put on a white suit coat, a pair of red, stiletto heels, grabbed my red clutch purse, and was seated in my living room by seven P.M., waiting like a nervous wreck and wondering why I was bothering at all.

He arrived at ten after seven. I opened the door and there he stood. And talk about a good-looking brother. Sex appeal was coming out of the man's ears. He was wearing a lamb's-wool crew-neck sweater, a pair of dark brown corduroy pants, Timberlands, and a leather bomber jacket. He had a cigarette between his fingers and was just taking a puff when I opened the door. He smiled awkwardly, as if I'd just caught him in an embarrassing moment, and tossed the cigarette to the ground. And almost immediately my heart started acting up again. I couldn't believe it. All he had to do was show up, and I was through dealing. And he was smiling too? Mercy. I couldn't help but smile. I couldn't help but watch his thick mustache lift up and create those gorgeous dimples on his cheeks, and smile too. And for once in my life I was glad I was in my hoochie mama outfit. I wanted to turn this brother on and I didn't care that my dress was so tight I was walking like a penguin. I was glad I had taken Scotty's advice and killed the African, at least for that night.

"Hi," I said, happy at the prospect that I might actually enjoy myself, and he, for a change, was upbeat too.

"Good evening."

I had the urge to invite him in, but I decided against it. I wanted the full treatment tonight. Dinner, a movie, the works. Any man who had me hating just about every piece of clothing I owned simply because nothing seemed good enough for him owed it to me.

I stepped out of my front door and just as I had expected, his eyes immediately began perusing my body. Normally I would have felt uncomfortable. What self-respecting woman wanted some man undressing her with his eyes? But this time was different. I wanted his attention. I probably needed it.

"I like your jacket," I said as I closed the door.

He looked down at his jacket but didn't respond. "Ready?" he said instead.

We walked slowly toward the parking lot. He began drifting farther back, which caused me to move in front, and I knew then that it was his opportunity to check me out. He didn't comment on my appearance, he just walked quietly behind me, and when we made it up to his car and he opened the door for me, I looked at his face to see if he was pleased. He was smiling, which wasn't easy for a naturally stern man like him, so I assumed he liked what he saw.

His automobile turned out to be one of those brand-new Cadillac Seville STS's, sky-blue and very elegant, but I couldn't help but smile when I saw it. Cadillacs were gorgeous and I'd been told that riding in one was like riding on air, but I always thought of Cadillacs as old people's cars. The retirees and senior citizens drove Cadillacs. The old white men in golf caps and the old black women with blue hair drove Cadillacs. But Benjamin Braddock? I thought he was cool. I thought he'd show up in a Vet or a Porsche, but certainly no old man's car. But that was how crazy my life was turning. I was expecting a tight-ass conservative like Benjamin Braddock to drive a sports car. And I was actually thinking that a man like him was cool. *Get a grip, Josephine,* I had to remind myself.

The drive to the restaurant was deliberately slow as Braddock was careful to obey all speeding laws, and neither one of us seemed particularly anxious to talk too much. For me it wasn't a question of conversation. I was too busy wondering why I was there at all. Braddock had always been the enemy in my eyes, the very incarnation of everything that I despised. Now I was going out with him? It was completely out of character for me. "You find a fool, you leave a fool," my mother always taught me, and I lived my life by that motto. If I didn't like you or your politics, I refused to have anything to do with you. Period.

But Braddock was different. I looked at him, wondering why he was different. And why did my heart feel funny around him? He was no Mr. Perfect. He was good looking, no doubt about that, but so were a hundred other men who'd asked me out. And they were young and eager men, ready to give me anything I desired if I'd only ask. Braddock was twenty years older than I, eager my ass, and wasn't ready to do anything for me except get on my nerves with his off-the-chain views. And he was a judge too? He was a man who had the power of life and death in his hands? A man who could decide that this one lives and this one dies and then continue his life as if those people he condemned weren't people at all but tiny specs of dust that somebody forgot to blow away? And if that wasn't enough he was crude, rude, and arrogant to the core.

But nobody else made my heart flutter. No one else had me wishing that I hadn't written so harshly about him. Nobody else had me sniffing for Faberge whenever a man crossed my path.

He took me to a jazz nightclub in Mayport called the Lighthouse. A large sister named EttaMae Cunningham was onstage singing oldies but goodies when we arrived. It wasn't exactly a senior citizens crowd, but it was close. I was the youngest person in the room, for one thing, and nobody else appeared to be under forty.

Braddock was apparently a regular because the waitress escorted us to a booth near the back without asking our preference, and when it was time to place our drink orders she didn't even ask Braddock what he would be having. "Sherry," I told her, for me, and she glanced at the judge before walking away.

Braddock pulled out a cigarette and was chilling, leaning back, bobbing to the beat, seemingly mesmerized by the singer. I tried to cross my legs and chill too, but in my penguin dress it was impossible. So I gapped open my legs and relaxed. I was just grateful we were in a booth.

The waitress finally returned with our drinks, sherry for me, scotch and soda for the judge, and took our dinner orders. But once again she glanced at Braddock in one of those *we've got a secret* looks as she walked away. She was thirty-something and easily a hot mama, one of those nearing-middle-age females who knew the only way out for them would be through a successful man, and I watched Braddock as she walked away. He took one of those sly glances at her ass, like he knew what the secret was too, but I didn't sweat it. I might have been practically a virgin for twenty-eight years but it was probably a safe bet that he hadn't practically been one for forty-eight.

"It Don't Mean a Thing If It Ain't Got That Swing," EttaMae sang, and then she started dowopping and dowopping and she was boring the shit out of me. *Let's get some Mary J. Blige up in here*, I wanted to say. But Braddock was strumming his fingers and all into it. This was his deal, this was what turned him on. I almost felt like a third wheel. The man and his music and me. But I didn't mind. At least he wasn't flattering me. At least he wasn't telling me that I was the most beautiful girl in the world and he would like nothing better than for me to have his baby. So I relaxed and tried to get into the groove too. I couldn't do it, I just couldn't get off on "Fly Me to the

Moon" kind of music, know what I'm saying? But I was enjoying how Braddock was enjoying himself, so all was not lost.

It wasn't until EttaMae finally took her singing ass a break, however, that I was able to get a little of his attention. I proposed a toast to the beautiful but cool weather we were having and he smiled and picked up his glass too. "Hear, hear," he said.

"So," I said, "this is where you hang out?"

He smiled slightly, as if the idea of him *hanging out* amused him. "Yes," he said. "This is it."

"I like this place," I said, looking around. And it was a nice place, cozy, the walls lined with great jazz artists, some I recognized, most I didn't. "I'm not too crazy about the music," I added, "but hey, you can't have everything."

"You don't like jazz?"

"I don't hate it. It's just not my thing."

"Have you ever tried to make it your thing?"

He seemed upset that I didn't like his kind of music, which offended me because last I looked it was still a free country, but I wasn't willing, not yet anyway, to ruffle his feathers. "To tell you the truth, no, I never really gave it a chance."

My honesty seemed to please him. "You should," he said. "You'll be surprised."

"Maybe you can help me to appreciate it. Maybe you can lend me one of your jazz CDs."

This seemed to upset him too, which upset me since I couldn't understand what I had said wrong, so I leaned back, folded my arms, and decided to chill. To hell with it, I thought. The brother was too moody for me.

He sipped his scotch and soda and puffed on his cigarette. Then he started talking. "Max Gerard had a press conference earlier today," he said, looking at his glass of scotch, not at me.

"I know."

"He said if Shepard's conviction is overturned the prosecutor's office will retry the case."

"Can you believe him? He is such a jerk. Shepard is obviously innocent. The DNA test proves it. What more do they want?"

Braddock sighed. Once again I was annoying him. "Did you attend the trial?" he asked me.

I paused. I knew what was coming next. "No," I said.

"Did you read the court's transcripts?"

"No."

He looked at me. "Then what the hell are you talking about?"

"That blood evidence was the linchpin of their entire case, Judge. No blood evidence, no case. Everybody knows that."

"Everybody who didn't attend the trial knows that. Everybody who never read the court's transcripts knows that. Max Gerard was there. And so was I. So before you completely conclude that we're both jerks, read the transcripts. And then talk to me intelligently like somebody who knows what the hell she's talking about."

I leaned back. I just couldn't battle Benjamin Braddock. His arguments were too concise, too sensible for me to even try to dispute. How can you argue with someone telling you to educate yourself? So I decided not to go there. "I take it then," I said instead, keeping my cool, "that you agree with Gerard's decision to retry?"

"Yes, I do," he said.

"But what about Shepard?"

"What about the three people who were murdered?"

"But what if Shepard's innocent?"

"What if he's not?"

I sighed. Braddock shook his head. "You don't see your problem, do you, Josephine? You decide that an injustice has been perpetrated and then you take the cause and run with it. But you never take it to that next level. You never go beyond the initial problem. That has always disappointed me about you. What about Shepard? you'll say, and then you exhaust all the wrongs that have been done to Shepard. But you never even consider the three people who died. What if Shepard's innocent? you'll ask, but you never consider that he's not. You're too smart a woman to be that narrowly focused. That has always disappointed me about you."

He said this and leaned back. Then he sipped more scotch. He didn't seem to care if I answered him or not. So I didn't. Except on one issue.

"You said I've always disappointed you because of my narrow focus, as you see it anyway. You talk like you know my work."

He hesitated, staring at his glass of scotch, his somberness returning. "I do," he said.

"Since when?"

"I've read everything you've written. For the *Gazette,* that is."

This surprised and excited me. "When?"

"After our first interview," he said. And then he looked at me. Our first meeting was hardly cordial. He accused me of prying into his personal life and I accused him of being an Oreo. It was not a date made in heaven, that was for sure.

But before we could even think about going there the waitress returned with our food. We ate slowly and hardly talked at all until, near the very end of our entrées, Braddock said: "Charlie Parker."

I tapped my lips with my napkin. "What about Charlie Parker?"

"That'll be a good CD for you. A good first jazz record."

I smiled. What an oddball. "Okay."

"We'll swing by my place afterward and pick it up." He looked at me when he said this, as if he was expecting a rejection, but I was too curious to see how the big man lived to turn him down. I okayed that too.

After dinner, EttaMae Cunningham was back on the stage to begin her second set. "Don't Get Around Much Anymore," she sang. And Braddock was grooving to the sound and to the woman who seemed to fascinate him, and was totally ignoring me once more.

Braddock lived in Neptune Beach, a small community east of Jacksonville's city limits. It was one of those border nooks surrounded on the north by Atlantic Beach, on the south by Jacksonville Beach, on the west by the Intracoastal Waterway, and on the east by the vast Atlantic Ocean. It was a place of pier fishing and spectacular sunsets and every time I drove there it was usually a relaxing experience. But this time was different.

Braddock lived in a large, two-story home on Portland Road. It was all brick, with a steep roof that reminded me of a church, a two-car garage, large oak trees casting a shadowy hue over the entire front lawn, all within a hundred yards of the majestic ocean.

He parked his Cadillac in front of his garage and we walked around a curved sidewalk to the front door. It was dark inside and I waited in the foyer for him to turn off his house alarm and flick on a light. When he did I was immediately struck by the somberness of the place. It was such a huge home, with vaulted ceilings, brick-lined walls, two fireplaces (one in the living-room area and one farther back, in the dining room), all surrounded by plush leather furniture and beautiful Persian rugs covering the glossy hardwood floors. But it didn't look lived in. It looked more like a showroom, a place the judge entertained his occasional guests, but as for him, he just ate and slept there. It was a home that was so pristine, in fact, that I could only conclude that I had a very hard-to-please brother on my hands.

"Have a seat," he said as he walked toward his huge entertainment center that was built into the wall. He took off his bomber jacket and tossed it across the arm of a chair, and then he began his search for Charlie Parker's CD.

I sat down in the seat nearest to me, which was a small, antique love seat facing the fireplace. I took off my suit coat and laid it across the back of the sofa. It was warm in Braddock's home, and I didn't want to look like I was uncomfortable there, so I decided to relax. But there was yet one problem. That tight-ass dress I was wearing. Since Braddock's back was to me, I sat on the edge of the sofa and pulled on my dress as hard as possible, trying to miraculously lengthen it, and I kept my legs tightly closed and cocked sideways, to ensure no sneak peeps, but it wasn't exactly a comfortable sitting position. He said I was narrowly focused, and he was right, because I hadn't given the next step a single thought. Did he really bring me here just to give me a CD, or was this his opportunity to, you know, get to know me better? It wasn't happening on no first date of mine, but that didn't mean the judge didn't have a notion.

He stood at that entertainment center searching through a large selection of CDs, his body straight, his ass tight, and it would seem implausible that a man like him wouldn't have a sex drive out of this world. Women had to want him. He was wealthy, successful, gorgeous as all get out. And the women who wanted him were probably just as experienced as he. Why in the world was he wasting his time with me?

"Here we are," he said as he finally found the CD he was looking for. He walked over and handed it to me. Then he sat beside me, the aroma of his cologne making me too comfortable.

"Thanks," I said, looking at the selections on the back of the tape as if I were actually interested in the damn thing.

"It's been digitally remastered," he said, "which isn't the best way to enjoy jazz. But it's a start."

Our eyes met when he said this. And then he leaned back. I was seated on the very edge of the sofa, just a sneeze from falling off, and

I was disappointed that I had done so. Now he could lean back and stare at me with abandon.

"When my dad was alive he was really into jazz too," I said. "But he didn't go out and buy any records or anything. He just always talked about how he liked jazz."

"What kind of music do you like?" he asked me.

I turned sideways, to at least be able to look at him, but he, in his leaned-back, relaxed position, still had the upper hand. "R & B mainly, some rap, some folk."

He smiled. "Folk?"

"You know, Tracy Chapman, Macy Gray, shit, I mean, stuff like that. I wasn't talking about no Joan Baez and Bob Dylan now, I wasn't going that far."

Braddock laughed. "Just checking."

"No way."

"You say R & B. Does that include old school?"

"You mean like Luther Vandross and The O'Jays and Gladys Knight and the Pips, people like that?"

"Right."

"Not really."

He laughed again.

"And I don't have anything against them either but—"

"Let me guess: they aren't your thing?"

I smiled. "Right."

"You shouldn't limit yourself that way."

"I don't think I limit myself. I just like what I like."

"But have you ever really listened to old school to render an opinion?"

"I heard some of that stuff, yeah. It just don't turn me on, that's all."

I could tell I hit a chord with him because he suddenly crossed his legs and laid his hand on my bare arm. I shivered when he did. "Just what turns you on, Josephine?" he asked me. I looked at him. I didn't know a lot about love, but I knew a lust-filled brother when I saw one, and brother man, at that very moment, was off the chain. The moment of truth, I thought.

"Many things turn me on."

"Such as?" He slowly began rubbing my arm. If I had any self-respect I would have pulled away from him and told him to hold on, not so fast, I wasn't practically a virgin for twenty-eight years for nothing. Nobody was going to hit and run on me that easily.

But I didn't pull away from him at all. I, in fact, started leaning more in his direction than away from him. His touch felt good, like a warm bath, like a splash in the pool on a hot, summer day. I actually wanted to close my eyes and enjoy the moment. "Food turns me on," I said.

"What else?"

"A good book."

"And?"

"A good story."

"Always the journalist. And?"

"And, I don't know, good music. My kind, anyway." I said this and smiled. But he was too far gone for smiling. His rubbing intensified, and when he exhaled, it sounded more like a lustful, almost plaintive moan than a sigh.

"Have you ever been married?" he asked me.

"Me? No."

"Any children?"

"Me? No."

"Have you ever been in love?"

I looked at him when he asked me this. "Sure," I said nervously. "Why?"

"You seem uptight."

I shook my head. What was he talking about? "Uptight? Why would you say that? I'm not uptight. Why would you say I was uptight?" He didn't respond, and it angered me. "Will you please answer my question?"

He continued to rub my arm but I could see the lust slowly sift out of him and his interest in me wane. Then he removed his hand altogether and pulled out a cigarette. "It was just an observation," he said and leaned forward.

"But I don't consider myself uptight at all, whatever that means."

"That's fine." He said this harshly, as if he was getting tired of me fast, and lit his cigarette.

I smiled, but I was defensive as hell. "I don't understand why you would call me uptight? I'm not uptight."

He took a drag on his cigarette and stared at me. Was I that obvious? Was his *have you ever been in love?* line a code phrase for *have*

you ever been laid? Then he called me uptight. What was that supposed to mean? I wanted to ask him, because it was tearing me up.
But I was wasting my energy because he looked as if he couldn't care
less.

He, in fact, stood to his feet. "Well," he said, "I'd better get you
home."

He walked over and grabbed his jacket. I stood up too. "It is late,
isn't it?" I said, although I was aching inside.

He unlocked the door of my condo and handed me the keys. I invited him in, but he declined. "I've got a long day tomorrow," he
said.

"I really had a nice time," I said.

This seemed to please him. "I'm glad."

"And I'll take very good care of your Charlie Parker."

"You'd better."

"And, Judge?"

He was already looking at me, but his interest was piqued. "Yes?"

"Would you be offended if I called you Ben?"

He laughed, a great, booming laugh. "Since that's my name, I
think it'll be okay."

"Did you read the article?"

His smile didn't fade, but it weakened. "Yes."

"What did you think?"

"I thought it was the kind of work you've been known to pro-
duce."

"Meaning?"

"More commentary than objective."

I sighed. I didn't know how to be objective? First Mel told me so,
now Braddock. I had a big-time problem. "I didn't mean to call you
an Oreo," I said.

"Yes, you did."

I smiled. "Okay, I did. But how did it make you feel?"

"Great. Wonderful." Then he frowned. "It made me feel like hell,
Josephine, how do you think?"

My heart sank. "I didn't mean to hurt you. I'm sorry."

"Don't be. How I feel is irrelevant. And it better stay irrelevant.
You're a journalist first. And don't forget it. If you think my views

are imbecilic, then you call it as you see it. You always have. And you always should."

"What about you?"

He hesitated. He seemed touched by my concern. "I can take care of myself," he said. "Just do your job."

"Even if I don't know how to be objective?"

"You know. And someday you will be."

I nodded. "Thanks."

He smiled. And then hesitated before speaking again. "Well," he said, "good night."

"Good night, Ben."

I don't know if it was my voice or the look on my face, but instead of leaving as it appeared he was about to do, he stood there staring at me. And then he walked closer and placed his hands on my arms. He seemed indecisive standing there, gently caressing my arms, as if he wasn't sure if he should hold me or get the hell away from me as fast as his good sense could take him. I wasn't exactly his type either. I wasn't exactly the kind of woman he imagined spending his winter evenings with. But to my relief, he didn't run away. He held me. He pulled me into his arms and held me closely against him. His touch felt so good, it was so warm in his arms, that I wanted to cry. It had been too damn long. Now it was torture. Now I wasn't just hugging him, but clinging to him, because this had to be right, because I was finally experiencing what the fuss was about and it had to be the real deal. It was a happy feeling, a wildly exhilarating feeling. But a terrifying feeling as well.

He removed his arms from around me and placed his hand under my chin. When he lifted my face to his, he stared into my eyes. I wanted him to kiss me, and he seemed to want it too, but he didn't. He just told me good night again, stared at me again, and walked away.

It took Mel Sanchez less than ten minutes to get back to me. He came into the newsroom, the article still in his hand, and walked up to my desk.

"Why are you doing this to me, Josie Ross?"

"Doing what to you?"

"Why you jerkin' me around like this?"

"What are you talking about, Mel?"

He waved the paper around in his hand. "This touchy, feely bull-shit!" My colleagues looked up. "You make this guy sound like Mother Teresa!" He read from the page: "*It was refreshing to know that there are still great men in our criminal justice system. Judge Benjamin Braddock showed his greatness when he admitted that even he could be wrong too and the Shepard case may need to be revisited.*" Mel looked at me. "Even he could be wrong too? Who the hell is he? He's Judge Oreo, remember? He's the enemy, remember!"

Mel was angrier than I had ever seen him. And disappointed as hell in me. I was his voice, his unyielding liberal voice, and I had let him down. "Clean this shit up and get it on my desk by five!" he ordered, as he threw the paper across my desk. He did not go back to his office, but out the door, slamming it as he went.

Helen was sitting in wait, her big behind eyes looking, her wide mouth smiling. "What?" I asked her angrily. But her smile would not cease.

"Don't this beat all," she said and sucked her lips. "Josie Ross actually tried to be fair and balanced in one of her articles." Some in the newsroom laughed. "I wonder what brought on this change of heart. How could His Oreo suddenly become His Greatness?"

"Maybe it has something to do with the fact that he's good looking," Cathy said.

"Oh yes," Helen said. "That he is. Very good looking. But I heard he doesn't dig the young ones. He likes his women to be mature and, how do I say it? Very well experienced."

Helen and Cathy laughed. I wondered how could she know anything about Ben Braddock's taste in women. But I wasn't about to ask her, or him for that matter. But given Helen's way, I didn't have to. "Not that he's my type," she said. "He's not. I saw him around town a few times, at banquets, dinner parties, and he always gave me the cold shoulder. I used to think that maybe he was gay. I mean look at me, okay? But one of his ex's said no way. I just wasn't old enough for him. And you're younger than me, Josie, so you can forget it!" She laughed when she said this, as if it were some clever line. "Tell us, Josie," she asked and sucked her lips once more. "Is His Honor's beauty behind this abrupt change?"

"Go to hell, Helen," I said. She laughed again.

I looked at my article. Mel was right. It was loaded with praises and platitudes of Ben, a man who had wined and dined me the night before but hadn't even phoned to see if I was alive the next day. And I was praising him? It was still my unfair, unbalanced style, but in the opposite extreme. I balled up the paper and tossed it in the wastebasket. I was a journalist first, even Ben said so himself, and I decided to act like it.

My story made the front page fold the next day and my coworkers, including Helen, couldn't stop congratulating me. I still reigned as the slash-and-burn queen, they said.

I waited all morning at my desk; waited for Ben to give me a call of congratulations too. I was hard on him for laying down Shepard's death sentence at all, but he had already made it clear that he was a big boy and nobody needed to hold their punches or preface their attacks. He didn't call me the day after our date, so I was certain he would call me today. But he didn't phone. I phoned his office a couple of times, and left messages, but he didn't return my calls. Then I spent the afternoon angry at myself for wanting him to phone in the first place. I had devoted my life to my independence, refusing to fall into that sickening love trap ever, and now I was wasting my entire day because some man wouldn't phone me, a man I hardly knew, barely liked, and whose views I could hardly stomach.

That was why, when the rest of the bullshit brigade came in from lunch and Helen was telling Andrea to forgive her cheating boyfriend and go on with her life, I could hold back no longer. We women were insane with the stuff we put up with. We couldn't keep making the same mistakes over and over again. "Listen to them if you want," I said to Andrea.

Helen leaned back, folded her arms, and sucked her lips. "Here we go," she said.

Andrea, no stranger to my harsh advice either, looked at me. "I love him, Josie," she said.

"Ain't that much love in this world."

"Don't listen to her, Boo," Helen said. "You've got yourself a good man. If you give him up, a hundred other women will be waiting in line to take him."

"That's the truth," Cathy said. She stayed with Curtis and gave in to his weird sexual requests, and since it didn't destroy her, as I had suggested, but rejuvenated her just like Helen said, Helen was now her new adviser and she was now Helen's most faithful disciple.

"Your man got a job," Helen said to Andrea.

"And he's handsome," Cathy added.

"And he's got a job," Helen said again.

"And he has a sweet personality," Cathy said.

"And he's got a job," Helen said once more and Andrea nodded her agreement. And then she looked at me.

"I love him, Josie. And Helen's right, I should give him another chance. Everybody deserves a second chance. But you disagree as usual, don't you?"

I looked at her, and I was determined to make my feelings well known, although they really didn't have anything to do with her. "Let me put it this way," I said. "A village is missing an idiot if you give that cheating dog another chance!"

Andrea seemed stunned by my bluntness, and Helen and Cathy too. The guys in the newsroom laughed. I grabbed my hobo bag and headed for the exit. Air was what I needed. Fresh air. Yet as I was leaving, Helen couldn't resist talking just loud enough for me to hear.

"Yeah, a village is missing an idiot all right," she said. "This village. Because the idiot just left!"

I closed the door behind me as the laughter in the newsroom grew. I stood out in the narrow hallway and tried not to cry. I felt like an idiot too. Not because of Helen or the others, but because I wanted Ben so badly. I wanted to see his beautiful eyes and great smile. I wanted to hear him laugh again and watch his mustache lift up and straighten out. I wanted to feel his touch against my bare skin again and anticipate his sweet lips pressed onto mine. I wanted him. And I was miserable and depressed and ready to do something desperate like run to the courthouse and demand that he feel as I do. And I hated myself for it. I didn't know who I was anymore. Just like that. I was slipping fast.

Only Scotty, I felt, could put a brake on my slide, so I went to him.

He was with a customer in the back of the store but he quickly excused himself when he saw me. I walked to the counter and we met up there.

"Hi," I said.

"I can't believe you, Josephine," he said.

"What?"

"I am so disappointed in you."

Another one. Get in line, I wanted to say. "What did I do now?"

"I called you all day yesterday and three times last night. And you got caller ID, girlfriend, so I know you knew it was me. Why didn't you answer your phone?"

Because Ben didn't give me a call at all after our wonderful night out and it bothered me, that's why, I should have told Scotty. But I didn't. "I was tired, Scotty," I said instead.

"So you couldn't pick up the phone and say you was tired?"

Fran came into the gallery carrying two small boxes. But she entered talking. "We simply must do something about the ambience of this place, Scott, dear. Every gallery I walk into is just bursting with kinetic synergy, artistic aroma everywhere, except here. Our gallery has the aroma of a shoe store. This will not do."

I looked at Scotty. How could he bear her?

"Stop being so rude, Frances," Scotty said. "You see Josie standing here."

"Hello, Josie," she said with no particular affinity. "But about this aroma."

Scotty shook his head. "You better leave me alone if you know like I know, girl, or you and your aroma are gonna smell real good unemployed."

She glanced at me, as if I were the one offending her, not Scotty, and then she headed for the back room.

"How can you stand her?"

"She's good."

"And nerve-racking."

"It's hard to find good help, okay? So you just leave Miss Thang alone; I know how to handle her. Besides, she wasn't the one who wouldn't answer my phone calls."

"I'm sorry."

"I just wanted to know how the date went."

"I said I was sorry. I guess I can't do anything right." I said this and turned to leave.

Scotty sighed. "All right, what is it?"

"Nothing," I said as I began walking away. Scotty walked up to me and held me from behind. I could feel him against me and I leaned into him.

"I said, what is it, girl? And don't tell me 'nothing.'"

I held my head down and then lifted it up, grabbing a handful of braids and slinging them out of my face. "He didn't call."

"Who didn't call?" He turned me toward his face. My eyes were watery. "Oh," he said. "Ben, of course."

"He didn't call yesterday."

"He could have been busy. He is a judge after all."

"I know. That's what I said. But he didn't call today either and I left two messages for him."

"I don't know, Josie, and maybe I'm a little naive, but perhaps that awful story you wrote about him that just so happened to have appeared on the front page of the *Gazette* this morning has something to do with it. I don't know. What you think?"

"He's not that kind of man."

Scotty released me from his grasp and looked sidelong at me. "Oh, he's not, is he?"

"He doesn't care what other people think about him."

"Baby, let me tell you something: those who claim that they don't care what people think, care most of all."

I closed my eyes and opened them quickly. "Oh, Scotty, what am I going to do? I hate feeling like this, I just hate it!"

Scotty considered me for a moment, and then he walked behind his counter. "Well," he said, "it's about time you showed some life."

I looked at him. "Excuse me?"

"It's love, Josie. That's all. And I keep telling you there's nothing freakish or weird about it. You're twenty-eight years old and this is the first time that you've been truly in love."

"I'm not in love, okay? I barely know the man and what I do know about him I don't like."

He smiled. "My girl's in love."

Fran appeared from the back room and walked behind the counter. "What are you smiling about?" she asked him.

"Nothing," I said.

"Josie's in love." Scotty said, still smiling.

"I am not in love. I have no interest in being in love. I am too strong a woman to allow some raggedy-behind man to have me all crazy."

Scotty slammed a stack of papers down on the counter and his smile left just as fast. "I am so tired of you and that bullshit, I 'clare 'fore God I am! Life without love is cold as ice, girl. And nothing can take its place. Nothing! Yeah, you're a big-time journalist now. And you can write all the stories you want. But in that midnight hour, when you're so lonely you actually appreciate the tick of the clock on the wall, those stories can't hold you and protect you and tell you that everything's gonna be all right."

Now Scotty's eyes were watery too. He wasn't angry at me, he was scared for me; scared that I would wake up one day forty years old, like him, and still be searching for a love that probably had passed me by years before.

But even if I was forty years old, I wasn't settling for what I could get. I hated the way I was feeling and if this feeling was love the way Scotty declared, then I couldn't handle it. I didn't want any part of it.

"I'd better go," I said to Scotty and he nodded. I glanced at Fran, who seemed disturbed by our emotionalism, and left.

I went home and got into bed. My energy level was zero. I tried to fight it, I got up and walked around. I watered my plants and dusted furniture. I tried to read, but I couldn't. I tried to listen to some music, was even trying to jam with J-Lo, but my rhythm was off. Scotty's voice kept echoing in my ear. *Life without love is cold as ice.* Over and over again. And man, did I have the chills.

So I lay across my bed and thought about it. What if Scotty was right? What if Ben found me attractive too but that DNA story turned him off? The more I thought about it, the more plausible it sounded. Scotty said his devil-may-care attitude was just a ruse, just a protective facade to keep enemies at bay. He cared. And the thought of it scared me. He cared?

I grabbed my shoulder bag and car keys and hurried for the door. I was in a pair of shorts and a T-shirt, but I didn't care. I had to ex-plain myself to him. I felt I had to make it clear to him that I was only doing my job. I felt desperate and impulsive and so filled with panic and dread that I could hardly contain myself. But I also felt en-ergized and determined and anxious to see what the next moments would bring.

*   *   *

I drove around Neptune Beach for nearly an hour before I worked up the courage to stop at Ben's home.

His Cadillac was not in the garage, but was parked alone on the driveway, and his home was dark, with only the outside lamp near the front entranceway giving it any illumination. It seemed like the kind of home that wouldn't be kind to uninvited, love-starved, panic-stricken sisters like me, and my every instinct told me to turn my behind around and go back to my comfortable, normal life. But I wasn't driven by instincts that night. Passion was driving me.

I rang the doorbell.

It took a while but the downstairs light inside the house eventually flicked on and, as my heart pounded almost uncontrollably, the front door was opened. And there stood Benjamin Braddock, wrapping the straps of his green, silk robe around his waist, his large, hairy chest revealed in stunning detail.

"Josephine?" he asked as if I was the last person on earth he expected at his door, especially at this time of night.

"Hey," I said. I was shivering, because it was cold as hell and I was wearing shorts, but I couldn't turn around now.

He stared at me. He was not about to make a move, not even one as innocent as inviting me in, until I explained why I was there in the first place.

When I started talking, I rambled, my words popping out so fast that I could hardly keep up with myself. "I didn't mean to hurt you," I said. "I was just doing my job. Mel, that's my boss, he told me that I had to stay true to my journalistic style. You even told me that. I couldn't sugarcoat it. I tried, but he wouldn't let me do it like that. I thought it was great the way you handled that first article I wrote on you, where I called you, you know, an Oreo. I thought it showed what kind of man you are. So I didn't think it mattered to you what I wrote, so I wrote the way I write about everybody. Negative, in other words. But then you didn't call me. I thought you would call me. But you didn't. And you didn't return my phone calls. And then Scotty said those who claim not to care, care most of all, and so I felt I had to come over here to tell you that I didn't mean to hurt you. I just didn't think you would care."

He stared at me, as if I were a stray cat and he were deciding whether to keep me or cast me to the dogs. After what seemed like forever, he made one step off of his foyer and onto the threshold.

Then he put his hands around my waist and pulled me into him. I laid my head against his bare chest and I could feel the tears trickle down. But I felt safe in his arms. Warm and protected. I felt as if I were coming out of the cold.

He held me and rubbed my hair and held me some more. We stood halfway inside and halfway outside his home clinging to each other. He tried to pull away from me but I would not let him. So he lifted me up into his arms and we entered his home.

I remembered holding on to him, as he carried me first into his living room but then upstairs. I was so terrified that I was trembling, and I knew he felt my tremble, but neither one of us could stop the ride. He did not slow down at all, in fact, until we were in the bedroom. His bedroom. And he laid me on his bed.

The pillow was already indented. It was the same pillow where, just moments before, he had laid his head. His sheets were bright blue silk and I knew I was lying where he had lain. Without saying anything to me he removed my tennis shoes and then my shorts, revealing my pink bikinis. He stared at them and I just knew that this was it, this was finally it, but it wasn't. He pulled the cover up on me and sat on the edge of the bed. I looked up at him and as quickly as I looked into his beautiful eyes, my tears returned. I felt as if I were a patient etherized on a table and were completely exposed and vulnerable. Any false move, I felt, and I was done.

But he made no moves at all. He just stared at me. Then he took his large hand and wiped my tears away. "Why are you crying?" he asked me.

I shook my head. "I don't know what's happening to me."

He smiled and pressed his hand against my cheek. "A reality check is happening to you, Josephine, that's all."

"What do you mean?"

"It's easy to despise someone from a distance because of his group affiliation or category of views. But it's quite another matter to despise that person to his face. Not because of your fear of what he might do to you, but because of knowledge. You've gotten to know that person and you now realize that he's no caricature or stereotype but a real, breathing individual with contradictions and feelings too."

He was right, on one level, but my problem ran deeper than that. Yes, I had gotten to know the judge, and he wasn't what I thought.

But I was also falling in love with that judge and those feelings were so unexpected, and so incredibly ironic, that I didn't know how to get a handle on them. That was my real problem. And he was the last person on earth that I could talk to about it.

"I don't want you worrying about anything you write about me," he said. "I already told you that."

"Then why didn't you call me?"

He seemed puzzled by the question. "I don't recall saying that I would phone you."

"You didn't say it, but . . ."

I couldn't continue. I felt foolish immediately. Ben, however, smiled. "You're a strange young lady," he said. "You know that? You project such an image of strength and independence, your own woman and all of that, but that's not what I see when I look into your eyes. I see a young, impetuous wildcat. You broke free from domestication, but your heart is still back home. So you roam the wilds projecting this image of strength for your own protection, because as soon as it's discovered that you, unlike the real forest beasts, never really belonged there, you're doomed. You wouldn't be of course, but you've convinced yourself that you would."

I touched his hand as it touched my face and he hesitated, staring into my eyes as if he could see through them, but then he leaned down and kissed me. I closed my eyes and felt the tender quiver of his lips against mine, and then my mouth opening up and allowing his tongue in. I held on to him and pulled him down closer to me, my body trembling underneath the covers as they craved this man's touch. I did not want it to end, I could not bear its ending, but he gently but firmly pulled back.

And I opened my eyes. He smiled at me, his mustache lifting up, the lines on the sides of his eyes slowly appearing again, and then he told me to move over.

I slid over in his bed and he stood up, removed his robe, and got in. He wore only a pair of green boxer shorts and the smell of his cologne turned me on too as he lay beside me. He then pulled me to him and I rested my head against his chest. I could have talked to him all night, about my feelings and my fears, and what in the world I was going to do about this damn love jones of mine, but I didn't. Because within a precious few minutes, and as if I had been awaiting this opportunity all of my life, I fell asleep in his arms.

* * *

When I woke up the next morning, he was dressed for work and bending down kissing me. "I'd better get up too," I told him.

"No," he said, his hands holding me down by the shoulders. "Take your time. Relax."

I smiled. "I will," I said.

He kissed me again, stared at me again, and then left.

I jumped out of bed, feeling wonderful, feeling as if I had discovered a treasure so precious that even I couldn't understand the depth of its value. And I wasn't regretful at all. I didn't want to know why it took me so long to discover love. I was glad I waited. I was glad I didn't jump onto every bandwagon that came along, every smooth joe who whispered in my ear. I was saving myself for Ben. A real man. A pro.

I pranced around his beautiful home in my T-shirt and panties as if I were the mistress of the house, in and out of rooms, in and out of closets, amazed at how tidy he was, looking and laughing and walking on air.

I even checked out his record collection. Jazz, jazz, a Frank Sinatra greatest-hits album, and another one entitled *Sinatra at the Sands,* and more jazz. From Dave Brubeck to Duke Ellington, Stan Getz to John Coltrane, nothing but jazz. I even pulled out one record, a Louie Armstrong recording, and placed it on the turntable. I slouched down in his wing chair and listened. Armstrong, in his patented Satchmo voice, was singing about a wonderful world where there's bright skies and beautiful birds and it suddenly wasn't jive jazz anymore, but music. Sweet music. Ben's music. So I chilled and grooved to the beat too.

My groovin' stopped, however, when Ben's front door was suddenly unlocked and before I could even stand up, the other woman entered into my world.

She stood at the door looking at me. And then she closed the door. "Hello," she said. I couldn't say anything. She was one of those beautiful sisters too, with the big eyes, the long hair, the perfect nose, mouth, ears, and body. Helen said Ben didn't go for the young ones, and she was right, because the sister was no spring chicken. She was older, she may have been as old as Ben himself, but that was her attraction too. There was an elegance about her, a sophistication, as if she was old enough and experienced enough to know what pleased a man and, equally as important, what didn't.

She looked around. "I didn't think Benjamin was at home."

"He's not at home," I said.

She checked me out, up and down, and it was only then that I remembered I was half naked. "I see," she said. Then she walked toward me, extending her hand as she came, smiling so grandly it seemed unnatural. "I'm Angela."

Nervously I shook her hand.

"And you are?"

"Josie."

"Nice to meet you, Josie. I didn't know Benjamin had a house guest. I do apologize. I certainly didn't mean to barge in." I didn't respond. What was I going to say? Barge out? "I'll just leave," she finally said, when she realized that I didn't appreciate this scene at all.

"No," I said quickly. "Let me get my things. I'll leave." I said this and hurried toward the stairs. My heart was in my shoe. I was devastated that there could be another woman on the horizon and angry with myself for not realizing it was a possibility. So I dressed quickly, with fire under my feet, looking at Ben's now empty bed, the bed we had shared together, and I couldn't believe I allowed myself to be used this way. What the fuck was I thinking? Ben Braddock, with the snap of a finger, could easily command the companionship of beauty queens and models or sophisticated ladies like Angela galore, and here I was thinking that he wanted me. Me. Young, inexperienced, and too rough around the edges for such a refined world as his. Damn.

I grabbed my tennis shoes and started heading down the stairs, putting them on, nearly tripping twice and breaking my neck. I wanted to cry but I was too angry to cry. This was love? All of this goddamn emotion was love? And Scotty was getting on my case for my refusal to let some bastard take me through this crap year in and year out like some damn weather vane, swinging hot and cold and mild and lukewarm based on whatever way the wind blows? Hell yeah, I refused. Who needed this?

And when I finally made it downstairs and Miss Angela actually tried to engage me in a conversation, as if we could all just be friends, I excused myself and kept on trucking. *You and Ben be friends. Y'all match. Y'all got it going on. Because as for me? See ya!*

LIFE IS EASY
LOVE IS HARD

I called in sick for the first time in my career and went home to bed.
My phone rang later that morning, around ten-thirty, but when my
caller ID displayed the courthouse as the location of the caller, I
didn't answer. He called once more, around lunch, but I still refused
to take his call. I took the plunge and was willing to finally give love
a chance, and what happened? Miss America, the girlfriend, showed
up. I wasn't about to take his calls.

Not even Scotty's calls. He called twice too. But unlike the judge,
who probably said to hell with it, Scotty came over. I didn't let him
in, but he had a key.

"You need to get out of this bed," he said, standing at the foot of
my bed, his long ponytail curled around and sitting across his shoulder. "You didn't do anything wrong, Josie. Everybody has a night
like that."

"Didn't you hear me, Scotty? He has a girlfriend. He let me sleep
in his bed when he already has a girlfriend. I hate him!"

"Okay, he sleeps with you. He makes passionate love to you. He's
a man, Josie. Some men are just like that."

Scotty didn't know, because I didn't tell him, that nothing had
happened last night. "Why did he invite me to dinner? And why,
when I went over to his house last night, couldn't he just tell me that
he appreciates my coming by but he's already involved with someone? Why couldn't he just say that?"

"Because maybe he's not involved with someone."

"Oh, Scotty, please."

"That woman could have been anybody, Josie."

"Sure she could have. His aunt. His cousin. A Jehovah's Witness."

"That's right!"

"A Jehovah's Witness who also happens to have a key to his home."

"A key? Girlfriend had a key?"

"Yes."

"Damn. He *is* a dog, ain't he?"

I sat up in bed and slung my braids out of my face. I lifted my knees up to my stomach and rested my chin on my knees. "Games," I said. "I hate games. I hear it all the time at work. What game can I play on this woman, what game can I play to wrangle this man? But I ain't going out like that. You hear me, Scotty? Nobody's twisting and turning me around like I'm some puppet on a string." Then I frustratingly shook my head. "Damn!"

Scotty sat down on the bed beside me. "Maybe she's just a friend, Josie."

"No way."

"I have a key to your house, and we're friends. It's possible."

"I saw the female, Scotty. No way is that witch just a friend of his."

He sighed. "I don't know what to tell you," he said.

I looked at him. Something about his spirit was even more depressed than mine. "You okay?"

"You've got your own problems."

"Scotty! What is it?"

He hesitated. "Bruce left."

No surprise there. I had tried to tell him. But no-o-o. Bruce was different. Bruce was the one. Yeah, right. Just like Ben was the one for me. "When did he leave?"

"Last night. He made some purchases on one of my credit cards and I confronted him about it."

"He stole your credit card?"

"Just long enough to make the purchases."

"That asshole. How much did he spend?"

Scotty crossed his legs. "Two thousand."

"What! *Two thousand dollars?* I know you called the police, Scotty, don't tell me you didn't call the cops on his ass."

"I just wanted to hear his side of things, Josie, that's all."

"His side? What side? He stole your credit card and charged two thousand dollars on it. Ain't nothing else you need to know!"

Scotty remained calm, which meant he was still upset by it. Why he kept taking himself through this crap astounded me. Once was enough. I mean really.

"When I confronted him about the card he went off on me, denying everything as usual, and then we had a little altercation, yes, we did. But he finally left."

"An altercation? He fought you? He beat you up, Scotty?"

Scotty looked at me. "Nobody beats up Scotty Culpepper, okay?"

I smiled. "You beat his ass, didn't you?"

"I was the drum major and he was the drum, honey."

I laughed. "Good. I told you Bruce was shady. And you still should turn his behind in for stealing your credit card, you can't let him get away with that."

"He didn't get away with anything. Trust me. He didn't take anything with him, and I'm talking not even his funky drawers."

I laughed. Scotty shook his shoulders and smiled. "You'll be fine, Scotty. You always are."

"And you're gonna be just fine too. You're strong. And tough as an ox."

I smiled, inasmuch as I could manage. "Ben said I wasn't strong at all. I was just a young, impetuous wildcat."

Scotty looked at me. "Yeah, you're wild all right. But that's what he said?"

"Yeah."

He shook his head. "I don't know, girl. You're stubborn. You've always been so damn stubborn. But you may be making a terrible mistake on this one."

"What kind of mistake? He has another woman."

"Maybe. But he seems to be such a good guy, you know?"

"What's good about him? He played me, Scotty. Let's face facts here. The brother played me! I tried that love thing you just kept begging me to try. I tried it. And what did it get me? Played, that's what. And *he's* supposed to be a good one? Please."

"Okay. Dang. He ain't good. Forgive me for even suggesting it! But enough about all this." He jumped up and clasped his hands together. "Let's go shopping."

I looked at him. "What?"

"Let's go shopping."

"Do I look like I want to go shopping?"

"You never look like you want to go shopping, and today least of all. That's why you've got to go. When I'm depressed—"

"I'm not depressed."

"When I'm depressed I go out and buy me a bag or a pair of shoes or even a nice little hat. Something. And that's exactly what you're going to do."

I shook my head. "Wanna bet?"

"Oh, I can cover the spread, honey," Scotty said.

We went shopping. I couldn't believe I had consented. But he was so insistent and he made it sound like it could actually be fun. But it wasn't until he promised to bankroll our little excursion that I agreed to go.

The Avenues Mall was crowded for a weekday, but it was mainly stuffed with older ladies and housewives, the types who shopped very methodically, who didn't grab a blouse and leave, as did their younger counterparts, but who inspected it for blemishes and tatters, and then spent another ten minutes deciding if they really wanted it at all. Scotty and I had a field day watching them operate. We'd follow a few of them into one of the ritzy department stores, for instance, and then stand back and try to predict the outcome. Scotty, of course, was always right.

"She'll buy," I said about one of our unsuspecting suburbanites.

"She's not buying a thing."

"Yes, she is, Scotty. Look at her face. She loves that scarf."

"You're right about that. She sure love it, girl. And she's gonna steal it, but she ain't buying it."

I looked at Scotty. "Steal it?"

"See?" he said and pointed to the woman as she cleverly tore off the tag and then slipped the scarf into her purse.

I started looking around. "Surely the security cameras saw her."

Scotty looked at me. "Are you out of your mind, Josie? Them cameras too busy looking at us to worry about her."

"Us?"

"Yes, us. Oh, honey, I assure you that every camera in this store is focused right over here. And we're the only people of color in this place too? Child, please. The Miss America Pageant don't get as many clicks as we're getting even as I speak."

"Come on, Scotty."

"You think I'm lying? If I was to do anything suspicious, anything, an undercover store detective would be over in a flash. Watch and learn, honey. Watch and learn."

Scotty leaned down, as if he were tying his shoe, and before he could stand up straight a white man in a trench coat was standing in the aisle beside us. I jumped, startled by his sudden, seemingly out-of-the-blue presence. But he didn't approach us. He started examining a rack of women's blouses instead.

Scotty nudged me with his elbow. "See what I'm saying?" he said. Then he looked at the detective. "That's cute," he said of the blouse the detective was viewing. "Is it for you or your boyfriend?"

The detective's already forced smile completely disappeared and Scotty burst into laughter. "Yeah, boy, you're a dick in more ways than one!"

I laughed too but I also had enough sense to grab Scotty by the arm and proceed to get the hell out of there.

I enjoyed myself with him. He took me to a late lunch too, at a burger joint, and we pigged out on fast food for a change. Then we hopped back into his Miata. But instead of taking me home, he took me to the *Gazette*.

"Don't do this," I said as his car stopped in front of the building.

"See ya later, alligator."

"But, Scotty—"

"But, Scotty, nothing. You don't need to be sitting home. You said yourself you wasn't gonna let anybody play you. Then don't play. Get to work."

"How am I going to get home?"

"I'll come get you."

"But what if I get an assignment?"

"All you gots to do is holler."

I sighed. "You still owe me," I said.

"Owe you?"

"Yes! You didn't buy me anything."

"You didn't want anything."

"How could I want something when we were so busy chasing terrified old ladies and unsuspecting housewives around the mall?"

Scotty laughed. And then he turned somber. "Listen to me," he said. I looked at him. "I still say that woman could have been any-body."

"Let it be, Scotty."

"I just would hate for you to make a mistake, that's all."

I nodded. "Thanks. But I'm not making a mistake."

"Sure?"

"Positive. Benjamin Braddock and Josie Ross never were, nor will we ever be, an item."

Scotty nodded. And then he sat erect. "Well, in that case," he said, "if you don't want him, can I have him?"

I laughed. "It's a free country," I said and got out of his car, al-though there was no denying that my heart still ached for Ben.

Within minutes of my arrival in the newsroom, Mel was calling my name. "Josie Ross, in here!" he yelled.

"I thought you were sick," Helen said as I walked past her.

"I am," I said. "Sick of you."

I didn't even care to look back at her expression as I hurried into Mel's office.

"Close the door," he said. He was standing behind his desk, his shirtsleeves rolled up, his face fatigued near burnout.

"What's the matter?" I asked him as I sat down.

"Did you hear the news?"

"What news?"

"And what's with this calling-in-sick business this morning? You've never been sick before."

"Mel, what news?"

He sighed. "I thought you knew. I thought that's why you called in. You were breaking my heart there for a minute, kid."

"What are you talking about? What's happened?"

"Civil rights have been set back fifty years, that's what's hap-pened!"

"Mel, please stop speaking Puerto Rican. What's happened?"

He sighed again. Then he sat down. "The governor of our great state of Florida has just announced his intentions to nominate your Judge Greatness, better known as Judge Oreo, to become the next justice of the state supreme court."

His words were clear but somehow I couldn't understand him.

Ben, a supreme court justice? And suddenly I didn't know what to say. "Really?" I said.

"Fifty years of struggle about to be tanked and what does our slash-and-burn queen say? Really."

"Are you sure?"

"I am positive, Josie Ross. It's a done deal. Your boy is about to become state royalty and not just screw you, but all of us."

I looked at Mel. How could he say such a thing? "Go to hell," I said.

"I'm sorry," he immediately said. "I was out of line. But this is some development, JR. The conservatives already have a four-to-three majority on the court with the chief justice always voting with them. But at least the liberals could occasionally cajole Justice Preston, the one moderate conservative, to see their side of the issue and swing a winning margin every now and then. But with Braddock there? With Braddock replacing the most liberal voice on the court? Forget about it. It'll be a five-two majority for the tank heads. Five-two, JR! That means our side would have to win over two votes every single vote. That's impossible the way that court is constructed now. And you know yourself that Braddock ain't gonna be no swing vote! We're doomed. Pure and simple."

I leaned back. It was true. What on earth was I thinking? Braddock was actually the enemy. The man I had spent the night with was actually the one human being I would least like to succeed, because if he did, if he had his way, he would set back the cause of civil rights by leaps and bounds. Mel wasn't exaggerating. We were in trouble.

"What can we do?"

"You can get over to that courthouse and get his reaction to the governor's announcement. Then get some opposing views. Hell, get a lot of opposing views. And then slash and burn his ass! The written word is the only weapon we've got now, JR. And we've got to get the word out that this is a terrible blow to every human being who believes in justice for all. We've got to create so much negative fire underneath this announcement that even Braddock's conservative buddies might run for cover. That's what we can do."

I stood up and nodded. I agreed with Mel one hundred percent. Benjamin Braddock had me off stride for a second once more, but never again, I decided.

* * *

I walked to the courthouse and arrived just as Ben was leaving the building. He hurried down the stairs and moved with an athlete's stride toward the parking lot, forcing reporters to chase him with cameras flashing and microphones and notepads shoved in his face. But he had no comment for every question hurled. So I decided to enter the fray. "Are you an enemy of civil rights, Judge Braddock?" I yelled above my colleagues. He stopped walking and turned toward me. He saw me. His beautiful eyes cast their light my way. And I remembered how he had leaned down and kissed me the night before. And again this morning. And now this.

He looked at me for a moment, but he didn't respond to my question either. He walked to his Seville, got in, and drove away. Some reporters were disappointed and felt he could have at least given a statement; others were rejuvenated and ran to their cars to see if they could tail him. But me? I wasn't disappointed or rejuvenated or anything. I didn't know what I was.

I hung around the courthouse getting comments from his colleagues and ended up writing a story that would have made my own mama cry. It was a scathing rebuke of Ben's appointment. Every opposing voice was heard. Ben's supporters, just barely. Mel loved the story and said that it would be tomorrow's lead: GOVERNOR TO NOMINATE BRADDOCK TO SUPREME COURT. MANY OUTRAGED. It was, of course, the outraged many that received almost all of the ink, but we didn't care. We were on a mission.

I went home that night, slipped on a pair of shorts and a halter top, and cleaned out my kitchen cabinets from top to bottom. I moved everything out, from pots and pans to plates and cups. I felt on edge for some reason, unable to rest, unable to stay busy enough. I even smoked cigarettes, something I only did when I was nervous as hell. And to top it all off, I had a Jackson Five tape on, the real old stuff, and I was trying to groove to songs about a rat named Ben (boy, was that familiar!), and one bad apple, and rockin' robins, but it all seemed forced and fake and just something to do to stop thinking about something else. And then the doorbell rang.

I looked at the clock over my stove. It was nine thirty-two. Not that late, I thought, but late enough.

I dried my hands on a towel and walked cautiously toward the front door. I looked out my bay window and saw Ben's Seville parked in front of my building. My heart dropped. "What in hell?" I said out loud and hurried to the front door. He had some nerve coming here, I thought. Some damn nerve.

I opened the door quickly. "What do you want?" were the words and the tone I had planned to use. And my lips were fixed and ready to do their thing. But then I saw him, standing there, his anger palpable, his agitation wrenching. And I couldn't say anything.

"You are really trying my patience," he said as soon as I opened the door. "I don't have time for this shit! Now what's wrong with you?"

It was his tone that shook my stare, and suddenly my anger was just as palpable as his. How dare he come to my home yelling at me, I thought, especially after what he did to me! "Excuse me?" I said to him. "Ain't nothing wrong with me. What's wrong with you?"

He wanted to lash back, the fire in his eyes made it clear, but he didn't. "May I come in?" he asked instead, not politely, but derisively, and without waiting for my answer, he came on in.

He whiffed past me smelling like a combination of Faberge and tobacco and walked toward my living-room sofa. It was his first time in my home but he moved as if he knew his way around. He moved past the sofa and walked behind the chair. Then he looked at me. I closed my door and leaned against it. He was either going to quickly explain his problem or get the hell out of my home.

"Now I don't know what kind of game you're playing," he said, and my mouth gaped open.

"Game?" I said. "Me? You got some nerve!"

"Okay, what is it? What has the world done to Josephine now? Or is it just me this time?"

"What are you talking about?"

"Why would you ask me a question like that?"

"A question like what?"

" 'Judge Braddock, are you an enemy of civil rights?' That's what!"

And it was only then that I realized who was actually standing in my living room. Benjamin Braddock. The next justice of the Florida Supreme Court. The next right-wing ideologue poised to roll back every program beneficial to the poor and disenfranchised. And he was a womanizing, snake-in-the-grass, cheating dog too? Hell yeah,

I asked if he was an enemy of civil rights. "I asked that question, Judge," I said, trying my best to remain composed, "because many people feel that way."

"Bullshit!" he screamed. "Nobody feels that way but you and that crowd at the *Gazette*. Because anybody who knows my record knows that I have never trampled on anybody's civil rights. Ever!"

He was so angry that he was shaking. I had asked him a tough question, what was the big damn deal? Every reporter at the courthouse was asking him tough questions. Why would he be shocked that I would too?

But as soon as his anger should have been rising, given his state, it began to deflate. Without seemingly any provocation from me, his gorgeous face went from grave agitation to a more subdued, irritated look. It wasn't a pleasant look either, but it was about as good as it was going to get with him. "Come here," he said to me.

I thought it was an odd command, an almost arrogant one, but since I couldn't just lean against the door all night, I decided to see what he wanted. I walked up to him. His hands were in his pockets and his face looked so distressed that I thought I was missing something. All of this damn emotion over one question?

I stood in front of him and folded my arms. I had on a revealing halter top and shorts and when I folded my arms he looked down at my chest, which annoyed me, so I unfolded them. "Yes, what is it?" I asked him.

"She's not my girlfriend," he said.

"Pardon me?"

"She's not my girlfriend."

"Who's not your girlfriend?"

He didn't respond. He and I both knew full well who.

"I don't know what you're talking about," I said, determined to see the charade through.

"Why didn't you just phone me? If you had a concern like that, why couldn't you just pick up a phone and ask me?"

"I don't know what you're talking about, Ben."

He looked up at the ceiling and sighed, and then he looked back down at me. "I'm not one of your playmates, you understand, Josephine? I don't have time for games. Now what's wrong with you? And you tell me the truth!"

I leaned against the chair. Something about his eyes, and the tone of his voice, made me cut the bull immediately. Here stood a man of distinction, a man whom the governor himself thought enough of to want to nominate to the state's highest court. And I was trying to jerk him around? I decided, right then and there, to get real. "You were right," I said.

He frowned. "I was right about what?"

"Me being uptight. Never being in love. You were right."

He looked down, at my chest, when I said it; then he looked into my eyes. Just the realization of what I had said saddened me, but I couldn't find any compassion in his eyes. He still looked hard and stern, troubled by my acknowledgment but not moved by it, and he still, even after it was obvious that I was on the verge of tears, looked irritated as hell.

He turned and walked, not toward me to hold me and tell me it would be all right, but away from me. I wrapped my arms around myself, like an addict in need of a fix, when he turned away from me. I remembered his touch and wanted to feel it again. I hated what he had done to me, and I hated that he wasn't standing up like a man and admitting that there was another woman, but I still wanted to feel his touch again. It was pitiful, but it was true. I would have sold out for a touch. I would have buried my differences with a man like Braddock just to feel his lips on mine again.

He, however, seemed to be at war with himself: walking over by the fireplace, and then toward the kitchen, pacing back and forth as if he were engrossed in his own battle. Then he walked toward the sofa, looked at it, and sat down. I didn't know what to do with myself either, so I walked around to the front of the chair and sat down too.

After a long stretch of silence, nothing said, nothing done, he pulled out a cigarette. "Mind if I smoke?" he asked.

"No."

"I should stop, it's a terrible habit. But there's always something, isn't there?"

"I guess so."

He lit his cigarette and took a long drag. Then he looked at me. "So," he said, "you've never been in love?"

"No, I haven't." And then I looked at him. "Until recently."

It was my moment of truth, my decision to finally admit what was obvious all along: I was in love. I was in love with Benjamin Braddock. I thought I could shake it. I thought my anger would keep me focused. And when Mel put it all in perspective, telling me, in essence, that I was sleeping with the enemy, I just knew that had settled it. But that hadn't settled a damn thing. I suspected it when I saw him at the courthouse and now, as he sat in my living room, there was no doubt at all. I was in *LOVE*.

I looked at him because I needed to gauge his reaction. But he didn't blink or in any way look away from me. And although my confession was monumental in my eyes, it didn't seem to register so much as a flicker in his. So I kept on talking. I didn't see where I had anything to lose. "That was why I came to your house that night. I just needed you to know how I felt. But then your girlfriend showed up. And that was the end of that."

He puffed on his cigarette again and leaned forward. "Where can I put my ash?" he asked.

What a letdown! I had just exposed my soul to him and he was worried about ash? The man had no conscience. I looked around. I only had one ashtray in the house, and it was in the kitchen where I had left it. So I went and got it, handed it to him, and then sat down on the opposite end of the couch.

While he tapped the ash off of his cigarette, I looked at his muscular biceps, how they seemed to bulge out of his suit and give it an almost tight look, and I remembered how warm those arms felt around me. And how badly I needed to feel that warmth again.

He looked at me and caught me staring at him, which made me appear even more vulnerable. I was through dealing. "She's not my girlfriend," he said.

"Sure she isn't," I said, deciding to mask my weakness with cockiness. "But it doesn't matter."

"It doesn't?"

"Not to me."

"Then why did you mention it?"

"Because it's a fact. Your girlfriend showed up."

"She's not my girlfriend, Josephine, and I'm not going to tell you that again!" He said this pointing his cigarette at me. Then he seemed upset at himself for getting upset with me and he leaned back. But he didn't apologize.

"Who is she?" I asked.

He paused. "Her name is Angela."

I waited for more, but he did not continue.

"Angela?"

"Yes."

"Who is she?"

"A friend of mine."

"With a key to your house?"

He looked at me with a combination of disappointment and disgust. He wasn't about to answer my question. To him, he'd answered it. She was his friend. Case closed. To me, he hadn't even begun to respond.

But the weight of his personality was stronger than mine and his refusal to say more won out. What could I do anyway? Demand that he answer me, and with a more complete response? He would have told me to go to hell. Nobody demanded him to do anything. So I decided to change the subject. Since I wasn't going to be fulfilled anyway, I thought, at least I could get a good story out of it. "Congratulations," I said.

He looked at me. "Do you mean it?"

"No, I don't. I think the governor has made a very big mistake."

He nodded. "Good for you."

"You agree with me?"

"No. But that doesn't mean you're wrong."

I smiled. He was smooth when he wanted to be. "You didn't answer my question," I said.

"I thought I had."

"I'm talking about the one I yelled while you were leaving the courthouse. Are you an enemy of civil rights?"

"The kind of civil rights you and your paper espouse? Yes, I believe I am."

I nodded. And then I stood up. "I see."

He frowned. "Sit down."

"I don't think we have anything further to say."

"Sit down."

I looked at his shoes for some odd reason, and noticed how expensive they were; then I sat back down.

"You're young and idealistic, Josephine. And those aren't bad things to be. But both limit you. You read about the civil rights movement of the sixties. I lived the movement. And I am not going to keep living it over and over and over again. It's done. We've won. Now let's move on."

I smiled. "We've won? How can you say that? We ain't won nothing. Our people are still on the bottom, Judge. Don't you realize that?"

"No, I don't. We have poor people in our race who will remain poor if all we do is tell them the secret to success is qualifying for this government program or that one, and they don't have the wherewithal to tell us to get the hell away from them."

"So the institutionalized racism that exists in this society is our fault?"

"It's not a fault, Josephine, it's a fact. A fact of life. Just as pollution and traffic jams and bad movies are facts of life. Nobody's telling you to like the pollution or traffic or movie, but sometimes you just have to endure it. That doesn't define you and it doesn't stop you. It's just one more hurdle to get over."

"Have you ever been poor a day in your life, Judge Braddock?"

"Totally irrelevant."

"It's completely relevant. It's easy to talk about jumping over hurdles, particularly the kind that keep getting raised higher and higher, when you've never been down there to jump. I've been poor, Judge. I know what time it is. People need your help. Not your judgment."

He looked at me, at the tears that began to well up in my eyes, and he nodded as if he understood. And then he grabbed my arm and pulled me to him, my little body sliding across the sofa limply until I was at his side. He lifted me and sat me on his lap. And I allowed it. "You have a big heart, you know that?" he said, and he stared at me unblinkingly until a funny look came over his face, a compassionate, sensual look. And then he kissed me. Tender at first, and then passionate and long and rough. I held on to him as if I couldn't let him go.

And it all happened so fast. The kissing led to fondling and before I could catch my breath he was lifting me up and removing my clothes. He unbuttoned and unzipped his pants, but he didn't remove them. He pulled out a condom, and I heard the rattle of paper. But when I thought to look down to see what was happening, he had entered me. It felt slow and easy moving in, and then so full and tight that I could hardly contain myself. I screamed and held on to him and he grabbed hold of me and pulled me back and forth, back and forth, as if I were riding a horse. And I rode, baby, rode. And when I thought I couldn't take any more and would stroke out from the feeling alone, it happened. Finally, it happened! Every muscle in my body clenched, my heart danced the watusi, and I jerked and jerked until I collapsed into the arms of Benjamin Braddock.

SO NOT ME

I was whipped. No question about it. Benjamin Braddock, the man who was supposed to be my nemesis, the man who was supposed to be public enemy number one given his extremist views, had me under his complete and unbridled control.

I didn't realize it more clearly than the day after. He left my condo around two A.M., his body language making it clear that he was well pleased with the outcome, his mustache lifting up as he smiled and kissed me again. I couldn't sleep at all after he left, so I walked around. My heart was leaping for joy, and every time I thought of him holding me, I craved for more. But I was terrified too. I loved him, there was no doubt in my mind that what I felt for Ben Braddock was nothing short of heart-wrenching love. But when I brought up that infamous question of where do we go from here, especially in light of the round of lovemaking we had just endured, he would change the subject, to the Shepard case, to my record collection, to the weather. And that Angela woman, that so-called friend of his with a key to his home, was still an unspoken mystery, still the one outstanding entity that could quickly turn my dream into a nightmare. It was all troubling and exciting at the same time. Sometimes I would feel so great that I wanted to run outside and dance on the side of the road. And then other times I would want to cry, because I was too happy, and too needy, and still too unsure if Benjamin Braddock was my knight in shining armor, or just a spook, a mirage, a hit-and-run flimflam scrub up to no good.

The signs weren't very hopeful the day after. Mel Sanchez had promised to make my blasphemous article on Ben's nomination to the state supreme court front page, above the fold news, and he kept his word. That bothered me, since I was raking over the coals the man I loved, but I had already warned Ben of what was coming and he told me not to worry about him, so I didn't sweat it. But when he didn't call me, not that morning, not that afternoon, and when he, like before, didn't return my calls, I didn't know what to think. The idea that he would make love to me and then act as if he didn't know I existed was confusing as hell. I wanted to phone him the moment he left my condo. I wanted to run out of my home and chase after him the moment he drove away.

But I held my ground. It was his job to call me, not the other way around. I was the one who gave it up last night. He was the victor. But instead of calling and thanking me for giving him the ride of his life (at least in my mind anyway), he went about his business as if last night didn't mean shit to him.

That was why, after work, I drove to Scotty's gallery. Scotty knew all about the craziness of relationships and I needed him to tell me if it was true, if I had been played by a master of the game, or was simply overreacting.

He was in his office looking over his inventory sheets when I arrived, but Fran, to my dismay, was seated on the couch beside him.

"Hey, girl," she said excitedly as I walked in, and just the sound of her voice irritated me. "Don't tell me you're giving up your Africanism."

Scotty peeped over his reading glasses when she said that. I was wearing a white keyhole top and a pair of magenta dress pants I had ordered out of a Spiegel's catalogue, and although Fran was correct to notice that I wasn't in my normal African attire, I felt too combative to agree with her. "Excuse me?" I asked.

"Your clothes," she said.

"What about my clothes?"

"They don't look African to me."

"Who said they did?"

Scotty sighed because he knew what kind of mood I was in and Fran, knowing too, abandoned her sorry attempt at small talk.

"Everything all right, Josie?" Scotty asked. I told him that it was, although it obviously wasn't, but that was enough to turn his attention back to his work at hand.

So I folded my arms and began pacing back and forth, sighing and patting my feet, and then pacing some more. I knew I was getting on Fran's nerve, which was good because I was hoping she would take her nosy behind on so I could talk with Scotty, but what I didn't know was that Scotty was tired of me too. He peeped over his reading glasses again, as if to throw me a hint, but when I kept on keeping on, he exhaled. "Will you please sit down?" he asked impatiently. Fran laughed like the childish broad she was, and that voice of hers made me want to hurt her.

"What's funny?" I asked. "You see something funny?"

She and Scotty both looked at me, and she was not amused. "Like, what did you say?"

"You heard me, heifer," I said, walking up to where she sat. "I said what's funny? What's so damn funny?"

She got off of that couch then. "You better get out of my face!" she yelled.

"And what you supposed to do?" I asked, daring her. But Scotty stood up between us.

"That is most certainly enough," he said with great exasperation, his inventory sheets barely manageable in his hands. "Fran, you can go. I'll see you tomorrow, girl. And, Josephine, sit your skinny ass down."

Fran laughed again, but I didn't care. Scotty told her to leave. Not me.

I sat down. Scotty at first hesitated, and then sat down too. "You need to get a grip."

"Me? She was the one acting like some stupid, giggling kid."

"Okay, what is it? What has he done now?"

I paused. "I didn't say he did anything."

"Is he mad at you about that article you wrote on his nomination, because if he isn't, he should be."

"He doesn't care about stuff like that, Scotty, I told you. I mean he cares, but he knew it was coming."

"He knew? How?"

"He came over last night." I said this and looked at Scotty. He smiled.

"And?"

"And?"

"One thing led to another, right?"

"Yes."

"And let me guess: he made passionate love to you and has not phoned you once again."

I nodded.

"Well, at least he's consistent. Love-'em-and-leave-'em Ben, that's him. But what about that other woman? That Jehovah's Witness with the key to his house?"

"He didn't say."

"What you mean he didn't say?"

"He didn't say."

"Did you ask?"

"Of course I asked."

"And?"

"He said she was a friend of his, but that's all he would say about it. Oh, Scotty, tell me it's not what I think it is."

"What you think it is, girl?"

"I don't know. I just don't know. All I know is that I love him, that's all I know." I looked at Scotty. My first true confession. He didn't seem surprised in the least. He just took his arm and placed it around my shoulder.

"I'm sorry it's been so complicated, sweetie."

"But he knows how I feel, Scotty. I told him everything last night."

Scotty removed his arm from around me and looked at me. "What you mean by everything?"

"I told him I loved him—"

"Whoa, whoa," he said and held up his hand. "Wait a minute here. You told him what?"

I was dumfounded. "That I love him."

Scotty shook his head. "No, you didn't, girl."

"What?"

"You don't tell a man you love him just like that. You barely know him. You love him, that's a fact, but it ain't none of his business yet."

"Oh, I get it now. Another game. Never let your true feelings show, is that how it's played? Well, I'm not down with that, you hear me, Scotty? I love him and he knows it. And if he can't deal with that, then tough."

"Well, he apparently can't deal with it, 'cause he gone. So all of your big talk don't amount to nothing but big talk. You told me you was through with him. After that Angela woman hit the scene you told me that was it. Now he shows up at your house, out of the blue, and it's on again? You're full of it, you know that, Josie? You talk a good game about what you will and will not take from a man but damn, girl, you taking more than most and you just getting started. And then you tell him you love him, that you're weak for him, and then have the nerve to say if he can't deal with it, then that's tough? You're the one, it seems to me, who can't deal, sister girl."

I leaned my head against the back of the couch. I felt exhausted and hadn't done much of anything all day, except, of course, worry about Ben. "What can I do?"

"I ain't wasting my breath because you never listens to me."

"Just tell me."

"Check him out. If you wanna find out what the good judge is up to at night and if he intends to do right by you, check the brother out."

"You mean spy on him, Scotty?"

"That's exactly what I mean."

"Please. I don't play games, I told you that."

"You never listens to me."

"Not when you're talking nonsense like that I don't. I'm not about to tip around town following some man. I'll never get that hard up."

"Okay! Goodness. Forget it."

"Maybe I'm just overreacting. Maybe he'll call later tonight, or even come over."

"He is, after all, a judge. Maybe he's just busy, right?"

"Right."

"Wrong, girlfriend. That is not right. Ain't no man gonna be too busy to call the woman he loves. If he loves her. I'm sorry, but you always telling me to face facts. You got to face 'em too."

My heart was like a bolt of lightning, and it was striking every chord, and hurting like hell when it did. "So there's nothing I can do. Is there?"

"You can wait and see what happens. Or pick up the phone and call him."

I looked at Scotty. "Call him?"

"Yeah. That's the only way you'll ever know what time it is. Call him. But don't be telling him that you love him and you miss him and all that scary stuff. No self-respecting man can take all of that this soon."

"So what am I supposed to tell him?"

"That you just called to say hey. That's all. And who knows, maybe that's all it'll take. He is a great-looking brother, even I have to admit that. He may very well be used to women chasing him."

Scotty's words made sense to me, probably because I wanted something to hold on to, and I decided, almost as quickly as he had suggested it, to give Ben a call. If he acted as if he was too busy to talk or had a prior engagement or just hung up in my face, I would know right then and there that my knight's shining armor wasn't shiny at all, but old and rusty, and I'd go on with my life.

So I did it. I picked up the phone and dialed his number, a number I had already committed to memory. It rang for what seemed like forever and I was just about to hang up when the ringing stopped. The voice on the other end said, "Hello," and my heart sank. "Hello," the voice said again. And I hung up the phone.

Scotty looked at the phone first, and then me. "He didn't answer?"

"No," I said. "But she did."

"She who?"

I looked at Scotty. My face said it all. "Oh, Josie," he said and hugged me. "I'm sorry."

But I wasn't interested in his pity. The more I thought about what Ben was doing to me, how I wasn't even myself anymore, the angrier I became. "How could I've been so stupid?"

"You aren't stupid, Josie. You're in love. And this is how love goes sometimes."

"I can't let him get away with it. I can't let him do this to me."

"Don't go there, girl. That revenge thing never works, trust me. Just forget about him, okay? It'll be hard, Lord knows it was devastating when I had to admit that Bruce wasn't worth a damn, but thank God this wasn't some long relationship. You've just got to find a way to get over it."

I jerked away from Scotty and stood up. Get over it? Was he nuts? "You don't understand, Scotty," I said. "I can't just get over this.

This ain't no everyday thing for me. Don't you get it? He knows I love him, Scotty. I told him I loved him. Now he's back in the sack with Angela or whoever the hell else he's messing with, and he can now brag to his friends how he did a number on Josie too? I can't handle that. I'm sorry. And you say get over it? I'm not letting some joker like Ben Braddock play me like this. I didn't wait twenty-eight years for *this*. Like hell I'll get over it!"

Scotty looked at me. And he knew I meant business. He knew I wasn't going to rest, he wasn't going to rest, this entire world wasn't going to rest until I had my say.

He stood up. "Okay," he said. "You're right. He was wrong to treat you this way and you should confront him to get it out of your system. But only if I come along too."

"I don't need you to hold my hand, Scotty."

"And I don't need to be reading in tomorrow's *Gazette* how their very own ace reporter beat the crap out of the unsuspecting middle-aged girlfriend of the next supreme court justice. Forget it, girl. I know you. You are the mouth of the South. Your mouth can be a deadly weapon when you're angry like this. And you think I'm gonna let you visit those white-bread black folks in your condition? It ain't happenin'. You ain't about to enter that world alone."

Scotty drove the only way he knew how, fast, and swerved his Miata against the curb in front of Ben's home. The Seville was there, but just as I suspected, another car, a blue and white Lexus, was parked in the drive too. The morning I had left Ben's home in haste, that same Lexus was parked on his drive. A personalized plate with *AC-1* written on it was an unnecessary confirmation. It was Angela's car.

I looked at the cars and the peacefulness of the neighborhood, and sadness overtook my anger. What was I doing? I wasn't myself anymore. I was no longer Josie Ross, the in-your-face, never-been-hurt-by-a-man ultraliberal, the woman who wore her independence as a badge of honor. I was some hurt kid, terrified of being alone, scared even to confront Ben, because my worst fears would then be realized. He didn't want me. No ands, ifs, or buts about it. That was why I wanted to turn around, to say to hell with this, but I couldn't.

He had made love to me. That was the problem. Of all the men who begged and pleaded for the opportunity, I gave it away to Ben.

He didn't even have to ask. And what happens? He's not grateful and ready to commit his life to me, as I had assumed it would absolutely be, but he was ready to kick me to the curb and move on to his next conquest. If Helen McCoy would have seen me at this very moment, so vulnerable that it was pathetic, she would have died laughing. "Not the slash-and-burn queen," she would have said. "Not *the village is missing an idiot* idiot!"

I stepped out of Scotty's Miata and as soon as my feet hit ground, I got in a hurry.

"You sure you wanna do this?" Scotty asked as we walked hurriedly toward the front door. It was six-thirty in the evening and the sun was just beginning to set. I looked at Scotty against the backdrop of an approaching sunset and he looked the way I felt: worried.

"I'm all right," I said to reassure him. But my mind wasn't on him. Ben and Angela, they consumed my every thought.

When we arrived at the front door I began banging on it with my fist, as if the doorbell were nothing more than decoration. My heart was pounding more intensely now, my palms were sweating bullets, and I could feel my anger rising the longer it took him to get to that damn door.

"Now slow down, Josie," Scotty said when I started a new round of banging. "This is a future supreme court justice's house. This ain't your girlfriend up the road's place."

"He better be glad this all I'm doing to his door."

"But you gonna bang it down, fool."

"Does it look like I care? Huh, Scotty? Does it look like I really care!"

Scotty threw his hands in the air and shook his head. I was in the zone and he knew it, and all the reason in this world couldn't turn back my charge.

After yet another round of bangs the door was finally opened by Braddock himself. He was wearing a pair of suit pants and his white dress shirt was not tucked in, but hung out loosely as if he was just getting ready to disrobe. Until I showed up.

"Don't you bang on my door like that!" he said angrily as soon as his door flew open. "What's wrong with you?"

I shook my head. The brother was good, I had to admit. He was standing here as if he could not possibly fathom what my problem could be, and then had the nerve to get angry with me because I didn't show respect at *his* home? I didn't show it because I didn't have it.

"Aren't you gonna invite us in?" I asked so bitterly that it sounded more like a command than a question.

"Not until you settle yourself down."

"Settle myself down?" I asked, and Scotty, knowing that tone of mine all too well, and also knowing that Ben had the look of a man not fond of confrontation, touched me on the arm. "Cool it, J," he said.

"I ain't coolin' nothing," I said in return. And then I looked at Ben. "You got some nerve, you know that? Telling me to settle down. You settle down! You don't tell me what to do. *Fuck you!*"

It was those last two words that did it. As soon as they rolled from my lips the judge lost all restraint and grabbed me by the arm, slinging me into his house as if I were a rag doll. Anger was in his eyes, great, sudden, violent anger, and his look alone terrified me. And when he released my arm and turned to close the door, the terror that was in my heart was showing all over Scotty's face. "Are you coming in?" Ben asked him, angrily, his fuse so short Scotty knew there was no time to contemplate a response. So he just hurried in.

Ben slammed his door shut and looked at me. Scotty and I stood like two mannequins, standing shoulder to shoulder, frozen in place as we witnessed the unleashed furor of Benjamin Braddock.

"Who do you think you are?" he asked me. "Don't you ever talk to me like that!"

"Where is she?" I asked, looking around, not in the least interested in his unrighteous indignation.

He could tell how little I thought of his fake propriety too because he gave me a priceless, deadly look. But I didn't even care. "Where is she, Ben?" I asked again.

This time he frowned. "Where's *who?*"

"Your friend girl. Miss Angela. Who the hell you think?"

Scotty once again touched me on the arm, but I snatched away from him. But before Ben could respond to me, or lash back at me, the subject herself walked into the living room from around the kitchen. She was dressed to kill in a gray pantsuit and heels, carrying a glass of what appeared to be red wine, looking gorgeous and obnoxiously happy. I wanted to throw up. "Oh," she said when she saw us, as if she was happily surprised by my presence, "Josie again. How are you, dear?"

I looked at the witch and shook my head. "What, you know me?" I asked, looking her up and down. "You supposed to be a friend of mine because you know my name?"

She didn't answer my questions, of course, but that nauseating smile of hers was gone. Ben, however, wasn't amused either. He looked as if it was taking all he had not to slap the shit out of me. "What's the matter with you?" he asked me, as if he didn't know. "And why are you talking to her in that tone?"

"And who is she supposed to be? I can talk to her in any damn tone I please!" Scotty nudged me by the elbow this time, but I wasn't thinking about him. Ben just stared at me, as if I never ceased to amaze him, as if he was seeing a side of me he didn't think was capable of existing.

"Look, Ben," Angela said, putting her glass of wine on a nearby table, "I can leave."

"You aren't going anywhere," Ben said to her angrily, although he never took his eyes off of me. "You apologize to my guest at once, Josephine."

I almost laughed. "Apologize? To *her*? Are you out of your mind?" Tears began to drop from my eyes. I didn't want to cry, but I couldn't help it. "You played me," I said. "You made love to me and now you act like it's nothing. Like it was just something to do! And you knew there was another woman. How could you do that to me? Why didn't you just leave me the hell alone, Ben? Why didn't you tell me you weren't interested and leave me alone? I was doing fine before you came. I had it together before your sorry ass came into my life. Now look at me!"

My tears were dropping like water and I knew I was a pathetic sight to behold because everybody in the room, even the other woman, had pity all over their faces. And Ben, who looked crushed, seemed to pity me most of all. But I didn't want his pity, and I lashed out even angrier because I didn't want it, and I felt cheap and depraved and so totally out of control that I could hardly see straight. It wasn't until Scotty placed his arm around my waist and told me to cool it, whispering, "They've got the message" in my ear, that I even thought about settling down.

Then Ben told his girlfriend to come by his side. She walked up to him with her hand on her chest. She seemed so flabbergasted by my outburst that she stayed a step behind him, for protection no doubt.

"Angela," Ben said, "this is Josephine."

Angela, this time, only nodded in my general direction.

"Josephine," Ben said, "this is Angela Caldwell. Fred Caldwell's wife. Freddie Caldwell, and you probably know this, was once a pro ball player, the starting tailback for the Pittsburgh Steelers before he blew out a knee. He's chairman and CEO of Caldwell Electronics nowadays. This is none of your business but Fred's my best friend. He and Angela are about to celebrate their twentieth wedding anniversary and she and I have been planning for weeks for the big occasion. I told you before that she is a very good friend of mine but she is not my girlfriend, and I will not say it to you again. And yes, you're right, I haven't been around to see you today. I was suddenly called away to a series of meetings in Tallahassee with members of the governor's selection committee. I returned to town less than an hour ago. I left a message on your home phone telling you that I would see you later tonight. I guess I could have phoned you from Tallahassee today, sure I could have. But I never checked in with anybody before and I'm not about to start now."

He said this calmly, in a rationed, measured voice, and I felt as if somebody had taken a sledgehammer and slammed it into my face, rendering me so embarrassed that I didn't know where to begin to know what to do. Of course I knew Fred Caldwell. Everybody in Jacksonville knew Dollar Bill Caldwell. He was one of their most famous citizens. As soon as I hit town I had heard about Caldwell. He played his college ball at the University of Florida, and Mike Cooper, our sports reporter, always compared every Gator back in the history of the school to Dollar Bill. Dollar Bill Caldwell. When he got his hands on the ball it was like money in the bank.

And I had just insulted his wife. Big time. I was so beside myself with shame that the only thing I could think to do was look at Scotty. He smiled. "This is where we back our behinds up and get the hell out of here," he suggested. But no way could I just leave.

I looked at Angela. "I'm really sorry, Mrs. Caldwell," I said.

She should have cussed me out and told me what I could do with my sorrow, but she had too much class for that. She smiled instead. "That's okay, dear," she said. "A good man will sometimes make us do some interesting things."

I smiled. She had made the understatement of the night. I looked at Ben, at the good man that stood before me. I was so relieved that there was an explanation for everything that I wanted to run into his arms. But the expression on his face was more grim than warm. I didn't think he would be receptive to a hug just yet.

"Well," I said, "I better go."

At first he didn't want to stop me, and Scotty and I actually turned to leave, but then he spoke up. My heart leaped for joy when he did. "Have you had dinner yet, Josephine?" he asked in his odd combination of concern and contempt.

I turned to him. "No," I said.

"I'm too tired to go out and eat so I think I'll whip something up for us."

"Okay," I said, inwardly delighted.

"You stay too, Angela," Ben said. "Fred, I'm sure, will grab something at the office."

"And I'm sure you're right," Angela said.

We stood there awkwardly, and then Scotty spoke up. "Y'all just forgetting about me?" he said, and we all looked at him. His face was serious. He actually felt left out. Then we looked at Ben. He smiled.

"Now how could I ever forget my man Scotty?" he asked. "I just assumed without asking that you would be staying for dinner." And that was all it took, because Scotty beamed. We laughed.

Dinner was spaghetti, garlic bread, and salad, all thrown together by Benjamin Braddock himself, and it was delicious. Ben and Angela spent most of the evening going over details about the anniversary party, and occasionally Scotty put in his two cents. I just ate quietly and listened. I felt I had said enough, thank you. I still felt bad about my behavior and I could tell that Ben was still a little pissed with me, so I stayed in the background.

After dinner Scotty insisted on helping Ben with the dishes while Angela and I relaxed in the living room. Angela, who, like Ben, smoked, pulled out a cigarette and offered me one. I declined and she smiled. "How old are you?" she asked me.

"Twenty-eight," I said.

"My goodness. Ben's forty-eight. Does that bother you?"

I looked at her. What was up with this? "Why should it bother me?"

"It shouldn't. That's my point. The fact that he has a female friend shouldn't bother you either."

She didn't have to go there, because I believed Ben. She was his best friend's wife. And I just knew a man like him wouldn't dare have a sexual relationship with his best friend's wife. But of course I didn't let her know all of this. I still felt she was a little too chummy with my man and she had that look about her, like she knew she had it going on and she could have any man she wanted. So I played it cool with the sister. "I don't follow you," I said.

"I've known Benjamin for almost thirty years now. He and my husband went to Florida together while I was a freshman at Florida State. Whenever I would go to Gainesville or he and Fred would come to Tallahassee, we'd have such fun. Not because there was so much to do, but because we, the three of us, truly loved each other's company. That's all. We still enjoy each other's company."

I still didn't follow her, but I nodded as if I did.

"You're very pretty," she said.

"Thanks. So are you."

"And so young."

I couldn't say the same about her, so I smiled.

"How long have you known Ben?"

"Not very long at all."

"I see. That explains it then. But may I offer you some advice?"

I braced myself for anything. Now I would know sister girl's true intentions. "Yes," I said, eager to hear this sage advice.

"Your fears are misplaced," she said. "I would suggest you relax. He obviously cares about you or he would have thrown you out on your rear—and you know what I mean."

I did. And she was right. "Did he tell you about me?"

"No. But that's not unusual. He rarely discusses his personal affairs with me. To my husband he tells more, but not to me. But relax, Josie. That's my advice. Relax. I've known Benjamin Braddock a long time. And I assure you he is not the kind of man you have to worry about."

I looked at her and smiled. I could only hope she was right.

But I was determined to keep my wits about me. He still could

have been playing the game, but he was too sophisticated to reveal it and I wasn't smart enough to figure it out. That was why, when the party was over and Scotty was handing me my jacket, I had already decided to refuse any offer to stay. I watched Ben after dinner, when he and Scotty joined us in the living room. I saw how he would sneak peeps at me when he thought I wasn't looking, and when I did look he'd look away. I wasn't well experienced, but I was experienced enough to know a brother in heat when I saw one.

And sure enough, as Mrs. Caldwell, Scotty, and I walked toward the front door to leave, Ben, who was bringing up the rear, touched me lightly on my arm and informed Scotty that he would be taking me home.

Scotty smiled, which I didn't appreciate since it seemed so locker-roomish, and then he said, "Okay, Judge," as if it were a decision that didn't concern me. I shook my head no as I turned around to set Ben straight. I couldn't continue to let him control this entire relationship. And if he thought I was that easy, then the whole affair was doomed. I even had my line predetermined. *Thank you, Ben,* I was going to say, *but I came with Scotty, I think I should leave with Scotty.* But when I turned and looked at him, and he was standing there looking so gorgeous that it made my stomach rumble, the words got twisted on my tongue, and instead of saying what amounted to *no way, Jose,* I said, "Okay, Judge," and handed him my coat.

He kissed Mrs. Caldwell lightly on the cheek, shook Scotty's hand, and bade them farewell. When they were gone and the door was closed, he leaned against it and looked at me. I felt awkward as hell just standing there, because I suddenly didn't know what to do with my hands, so I began walking toward the living-room area. "It was a delicious meal, Ben," I said as I walked, trying my best to convey the image of somebody who knew what she was doing. I looked back, to see if he was following me, but it wasn't until I sat down on his sofa that I saw him appear at the entranceway into the living room. His hands were in his pockets and he seemed preoccupied, maybe even impatient, as if my desire to chitchat on the sofa wasn't at all what he had in mind.

"Did you hear me?" I asked him. "I said dinner was delicious."

"Thank you," he said. Then he walked over by the sofa and sat next to me. "I'm glad you liked it."

"I did."

He looked at me and smiled. Then he slowly slipped his arm around my waist and nudged me closer to him. "You looked like you could use a good meal tonight."

I laughed. "Was I that bad?"

"You were pretty bad."

"I'm sorry. I just thought she was, that you and she . . ."

"I told you she wasn't my girlfriend, Josephine."

"I know. But you know how I am."

"I'm beginning to learn, yes."

His hand reached in under my blouse and he began to rub my stomach. It felt so good I leaned back and closed my eyes. "Who taught you how to cook like that?" I asked him.

"Necessity."

I opened my eyes. "Necessity?"

"My wife wouldn't. The maid couldn't, good anyway, so I had to."

It sounded so pitiful, his life before I came along, so I smiled. "You can do it all, can't you?"

He seemed baffled by my question, he even raised his eyebrows as if he was truly confused. "It's called surviving," he said. "Nothing remarkable about that."

I touched his hand as it massaged my stomach. He looked at me. "You really don't think you're a big deal, do you?" I asked him.

"I'm not a big deal."

I smiled. "Yes, you are. You're hot stuff, man. And it doesn't even faze you. That's why I love you so much."

His facial expression immediately changed when I mentioned love. He became so disconcerted that I began to worry if I had said something wrong.

"What's the matter, Ben?" I asked him.

"Nothing's the matter."

"Are you sure?"

"I'm positive."

"But . . ."

"But what?"

"But I don't understand."

"There's nothing to understand, Josephine. Everything's fine." Then he removed his hand from around me and stood up. "But I am tired and I've got to get an early start in the morning. I'd better take you home."

I looked up at him dazed. Did I miss something? He didn't love me, was that why he hated when I mentioned the word? When he thought I was interested sexually, he was fine, rubbing on my stomach and ready to rub more than that. But as soon as I mentioned that little four-letter word it was suddenly time to get rid of me. I stood up quickly too, because I refused to let him see how I really felt. I even told him that he was right, that it was late after all and I had to get an early start myself. Then I looked into his eyes. And he looked into mine. But my lie and his lie kept us from saying another word.

It was a painful ride home. My Mustang still sat in front of Scotty's gallery, and I should have told him to drop me off there, but I couldn't speak. I felt like a failure. I felt like a woman who talked the talk, but it was now exposed, not as wisdom and self-assuredness, but hot air. I looked at Ben, as he drove along the quiet streets of Jacksonville, his eyes riveted on nothing more than the dark road ahead, and I knew I was out of my league. He was a man who didn't have time for weakness, who probably wanted me because I was supposed to be this tough chick who would stand up to him, not some lovesick puppy. He wasn't a rigid conservative by accident, but by nature, who blamed the victim for acting like a victim, who didn't suffer fools well. A man like him wanted a rock, a boulder, not a pathetic, emotional wreck like me.

When we arrived at my condo I got out of his car quickly, before he could even think about saying a word to me. I slammed the door of his expensive Seville as if it were a junk car. My sadness had turned into anger, and it wasn't about him, but me. There was a reason I had avoided love so long, and this was it. I couldn't be myself and be in love. Being in love meant *falling* in love. And I'd fallen head over heels. Completely off balance. My very sense of being was upside down. Everything I thought was right was wrong, everything I thought I was, I wasn't. I believed I was winning by avoiding the game, but now, of all times, when I should have picked up my marbles and gone home once more, I didn't. I stayed. I allowed my feelings to show. Now I felt cheap, like a prostitute, and exposed, like a traveling shell-game artist ready to display her wares to a customer who knew exactly what she was up to.

I unlocked my condo and hurried inside. I leaned against the door and listened for Ben's car to drive away. And he did, slowly at first, and then quickly, backing up and speeding off as if he couldn't get away fast enough. My body felt weightless after he left, as a sense of being drained overtook me. And before I realized what was happening, I slid to the floor as if I were being deflated, and I couldn't hold back any longer. I cried. I cried like a baby. I cried for my mama. I cried for the woman I never really was.

IT DOESN'T TAKE
ALL THAT

A new day. Thank God for another day. I was up early, just after six, and had showered, dressed, made me a cup of cappuccino, and was in a cab heading for Scotty's gallery before eight A.M. I still felt the sting of the night before. There was still a lump in my throat whenever I thought about Ben, and my heart still felt as if it had a hole in it the size of a basketball. But this was a new day, and I was determined to live this day for me, about me, and on my own terms.

My Mustang stayed the night in front of Scotty's gallery, and I was relieved to find it undisturbed as the cab drove up and dropped me off. Once inside, I popped out that Charlie Parker CD Ben had given me, and popped in the Baha Men. They were singing "Who Let the Dogs Out?" and their *woof* dog sounds were loud and the beat deafening and I loved it. I needed it! And I blared it to the max, the bass so deep that my car felt as if it were bouncing, and I pumped my fist in the air and moved with the groove. To hell with Benjamin Braddock, I decided. To hell with his jive-ass jazz and off-the-wall politics and that whole damn scene called love. Who the hell needed it? Not me. I had my job, my Mustang, my condo, and my music. It worked for me before Ben Braddock, and I was going to keep working it after Ben Braddock.

Mel was sitting at my desk when I arrived at work. The newsroom was quiet, with just a handful of reporters scurrying about, and of all the empty desks in the room he picked mine to sit behind.

His legs were crossed and he was leaned back smoking a cigar and playing solitaire on my computer. I hesitated when I saw him, because his affection for me was scary too, but I quickly reminded myself that my days of being afraid were gone. If Mel liked me in a way that went beyond our professional relationship, then that was Mel's problem. If Leroy the security guard or Coop or Eddie or any other human being had any designs on me whatsoever, that was their problem. Benjamin Braddock had taught me well. It was my fault that I fell in love with him, and it was their fault if they were falling for me.

"Good morning, Mel," I said with little energy as I slung my shoulder bag on my desk and dropped my keys down beside it. I wanted to make it clear immediately that I didn't appreciate his intrusion.

"Aren't we in a foul mood this morning," he replied without taking his eyes off of the computer screen. I checked him out. He had on a light blue shirt, a pair of red-and-green-striped pants, and a fat, dark gray polka-dot tie. A fashion disaster, in other words. Helen once told him that all he needed was a woman's touch, but when I jokingly suggested that she could be that woman, he cussed me out. "Pigs will fly," he warned, "before that stinkin' woman touches me!"

I looked at Mel to see if he would get my drift and get on out of the way, but he was too engrossed in his computer game to pay me any attention. I picked up the small stack of mail that sat in the middle of my desk and skimmed each envelope. Then I tossed them on the desk. "Come on, Mel," I said, but he continued to play his solitaire as if he didn't hear me, moving the jack on top of the queen and the king underneath both of them. It seemed like such a ridiculous game to me, moving cards around like that, but I guess that was why they called it solitaire. Alone. Nothing to do. Do this.

"Mel, come on, I've got work to do," I said, but this time I nudged him with my hip. That got his attention, as I was sure it would, and he immediately looked at me. I was wearing a pair of tight jeans and a Gap T-shirt tucked inside. African attire was still my thing, but I wasn't feeling it today.

Mel's eyes were, at first, fixated on my hands for some reason, but then he slowly stood up and we were eye to eye. Now there was a face of compassion, I thought, because his face beamed with it, and I wondered why it was that I could fall madly in love with a man like Ben, who viewed compassion as a weakness, and not fall at all for

Mel, who, like me, viewed it as a duty. But such is life, as my mother always said. Such is life.

"Where were you last night?" he asked as we stood so close I could smell the tobacco on his breath.

"Excuse me?" I asked. For some reason, maybe it was the way he asked it, it seemed like a strange question to me.

"I phoned you last night, but I didn't get an answer."

I could see Helen peripherally as she turned her head sideways. She had heard Mel's comment and wanted to gauge my reaction. She was so nosy that I thought about putting on a little show for her, maybe even flirting with Mel big time so she could run and tell that, but I couldn't do that to Mel.

"I was out last night," I said. "I went to dinner."

He nodded. "With Scotty?"

Mel had found out somehow, maybe bigmouthed Scotty told him, that my relationship with Ben had taken an unexpected turn, but instead of asking me directly, he insinuated like hell. But I didn't play games with Braddock, so I certainly wasn't going to play them with him.

"Yes, with Scotty," I said. "What did you want?"

He looked at me, as if he knew I was technically correct but not completely honest. "Nothing," he said. "Just wanted to talk." I nodded. I should have asked what about but I couldn't. I knew what about.

He looked at me longer. Maybe it was a deception. Maybe I should have mentioned that I had had dinner not only with Scotty, but with Ben Braddock, the enemy, too, but I couldn't go there anymore. It was none of his damn business who I had dinner with.

My face apparently made my defiance known because he didn't linger around my desk the way he normally did. He began walking away, moving past desk after desk, until he was in his office.

I sat down. He was pitiful, I thought, but I couldn't do anything about that. I wasn't there to pity him or nurse his romantic idealism, I was there to work. And that was exactly what I decided to do.

My shaky-at-best confidence was shot, however, when I went to the rest room and returned. It took me less than five minutes. Five short minutes. But when I returned, Benjamin Braddock was in the house, leaning against my messy desk.

Helen had completely turned her chair around, as if she was searching for a file on the desk behind her, so she had a ringside seat. Cathy and Andrea, her two partners, were less obvious, but their eyes were riveted on us too.

I stopped cold in my tracks when I saw him. I didn't mean to be so obvious, but he was the last human being I expected to be standing at my desk. And why did he always have to look so gorgeous? Why couldn't his hair be out of place or his suit ruffled or his shoes mismatched? Why did he always have to look so perfect? "Ben," I said after I regained my composure and began heading for my desk.

"Good morning," he said and stood erect.

I walked up to the desk and stood beside him. He smelled good too. Damn. "What are you doing here?" I asked him.

"Let's go someplace," he said. "I need to talk to you."

"Now?"

He looked down as if I had once again said the wrong thing. "Yes, Josephine. Now."

His impatience was definitely his weak point, but that was his problem. I was at work. I couldn't just pack up and leave. But he was acting as if I were just hanging around the newsroom because I had nothing better to do. I glanced at Mel's office. I didn't see him, but I knew he was there, fuming, wondering what the hell was up with this. Me and Braddock together? In the flesh? On *his* turf?

"I can't now," I said. "I don't think my boss would like it."

"Well," Ben said, "I know *his* boss, and he wouldn't mind at all."

He was referring to his buddy, our publisher. Guys like him had the power and they loved the power. And they wouldn't hesitate to use it to their advantage. So why should I complain? I figured. Besides, I was curious as hell to know what he had to say. And it had better include an apology.

So I agreed to go across the street to Polly's, a small café that was still in business because the *Gazette* folks and a few of those 65,000 additional downtown office workers frequented it so much. We took a table beside the jukebox and I walked over and pressed on a tune. And it wasn't jazz. It was Eminem's "The Real Slim Shady."

When I sat down I could tell Ben was irritated with my selection, but I didn't care. I felt just that rejuvenated. If he wanted to listen to some damn Miles Davis, then he could go home and listen to him.

"Hey, girl," Sandy, the waitress, said, coming up to our table. "I knew you was in here when that rap music started. You're the only customer we got who listens to that stuff."

"I know. It ain't easy being me."

Sandy laughed. She was a dirty blonde who smoked so much that her voice always sounded as if it was a drag away from a certain diagnosis of emphysema. "What y'all having?" she asked, cutting off her laughter on a dime, as usual.

"A half-caff no-foam latte for me," I said. "You know me."

"Yeah, I got you." She looked at Ben. "What about you, sir?"

"Ah, a Coke, please," he said.

"A simple man. I like that." She said this and then walked away.

Ben pulled out a cigarette. He was real hesitant to talk, which surprised me, but then he got to the point. "About last night," he said. I didn't say anything. "Not my finest hour, was it?"

He asked this question and then stared at me anxiously, as if my response alone would determine everything. I hated being on the spot like that. He didn't play games the way I had expected them to be played. None of that flip-the-script lowdown for him. His games were chesslike, where every move determined the next move, not by picking up a piece and setting it down, but by sleight of hand, where a move was made before you even knew that a move was being contemplated. It was all about manipulation, in my view, and I wasn't wit it.

"No," I said, "it wasn't your finest hour."

"It had been a long day. The selection committee in Tallahassee drilled me on everything I ever did in my entire life and I just. . . I was tired, Josephine. I wasn't trying to be disrespectful."

"All I said was that I loved you and you acted as if I had offended you or something. What was up with that? I was just being honest. It's not like it's a secret anymore."

He gazed at me with a piercing look, as if he was trying to decide if I was worth the bother. And it could have gone either way. He exhaled. "Is it too late now?" he asked, his bright brown eyes appearing to search mine for clues.

But it sounded like another question within a question to me. So instead of trying to figure out what he meant, I decided to asked for clarification. "For us or for the apology?"

His mustache lifted up and he smiled. I was finally catching on.

"Both," he said.

"For the apology it's definitely not too late. For us, I recommend one day at a time."

He nodded. "Good answer," he said.

He walked me back to the *Gazette* and we stood at the elevator talking a few minutes longer. Leroy the security guard acted as if he didn't see us, but he couldn't help but see. He was still hitting on me, every day he saw me, but maybe now that he knew he wasn't my type by a mile, he'd leave me alone. But it wasn't like I cared. I had Ben.

He didn't exactly apologize for how he treated me at his house, but he did apologize for not being more patient with me. He wasn't used to a woman like me, he said, and he didn't clarify himself either. But that was cool too. One day at a time, I kept telling myself. One day at a time.

He invited me to dinner with the Caldwells and said he would call me later with details. And then he kissed me on my lips, gently, and I trembled for more. He smiled. He rarely smiled, so when he did it warmed my heart. I had no choice but to smile too.

I hurried back into the newsroom expecting fireworks from Mel. *Where the hell were you?* I expected him to say. *I had an assignment ready to go and I couldn't find you anywhere!* But he didn't say a word. He stood there, looking out of the plate-glass window of his office, staring at me as if he could not believe that I, his liberal side-kick, his crush-the-conservatives protégée, would allow a man like Ben Braddock within a hundred feet of my heart.

Fred and Angela Caldwell lived on Fleming Island in a sprawling Tudor-style home with big, bay windows of smoked glass, round, towerlike structures on either side of the front end, and thick, white-column posts with pink capitals and green plinths, sitting like a modern-day castle at the end of a steep, fifty-foot incline.

I drove up cautiously. Ben had phoned earlier and told me to meet him there, but his Seville was nowhere to be seen. A Mercedes was there, a Saab, and Angela's Lexus, but Ben, as usual, was late.

I felt foolish coming to their home without Ben already present, since my introduction to Angela Caldwell wasn't exactly reassuring, but I wasn't in the kind of neighborhood where you could kill time by hanging out at the 7-11 around the corner. So I got out of my car, walked up to the heavy wooden door, and rang the bell.

This was my first official date with Ben and I started to go all out, first in a beautiful evening dress and then I considered wearing a gown, but then I felt such extravagance would send the wrong signal. He seemed to like me best when I was my regular feisty self, so I was determined to stay the course. I wore a white pantsuit with white and yellow pumps, carried a white clutch purse, and tossed a yellow scarf (Scotty's idea) around my neck. My hair remained in braids but I had my stylist lift them up for a change, and although it was evening time I wore a pair of yellow transitional shades to help give me a more grown-up, mysterious woman appearance. I was hanging with the big shots tonight. I wanted to at least look old enough to be there.

The butler, a burly black man in a tight-fitting white jacket, opened the door after my second ring. I exhaled.

"Good evening," I said smilingly.

"Good evening," he said dully.

"Is this the Caldwell residence?"

"It is."

"Hi, I'm Josie Ross. I'm supposed to meet Judge Braddock here tonight but I see he hasn't arrived yet."

The butler just stood there.

"I would have waited in my car but I didn't want you to mistake me for an intruder or a Peeping Tom or something. So here I am."

He stepped aside. "Right this way, madam," he said.

That was simple enough, I thought, as I stepped into the white-marble foyer of the breathtakingly beautiful home. From the crystal staircase to the elegant all-white furniture to the glass elevator, nothing about the place was understated. Talk about black folks having arrived. The Caldwells had arrived, gone back, and arrived again the way they had their crib hooked up. And there were no Ma and Papa Gus type of paintings on their walls, no Norman Rockwell feel-good shit either, but only the most extravagantly expensive. From Monet to Renoir, Delacroix to Matisse, almost a room too crowded with artistic beauty. The art in Scotty's gallery, art I used to think was just perfect, looked like something out of one of those everything's-a-dollar stores compared to the art in the Caldwell home.

The butler escorted me into a huge sitting room and told me that someone would be with me shortly, and he left, closing the sliding double doors behind him. I walked around the room because it was gorgeous too, with more lavish furniture, all Victorian, all with that glossy satin mahogany finish, and even more expensive paintings. There were photographs in gold picture frames on top of the fireplace mantelpiece and I searched for familiar faces. Angela Caldwell was prominently displayed, her beauty so radiant that it glowed on camera too. The man always with her was Fred "Dollar Bill" Caldwell, her husband. I recognized his picture from all those I'd seen in the newspapers through the years. He was one of Jacksonville's most famous citizens and he was Ben's best friend. *My* Ben. I felt honored.

There were numerous other pictures of pretty strangers, and then there was Ben. He figured prominently in this family too, because he appeared in quite a few family photos, looking stunningly handsome in his wonderful but seldom-displayed smile, a smile so contagious that I found myself smiling too. And I found myself feeling fortunate that somebody like Ben could have chosen somebody like me. I was just a poor girl from Alabama after all, who could have been just like my siblings, still stuck and bitter, but who got away, and ended up here. Of all places. What else could I do but smile?

The doors of the sitting room slid open and a young man, perhaps eighteen if that old, entered quickly. He was wearing a blue short set and appeared agitated. "Have you seen my racket?" he asked me.

"Your racket?"

"Yes. As in tennis."

I shrugged my shoulder. "I don't live here."

"That's the craziest thing I've ever heard. Of course you don't live here. What an idiotic thing to say. Do you even know what a tennis racket looks like?"

His flippancy wiped the smile from my face. "Yes."

"Well?"

"No, I haven't seen your racket."

"Terrific," he said, and then he gave me the once-over. "Who are you anyway?"

"My name is Josie."

"Oh. Uncle Ben's old lady."

What an asshole, I thought. "Yes," I said.

"You're certainly the youngest one so far. I didn't think he was the kind of dude who went for that sort of thing. But you're pretty, so I guess he made an exception."

I didn't know if he was being nice or nasty so I didn't respond. He looked at me a little longer, as if he was waiting for me to say something, and then he left. He was easily Fred Caldwell's son; they had the same square forehead, the same turned-down mouth, and if his behavior was any indication of what kind of man his father was, I figured I was in for a long night.

I sat down and hoped that Ben would get here before I had to meet the legend of the house. His wife was nice enough, although I couldn't say that she and I had hit it off to such a degree that we were now girlfriends, but she and he could be a study in contrast. Ben and I certainly were. But before I could ponder it further, or even plot a strategy, a female walked in, not Angela Caldwell, but a younger version of her. Unlike the boy before her, she didn't enter talking. She entered looking.

"Good evening," I said to her when it was apparent that she wasn't interested in speaking. She kept walking and looking, and then she plopped down on the couch that sat directly across from mine. I thought her childish and even silly, so I decided to see how far she'd take it. I didn't know why, but females always seemed to view me as some threat to their womanhood when I wasn't even thinking about them.

I slid my shades down the bridge of my nose and checked her out from over the rim. "I'm Josie," I said. "You must be Angela's daughter." I said Angela carefully, because we weren't exactly on a first-name basis, but Miss Thang didn't know that.

"You're not his type," she said.

Her bluntness at first surprised me, but I quickly regained my composure. "I'm not?"

"No."

"And why not?"

"Because you ain't!"

Her sudden flash of temper angered me too. "Well," I said, "that's your opinion, isn't it?"

"He likes women with meat on their bones. You're skinny."

"I have meat on my bones."

"He likes grown-up women. You look like a little kid."

"However, I'm not a kid, unlike some of us in this room."

She glared at me and she probably would have told me some-thing, but a back door in the room opened and Ben, Angela, and Fred entered talking. I stood up, astonished and relieved, because I didn't realize Ben was already there. My little visitor, however, jumped up and ran to him. "Hi, Ben!" she said gaily and kissed him on his lips. He placed his hands around her waist and smiled.

"That's Uncle Ben to you, FassyMae," Angela said.

"He's not my uncle," Miss Thang said as she stared adoringly at my man.

"He's the closest you'll ever get to one," Fred said. He was the first to hurry toward me, his hand extended as he came, his smile al-most as infectious as Ben's. "You must be Josie."

"Yes," I said smilingly and shook his hand. Ben and Angela made their way toward me too, with Miss Thang still clinging to Ben as if she were a blower on the side of a vacuum. Girlfriend was ready to clean up, particularly me, but I wasn't having it. I moved next to Ben and placed my arm around his.

He looked at me as if he was surprised by my public display. "Hey," he said to me.

"Hey yourself."

"You look radiant," Angela said, and I smiled and returned the compliment.

"You're a knockout," Fred said. "Benjamin is a lucky man."

I smiled and thanked him too, and then I thanked God that he wasn't as horrid as his children. I, in fact, liked him immediately. There was a genuineness about him, an earnestness, as if he was going to be in my corner and was going to make sure that Ben stayed there as well.

"Sit down, dear," Angela told me, and we all sat down, Angela and Fred on one couch, me, Ben, and FassyMae on the other one. I had removed my arm from around Ben's, since it was an unsolicited move on my part anyway, but FassyMae still held his hand.

We talked small talk for maybe ten minutes or so, until Angela announced that she was famished and we should get going.

"Where?" Ben asked Angela.

"Where?" Angela asked Fred.

"Where?" Fred asked FassyMae, and she giggled. Then he looked at me. "You pick a place."

"Oh, Fred," Angela said. "You didn't make a reservation?"

Still looking at me, he said: "Now what is wrong with that question, Josie? Let's examine it. I work. Sometimes eighteen hours per day. I leave the house at five-thirty every morning and return sometimes as late as midnight. My wife, on the other hand, doesn't work, usually leaves home around eleven to get her hair and nails done or to mall-hop, she is home well before dark most nights, yet she wants to know why it is that I—I, mind you, the workaholic—didn't make a reservation for this evening's dinner."

Angela hit him lightly on his arm. "Not you, silly," she said, "but your secretary, or one of your assistants."

"Now what is wrong with that observation?"

"Not again," Ben said.

"You pick a place," Fred said to me.

I smiled. "I'm sure you wouldn't want me to pick the place."

"Sure we would. Don't we, Benjamin?"

Ben looked at me. He still made my heart drop every time he looked into my eyes. Yet he still seemed suspicious of me, as if he wasn't yet sure what I was all about. "Do you have a favorite restaurant, Josephine?" he asked me.

"Yes. But I'm sure—"

"It's settled then," Fred said and stood up. We all stood up too. "Do you think we'll need to phone ahead?"

"You don't understand—"

"We need a reservation then?"

I smiled. "No, but—"

"Good," he said, and placed my arm across his. "Stay out of trouble," he warned FassyMae, and then he and I began walking toward the exit.

"Bye, Benny," I heard FassyMae say, and when I turned she was kissing him on the lips. I could deal with her schoolgirl flirtatiousness because most kids her age had that silliness about them, but what I couldn't understand was why Ben would allow it.

He took Angela's arm and they began walking behind us, but not fast enough for Fred. "Come on, sweetheart," Fred said, looking back. "You too, Angela." We all laughed.

We drove in one car, the Mercedes, and I was surprised when Ben got behind the wheel. Fred and Angela settled in the backseat and I sat up front with Ben.

"What happened to the Seville?" I asked him.

"Nothing happened to it."

"What," Fred asked, "you didn't know your boy drove a Benz?"

"No. I just thought he had a Seville."

"Oh no, honey. That Seville is his work car. It's a forty-thousand-dollar work car, to be sure, but it ain't no Benz."

"Forty thousand dollars?" I asked, unable to conceal my shock.

"You think that's too much money, don't you?" Fred asked.

"Yes. Matter of fact, I do."

"Oh, I love you. I love her, Benjamin!"

"I'm sure you do," Ben said.

"Given the level of car we're talking about," Angela said, "I think forty thousand is about right."

"This from a woman who goes through two thousand dollars a week," Fred said. "Do you realize what that means? If we get a divorce I would have to pay her eight thousand dollars per month spousal support, and that's just for her little spending change. And given the state of the law profession these days they'll probably throw in another ten thou per month as a final, sucker punch. That's eighteen big ones every month. No sirre, Bob. We ain't never getting a divorce!"

"It's cheaper to keep her, Fred," Ben said.

"Absolutely."

"But it's not cheaper for me to keep you," Angela said. "I'll be an extra ten grand per month richer if I get rid of you."

Angela and I laughed, I even turned around and high-fived her. Ben glanced at me with that old disapproving, stern look of his, but I didn't care. I liked a woman who wasn't afraid to flip the script. Angela didn't get to be Mrs. Caldwell by cowering up, and I wasn't going to be Mrs. Braddock by cowering either.

"Josie?" Fred asked.

"Yes, Fred?"

"Where's the pussycats?"

Ben was the first to laugh, and then Angela, and then I joined in too.

I took them to the Cut, a nightclub bar and grill that served the best ribs in town. It was my undisputed favorite eatery and I decided to give these uptown black folk a taste of downtown for a change. It was in the heart of the hood, however, on A. Phillip Randolph Boulevard, and it was sandwiched between a funeral home and a pool hall. Parking was in the back, on an unpaved strip of land, and you had to go through a metal detector to get inside the place. Ben didn't seem to mind, and neither did Fred, but Angela wasn't feeling it.

"Why in the world do we have to be scanned?" she asked the man at the door as he lifted his handheld metal detector and prepared to slide it over her body. "We aren't loaves of bread, or boxes of Cheer."

"Tide, dear," Fred said.

"What?"

"You said we aren't boxes of Cheer. I say we aren't boxes of Tide."

"What are you talking about?" Angela, obviously annoyed, asked her husband.

"Tide detergent."

"I know what it is. But why Tide?"

"Why Cheer?"

"That's a silly question."

"No sillier than you comparing us to detergent in the first place. No sillier than you standing up here questioning this man about why is he doing his job in the second place."

"It's not a silly question at all," she said and then turned back toward the employee. Some of his fellow scanners walked over and looked at us, undoubtedly finding some of us an odd mix for their kind of club.

"I ask you again," Angela said to the employee, "why must we, human beings, mind you, be scanned?"

"To make sure you ain't packin'," he said. "Why you think?"

"Let's not get smart there, young man," Fred said, moving in front of his wife.

"I'll get smart if I wanna get smart."

"Now look here—"

Ben stepped forward, moving in front of Fred. Then he looked at Angela. "Let's get it done, Angela," he said impatiently.

"It's just so demeaning," Angela said.

"I know. But let them do it."

Angela looked at Ben and like everybody else, I guess, those eyes of his could not be denied. She allowed the man to run the scanner across her body.

Ben and Fred underwent their scans after Angela and I, but Angela was still fuming. "Leave it to black folks," she said, "to come up with this. A metal detector in a restaurant!"

"Nightclub," I said.

"Whatever it is. I have never heard of such an outrage. To make sure I wasn't packin', he said. Does it look like I'm packin'?" She said this and opened her arms, as if to demonstrate that her body was too perfect to mess it up with a bulky weapon. The men who stood nearby were more than happy to see what she meant.

We took a booth near the back of the club and the place was wired. A hyperactive DJ was on duty, playing a little bit of everything, but the dance floor was most crowded when the new stuff came on.

When we arrived he was getting down on Motown, playing old standards like "Ain't No Mountain High Enough" and "Papa Was a Rolling Stone," which pleased Angela mightily and helped to calm her down. Fred, on the other hand, liked everything, and even when they switched to the new stuff (my kind of music), he asked his wife if she wanted to dance. It was Will Smith's "Gettin' Jiggy Wit It," but Angela wasn't jiggy with anything that night.

"No, thank you," she said and sipped her wine.

Then he looked at me. I actually wanted to dance, so I looked at Ben. He was too busy perusing the menu to pay me any attention, so I took a chance and said okay to Fred's unasked request.

We got out on the dance floor and tore it up. Fred wasn't as fast as I was, but he knew how to bust a move. The floor was crowded and we were bumping hips, moving up, moving down, and I was having a ball. I glanced over at Ben, who had on his reading glasses still, and he looked so out of place that it astounded me. He looked like a judge. He carried that distinction with him as if it were a mark. And it saddened me. Fred was successful too, even more so than Ben in a lot of ways, but he knew how to have fun. Angela, of course, was sweet when she wanted to be but she was pretty much a lost cause. But there was hope for Ben. There had to be.

Fred and I stayed on the floor through Missy Elliott's "One-Minute Man," but when the DJ flipped on Whitney Houston's "Heartbreak Hotel," we left the floor and I asked Ben if he would like to dance.

"I ordered you the riblet basket," he said and took off his glasses. "The waiter declares it's their most popular dish."

"It is. Thanks. Wanna dance?"

He looked around, at the youthful crowd on the dance floor, and he shook his head. "I don't believe so, no," he said.

I tried to maintain my smile as I sat back down, but it was a fake display. It wasn't like I was asking him to do the electric slide across the floor, or break-dance on the table. I just wanted to show him off a little, to see what he was like when he allowed himself to cut loose. But that damn dignity of his, that always His Honor distinction, made me worry. We had nothing in common philosophically. Nothing in common generationally. Nothing in common culturally. We had nothing in common!

But at least the evening ended on a positive note. They all loved their meals. I was grateful. And after we dropped off Fred and Angela and Ben walked me to my car, he stood at the car door and told me something wonderful. "I don't rock n' roll," he said, "but if you really want me to, I'll try."

I smiled. He was willing to change for me. He was willing to, in his eyes anyway, make a fool of himself just for me. I had never felt more special in my entire life.

But I couldn't let him do it. Just like I didn't think it was right that I should have to change for him, it wasn't right that he should have to change for me. "Thanks anyway," I said, "but being able to rock n' roll isn't a requirement for being with me."

He smiled. "Good," he said as if he was relieved. I was so thrilled to know that there was hope for him, that he wasn't as rigid as he seemed, that I leaned my head out of my car window and gave him a quick peck on the lips. I was smiling after the kiss, and then he smiled too.

"Good night, babe," he said.

"Good night."

He tapped me lightly on the nose, stood erect, and then, with the look of a man completely happy and satisfied, walked back to his Mercedes.

NOT ALL GOOD,
BUT CLOSE

I was already in love, but I think Ben was catching up. He'd phone me every night, just to say hello, and we'd end up talking to midnight. And on weekends we'd take long strolls around the Riverwalk and watch the boats dock and sail in the marinas, or we'd drive over to Fernandina Beach for one of their famous festivals, or we'd just chill at his place, on his patio, where his backyard is the Atlantic Ocean. One Saturday, on my birthday, he went with me to the hairdresser's.

It was seven A.M. and I had fallen asleep with my television still on. I was awakened by my doorbell ringing to the odd sounds of the Road Runner beep-beeping. It took me a few seconds to realize that it was actually my doorbell ringing and not just another Road Runner noise, and it rang again and again before I could crawl out of bed, throw on a robe, and hurry downstairs to answer it.

It was Ben. "What time is it?" I asked as I stepped aside and let him in. He brushed against me as he entered and kissed me on my cheek.

"Seven," he said.

"Damn," I said and closed the door behind him. Saturday was my sleep-in day. I didn't even turn over before ten. "What brings you out this early?"

He stood in the foyer and shook his head. "What day is it, Josephine?"

"Saturday."

"And?"

"What?"

"Josephine, it's your birthday."

"My birthday? Oh yeah," I said, scratching my neck and yawning. "I forgot. I must be getting old."

"You aren't getting old," he said. "You never forget your own birthday when you're getting old." Then he smiled and shook his head. "You forgot your own birthday?"

I didn't know what to say. When I turned twenty-five, it just stopped being a magical day for me. I spent most of those days alone anyway, which didn't bother me when I was younger. Back then my birthday was my just-for-me day and I'd take walks or trips and just have fun alone, but when I hit twenty-five, I lost interest. For the last three years my birthday was an everyday day, and if Scotty didn't bring me a gift or just call to say happy birthday, sweetheart as only he could, I'd usually let the day come and go without even remembering that it actually wasn't a regular day. And since Scotty was out of town on a business trip this weekend, it seemed like a sure bet that this birthday was going to be one of those gone-before-I-knew-it-was-here days too.

But Ben was here and he knew all about me. Our talks to midnight were usually all about me and my childhood, where my birthdays back then always ended up with one of my crazy siblings fighting the kids at my party because they weren't poor like us and they, unlike the kids who came to my siblings' parties, actually bought gifts. My siblings couldn't deal with that. Who did I think I was? they'd ask, and then start terrorizing my guests. So Ben knew the date of my birth, although he never acknowledged that he did, but that was the kind of man I had lucked upon. A thoughtful man. A considerate man. But an impatient-as-hell man too. His seven-A.M. visit was no accident. He was up before the crack of dawn every single day, work or no work, mainly because he just didn't have enough patience to wait, to give his body a little R&R, before he thrust himself upon the busy business of another day.

I, however, didn't have that problem. One Saturday I slept until three P.M. and another Saturday I didn't get up at all. But Ben didn't care about all that. This was my special day. And the way he saw it, you just didn't sleep away your special day.

He looked down at my chest, since my robe was one of those

skimpy wrap-over deals that was poorly wrapped over, revealing half of my breasts, and then he walked up to me and held me. I leaned my head against his chest and closed my eyes. I could have fallen asleep in his arms, and wanted nothing better than for him to take me to my bedroom and let me do just that, but as I said, lying around in bed wasn't something he did. He kissed me instead. And that was more than enough. I'd never loved kissing as much as I did with Ben. He knew how to do me. I found myself so aroused, in fact, that I managed to slip out of my robe and let it drop where I stood. He held me tighter and kissed me harder when he realized I had disrobed. Then he lifted me up and I wrapped my legs around him. And he kissed me longer.

But he didn't take me upstairs. I wanted him to get moving, I even started hitting his back with my feet as if he were a horse and I the jockey, but he didn't budge. Then the kissing slowed down and eventually came to a stop too. I let my head fall back exhausted by the feeling, and he rubbed my neck with his big hand, and then he put me down.

"Go get dressed," he said, hitting me on the behind and then walking toward the kitchen. "I'll make breakfast."

I stood there momentarily, because it sounded like Greek to me. Breakfast? At this time of morning? He must be out of his mind. I was getting nauseated just thinking about eating at seven A.M.

But by the time I had showered and put on some clothes, a very short yellow shift dress was about all I could manage, he had a plate filled with sausage, eggs, and grits sitting on my kitchen table, hot and ready for me to devour. And I ate. I ate until I couldn't eat anymore. He, however, had coffee only, which surprised me, but I didn't sweat it. The food was too good.

He leaned against my kitchen sink, sipping his coffee and staring at me. I was so used to his stares by now that I would often forget he was looking and not feel uncomfortable at all, and sometimes, like now, I would even stare back at him. He was dressed casually, in a pair of brown chino pants and a white polo shirt, and was wearing a pair of his expensive Bruno Maglis but had one shoe crossed over the other as if they were nothing more than a plain old cheap pair of desert boots.

"This is great," I said. "I haven't had breakfast in years."

"It's the most important meal of the day."

"I know. But dang. It's also the most inconvenient meal of the day. I just can't see myself eating all this food this time of morning on no regular basis."

"You don't have to eat it all. But you should eat something every morning."

I didn't say anything. I could tell in his voice that he wasn't pleased and was just one cross word away from lecturing me on the virtues of good nutrition. And I wasn't in the mood for a lecture. So I stayed quiet. I was learning how to avoid confrontation with him. Staying cool sometimes did it. Changing the subject always did.

"What did you have planned for my birthday?" I asked him.

"It's your birthday, honey. What do you want to do?"

I thought about it. "Well," I said, "I did have this hair appointment today."

"Okay. What time?"

"Twelve."

"Good. That'll give us enough time to drive over to Fleming Island. Fred and Angela have a gift for you."

"They do?"

"Yes. They're my friends so that makes them yours too. Don't you think?"

"Sure," I said, excited that I could have a friend like Fred Caldwell, who wasn't just rich and good looking, but was also funny and down to earth and somebody I felt was in my corner.

"We'll pick up the gift and then go to the beauty parlor."

I looked at Ben. "You mean you're going to the hairdresser's with me?"

He seemed confused by my question. "Certainly. Is that a problem?"

"No, but I don't think you understand what you're getting yourself into."

"What do you mean?"

"It could take hours. And I mean *hours*."

He nodded. "I see. Well, it's your birthday. And I'm spending it with you. And if a nice chunk of it is spent in the beauty salon, then so be it. I'm game."

I smiled. Sure he was.

*   *   *

Fred and Angela had my gift wrapped and sitting on the coffee table in the parlor. I ran up to it like a little kid and unwrapped it quickly. Fred laughed and told me not to break my neck and Angela said it was refreshing to see somebody who still appreciated a simple gift. Ben didn't say anything. He sat in the chair and started his staring-at-me routine. I looked up from unwrapping my gift and smiled at him, but I felt bad after I did it. There was something about his stare. It wasn't his usual *who is this person?* look, but it was more intense, as if he was still trying to figure out if I fit into his world, a world of rigid traditions and conservative values, where his best friend was a man of such high esteem as Fred Caldwell, and where the good life wasn't a privilege, but a right.

I looked back at my gift. I couldn't tell him if I fit or not, because I didn't know myself. I wasn't refined like Angela, or talented like Fred, I was wide open, mouthy, full of opinions and contradictions. If I did fit, it was going to be a loose fit, to be sure, where I would probably always be on the verge of not fitting at all.

The final paper was torn away and then I removed the inside wrappings. And my heart leaped with joy. It was an African pantsuit, made out of the most exotic-looking kinte material I had ever seen, in a gorgeous periwinkle blue. "Ah, shit!" I said as soon as I saw it, and Fred and Angela laughed.

I glanced at Ben. He wasn't frowning but he wasn't smiling either. So I decided to calm my behind down. "It's beautiful," I said to my friends. "Thanks, guys." First I hugged Angela, and then Fred. And then I moved over and hugged Ben too. "What was that for?" he asked. "It's for introducing me to such wonderful people," I said. Angela and Fred said "aah" very sweetly and Ben smiled. And then he hugged me without inducement.

Loretta sat me in her chair within minutes after I got there because she knew I didn't play that waiting game. We were in the Primp Salon, which was owned and operated by Loretta and was one of the most popular salons in J-ville. Ben sat in the waiting area, which was naturally loaded with females, and every one of them kept taking peeps at him as if he were a hamburger and they were the bun. Even Loretta couldn't stop looking around the curve and checking him out. It wasn't until she had loosened half of my braids, however, that she got up the nerve to ask. "Okay, girl," she said, "are you gonna tell me or make me pry it out of you?"

I smiled. "Tell you what?"

"Come on, Josie."

"What?"

"Who's that sexy hunk of man you brought in here, child? That's what! Look like somebody took gorgeous and melted it in a bottle and it suddenly became him."

I laughed. Loretta always did have a way with words. "His name is Ben," I said.

"Ben?"

"Yes."

"And he's your boyfriend?"

I smiled. The idea that Ben could be somebody's boy anything was amusing. "Yes," I said.

"Damn, girl. When you bust loose you bust loose. The rest of us fooling around with these jive-ass Negroes who get a job at the bank and then think they're too good to be with somebody like us. But not you. Not Miss Josephine. She don't get no raggedy assistant bank manager. She gets the dude who looks like he owns the bank! That's right, girl. If you gonna go, go all out. That's what I say. Got you a distinguished gentleman. Everybody ain't able. But do he got a brother, child? Or a nephew? Or hell, a next-door neighbor who looks half as good as he does?"

I laughed out loud and looked at Ben. She was right. He was gorgeous and distinguished and all mine. I couldn't believe it either.

We left Loretta's by five-thirty. Ben looked tired as we sat in his Mercedes, but he tried to keep smiling and playing the good host. He even complimented me on my braids, which was unusual. "They're always so neat," he said. "You don't go for that Whoopi Goldberg look, do you?" I laughed. A little of me was rubbing off on him. About time, I thought.

"Okay, what's next?" he asked as he cranked up the car.

"Dinner, I guess," I said.

"Dinner it is," he said.

We went to the Olive Garden in Arlington and we both ordered a seafood alfredo. A nap would have been nice afterward, I was just that stuffed, but Ben wasn't the napping kind of man. We went shopping instead, to the Regency Mall, and everything that I even intimated that I wanted, he bought for me. We ended up with over seven bags filled with jewelry and shoes and perfume and scarfs and blouses and hats. Total bill: One thousand seven hundred dollars. And it didn't even faze Ben. I stood back and let him write the checks. What planet was this brother from? I wondered. I'd never met anybody so generous. And even later that night, when we were back at my condo and he gave me the gift he had picked—a gold tennis bracelet with diamond studs—and I told him I just couldn't accept it, that he had done too much already, he looked at me as if I were crazy. "This is the least I can do for you, Josephine," he said. "You understand me? This is nothing. Never let a man think that what he does for you is the best he can do. Or it will be."

I smiled and nodded and cried. Yes, I cried, damn it! I always cry. And he held me close to him. For hours we sat on my sofa and he held me in his arms. It was the perfect birthday.

Except he didn't make love to me. I asked him to, because I was horny as hell, but he said no. We had to take it slow, he said.

"But why?"

"Numerous reasons."

"Give me one."

"Do you believe in God?"

"Of course I believe in God."

"Well, so do I."

"And?"

"And I'm not pushing it."

"Pushing what?" And then I smiled. "You mean the sin thing? The *it's better to marry than to burn* thing?"

He wouldn't respond.

"Is that the only reason?"

"No."

"Then what?"

"We need to take it slow."

"Don't you think we are?"

He leaned his head against the back of my couch. "You ask a lot of questions, do you realize that?"

"Yes, I do, but—"

"But nothing. Stop playing journalist with me. Okay?" He said this looking as serious as he could look, and then he smiled. Which meant, of course, that I smiled too.

"Okay," I said, although there were a lot of questions left unasked.

So we took it slow, and it was a good thing. At first. I didn't want to lose myself in the relationship, which wasn't that hard to do since I had a love jones out of this world, and Ben couldn't take another heartbreak. At least that was Fred's explanation for Ben's slowness. I was concerned, after a while, when date after date and he would never go all the way with me. He'd kiss me, and always passionately, but he wouldn't take that next step. It was a complete reversal from that night at his house when the only thing he seemed interested in was sex. That is, until my big mouth mentioned love. Scotty said he may have been punishing me for insinuating that he didn't love me back and that he only wanted me for the sex. "I'll show her," Scotty said he may have decided. "We'll see who wants it now!"

That was why I went to see Fred. He was Ben's best friend for nearly thirty years. They were closer than brothers. If anybody could give me some insight into the mystery that was Benjamin Braddock, he could.

Caldwell Electronics was a large office complex in Mandarin, just beyond Sunbeam Road. I had scheduled an appointment with Fred for eleven that morning, but my usual lateness didn't find me walking into his office until well after twelve.

He was in the middle of a conference call when I arrived, so I had to wait nearly an hour longer, but given that it was my fault for running late in the first place, I was grateful that he would see me at all.

His secretary sat me down in the waiting area of her office and asked if I wanted something to drink. She was a thirty-something woman with big breasts and small eyes and a flirtatiousness about her that seemed slutty to me, but was probably welcomed by men.

After I declined her offer for a drink, she went back behind her desk, seemingly to work, but every time I looked up she was looking at me. When I first saw her I wondered if she and Fred were more than professional acquaintances (she had that mistress thing about her, that proud-to-be-the-other-woman look down to a science), but now, the way she kept her eyes on me, I was certain of it. She viewed me as her competition. I didn't even know the female but I was supposed to be in competition with her. Terrific, I thought, as I crossed my legs and flipped through a *Black Enterprise* magazine. I was worried about my relationship with Ben while girlfriend thought I was plotting some takeover of Fred. Love was nuts. Love was too crazy for me.

After over an hour of these looks from the secretary, Fred finally called me into his office. He rushed up to me gaily and kissed me on the cheek. "You look grand!" he said, and offered me a seat.

We sat down on a long leather couch and he unbuttoned his suit coat and sat next to me. Understanding that he was a busy man, I attempted to get to the point right away. I treaded lightly, however, because it was a very delicate matter I was trying to discuss. Fred, however, decided to skip the bull.

"In other words," he said, "Benjamin ain't giving it up and you want to know why the hell not?"

"Oh God. Am I that transparent?"

"You needn't worry, Josie. He's not taking it slow to get back at you. He just can't bear another heartbreak."

"What do you mean?"

"His wife died ten years ago. Did he tell you?"

"He told me. But what kind of woman was she, Fred?"

He shook his head. "Horrible," he said. "I couldn't stand her. She was Satan's daughter before she got sick, but, baby, let me tell you, after she got sick, forget it. She was Satan himself. Just a terrible woman. Nothing was good enough for her. Nobody was good enough for her. Every maid he hired, she fired. Every nurse with the courage to show up, she ran away. She almost burned down their home twice. She tried to kill Benjamin two or three times. She accused him of sleeping with the maid, the nurse, the next-door neighbor, my wife, the female star on whatever television program she was watching, even me."

"You?"

"Even me. Oh, I was his lover boy, she would say. I would play right along too. 'That's right, Liz,' I'd say, 'so where does that leave you?' Oh, she couldn't stand me. I know Benjamin told you she was sick, and she was, but it wasn't a physical illness. She was nuts. And I mean off the chain. And wouldn't take her medication. She'd hop a plane to Paris on the spur of the moment, or go on elaborate shopping sprees, or sit in a corner and rock all night long. Benjamin didn't know if he was coming or going. It was a nightmare. Angela begged him to put her in an institution and go on with his life, I begged him too, but he wouldn't do it. 'For better or worse,' he'd say, and they stayed married for eighteen years. But even Benjamin would admit it was all worse."

He had said a mouthful. I leaned back. "She's been dead for ten years and you're saying he would still feel disloyal to her if—"

"Oh no. He's been in love many times since Liz died. But every one of those women were using him for their own selfish gain. It's the damndest thing. Benjamin has everything in the world going for him, the looks, the brains, everything, but he always, and I mean always, picks the wrong woman. And she always, in the end, breaks his heart."

I shook my head. "Well, if that's the case, then it would stand to reason that I'm the wrong woman too."

"God, I hope not."

"I'm not. But if he won't give me a chance to prove it . . ."

"He will. But he can't take another heartbreak, and I mean this with all sincerity. I was there with him. He can't survive another let-down. He's had thirty years of letdowns. He's got to take it slow."

I sighed. I felt burdened down, as if loving Ben was going to be a lot more complicated than I had hoped. "What can I do?" I asked Fred.

"Tell him how you feel. Let him know that you'll remain true to him. He'll come around."

I smiled. It was reasonable advice, I thought. Then I thought about Ben. "You won't tell him I came to see you. Will you?"

"Only if he asks."

"I don't think I like that answer."

"You don't have to. But I'm gonna look out for Benjamin."

I nodded. He was a good friend. I could respect that.

I held on to his words later that night, when I had sipped enough sherry and grooved to enough Arrested Development to get up the nerve to phone Ben. We needed to have what my mama always called a *come to Jesus* meeting, where we'd get serious as hell and lay it all on the line. And then, if all went well, we'd make passionate love all night long.

I tried at nine, again at ten, and again at eleven. It was a Tuesday night and I began to wonder where could he be. And then I panicked and started phoning his home every five minutes. I lay on my lounger, with my cordless phone sitting on my exposed stomach (I was wearing only a bra shirt and a pair of shorts), and I was mad, sad, and concerned all at the same time. And all kinds of thoughts started rushing through my head. He was with another woman, was the main thought, and the more I thought about it the more specific the other woman became. Maybe his secretary or one of those sassy law clerks of his. Maybe Fred's secretary. Maybe Fred's wife. Which led me to obsess on Angela. Then I became convinced that she was the one. It all fit. They stared at each other too often, and each was always touching the other's hand, and would lean against each other while laughing at some private joke of theirs. Although they did have a big surprise anniversary party for Fred, I began to wonder if maybe that *planning the party* line was a ruse to cover the fact that I had caught her at Ben's home one time too many. They did take forever to answer the door. Maybe they were naked in bed and my surprise drop-by foiled all their nasty little plans.

And Fred. He spoke of Ben as if he were some kind of saint, but maybe that was a ruse too. Maybe Fred was fooling with his own secretary and therefore didn't mind Ben fooling with Angela. They were, after all, of that free-love, swingers generation. Maybe they had an understanding. And they were Republicans too? The pious adulterers? The ones who did it more than anybody else but acted so offended when others wanted some too? Maybe everybody knew exactly what was going on, and relished in their clandestine activities, except me.

I closed my eyes and shook my head. *That bastard*, I thought. If I found out that he had me falling in love with his behind while he was fooling around with somebody else, I would not be responsible for my actions. And heaven help the woman. Angela Caldwell would be minced meat before I was done.

But my anger couldn't temper the ache in my heart. I loved him. That was the problem. And it was my problem. He never said he loved me. He never even said he liked me. Hell, he may have hated me for all I knew. He may have dared me to fall in love with him just to get back at me for writing all those horrible stories about him. I always felt there was a part of him that was locked from view, and it could have been sensitive or it could have been sinister, but I would never know because he wouldn't dare allow me to see it.

But Ben was the victim, according to Fred. Every woman Ben ever loved broke his heart. Every one. And Fred declared Ben didn't do anything wrong. It was always the woman's fault. But my mama told me long ago to watch out for that tale. If a man keeps having doomed relationships over and over again, she said, then something is wrong with that man. He's the common denominator. Besides, actions speak louder than words anyhow. And his actions were clear: he was out on a Tuesday night, it was late at night, and he had not mentioned any prior engagement.

I dialed again, angry as hell. It was my time to flip the script. I was going to smoke the brother out if I had to. I couldn't let him get away with this. I couldn't let him think for one second that my heart was a toy that could be tossed around at will, and not break, and not get so jumbled up that it was just as good as broken. I had to make it clear to him that when I played, I played for keeps. None of that open-relationship, anything-goes bullshit with me. We had to come to Jesus. Right now.

He answered his phone by eleven forty-five. "Yes?" he said as if he was annoyed that somebody would phone him at this time of night.

"Hi," I said, "I hope I didn't wake you." I closed my eyes. If he claimed I had awakened him I was going to cuss his ass out. He wasn't asleep three minutes ago, or three hours ago either. He couldn't have been. He wasn't home.

"No," he said, "I wasn't asleep."

I exhaled. At least he didn't tell me a bald-faced lie. But he didn't mention the fact that he was just getting home either.

"Is there something wrong?" he asked.

I hesitated. "Can you come over?" I asked this and shook my head. The evening had gone horribly wrong. My plan was to invite him over, explain to him that he needn't worry about me breaking his heart, and then make passionate love to him. Now I was inviting him over to crucify him, to tell him in no uncertain terms that he picked the wrong one to mess with this time.

He didn't answer me right away, as if he knew that my request wasn't driven by love. "It's almost midnight, honey," he said.

"I know it's almost midnight. But I need to see you."

Again, he hesitated. He didn't want to come. The pause was too long and agonizing. And when he finally spoke up, it was with little enthusiasm. "I'm on my way," he said, and then he hung up.

I started to get up and put on one of my more alluring outfits, just to show him what he could have had if he had played his cards right, but I didn't move. I lay there, staring at the ceiling, realizing by default that there was a reason why I kept my heart on guard. For twenty-eight years I did it. It was my greatest accomplishment. But then I met Ben. And I threw all caution to the wind. And this was my reward.

He arrived an hour after I had phoned him. He wasn't casually dressed, as I assumed he'd be, but he wore a black suit, white shirt, and thin black tie. Still in his work clothes. Almost midnight and he was still in his work clothes. And he looked tired too, so tired that it seemed as if he could barely stand up.

"Hey," he said and tried to smile.

"Come in," I said and stepped aside. No smiles, no warm greetings from me.

He walked in slowly. He kept looking at me as if my face would reveal the answer to the riddle of the night. But all he saw was a blank look, not of anger, not of bitterness, but of a sister with a made-up mind.

"Have a seat," I said as I closed the door and walked past him back to the sofa. I was scantily clad in my bra shirt and shorts, revealing all of my stomach up to my chest, but I didn't care if it turned him on or not. I plopped down on the sofa, folded my arms and legs in an Indian pose, and looked at him. He stood there, still staring at me, and then he slowly walked to the chair next to the sofa and sat down.

For a few moments nothing was said, as he looked around, at my walls for some reason, and I looked at him. There was an anger in his manner, as if he couldn't wait to lash out either, but he had the kind of self-control that allowed him to wait his turn. My self-control wasn't as contained, but I managed to at least keep it in check. Any false response from him, however, and all bets were off.

"How was your day?" I asked him, playing one of his double-meaning-in-every-question games.

"Fine, and yours?" He asked this and looked at me. He seemed oddly disappointed, as if he knew what I was doing and was hurt that I was doing it.

"Not so fine," I said, deciding to stick with my script. "I needed somebody to talk to tonight. I phoned you." He didn't say anything.

Just looked at me. "I was surprised that you weren't at home. You never mentioned any engagement."

This was supposed to be the line that would force him to explain himself and I could see what kind of clever lies he could tell. But he didn't explain anything. He just stared at me. "What did you need to talk about?" he asked.

"Us," I said.

"What about us?"

I shook my head as if surprised that he didn't know the answer himself, and then I lifted my arms up over my head. My body stretched with the pull and Ben's eyes looked down at my body and stayed there. I expected a quick glance, that was normally his style, but when it was apparent that his eyes weren't going anywhere, that he was undoubtedly undressing me with those eyes of his, I became self-conscious as hell and dropped my arms back to my side. It was only then that he looked away.

"Something isn't right with us," I said. "Don't you realize that?"

"I wasn't under that impression, no."

I smiled. "Okay," I said, my self-control beginning to unhinge. "You wanna play dumb, let's play dumb: where were you tonight?"

His tired eyes looked down, and then they looked back up again. "Excuse me?"

"You heard me."

He frowned. "Who do you think you're talking to?"

"Let me see: there's you in the room, and there's me. Either I'm talking to myself, or guess what? I'm talking to you."

He pointed a finger at me. "Watch yourself."

"No, you watch *your*-self," I said, pointing a finger back, my self-control now gone. My head was bobbing and my hands were moving and I was taking no prisoners. "First of all," I said, "you know what the hell is up. Waltzing in here like you don't know what time it is. Who the hell is it, Ben? Angela again? Or some new chick?"

He rose to his feet so quickly and angrily that I actually leaned back in fear. He pointed at me again. "You don't know what you're talking about!"

"Then enlighten me," I said and folded my arms. "But tell the story straight because I know bull when I hear it."

He stared at me, disappointed, angry, and then he started heading for the door. I stood up desperately. "Don't you dare leave!" I yelled. "I'm not finished!"

He stood at the door, his tall, straight back to me, and then he slowly turned around. The tears had already started before he turned, but now I couldn't control them. He stood there, staring at me, his face more frustrated than compassionate, more tired than concerned.

"How could you do this to me?" I said. "You know how I feel about you, but you act like you don't give a damn. You made love to me, Ben. I have a right to question you."

"You weren't questioning me. You were accusing me."

"Where were you tonight?" I asked this and wiped my tears away quickly, as if they had not been detected, as if this man had not seen me, once again, at my most vulnerable.

"I was visiting a friend."

"A friend? Who?"

"A friend of mine."

"A woman?"

He sighed. "No."

"Fred?"

"Is there anything else?"

"Who was this friend if it wasn't Fred Caldwell?"

"I am not playing twenty questions with you. Now is there anything else you wanted?"

I didn't respond.

"Good night, Josephine," he said and turned to leave. I wanted to run to him and beg him not to go, to explain to him that this love thing was new to me and I couldn't help being petty and desperate and scared. But I stayed put. I didn't have the energy to move. The tears flowed freely and I let them flow.

"Good night," I said, my voice cracking in pain. He turned back around when he heard my voice. I felt so exposed that I wanted to hide from sight. He saw what I felt because his anger and frustration left. Just like that. And compassion came. One of the few times I'd seen it in him. And it walked with him toward me. First he lifted my face up to his and then he pulled me into his arms. He held me as tightly as I held him. I wanted to apologize, for questioning him, but I couldn't. It felt too good in his arms, his sweet cologne making me so relaxed that I was getting drowsy, his warm body like a harbor to my heart.

I looked into his eyes. His compassion for me was so intense that one false move would render him teary eyed too. "I love you," I said to him. He smiled, the wrinkles of age appearing on the side of his eyes like reminders. He'd seen it all before. "I know," he said. "But you're worrying for nothing."

"I love you so much."

He closed his eyes and opened them back. Something about my desperation seemed to unnerve him, and he released me. "You need to stop worrying and get you some rest, Josephine. Can you do that for me?"

I nodded. "Yes," I said.

"Everything is fine. Okay?"

I nodded again. "Okay."

"Good. Now I'm going to take my own advice and go home and get some rest too. I'll call you tomorrow."

"I'm sorry for bringing you all this way—"

"Stop apologizing," he said with a flash of anger. "Just stop it, Josephine. You have every right to ask me to come see you. It's up to me to come or not. You understand?"

"Yes, I do," I said. And my response, for some reason, seemed to touch him again and he pulled me into his arms once more. And he kissed me.

When we released I was virtually out of breath. He was too, as he staggered toward the front door. I had gone to see Fred because I needed to know why he wouldn't go all the way with me. Now I understood why he wouldn't. I couldn't handle it, that's why. He was my first true love, and he was no kid but a well-experienced, middle-aged man. He wasn't any more accustomed to somebody like me than I was to him. We *had* to take it slow.

He opened the door and turned once more. This time, however, his sternness had returned. "I want you to take some time off work," he said.

"Okay," I said without even thinking about it.

"Don't you want to know why?"

I smiled. Where the hell was that independence of mine now? "Sure."

"I want you to go with me to Key West. My sister is getting married in a couple of weeks. I thought it would be a good opportunity for you to meet the parents."

"Okay," I said nonchalantly, as if such invitations came my way every day. He looked at me a few moments longer, and then he left.

As soon as the door closed I dropped down on my sofa and screamed into the pillow. "He wants me to meet his mama!" I yelled. "Yes! Yes! Yes!"

Mel, however, didn't share my excitement. "A vacation?" he asked. We were in his office. He was seated behind his desk, I was standing in front of the desk.

"Yes, Mel, a vacation."

"Why do you all of a sudden need a vacation?"

"It's not all of a sudden."

"But why do you at this point in time want a vacation?"

"I don't know. Maybe it's because I never had one."

"But why all of a sudden?"

I sighed. "Are you going to approve it or not, Mel?"

"Absolutely not. We've got assignments up to here—never enough reporters. No way, JR! Tell your boyfriend you can't make it this time."

I stared at Mel angrily. It was personal with him now. He didn't know jack about my plans, or whom I would be spending my vacation with, but he assumed it had to be Ben. I figured it was none of his damn business, so I left the office.

I went into the rest room—my sanctuary—and called Ben on my cell phone. As soon as I heard his voice, I began to cry. "He won't let me," I said.

There was a moment of silence that lasted too long and I could feel his irritation. "What are you talking about, Josephine?"

"He won't let me take time off."

"Who won't let you?"

"Mel Sanchez, my boss. And it's only because he hates you, it has nothing to do with the job."

"Okay," Ben said calmly.

"What am I gonna do?"

"Don't worry about that now."

"But he said I can't take any time off, Ben."

"Don't worry about that now."

"But—"

"But nothing, Josephine. Now listen, I've got to go. I'll talk to you later."

And he hung up, quickly, before I could even say good-bye.

The Culpepper Gallery was packed at noontime, as tourists flocked in from the Landing and Metropolitan Park to purchase a stack of Scotty's unique prints of the city and to check out other collectibles. I squeezed in and made my way to the back room, where Fran motioned that Scotty was. He was on the phone yelling at one of his distributors, and I took a seat on the front end of his desk.

"Idiot!" he said as he threw the phone on its hook. "Everybody wants to screw Scotty, but I tell you what: they will get screwed if they keep playing games with me!"

I shook my head. It wasn't exactly the mood I'd hoped he'd be in when I decided to drop by.

He stood up and walked around next to me. "Why aren't you working?" he asked and kissed me on the lips.

"I just came from an assignment. And it's a trip. Ambri Corporation is accusing Councilwoman Hughes, the city council president, of embezzlement."

"Are you serious?"

"Can you believe it? But Ambri is sticking to their story. They claim she misappropriated funds when she worked for them in the eighties. She, of course, denies all allegations."

"Good for her," Scotty said and sat beside me on his desk. "They're just trying to scare her out of running for mayor next year."

"That's what she says. And she was quick to point out to me that the mayor has a lot of his cronies on Ambri's board of directors, was once on there himself in fact, and they would like nothing better than to see him reelected."

"I hear that," Scotty said and then looked at me for a prolonged period of time. "You all right?" he asked.

"Yes."

"Sure?"

"I'm fine."

"Mel Sanchez came by here looking for you."

I looked at Scotty. "When?"

"Not an hour ago."

"He knew I was on that Ambri assignment, what's his problem? What did he want?"

"You, as usual. And he was highly upset. He said your boy-friend—"

"My boyfriend?"

"Ben Braddock, child. He said your boyfriend phoned Marshall London, whoever he is . . ."

"He's our publisher. And Ben called him?"

"That's what Mel said. And Mr. London called Lawrence some-body."

"Lawrence Dinkle, our managing editor. Go on."

"And he told that Dinkle man that Mel, for personal rather than professional reasons, refused to allow you vacation time. Well, that Dinkle man told Mel to allow you all the time you need, and Mel is hot."

"He would be."

"He said you're sleeping with the enemy and you'll pay for it in blood."

"What is that supposed to mean?"

"Now you know Mel. Everything means the end of the world is near. You were his good little liberal girl. Now you're not his at all. He's hot."

I shook my head. "He can stay hot for all I care. He never should have turned me down."

"And you ran to Braddock?"

"Hell yeah, I ran to him! Mel was wrong, Scotty, that's all there is to it. He hates my relationship with Ben, that's what made him say no."

"So," Scotty said, "is it true? Are you really going on vacation with Ben?"

"Yes."

"Where?"

"Key West."

"How nice."

"His sister is getting married."

"Even nicer"

"And he wants me to meet his parents."

Scotty smiled. "What? He wants you to meet his mama?"

I nodded.

"Uh-oh," Scotty said. "It's on, girl!"

I smiled too and allowed Scotty to nudge me playfully. "Go, Josie, go, Josie, go, Josie!" he kept nudging and singing, and singing and nudging, until I slid from his desk and fell to the floor.

THE GOOD, THE BAD, AND DESIREE

It was six and a half hours from Jacksonville to the Florida Keys and Ben drove nonstop all the way. We were in his Mercedes, his "good car," having left the Seville in the garage with my Mustang parked beside it.

I arrived at his home early, before seven A.M., and he took his pretty time coming downstairs to open the door. I was dressed comfortably, in a green short set and sandals, ready to take on the March wind and Florida sun in style, while Ben opened the door wearing a brown suit and tie. I smiled and shook my head. He looked as if he were leaving for a business trip rather than a vacation.

He seemed pleased when he saw me, however, as he wrapped me in his arms. "You always smell so good," I said.

"Just be still and let me hold you for a moment," he said.

I did as he requested and lay against his chest. I could hear his heartbeat and it was deep and vibrant and steady. We both seemed to understand that, by going on this trip together, we were about to take our relationship to the next level. It was an exciting feeling but it was scary too. I looked up into his bright brown eyes. We had had sex but once and my body was craving for more. On this trip, I fully expected to get some. I also fully expected to hear him say, for the first time, and without coaxing from anyone, that he loved me.

So it was a trip of expectations for me. We had played the take-it-slow game as well as it could be played, I thought, but now I was ready to take it so fast that the only reason we would stop would be to catch our breath. That was how I felt anyway. Ben wasn't telling. I knew he cared about me, he spent too much time with me for a man who didn't care. But a part of him was still locked from view. Maybe Fred was right, maybe it was because he had had too many heartbreaks. But maybe there was more to it than that.

He seemed to read my heart through my eyes, because as soon as I started thinking about our relationship and where it was headed, he immediately released me.

But I didn't sweat that either. I was determined, on this trip, to have me some fun. "Well," I said, smiling and turning around as if I were some supermodel on a runway, "how do I look?"

He gave me the once-over and then he nodded. "You look fine," he said, and hurried to the foot of the stairs where his suitcase stood. I shrugged my shoulder. Nobody was going to confuse him for a touchy, feely brother, that was for sure.

"You're dressed so formally," I said smilingly. "Don't you have some shorts you can throw on?"

"Don't be ridiculous," he said and told me to lock the door, we'd leave through the garage.

It was a fast trip and I was astonished at how many traffic laws the good judge broke. He was driving as if the road were an obstacle course and all the other cars on that road were the obstacle. At one point, while we sped along the I-4 Corridor, I looked at the speedometer. We were doing ninety with a bullet. I looked at him and laughed. "Damn!" I said.

But it was serious business to him. He didn't talk much, and when I would try to carry on a conversation with him, even a superficial one, he seemed annoyed by me. So I gave up and just leaned back and relaxed. "You talk too much," my mother once told me. "Just be quiet sometimes." I decided to heed her advice.

We arrived in Key West before noon. It was a remarkably quick trip. When I woke up (between the silence and the jazz I had long since fallen asleep), we were pulling into the driveway of one of those beautiful southern homes with huge lawns and exterior staircases. We were in the Old Town section of Key West, where the big boys lived, at a big white house with a second-floor balcony and an American flag flying on the post.

"This is your childhood home, I take it," I said jokingly.

"Yes," he replied, and got out of the car.

Cars abounded in the driveway, every make and model imaginable, and a crowd of people hurried from around the side of the house when Ben stepped out. They were all calling his name and running to him, from small children to adults, men and women. Ben, true to form, stood there and soaked it all in, smiling like the god they took him for, and they smothered him with hugs and kisses and double-grasped handshakes. I stepped out of the car slowly. This was it. I was going to meet the family. I was finally going to find out if I could fit into a world like Ben's.

I wanted to go and stand beside him, but the crowd made that impossible, so I lingered where I stood, waiting for him to remember that I existed too. And he did. Eventually.

"Josephine, come here," he said, while his people continued to ask him a zillion questions and he continued to try and answer them. Nobody even looked my way when he called my name, and I was grateful, so I moved quickly near him. When he saw me coming he had to reach through the crowd to take my hand. He gently pulled me until I stood beside him.

"Everybody," he said and the crowd quieted down. "This is Josephine."

"Hello, Josephine," they said in robotic unison, stared at me from head to toe, quickly finding me uninteresting, and then turned their attentions back to the man of the hour. He was engrossed in them too, as he asked about this one's husband, that one's son, this one's business venture, that one's college major. And I stood there, smiling, listening, wondering why he didn't tell them that I was his woman. Not just Josephine. Josephine could be anybody. Josephine, my woman, could not.

But while I pondered what I perceived to be a slight, they gathered around Ben and began to move him toward the house. I grabbed his hand and made him hold on to mine. He looked at me, no doubt because I was squeezing the mess out of his hand, but he didn't let mine go.

So we all gathered together like a herd of cattle and headed toward the big house. Ben loved these people, it showed in every move he made. Gone was that stuffiness. Gone was that agitation and irritability. He was relaxed here in the Florida Keys, where the sun shone intensely and the blue sky hovered over the big house like a painting on a massive wall. And this was his childhood home, this paradise of a place. While my childhood had me running down dirt roads and eating PB&J for breakfast, lunch, and sometimes dinner too, his had him skipping on easy street, chilling in the sun, and understanding even as a child what it meant to live the good life. From this vantage point it wasn't hard to see why he thought the way he did. From this vantage point everybody did pick themselves up by their bootstraps and jump over every hurdle that got in their way. And if they didn't pick themselves up or jump the hurdles, then it *was* a personal problem. There was no excuse.

We settled in the large living room, where there was so much in-and-out activity that I couldn't keep up. Ben was the head of the clan, however, as he sat in the chair of choice and everybody flocked to him for all of his worldly advice and wisdom. I sat at the end of a couch and smiled and nodded and accepted tea from the butler's tray. Two college girls—teenagers—sat next to me, believing, I supposed, that I was a teenager too. I was upset at first, that they would think of me as some kid, but they were nice girls and very hard to dislike, so I chilled. They were two sisters, Wendy and Mindy, and both were pretty, petite, and smart. In fact the first thing I noticed about Ben's relatives was that all of them were pretty, petite, and smart. Ben was easily the biggest thing in the room.

Before too long the girls and I were joined by more and more young people. One young boy in particular, a seventeen-year-old named Jeremy, Ben's nephew, wasn't wasting any time trying to come on to me. I was polite, because he was very cute and sweet about it, but after a while he was beginning to grate on my nerves. So I started ignoring his *you're so pretty* and *why don't we go for a walk?* remarks and began looking around. And right away I noticed a trend. There were exactly three groups in the house. Ben's group were the jet set, the older folks who were bankrolling the get-together. Then there were the middle group, the thirty-something yuppies who found the young set too young and the jet set too boring.

And then there were my group, the young and the restless. And I mean very young. I was the oldest thing in this group. For some reason they flocked to me and wouldn't let me go. They surrounded me on the couch, all very talkative, all full of fun and jokes. And I enjoyed them too. Soon I even forgot about Ben and just leaned back and laughed until my belly ached. I had forgotten what it felt like to be this young, where everything and everybody was a trip, where you didn't want to hear anybody over the age of twenty-one tell you anything. So I didn't tell them anything. I just leaned back and let them tell me.

When I bothered to look around again, I saw where Ben's group had made their way into the dining room, playing some card game and drinking beer, and the thirty-somethings were making their way out the door, usually in groups of threes, going to visit this museum or that friend's house or this art gallery. These were some of the most Brady Bunch black folks I had ever met. No cussing and fighting and fussing over who was drinking up all the liquor. In fact, there wasn't a ghetto-fied person in the house. If you didn't count me.

But everything changed when the music started. Jeremy came downstairs with a boom box and Mindy and Wendy popped in some CDs, first DMX's *Party Up* and then Ja Rule and Nelly, and they started getting down, dancing like the black folks I didn't think they could be, cuttin' up and having fun. Jeremy dragged me onto the dance floor, and at first I felt pretty foolish dancing with all those teenagers, but that feeling didn't last long because I was having too much fun. It wasn't long before everybody else stood back and gave us room, and we tore it up. Some of the jet setters even came over to watch us bump and grind and dance until we were stooped down and then we'd move back up until we were doing the electric slide. I danced so hard that I was laughing. And I knew I looked good. Every man in the room had his eyes on me.

The only problem was, I had forgotten about Ben. And when I finally realized that I wasn't in some nightclub somewhere but was in the family home of a man who was about to become a justice on the state supreme court, a man who I just knew didn't appreciate my display one bit, I sat down. I didn't look his way, but I guess you could say I could feel his stare.

Jeremy tried to pull me back up, and some of the other guys, but I wouldn't budge. I leaned back and pretended that I had to catch my breath. When they gave up and went back to the dance floor, I took what I thought would be a very casual glance Ben's way. And there he was, sitting at the dining room table supposedly playing cards, sitting at the head of that table, staring at me. And if looks could kill I would have been dead.

But I quickly looked away as if I didn't see him. He was a tight-ass, not me. And I wasn't going to start being one either. He didn't like to dance. That was his deal, that was his thing. But damn it, I loved to dance and sometimes I was cuttin' loose whether he liked it or not. I even thought about getting back on the dance floor, to make it clear to him that this was who he was getting if he wanted me. I was loud and wild and full of life sometimes. Take me or leave me. Then I smiled. *Cool it, Josie,* I said to myself.

"What are you smiling about?" Mindy asked as she and Wendy came over. The dancing was winding down and Jeremy and his boom box started heading outside.

"I'm just smiling," I said.

"Look at Aunt Miriam," Wendy said. "She's going to talk Uncle Ben to death."

I looked into the dining room. Aunt Miriam, a woman who appeared to be in her mid to late fifties, with sandy red hair and a pretty face, was sitting beside Ben talking nonstop. Ben was playing cards and listening to her, but it didn't take a genius to see that he would rather she shut the hell up.

"And you can tell Uncle Ben is bored to tears," Mindy said and they giggled. Then she looked at me. "You're one of his interns or something. Right?"

His intern? Where did she get that from? "No."

"You're not one of his law clerks?"

"No, I'm not."

"I thought for sure Granny said Uncle Ben was bringing one of his law clerks with him."

I found it strange that Ben's mother—whom I had not yet met and was dreading the encounter—would say such a thing unless Ben specifically told her that I was one of his clerks. I looked again at Ben, as he listened to Aunt Miriam, and I wondered if his decision to keep his distance with me wasn't entirely spur of the moment. I was young after all, and wasn't exactly mainstream in my appearance. Maybe he was embarrassed to have a young, liberated girlfriend like me. "No," I said to Mindy, "I'm not a clerk at all. I'm a reporter."

"Really?" Wendy asked.

"That's how Ben and I met," I went on, refusing to participate in my own public shunning. "I had to write a story on him for my newspaper."

"Your school newspaper?" Mindy asked, by far the more astonished of the two. The idea that somebody she perceived as her equal could be an equal of her beloved Uncle Ben didn't sit right with her. But that was her problem.

"I'm a reporter for the *Jacksonville Gazette*," I said.

"Really?" Wendy said again, her brown eyes wide with admiration. "And you're Uncle Ben's girlfriend?"

"Nonsense," Mindy said before I could open my mouth. "Uncle Ben is almost fifty years old. He's ancient. That would be absurd. And can you imagine what Desiree would say?"

"Oh yes," Wendy said and giggled. "Desiree wouldn't like that."

"Thank you," Mindy said.

Desiree? Who the hell was Desiree? I wanted desperately to ask about her, and would have if Mindy weren't there. But Mindy was there.

"Anyway," she said as she stood up, Wendy standing too, "let's go to the club and see what Mike and Skip are up to."

"Sounds good to me," Wendy said.

"You'll come too," Mindy said, looking at me.

Imagine me going to some country club to see what somebody named Skip was up to? I passed, for my sake as well as the club's.

"You're sure?" the sweet one, Wendy, asked.

"Positive," I said with a sweet little smile of my own, and they left.

I leaned back and crossed my legs. The young people were all gone by now and Ben, after a long while, moved away from the talkative Aunt Miriam and started hanging with a small group of men. Everybody, it seemed, was cordoned off into small groups. Everybody, it seemed, but me.

I watched Ben operate, as he carried on various conversations with different people, and I was amazed at how adapt he was at ignoring me. I was sitting on a couch alone, totally alien to the people and my surroundings, but he acted as if he didn't give a damn. I wanted to talk to him about a lot of things, particularly who this Desiree woman was, but he wouldn't even look in my direction. And the females in the room were just as horrible. Only they'd stare at me until I looked at them and then they'd roll their eyes or shake their heads or look me up and down as if there was something about me they just didn't like.

I wanted to leave, to get as far away from that crowd as my feet would carry me, and would have, but Carolyn came to my rescue. She was Ben's thirty-five-year-old baby sister and was the reason for the get-together in the first place.

"Hi," she said, as she sat down beside me. She was too perfect looking, with a small, narrow face, big brown eyes, and a smile out of this world. I could tell as soon as I saw her that Ben worshiped the ground she walked on.

"Congratulations," I said.

"Thank you. I'll be married in four days, can you imagine?"

"Is this your first marriage?"

"Yes. My very first. I wanted it to be right, you know?"

I nodded. I definitely knew what she was saying.

"I meant to come by earlier, but you seemed to be having such fun."

I smiled. "I guess I overdid it on the dance floor."

"Not at all. Why would you say that?"

"Ben didn't seem that pleased."

"Ben's never pleased. You mustn't let him curtail your fun."

I wanted to ask her so much about him, not to mention that Desiree woman, but I didn't have the nerve.

"You hear me?" she asked. "You enjoy yourself."

"I will. Thanks."

"And thank you for coming, I appreciate it. Maybe before the wedding we can spend some time together. I would love for you to meet some of my friends."

"I'd like that, Carolyn. That's nice of you."

"Good." And then she smiled. "Ben tells me you're a reporter."

At least she got my occupation right, I thought. "Yes."

"That sounds so fascinating. Do you like it?"

"Yeah, I think so."

She looked up, over my shoulder, and smiled. I turned around. Ben was standing behind me. "She loves it," he said.

"I think the journalism profession is a worthy calling," Carolyn said. "You have excellent taste, big brother."

I smiled. It was good to know that she was on my side. Ben, however, just stared at me. And then he reached out his hand. "Come on," he said.

I took his hand and stood up. "Where?"

"Don't question it, Josephine," Carolyn said, standing too. "He's got to show you off a little, that's all."

Ben smiled and looked at his sister. "What do you know about it?"

"I know you, that's what I know about it," she said playfully. "She got it going on and you're proud to point it out. I think it's so romantic."

"Oh God," Ben said and began guiding me away. "Let's just get out of here."

I looked back at Carolyn and smiled. She shook her head approvingly.

Key West is the southernmost city in the continental United States and we drove along the edges. Although it had a reputation of glamour, it seemed more sedate to me, like a quaint little fishing village with the occasional tourist spots. And we hit them all. Sloppy Joe's Bar, Mallory Square, Truman's Little White House, Hemingway's place. We also hit the lesser-known hideaways such as the Lonely Lane Hot Spot and Spider's, where the best crab legs I'd ever eaten were fried on a grill and tossed on my plate. We even danced together at Spider's, which was wonderful, and it was the first time I slow-dragged in my life. Ben held on to me and led the way, and I leaned against him and let him do his thing. Most of the music, such as Andy Williams singing "Moon River" or Dean Martin singing "That's Amore!", didn't exactly turn me on, but one song, Rod Stewart's "Tonight's the Night" with that edgy, sexy voice of his, was perfect. I looked up at Ben as he held on to me and smiled that rare smile of his, and it was the best dance I'd ever had. But then, and so suddenly that it startled me, he slung me around as if I were a ballerina and dipped me across his arm. I looked at him, to make sure he knew what he was doing, and he smiled even wider. "This, my dear, is what you call dancing," he said. I laughed.

On the road again and we were heading back to Old Town. At least that was where I thought we were heading. We detoured, however, and ended up driving down some shadowy streets and quiet lanes that eventually let to a place called the Motel Deluxe, a kind of Motel 6 without the brand-name backing. Ben pulled up to the main office area and I looked at him. I knew what time it was, he wanted a quick hit before we returned to his parents' home, but I just couldn't resist playing crazy. "What do you need from here?" I asked him. "This doesn't look like your mama's house to me."

"I thought I'd show you what one of these rooms look like," he said, and with a straight face too.

"You're going to show me what a room inside this motel looks like?"

"Right."

"Why?"

He almost smiled. "I thought it would be something interesting for you to see."

"Have you ever stayed at a motel before in your life, Benjamin?"

He smiled. He couldn't hold it in any longer. "Okay, you got me. But I came close once." He said this and looked at me. His bright brown eyes trailed down, to my chest, and when he looked back up at me, his smile was gone. "I thought we'd take an hour or two and relax."

"Relax?"

"Yes."

"Not that I have anything against this Motel Deluxe, but I would relax better at the Marriott."

He laughed. "Okay," he said and began to crank up his car.

I touched his arm. "I'm just kidding, Ben."

"We can go there. This was just on the way."

"This is fine. Really."

"You sure?"

"I'm positive."

"Okay," he said, looked at me again, and then hurried to get the key.

We needed a radio to mute the sound, but there was no radio. The television would have to do. I grabbed the remote and quickly started clicking through the channels, searching for a noisy channel, like MTV, and Ben was on top of me, moaning and groaning and pumping, the bed squeaking loudly from our weight and bounce, the sweat pouring from both of us and feeling slippery, like oil, turning us on even more, but MTV had on a commercial and BET had on a movie, so I clicked on VH1. A tribute to Michael Jackson and his groundbreaking videos was on, and they were going way back, to when Michael had a short jheri-curled Afro, dark skin, didn't have his dance moves down yet, and was singing "Rock With You." But his voice was so soft that I had to turn the volume up as loud as it could go, because I knew my time was near and I would be carrying on as if somebody were killing me. I threw the remote down and grabbed on to Ben, my legs curled against his back as he moaned and groaned and pumped his ass off. And I was grateful for the music because it was clear that Ben's sexiness, and the way he felt inside me, was too much to contain, and I preferred that our motel neighbors believed we were partying too loud, than for them to hear what was really going on. And then it came. First as a high-pitched groan that grew louder and louder until containment was no longer possible. My body lifted up, Ben slammed it down, and that already out-of-control groaning went to an even higher place of refuge and became a soulful, thrilling, blissful wail.

We didn't make it back to his parents' home until the next day. Around noon the next day. Our room at the motel didn't require checkout until eleven A.M., so I talked Ben into sleeping in for a change. But when we arrived at his parents' home, our peaceful time together was about to get a little rocky.

We weren't back a good hour when it started. Ben was in the living room talking with some other men about the Dolphins, Buccaneers, and Jaguars, and which of those Florida teams was the best team. It was a wash as far as I was concerned, but they all had strong opinions. Carolyn and I were in the dining room, along with her bridesmaids, going over some of the details of her wedding. She asked that I sit in on the get-together, and I appreciated it, but her bridesmaids seemed very disturbed by my presence. They were civil with their disgust, they didn't rag on me or anything, but those damn looks. *What is she doing here? Why would we have anything to do with her? Who does she think she is?* I could never mistake those looks.

But they couldn't hold a candle to one woman's look in particular. It was a sudden entrance. Carolyn had asked my opinion on whether she should play Luther Vandross's "The Power of Love" or Mariah Carey's "I'll Be There" after she threw the bouquet and they were leaving the reception. Before I could respond, the front door flew open and a woman walked in as if she owned the joint. She was tall and bosomy and had that supermodel thing going big time, with all the right curves, the red dress and heels, the gloves (yes, gloves) that she whipped off of her hands, and the look. Lord, the look. Jesus, the look. Smart, confident, and drop-dead gorgeous. I could only pray that she wasn't the mysterious Desiree.

"Desiree!" Carolyn yelled and left my side with the quickness. She ran to Desiree, and Desiree ran to her. Others started heading toward her too, especially the men, who were almost knocking over their wives and girlfriends to get by her side. If Ben was the man of the hour, she was the woman. She was it. I looked at Ben.

He was actually straightening his tie and rubbing his hair in place as he moved more slowly toward the great woman. I sat back, folded my arms, and watched. All eyes were on this one person. His eyes were on this one person. Desiree.

Everybody seemed to move aside and make room for Ben when he walked up. Desiree said, "Ben, hi!" with a great force of excitement and she rushed into his arms. He grabbed hold of her and lifted her off the ground. She tilted her head back and laughed that laugh of confidence, as if she knew she was pleasing everyone in sight and was going to milk it for all she could.

Ben eventually released her and her feet touched down again. Then he looked at her entire body, slowly, painfully slowly. "You look wonderful, Desi," he said to her. I looked okay this morning, according to him, but she looked wonderful. I was doomed.

"I didn't know you would be here this soon," she said. "Carolyn, why didn't you tell me?"

"I wanted it to be a surprise," Carolyn said, and the little hope I had for her was gone. She wasn't on my side after all. She knew I was coming with Ben. Why would she want to surprise another woman when she knew I would be there? Probably for the same reason that all those other females were giving me the cold shoulder. Desiree, or *Desi* as Ben called her, wasn't a loose fit in their world. She fit right in. Anybody who looked at her would not be surprised in the least if she became the wife of a supreme court justice. Whereas if I became such a person, they'd be shocked as hell.

And she and Ben looked great together. Even I had to admit that. Both were tall and athletic and filled with that *can't touch this* sex appeal that should have been bottled and sold.

"So how have you been?" she asked Ben.

"Good."

"So I've heard. Congratulations, my dear." She said this and hit him playfully on his shoulder. He touched his shoulder and smiled. "Thanks," he said.

Then she turned serious. She knew how to play that role too. "I'm so very proud of you, Benjamin. Or should I say Justice Braddock? You've worked so hard your entire life. It's a wonderful thing. It's just you, you know what I'm saying?" Everybody around her laughed. I wondered what the joke was about. But of course it wasn't a joke. It was just the way she said it, all cute and cuddly, as only she could.

The more I watched her operate, the more I wondered what it was about her that seemed so familiar. I'd never seen her before, that was for sure. You don't forget meeting a woman like Desiree. But she *was* familiar. Then she said: "This is so beautiful, all of us together, this is what life should always be about. Family. Friends. Good times." And I realized at once what it was. She reminded me of Mary Richards from *The Mary Tyler Moore Show*. Some nights, when I couldn't get to sleep, I'd turn on Nick at Nite and watch all the oldies but goodies. And that was whom Desiree reminded me of. Mary Richards. She had the same quirky mannerisms, the same jovial expressions, and that same All-American girl smile. At any moment I expected her to toss her hat in the air, rear her head back, and proclaim that she was gonna make it after all too. When I made the connection, I understood. It was the easiest thing in the world to see why Ben would want her. What man wouldn't?

That was when I decided to get up and join in the fun too. If you can't beat 'em, join 'em. I joined. I walked up beside Ben, smiling from ear to ear, as if I were just as thrilled to see Desi too. Some of the females in the group looked at me with their *who does she think she is barging into our world like this?* look, but I didn't care. I felt defeated, not triumphant the way they were thinking, but I wasn't about to let them know that.

When I came up beside Ben, he seemed a little uncomfortable himself, but then he stepped back slightly and introduced me. "Desi, I want you to meet Josephine," he said. Still no I want you to meet *my woman Josephine,* or J*osephine, my woman,* but what the hell. Ben was Ben.

"Desi, hi," I said, moving up toward her, my smile so exaggerated and phony I could have won a contest.

"Hello, Josephine," she said, still playing the role, still knowing how to handle every situation that came her way. "How are you?"

"I'm great. And you?"

"Fantastic."

"Perfect," I said.

"She's cute," Desiree said to Ben, as if I were some little puppy he had found and although it was a cute puppy, she knew he wasn't about to keep *that*. Ben, however, didn't say anything. I felt horrible that he didn't, he could have at least said *thanks,* or *she's more than cute, she's my lady,* something. But who was I kidding?

I stepped back and away from Desiree, and hopefully out of the spotlight, but I found myself backing into Ben. I fully expected him to move aside and out of my way since he didn't seem, at least when Desi was around, to want contact with me, but he didn't. He even placed his hand on my arm and pulled me closer to him. Those females, who had that *who does she think she is?* look on their faces, looked at each other. *This is who I am,* I wanted to tell them.

"So," Desiree said, and I knew what was coming. She had to find a way to belittle me, to regain the ground she thought she'd lost. "You're from Jacksonville too?"

"Yes," I said, my smile still uncommonly grand. And Desiree knew it too. And it was eating her alive.

"What do you do?"

"She's a reporter," Carolyn said as if she was proud of me. I didn't need her kind of pride.

"A reporter? My. Front-line work, isn't it?"

"Excuse me?" I asked. My smile was still there, but my rising hot temper was weakening it. Desiree was winning again.

"What I mean is, you're not like the managing editor or the publisher, correct?"

"The publisher owns the newspaper," I said.

"Right. And that's not you."

The smile was gone. A frown came instead. She'd won. "I don't understand what you're getting at."

Desiree smiled and looked around. They all smiled back. "I'm not getting at anything," she said. "Nothing at all. Some of us are testy, testy."

The crowd laughed. I wanted to ask them what was so damn funny, and Ben knew I wanted to, so he squeezed my arm. But he didn't stand up for me. He didn't play that. He liked his women strong. If I wanted to be some weakling, then I was going to be it alone. To him I was a big girl. I could take care of myself. And he was right.

My smile returned, bigger and grander. Desiree was surprised. She didn't expect a comeback. "You're right," I said. "I am so sorry. This is too grand an occasion for testiness, now, isn't it?" Now her smile was gone. And I had won. And those females, although they didn't want to admit it, had to admit that I was right. Of course Ben holding on to my arm, in a kind of low-key *this is my woman* demonstration, didn't hurt. They figured if Ben liked me, then I couldn't be all bad.

I felt vindicated. I felt as if I could stand up to the best—and Desiree was the best—and hold my own. Ben even seemed proud of me. He smiled at me again, and held my hand, and when we all went out to the pool in the backyard, he sat beside me on the patio. I thanked God I didn't sulk when Desiree hit the scene. Sulking would have gotten me nowhere with Ben. He liked strength. He liked powerful women. I knew he was still nuts about Desiree and there was no doubt in my mind that they were once lovers, but I also knew that he was nuts about me too. And I was behaving the way a woman of his was supposed to behave: with class, dignity, but always, always, with strength. I was beginning to show some signs.

Almost, anyway. Everything was fine. We were all out on the patio, some in the pool, most just chilling and enjoying the sun, when Carolyn came up with this bright idea of putting steaks on the grill. Then she asked Ben of all the men out there if he would go buy some steaks. Ben quickly obliged his beloved sister and stood up. Then she asked if I would help prepare the side dishes. I gladly agreed. And as soon as I stood up, committed to helping Carolyn with her damn side dishes, Miss Desiree went to work. "I'll go with you, Ben," she said so quickly and so casually that before I could fully appreciate what was happening, she and Ben were heading for the front yard.

One hour later. The side dishes, baked potatoes, and corncobs were buttered and foiled and ready for the grill. But no Ben and Desiree.

Two hours later. Ben's parents came home, and the groom who

had been chauffeuring them around, and I finally met them, but I had to do it alone. Carolyn introduced us. The mother, Margaret Braddock, was a radiant woman of sixty-seven with pure white hair and a kind, pretty face. I knew instinctively when I first laid eyes on her that she was Ben's mother. They did not favor each other at all, her features were more subtle than Ben's, but she carried that quiet dignity that defined him and that I knew had to come from somewhere. Ben said she had once studied at the Sorbonne in Paris, while his father, then in the diplomatic corp, did some work on behalf of the French government, and the gracefulness showed. Her walk, her talk, her smile, all demonstrated her background and breeding. This was no ordinary sister, her very demeanor seemed to say. And his father, William Russell Braddock, was no less refined. He spoke in deep, every-word-pronounced-completely-correct tones, and the handsomeness that was still a part of him, even at seventy, made him an awesome figure to behold. They were pleasant with me, but were preoccupied with so many others who wanted their attention too that my big meeting with the parents wasn't what I had expected, especially since Ben wasn't there to prove to them that I was worthy of their time. But his actions said it all. He was gone. He didn't give a damn. Why should they?

Three hours later. Still no sign of Ben and Desiree. Omar, Carolyn's husband-to-be, hit the nail on the head. "What are they doing," he asked, "killing the cow?" Those females looked at me, and some of them even giggled, but I just turned my head. This was a game to them. And maybe it was. But I wasn't wit it.

Three hours and twenty-two minutes after Ben and Desiree left to go get steaks, they arrived in the backyard. Ben seemed nervous, hurrying into the kitchen with the steaks without even acknowledging my presence, but Desiree was giddy. She looked at me and smiled greatly. *See, bitch?* her expression seemed to say. *You can't compete with me!*

I went into the kitchen. Ben and Carolyn were hovered over the sink cleaning and seasoning the steaks. Carolyn said to him, "That's not right," just as I walked in. She turned quickly when she realized I was there, but Ben didn't turn at all. He just kept cleaning.

"Josephine!" Carolyn said gaily, but I wasn't thinking about her. She was a co-conspirator as far as I was concerned. She was the one who had me buttering corncobs while my man was out humping that obnoxious female. I walked up to the sink counter and stood beside Ben. At first he didn't look at me but I wasn't moving until he did. And he did. And his eyes said it all. They were regretful. Disappointed in himself. Guilty as sin.

I held out my hand. I wanted to cry, but I refused to allow it. "Give me the keys," I said.

He frowned. "The keys to what?"

"Your car."

A look of concern crossed his face when I said this. I had never asked something so personal of him before. "Why would you need my car?"

"To go somewhere."

"Where?"

"Off."

He sighed. "Off where, Josephine?"

"Are you going to give me the keys or not?"

"You don't know this town. I can't have you out there getting lost."

"Spare me, please."

"What did you say?"

"I just want to borrow your car, is that so hard? I don't ask for much." When I said this, the tears were just one exhale from dropping out. I wasn't lying. I didn't ask for much. Just kindness and truth. Faithfulness. He knew it too. That was why he wiped his hands and pulled his keys out of his pocket.

"Do you want me to go with you?" he asked.

"No," I said and snatched the keys from his hand.

I drove around Key West for hours, and the harder I tried to get my mind off of Ben, the harder it became. His car smelled like him, the jazz on his CD player reminded me of him. I hated that he would have slept with that witch Desiree, but his eyes never lied. He had done something with her. He told me I didn't have to worry, that he wouldn't hurt me. But what did he think he was doing? I drove around and around. I saw a million sights. Heard a zillion sounds. But I couldn't remember one.

When I returned to the Braddock home, most of the cars were

gone. I parked in the drive and hurried into the house, anxious for some reason to see Ben. I should have rung the bell, I suppose, but I didn't. I just walked right in.

No one was in the living room, but Ben was seated at the dining-room table smoking a cigarette. Aunt Miriam was also in the dining room, seated on a chair against the wall talking on her cell phone, and two females I didn't recognize were at the opposite end of the table talking quietly between themselves.

I walked up to Ben and placed his keys on the table. I turned to leave, but he grabbed my hand and held it. "Where did you go?" he asked me.

"Off," I said.

"Where, Josephine?"

"How should I know? I don't know this town, remember?"

He studied my face, and then he took a quick drag on his cigarette, all the while refusing to release me from his grasp. "What are you upset about?" he asked me.

"I'm not upset about anything."

"Nothing happened."

"It never does, does it?"

He frowned. "What's that supposed to mean?"

"You know what it means."

His face grew more flustered and he pointed his cigarette at me. He was hot. "I don't like bullshit, Josephine!" He said this so sternly that Aunt Miriam looked up momentarily from her cell phone conversation and the other two women glanced over as well. "Now I told you nothing happened. And I'm not going to keep repeating myself."

"You were gone for three hours, Ben. Three hours to pick up some steaks?"

"I ran into a friend of mine. Now I'm sorry but I did. I would have ended the conversation more quickly if I had known I was being timed."

How could I believe that? I would be the biggest fool this side of living if I believed that. That was the oldest excuse in the book. He ran into an old friend. Yeah, right.

Ben could see that I wasn't buying it, so he shook his head and released my hand. I left the dining room and went into the living room.

I would have left the house altogether but Ben's parents came downstairs and asked if I would sit with them for a while.

So I did. Mr. and Mrs. Braddock sat beside me. One on either side, in fact.

"Would you like something to drink, Josephine?" Mrs. Braddock asked me.

"Water would be nice. Thank you."

She lifted a bell from the coffee table and rang it gently. "What about you, Benjamin?" she asked, looking toward the dining room.

"Nothing."

"Are you sure, dear?"

"Nothing," he said again just as the butler arrived from the kitchen.

"You rang, ma'am?"

"Yes, Dawson, we would like a glass of water for the young lady, please."

"Yes, ma'am," Dawson said and headed back toward the kitchen.

We chitchatted for maybe fifteen minutes, mainly Mrs. Braddock and I with Mr. Braddock occasionally chiming in. Ben sat quietly in the dining room, but I could tell by his furrowed brow and anxious demeanor that he was raging inside. But Ben was hard to read sometimes. His moodiness was unlike anything I'd ever experienced. I didn't know if his rage had to do with me or nothing at all to do with me. Maybe seeing Desiree again fired him up. Maybe he was still steaming because I refused to believe his running-into-a-friend nonsense. Maybe it was some past issues he had with his parents. Maybe it was none of the above.

But whatever it was it ate at him all evening. And even when Desiree and the bride and groom and a host of other family members assembled with us, his mood did not completely lift. He smiled and was cordial, especially toward Desiree, who sat in the dining room with him, but when the conversation shifted away from him I could still see the anger in his eyes.

But that was not the worst of it. Desiree, at one point, rose and walked into a side room. It was an office or a study of some sort, but close enough and accessible enough that she could slip away virtually undetected. I detected her, however, because I had been checking her out just waiting for her to make her move. And, as I also expected, within moments Ben rose too and went into that same room. The gaiety of the crowd, as Ben's nephew Jeremy told jokes that had everybody in stitches, kept my anger suppressed. I didn't feel angry at Ben. I just felt sad. I thought he was different. I thought he was a good man, a decent, principled brother. But I was deluding myself. I deluded myself into mistaking a dog for a man.

I decided to leave. All of this roller-coaster bullshit, when I swore I'd never let some man ride me like this, turning my very existence upside down, wasn't for me. I wasn't feeling it. I was about to stand too, and by standing make a stand, but Mrs. Braddock held my arm. I looked at her. I was on the verge of tears and she knew it, but her smile kept me strong.

"Will you please tell Benjamin to come here?" she asked. "I believe he's in the study."

She knew what she was doing, although I didn't understand it, but I didn't fight it. "Yes, ma'am," I said lowly and reluctantly walked over to the study door. My heartbeat quickened as I walked, because I fully expected to catch Ben and Desiree locked into an embrace—or worse—when I opened the door. I opened the door quickly but not melodramatically—I didn't fling it open, anyway. But it didn't matter how I entered because the result was the same. They were embracing.

Ben was facing the door and he saw me enter. He did not push her from him, as most busted dogs would do, but he released her slowly, gently. She glanced back at me and I could see that she was crying, and then she walked over by the window, her back to Ben and me.

I looked at Ben. I didn't see guilt on his face, just weariness. "Yes?" he finally asked, but I didn't know what to say. I felt so inexperienced, so out of my league, so young. He hated it when I behaved like a child, and crying over a man who didn't want my tears certainly would have qualified, so I decided to hold back every emotion in my body. I even inhaled and erected my shoulders. He wanted Desiree, he could have Desiree. I couldn't compete against someone like her and I wasn't about to try. I got stronger with every defiant word that floated through my brain. I thought about all the grand advice I gave to my colleagues when they were deluded and actually believed that their cheating dogs were men too. My resolve, right then and there, made crying seem like a fool's game, like child's play, like ridiculous nonsense. Never again, I boldly proclaimed to myself.

Never again would I shed another tear over Benjamin Braddock or any other human being.

"What do you want, Josephine?" he asked in his normal, impatient voice and immediately, as if somebody had opened the floodgates of my heart and released the valve, the tears came. Desiree quickly turned around, crying too, as if she wanted me to know that she loved him too, and was more than willing to do whatever it took to get him back.

And there we stood, the three of us. I stood in front of him crying, she stood behind him crying, and he was in the middle. But he was stuck because he did not advance toward me or backtrack toward her. But something had to give.

It was Ben who spoke up. "I'm going to take Desi home," he said. "I want you to come with me."

Desi looked at me. I would have told Ben a thing or two about going anywhere with him, if Desi would not have looked at me. The fix was in and Ben was fooling himself if he didn't realize it. The last thing that woman wanted was for me to tag along. And that was exactly why I agreed to do it.

But it went downhill from there. Ben ran over to a car across the lawn to say good-bye to one of his nephews. That left Desi and me to put ourselves in his car. Desi put her long legs to work and outstepped me so decisively that she was sitting down in the front seat of Ben's Mercedes before I made it up to the door. When I finally arrived, she had the nerve to lean her body forward so that I could squeeze into the backseat. I looked at sister girl as if she had lost her mind. And I stood right there. I even folded my arms. If anybody was going to be squeezing into the backseat, I thought, it was going to be she.

But as usual, I thought wrong. Ben finally said his good-byes and came over to the car. Desi was smiling and putting on the best *I'm just so perfect* look she could muster. I was too far gone to even think about smiling. But Ben was Ben. He didn't seem to understand what all the fuss was about. Riding in the car was the point, in his view. What difference did it make *where* you rode? But it made every difference in the world to me that day. That was why, when he eased beside me and pulled the passenger seat forward, to make room for me to hop my behind in the back, I took my behind away from that car and started heading for the house.

"Josephine?" he yelled after me, as if he couldn't believe I was walking away like that. But I did it. I didn't look back.

Two hours on the patio alone and then Mrs. Braddock came outside. "I've been told that you're not eating," she said to me. I was out by the pool chillin' in a lounge chair, wearing shorts and sandals, trying to enjoy a breeze that was too strong and only served to remind me of my tumultuous days with Ben.

"I'm not hungry," I said.

"Not a good idea."

"I know."

She sat down in the chair beside mine. First she didn't say anything, and then she said a mouthful. "I'm sorry you had to fall in love with my son," she said, and I looked at her. "You're too fragile for a man like him."

"But why is it always about being strong all the time with him?"

"It just is, young lady. Make no mistake about it."

"But why?"

"I can't answer that. Benjamin is odd. And he's restless. He always has been. Unfortunately, nobody seems to keep his attention for very long. But I keep sensing that he sees you differently. There's something about you that scares him, I think. That's why he keeps you at bay and treats you the way he does."

"Do you think he loves me?"

She hesitated. "I don't know."

"But what's the point of the rest of it if he doesn't love me?"

"Josephine, I can't answer your questions. Only Benjamin can. And he won't."

I sighed. "What did he tell you about me?"

"He said that you were young."

"That's all?"

"Yes."

Great, I thought. A ringing endorsement. And then I thought about where he was. "Desiree was his lover once, wasn't she?" I asked her.

She paused. "Yes, she was."

"He broke her heart?"

"On the contrary."

"She broke his?"

"Yes. Just as every woman he's ever loved has. Just as you will someday."

"Me? I could never break anybody's heart. Never! If I love somebody, I love him completely. If I don't, I don't even give him the time of day. I don't play games."

"Oh, it won't be a game. It is never a game."

"But how can you believe that, Mrs. Braddock? He's the one who invited me here and then proceeded to treat me like I was second to that Desiree chick. And I had such high hopes for this trip."

"Maybe that's why. Maybe your high hopes scared him."

"He's too old to be getting scared, okay? Besides, he didn't know about my hopes."

"He knew. He's like me. He senses things. And if your high hopes were realized and he totally opened himself to you, he probably believes that will be the end of it. It always is."

"This is crazy. I'm sorry, but it is. He's scared of me breaking *his* heart? Me? It's stupid. Unless he's got some dark secrets he's hiding . . ."

"Nothing like that. We are all blessed and cursed, Josephine. I'm convinced of it. Benjamin is blessed with his looks, his brilliant mind, and what was once described to me as a commanding presence. He walks into a room and immediately dominates the room by the force of his presence alone. Even I sit at attention when he comes near me, my own son, can you imagine? But he's cursed too. He's cursed with the burden of always, always falling in love with the wrong woman."

I shook my head. Was there any hope? "A friend told me that Ben's wife became mentally ill during their marriage. . . ."

"No. He was wrong. She was already ill before he married her. We just thought she was full of life and impulsive, maybe even perilous. But that woman was seriously ill. And she wouldn't take her medicine, she'd pretend to but she couldn't have been, and Ben wouldn't put her away. For eighteen years he suffered. And then she died. But the pain continued woman after woman after woman."

"Including Desiree?"

"Including Desiree."

"What did she do to him?"

"Oh, let me see. Ah, yes. She got angry with him one weekend when he didn't show up for something or other, so she went and married another man."

My eyebrows stretched. "She *what?*"

"Yes."

"She's still married then?"

"No. Long since divorced. Within weeks of the marriage, I think."

I leaned back. This was too much. I thought love was a piece of cake, just sitting there if you cared to taste it, but I could not have been more wrong. Love was a science, very exacting, and one misstep could lead to so many others that the whole thing gets thrown out of whack.

My cell phone began ringing, and it was a welcomed distraction. I reached into my pocket, pulled out my phone, and flipped it open. It was Scotty. "What's up?" I asked.

"How you doing?"

"Don't ask."

"What's the matter?"

"I'm okay."

"Are you sure, darling? 'Cause I can get there."

"I'm okay, Scotty, really. What's up?"

"Your sister called me."

"Which one?"

"Martha, of course. She's been trying to get in touch with you all day. I started to give her the number to your cell but I thought about that and decided against it. The way you talk about how crazy your siblings are, I wasn't about to give up your number, girl."

"Good. What did she want?"

"She said you need to get to Alabama quick because your mama is sick and she's been asking for you."

"Oh God. Is it her heart again?"

"I asked her that. She said yes. But it's not another heart attack or anything like that. So I don't know what Martha was talking about. Your mama just sick, she said."

"She's probably sick and tired of my siblings."

"That's what I think."

"Okay, Scotty. Thanks."

"Call me later."

"I will."

"Love you."

"Love you too. Bye."

I flipped close my phone. Mrs. Braddock was standing up now, staring at me. I immediately felt defensive. "That was Scotty," I said.

"Scotty?"

"Scotty Culpepper. My best friend."

She nodded.

"He's gay," I quickly added.

She smiled weakly. "What did he want?"

"My mother is sick and I need to go see about her."

"Oh my. Is she in Jacksonville?"

"Alabama."

I got up and started heading for the house as I flipped open my phone and dialed the number to my mother's home. Mrs. Braddock, to my surprise, followed me. I hurried inside the house, up the stairs, and into the bedroom reserved for Ben and me, the bedroom where our suitcases were stored. Mrs. Braddock followed right behind me, asking me constantly if there was anything she could do.

My mother's phone was disconnected. Every other month, it seemed to me, my siblings would run up her phone bill to such an extent that she had to have it turned off. Then she'd find the money somewhere, from one of her male friends, no doubt, and have service restored. It was the craziest thing in the world to me, the way she put up with my lazy-behind siblings, but I couldn't tell her anything when it came to her babies, her grown-ass, not-worth-sweeping-out-the-door babies. I flipped closed my cell phone.

"Couldn't get anyone?" Mrs. Braddock asked me.

"No, ma'am."

"Well, is it an emergency?"

"Oh no. I'm certain of that."

"I see. When do you plan to leave?"

That was an easy question. I had no reason to stay here. "I'm going to try and get a plane out now."

"Now? But I thought you said it wasn't an emergency."

"No, but I'm going to just go. Do you have a phone book? I need to make a reservation."

She moved over by the telephone in the bedroom. "Dawson will handle that."

"No, ma'am, I can do it."

She began dialing a seven-digit phone number. "Dawson will take care of it."

"Who are you calling?" I asked her. I felt compelled to ask, feeling somehow that her sudden need to make a phone call was intricately linked to my sudden decision to get out of Dodge.

"I'm calling Benjamin on his cell phone."

My heart dropped. I was hoping for a clean getaway. "Don't do that please."

"He needs to know you're leaving."

"Mrs. Braddock, please don't. I don't want his pity."

"Hello, Benjamin?" she said into the phone. "Benjamin?" Then she looked at me. "May I speak with Benjamin please?"

I shook my head. Desiree, no doubt, had answered his phone. "Hello, son," she said into the phone. "Nothing's wrong. I'm letting you know that your guest is preparing to leave. Yes. As soon as she can get a flight out. Her mother is ill. Well, she said it wasn't an emergency but she wants to leave right now. Yes. Yes, Benjamin. I don't know, she insists she's leaving at once. What?" After a moment she pointed the phone in my direction. "He wants to speak with you," she said.

I hesitated, because the idea of talking to Ben terrified me. What could he say to me? Let me get out of my lover's bed and come say good-bye? "Hello," I said nervously into the phone.

"You're leaving?" he asked. He sounded almost hoarse, as if he had been awakened from sleep.

"Yes," I said. Hearing his voice made me want to cry.

"Why?"

"My mother is ill and I've got to go."

"To Alabama?"

"Yes."

"When is your flight?"

"We haven't, I don't know, we haven't made the reservation yet."

"It'll probably be morning before you can get a flight to Alabama, honey."

"I'll take the bus then," I said, purposely defiant.

"You'll do no such thing," he replied, equally defiant. "Don't get cute with me."

I closed my eyes and said nothing.

"I know you want to be by your mother's side and I respect that. But you're going to do this right. Dawson will find out what time in the morning is the first flight out for Alabama. He will make a reservation for that flight and I will drive you to the airport. Understood?"

"Sure," I said bitterly. It was the only way I knew how to respond to his orders. I should have cussed him out and handled my business, but love had me practically crippled with weakness. Scotty had said it best. When love hit me, he said, it was going to knock me down. And it did. I was wallowing on the ground.

"Put my mother on the phone," he said, and I handed his mother the phone.

He barked out a series of orders to her too and then she hung up. "It's the best way, Josephine," she said. When I didn't respond, because I couldn't, she left.

I lay across the bed, believing that all of my strength would be needed to confront Ben. And I decided to indeed confront him as soon as he arrived.

But he didn't come. Not at ten, not at eleven, not even at midnight. The longer he delayed, the angrier I became. After my phone conversation with him I just knew he would be on his way. I didn't even consider that he wouldn't. This was messed up. But I was the fool, not he. I was the one lying across a bed waiting for the morning to come, just because he told me to wait, while he probably hung up the phone, turned over, and went back to sleep, his girlfriend all snuggled in his arms. My anger kept rising and rising until I could slowly feel my old self begin to emerge. And I immediately felt like the biggest idiot that ever walked the face of this earth. What was I thinking? I was going to confront him, I said. Confront him for what? He was a free man. He could come and go as he pleased. And guess what? So could I.

And that was when my inaction became action, and before one A.M. rolled around I had packed my shit, phoned for a cab, and had my whipped behind in front of the Braddocks' home awaiting my ride.

The cab drove up quickly, before anybody in the dark, quiet home could detect that I was leaving, but as I walked toward the street with my luggage, a few feet from getting out of Dodge finally, Ben's Mercedes drove up. At first the sight of him stepping out of his car and walking toward me stopped me cold in my tracks, but I gathered my nerve again and headed for the cab.

"What do you think you're doing?" he asked angrily as he hurried across the lawn. I ignored him and prepared to hand my luggage to the taxi driver, who was standing at the cab's opened trunk. Ben attempted to take the suitcase from my hand just as the taxi driver reached for it, but I was angry too and snatched it from Ben's grasp. He looked at me, as if anger were an emotion no one could display but him, and then with brute force snatched the luggage from me.

"Get in the house!" he ordered, but I just stood there, my arms folded, my determination strong. "Now!" he yelled as he grabbed my arm and slung me toward the house, letting my arm go just as I began to stumble. I stumbled, but I did not fall. And I did not move another step.

He paid the taxi driver and apologized for the blank trip, and then he hurried toward me. He looked weary still, and angry as hell, and when he reached me he grabbed my arm tightly and pulled me up to the front door, into the house, up the stairs, and into our bedroom. Then he flung me onto the bed.

After setting the suitcase down and slamming the door, he stood at the foot of the bed staring at me, his suit coat wide open, his hands resting on his hips. He looked exhausted but he stood there for the longest time. And when he did talk he spoke haltingly, as if he was battling within himself to contain his anger.

"I told you I would get you to the airport."

"I wanna leave now," I said.

"Why is it so important for you to leave this very moment? You said your mother wasn't that ill. What's wrong with you, Josephine?" His face was so puzzled that it looked pained. He really didn't get it.

"Ain't nothing wrong with me," I said. "I just wanna get out of here now. And I will get out of here now!" I quickly stood up to leave, but he just as quickly grabbed me by my shoulders and pushed me back on the bed.

"I was spending some time with an old friend. I told you to come with me."

"You didn't want me to come."

"I didn't?"

"No. You was caught off guard and felt guilty, that's why you invited me along."

"So you're a mind reader now? Miss damn Cleo now?"

"Did you fuck her, Ben?"

He closed his eyes and exhaled. Then he tilted his head back and sighed. "I can't do it," he said.

My heart sank. "Do what?"

"This. Us. You limit your focus and that's all you can see. Stop going for the obvious all the time, Josephine. I told you that! Most of the time the obvious is the wrong answer."

"What are you talking about?"

"This goddamn child's play, that's what! I can't do it. You ask me a question, I answer it. Then you don't believe me. The answer isn't unusual enough. The answer isn't creative enough. A lie is usually the most creative tale of all, Josephine. Don't you realize that? But you don't. You see what you see and that's all you see. The truth? Well, that's beside the point. I take a friend home. You could have come too, but no. You want to lie in some bedroom feeling sorry for yourself. Well, I wasn't interested in a pity party tonight. So I had a few laughs and a drink with an old friend. And yes, she was my lover once. But not now. Yet you act as if—"

"As if what, Ben? As if you were out fucking that ex-lover of yours? You're damn right I'm acting that way. It's one A.M., Ben! You ain't gonna tell me you were just talking about the good old days with a buddy of yours. I'm not that damn naive. And you're right. I do see what I see. I've based my entire career on following facts, not fiction, and I'm not about to change that now. And you have the nerve to ask what's wrong with *me?* What the hell is wrong with you? I don't deserve this treatment! You hear me? If you don't want me here, tell me that. If you hate the sight of me and want me out of your life, say so! I don't know how to handle this, Ben. Sometimes you act as if you really care for me and then other times you seem as if you can't stand me. As if you hate me. What's up with that? I see you embracing another woman, what do you expect me to think? You've got to tell me what you expect from me. You've got to stop taking me through this shit and tell me something!"

The tears didn't come and I was thankful. I was too angry to cry anymore. I was too confused to get all mushy too. I looked at Ben and he was trippin'. The pain was all in his face. And I realized for the first time that this ride was bumpy as hell for him too.

He shook his head. "Is that what you think?" he asked me. "You think I don't care about you? You think I *hate* you?"

"Sometimes, yeah."

He sat down on the bed beside me so quickly that his sudden movement startled me. Then he placed his hands on my shoulders and turned me toward him. He wasn't confused or angry or even mildly irritated anymore. He was panic-stricken. "You are the most important person in this world to me, Josephine. Don't you realize that?"

"How am I supposed to realize it? You never told me."

"But I showed you. I spent all of my time with you. I brought you here."

"And then Desiree showed up."

"Forget her! She means nothing to me. I have loved you, Josephine, from the first time you walked into my office and called me a sellout." He smiled when he said this.

"You love me?" I asked him, stunned and thrilled at the same time.

"Of course I do. And you're going to break my heart." Lines came across his forehead when he said this. "But I've got to take that chance."

I was nodding no before he could finish talking. I threw my arms around him. "I will never break your heart, Ben," I declared. "Never!"

He didn't say anything. He just held me closer and closer to him. He looked into my eyes and kissed me. And then we began removing my clothes. And then his. And without saying a word he lay on top of me and eased into me. I pinched his back as his movements quickened, my entire body gyrating from the force of his sex alone. I wanted to scream, to shout out how I was feeling, but he covered my mouth and smiled. And just like that I had forgotten where I was, that I wasn't in Kansas anymore, but was in a different place, in a different time, and was about to become fully entrenched in Ben's world now.

NOT STUPID,
JUST CRAZY AS HELL

My family home was a small clapboard house on Hempley Street, one of those true-blue shotgun shacks surrounded by similar shacks, roaming dogs belonging to no one and everyone, and front yards that were more dirt than grass.

We arrived in Tuscaloosa around one that afternoon. We had caught the eleven-A.M. flight out of Key West International and had every intention of flying back that same day. Check on my mama, and hightail it back. That was the plan. Carolyn's wedding wasn't until the next day, and in the evening, so our every intention was to get back with plenty of time to spare.

This was Ben's chance to meet my mama and I was apprehensive as hell. I loved her and all that, but she was no Margaret Braddock. Her idea of somebody with background and breeding was somebody with good teeth and a steady job. And if I was to mention the Sorbonne to her, she'd just know I was talking about the newest restaurant in town. She was a good woman and a great person to know, but I didn't have a big mouth by chance. I inherited it from her.

Ben rented a Cadillac Escalade SUV, of all things, and it was big and black and lumbered like a Hum-Vee up to the curb in front of my mama's house. Ben leaned against the steering wheel and stared. I was staring too, at that same old house that was my childhood home. The old boards stacked on top of each other so flimsily now that I could only think of a house of cards. One wrong move and the whole thing would cave. I wondered if the bedroom ceiling still leaked, or if you still had to jiggle that damn toilet handle every time you used the toilet. My visits home used to be regular; the need to know that I, too, had roots, kept calling me home. But as time went by and the uselessness of it all crept in, my visits became less and less frequent, and when I did go home it was a short stay, declaring almost immediately that I couldn't stay, but was just passing through. In truth, I wanted to see my mama, wish her well, and get out.

"This is it," I said to Ben as I stepped out of the truck. I was certain that he was stunned; this wasn't exactly middle America we were about to embark upon, after all. I watched his face as he stepped out and looked up and down Hempley Street, at the dirt road and shotgun houses and the stray animals that roamed so freely, a neighborhood that easily looked like a third world country, so foreign to his point of reference that even he couldn't help but cringe. He thought he knew what poverty looked like, and philosophically, and from where he sat, he did. But up close and personal was the bitch. This was where the *pull yourself up by the bootstraps* folks really lived. I wanted him to tell me now just how many bootstraps these people were going to pull themselves up by, and just how many hurdles these folks were going to jump.

He held my hand as we walked across the dirt yard to the front porch, his expensive Italian shoes sinking in the sand, but he didn't even look down. When we got to the half-dilapidated wooden steps, he touched me gently on the arm. "Your mother lives here?" he asked, unable to conceal his shock.

"Yes," I said. "And so did I."

A pained look crossed his face. He looked down the road, at a small group of kids playing kick ball in the dirt, and then he looked at me. His astonishment wore him down. He exhaled. He didn't know what to say.

But he didn't feel as bad as I did. I had lived this life. I had family still living this life. And if he thought the surroundings were a trip, he didn't know the half of it. My mama's house was a palace compared to the ghetto-fied-to-the-bone nature of my crazy siblings.

First there were the twins, Mary and Martha. At thirty-four, they were the oldest of us Ross children, and both were heavy-drinking, loud alcoholics. Mary was mean when she got drunk—you didn't want to mess with her. But Martha was gentle when she drank. All she wanted to do was talk.

Then there were my brothers, Joseph and Jarvis. Joseph was thirty years old, he and I used to be real tight, and Jarvis, the boy we called psychobaby when he was a kid because he was so damn crazy even then, was the youngest of us at twenty-two. Both he and Joseph were high school dropouts, neither could keep a job, and both had babies by so many different mamas that I stopped keeping count.

I knocked on the front door, which I guess Ben found odd, but I knew my family better than he. You don't just barge in on my people. Joseph would probably pull his gun, Jarvis would pull his knife, and Mary, the original slash-and-burn queen, would give you a tongue-lashing you wouldn't soon forget.

I looked at Ben. He was in a suit and tie, as usual, and had both hands in his pockets. Mary was going to have a field day with him. I wanted to warn him, and I would have, but then Martha opened the door.

She had a can of beer in one hand and a cigarette in the other. She was wearing an old housedress, a pair of talking slippers, and a baseball cap on her head. She was once a very pretty girl, all the boys on the block wanted her, but bad relationship after bad relationship had unhinged her. Her self-esteem, which once was enormous, sank, and so did she. Now she looked old, and haggard, and believed in her heart that she deserved every bad turn her life ever took. "Ah, shit," she said when she opened the door and saw me, "baby girl home, y'all! Baby girl home!"

She ran into my arms and I hugged her gently. She reeked of alcohol but it wouldn't have been Martha if she didn't. "I'm so glad you came, honey chile, let me tell you," she said as she stopped hugging me. "And look at you. All grown-up lookin' and everything. Still wearin' that African shit, I see."

I looked down. I was wearing my green pantsuit. "Yep," I said.

"And you keep wearin' it too. Everybody can't wear that stuff and look good, but you can."

"Thanks, Martha. So how you been?"

"I ain't complainin', girl," she said. "Don't see no point in all that." And then she looked at Ben. "Damn," she said. "Where you get this piece of meat from?"

I exhaled. *Here we go*, I thought. "This is Ben," I said. "He's a friend of mine."

"Well, I hope he ain't an enemy of yours." She said this and laughed so loud that I knew the beer was kicking in, propelling this gaiety of hers.

Ben reached out his hand to her, but she grabbed him and bear-hugged him instead. He smiled at her display but immediately released himself from her grasp.

"I'm sorry," she said, giggling. "I don't know where my manners at."

"Behind the preposition *at*," I said. Ben smiled. Martha looked at me as if she didn't have a clue.

"Nice to meet you, Martha," Ben said.

"You one fine-looking brother," she said. "Got to hand it to you." Then she yelled to those inside the house. "Baby girl got her one fine-looking brother, y'all!"

"You and baby girl better close that door!" Mary's unmistakable voice could be heard from inside the house. "Lettin' all them flies in here!"

"Come on in, y'all," Martha said. "And don't mind Mary. You know how she is."

So we walked on in. And the smell in the house almost knocked us back out. I knew the smell. Smelled it all my life. It was that nauseating combination of liquor and stale cigarette smoke, a smell that came together like a toxic fume, so heavy and dominant that it stayed strong in your nostrils even after you'd left the area. And poor Ben. I could only imagine his shock. His family home always smelled of fresh-baked bread, or cinnamon, or any other pleasant country scent. But he didn't sweat it. He didn't even show his repulsion.

There were three sofas in the living room and all three were badly stained and sunk-in because of missing springs and board support. My two brothers, Joseph and Jarvis, were on one couch, playing some video game, and Mary sat alone on another couch, a beer can sitting between her legs, a cigarette hanging from the side of her mouth.

"You took yo' pretty time getting here," she said as soon as I walked in. We never got along. Not as kids, not ever. Yet oddly enough it was Mary, not Martha or I, who was once the pride and joy of our family, the smartest, the prettiest (her looks were more exotic than Martha's), the one Mama just knew would make it out.

But she fell in love. And suddenly school and ambition and even her own hopes and dreams didn't mean a thing to her. Even after the guy had dumped her, and after the first of her many suicide attempts, Mama still believed that Mary, our leader, would make a comeback. But she never did. And then she discovered liquor, her new pain reliever, and her hopes and dreams, once again, were deferred.

"Hello, Mary," I said dryly.

She shook her head. "Why you always got to wear that African shit?" she asked, ignoring my salutation. "You ain't no African. Just a black nigger from Alabama. Same as the rest of us. Always tryin' to act like you so cute, and educated. An educated fool, that what you are. You ain't about Nathan Jones, you hear me?"

Ben seemed surprised by her venom, but I wasn't. Once Mary lost her way I became her target, as if she couldn't deal with the fact that she had made a shipwreck of her life while mine still held out possibilities. So I ignored her, the way my mother always taught me, but those cruel words of hers still stung.

But instead of stinging back, I turned to Joseph and Jarvis. It was one in the afternoon and my two big, healthy brothers were playing a game. Yet both of them, not working and undoubtedly broke as hell, still managed to have a bottle each of Mad Dog 20/20 sitting on the floor beside them.

Joseph, the oldest boy, named after Daddy even though he didn't deserve to be, looked at me. "Hey, sis, what up?" he said, and then quickly resumed pressing the buttons on his video game. Jarvis, a psychopath if ever one existed, didn't even bother to look my way.

"Hello, Jarvis," I said.

"What up, dog?" he said without moving an eyebrow away from the television screen, his button pressing more calculated than Joseph's, more intense, as if he would die if he lost.

"I want y'all to meet Ben," I said. Joseph glanced at him but just long enough to nod his head, and then he returned to his passion. Jarvis didn't bother. I shook my head and told Ben to have a seat. And I sat beside him.

We ended up on the third couch, so close together that we utilized only one cushion. "Where's Mother?" I asked.

"*Mother*," Mary said, trying to mock me, "had to run an errand. But *Mother* shall be back directly."

"I thought she was sick."

"She is sick," Mary said and then she looked at Martha as Martha sat on the couch beside our brothers. "Lovesick," they said together.

I should have known it would be something like that. Our mother wasn't exactly the Mother Teresa type. She dated more than me, Mary, and Martha combined. But at least she was well, I thought.

"Who you supposed to be?" Mary, who was on the verge of inebriation, asked Ben. Ben did not respond. I braced for the worst. "You heard me, motherfucker," she said. "Who you is?"

Ben stared at her, sizing her up in his methodical way.

"What you lookin' at? Cat got yo tongue?"

"No, it doesn't," Ben said.

"Then why you ain't answering my questions like you all that?"

"When you learn how to address me, then I'll answer your questions."

Joseph glanced at Ben and Mary gave him her patented once-over, her evil way of looking you up and down. "Oh," she said. "So it's like that? And who you supposed to be? The big man? Driving around in your big car and wearing all of your expensive suits and I'm supposed to bow down to your ass? Right? Wrong. I ain't bowing down to shit! If you ask me, you ain't nothing but a drug dealer. I know yo type. An old-ass drug dealer!"

I wanted to tell Ben to ignore her nonsense, that in her ignorance she had no clue whom she was speaking about, but I didn't have to tell him a thing. He wasn't thinking about Mary.

A sudden crash was heard in the kitchen area and I almost jumped out of my skin. Ben didn't even flinch. Then three small children, two boys and one girl, ran into the living room and began chasing each other around the sofas. I looked at Mary. And just as I suspected, she wasn't having it.

"Oh, no, ma'am," she said. "Oh, hell nall! Where y'all think y'all at? Y'all better cut that shit out. Buddy, you and Stanka better quit that runnin' in my house or I'm gonna hurt y'all. I'm gonna murder y'all! I'll shoot y'all dead! Oh, you laughing? This shit funny to y'all? Okay. I'll show you funny. Mojo, go get my pistol. That's right, baby. It's on my dresser. Go get it, go get it, go get it now!"

Buddy and Stanka, on learning that they were soon to be shot, made one more mad dash around the room and then hightailed it out the back door. Mojo was the littlest boy and he just stood there, staring at Mary as if he didn't know what a pistol was. Martha crossed her legs and laughed.

"You need to stop telling that baby to go get yo pistol. Go on outside and play, Mojo." Mojo gladly ran off. "You scarin' that boy half to death, Mary, when you do that. And besides, you ain't got no pistol anyhow."

"Like hell you say. Got me three pistols, for yo information."

"Quit lying, Mary. Who gon' give you a gun? Please."

"Those your children, Mary?" I asked her, to change the subject, knowing full well they weren't.

Mary, however, wasn't amused. "You must be out of your goddamn mind," she said. "Them savages? *Mine?* I ain't got no goddamn children, and if I had some they ain't gonna be wild like those animals!"

"Them Bebe's kids," Martha said and I nodded. Bebe (pronounced Bay-bay) was Joseph's longtime girlfriend. Her real name was Kenya and she was a sweet girl but Joseph treated her like dirt. "Joseph was supposed to be baby-sitting," Martha added. "I told Bebe she need to stop leaving them kids with Joseph. He don't be stuttin' them."

"Joseph's the father?"

"Hell nall," Joseph said without looking away from the television screen.

"Yeah, he is, girl, he just frontin', he know he's them babies' daddy."

Mary shook her head. "That's some scary shit," she said, and I couldn't agree with her more. The idea that our brother, who had dropped out of school, who worked so sparingly, an hour here, two hours there, you might as well say he never worked a full day in his life, who was in and out of jail, could be somebody's daddy, was terrifying.

"What's got Mama so lovesick?" I asked Martha.

"Titus Kirkpatrick," Mary said. "The weasel."

"He's a mechanic she's all in love with," Martha said. "But he don't mean her no good, Josie. He just wants what she got."

I looked around and then back at Martha. "And what is that?"

"He wants this," Mary, the drama queen, said, standing, with a sweep of her hand. "He want our daddy's house."

"What do you mean he wants it?"

"He want it, girl, don't you understand English no more? He

wanna run this here. He wanna move his shit up in here and take the fuck over."

"But that ain't gonna happen," Joseph said without looking away from his video game.

"Don't you need to be outside checking on those children, Joseph?" I asked him.

"Them ain't my kids. Them Bebe's kids. Bebe better check on 'em."

"They all right," Martha said as she finished the last of her beer and tossed the empty can into the large trash bag that sat like a piece of furniture in the middle of the living room. She then doused out her old cigarette, pulled out another one, and began feeling her breasts as if she were searching for something. A lighter was the only thing I could figure. "There's a thousand kids out there," she said. "They all look after each other."

"But back to this Titus Kirkland," I said.

"Kirkpatrick," Mary corrected me. "Titus Kirkpatrick. And there ain't nothin' to get back to. He ain't comin' here, that's all there is to that."

"He wants to marry Mama?"

"I don't know. And I don't care. But he ain't comin' here."

"Now come on, Mary. If they get married he'll have a right to stay here."

"See what I'm talking about?" Mary said to our siblings. "I don't know why y'all called her."

"Martha called her," Jarvis said.

"That's right I called her. She's a part of this family too."

"She just gonna take Mama's side, watch what I tell you."

"Not after she understands what's going on."

"What's going on?" I asked them, although I knew full well what was going on. Mama had her a real man this time. And no real man was going to allow my grown-behind siblings to sit up in a house all day, never work, never pay a single bill, and just drink and eat to their hearts' content. Titus, although I had yet to meet the brother, represented a clear and present threat to my siblings' way of life. That's what was going on. "Y'all ain't telling me nothing," I said. "All y'all saying is that Mama is in love with some dude named Titus and he's a mechanic, that's all y'all telling me."

"He's a weasel that's trying to worm his way into this house, that's what we tellin' you, fool!" Mary said this in her particularly nasty way and I almost shined back on her. But I let it slide. Sister girl was on the verge of drunkenness and her true self was beginning to emerge. And before my true self emerged too, I decided it would be best if I hit the road.

I stood up. Ben stood up too. "Call me when Mama gets back home," I said. "We're going to check into the hotel."

"Then get to going," Mary quickly said. "Don't nobody care about you checking into no damn hotel!"

Martha stood up too. "Don't go, baby girl. Mama gonna want you to stay here with her, you know she will."

"Let her go," Mary said. "Don't be beggin' her. Think she Miss America as it is. You ain't no Miss America. You just a jive-ass nigger with a little education. That's all you is. You ain't nothin'!"

"Yeah, whatever," I said and headed for the front door. Martha followed behind me.

"Yeah, you better leave," Mary said. "Whatever. Whatever, yo ass!"

Just her voice did it. Just the way she spoke her big talk. And I turned around and headed in her direction. "What's your problem, Mary?" I asked her, and she stood up. It was on, we both knew it too, but Ben grabbed me by the arm and pulled me back.

"What do you think you're doing?" he asked me, his once ambivalent face now frowned and annoyed.

"Nall, she bad, she bad, let her back it up, man, I ain't scared of her!" By now I was trying to break away from Ben to get to my own sister, but he pulled me back in front of him and then pushed me toward the front door.

"Let's go!" he said.

"Yeah, you better get her ass out of here," Mary yelled and I tried to break free again. But he pulled me against the door.

"What do you think you're going to do, Josephine? Fight her? Is that what you plan to do?"

In other words, how could the future wife of a potential supreme court justice behave so savagely? She couldn't. He knew it and I knew it. That's why he was shocked. Not because I wanted to beat my sister's ass. But because he even would have considered being with somebody who could.

We checked into the Sheraton on the campus of the University of Alabama, next to the Bear Bryant Center, and spent the rest of the afternoon lying in bed. Ben was exhausted, and was on the verge of falling asleep. I lay in bed watching him, his eyebrows and eyes and straight nose and thick mustache. I had a lot on my mind and he seemed to sense it.

"It's not your fault," he said, his eyes still closed.

"What's not my fault?"

"She provoked you."

"She always does. That's how she lives her life. It's like she's so jealous of me. But sometimes I swear to God I want to just . . ."

"Strangle her?"

"Beat her ass!"

Ben laughed.

"I'm serious. She's something else."

"You don't have to tell me that, Josephine. I saw it with my own two eyes."

"They're awful people, aren't they?"

He paused. "Yes," he said.

"I'm sorry."

"Don't be. We're not responsible for what our family members choose to do."

"But you're going to be a supreme court justice. You can't be associated with people like me and my siblings."

"Why? What's wrong with you?"

"I come from them."

"You overcame them, Josephine. Okay? You're worrying about nothing. We're together. Period. End of discussion."

I touched his face with my hand. I loved him. I really, truly loved him. "Yes. Okay," I said, and decided to chill out too.

We returned to the house around five that afternoon. Martha had phoned and told me that Mama had finally made it back and she was highly upset that I was in some hotel somewhere. Our plan was to check on Mama, wish her well, and then hit the road.

But when we arrived at the house all bets were off. The situation was far worse than I had thought. My entire family, for one thing, were in the front yard having it out. There was Mama, Martha, and the man I assumed was Titus on one side; Joseph, Jarvis, and Mary on the other. Martha was trying to be the voice of reason, but she was plastered, so all of her suggestions came out as slurred words uniquely strung together, starting out as understandable statements and then quickly lapsing into pure incoherency.

I looked at Ben. He smiled and shrugged his shoulders. "Ready?" I asked.

"You bet," he said as if he was a pro at these kinds of situations.

We walked across the dirt yard toward Mama. When she saw me, she hurried over, and I went to her. My mama. Her name was Irene. Irene Betty Ross. She was fifty-one and still beautiful and sassy, still had her figure, her big hair, her long nails and fake eyelashes that fluffed out, and she still knew how to work those hips. "Hey, baby," she said as she hugged my neck. She was so flustered that she looked to be on the verge of tears. My heart went out to her. "You okay, Ma?" I asked her.

"It's a mess, baby girl. Just a mess." Then she looked at Ben, from his expensive shoes to his nine-hundred-dollar suit, to that Cadillac Escalade parked in front of her home. Then she looked at me. "What's this I hear about you dating a drug dealer?" she asked. Ben smiled.

"He's not a drug dealer, Ma. That's just Mary being her regular hateful self. This is Ben. Benjamin Braddock. He's a judge."

Mama was immediately impressed. She eagerly shook Ben's hand. "A judge? You mean like court?"

I smiled. "Yes, Ma, that's what I mean."

"My, my. A real live judge. And a fine-looking one at that. You taking good care of my baby?"

I rolled my eyes. How could she ask that? But Ben smiled. "I'm trying to, ma'am," he said.

"Irene, honey. I don't play that ma'am stuff. Irene all the way."

"I beg your pardon, Irene," he said and kissed Mama's hand. She beamed.

"What's going on out here, Ma?" I asked her.

"They crazy, precious. They just done lost their minds."

My siblings, hearing the word *crazy* and rightly figuring it meant them, began walking toward us. The man I assumed was Titus followed at a distance behind. He looked so bewildered that I wondered if he would pass out.

Joseph and Jarvis did not have on shirts and looked like a couple of thugs. Mary was fully stoned by now, which meant she was louder and even more obnoxious than normal. She still had a beer in one hand and a cigarette in the other, and she was stumbling as she walked. But that didn't stop her from being the leader of the pack. I looked around at the folks in our third world neighborhood. These arguments at the Ross home were apparently so commonplace that nobody was even giving us a second look. Now that was sad.

"What the fuck you want?" Mary asked me as soon as she reached our side. Ben immediately placed my hand in his.

"We gonna settle this once and for all," Joseph said. "Titus," he said, and everybody turned and looked at Titus. He looked as if he wanted to run as far away from us as his feet could carry him. Joseph continued: "We don't know what kind of man you are."

"Yes, we do," Jarvis said. "He's a blood-sucking leech."

"He's not a leech," Mama said. "He's a good man. You're the leech."

Why she wanted to say that? She knew how Jarvis was. And sure enough, the psychobaby in Jarvis started to come on out. "Oh, I'm the leech?" he asked. "Is that it? Jarvis is the leech? I'll be damn. I'm the leech now. Shat the fuck up, Jarvis. They calling you a leech but shat the fuck up. You don't wanna hurt these motherfuckers."

"Yeah, you better shat up," Mama said.

"The point is," Joseph said, getting back to the original discussion, "it don't matter what kind of man you are, Titus. And you might love my mama just like you claim. That's cool too. But yo ass ain't moving in here. That's the point."

"Amen," Mary said.

"Let's not do," Martha said, her words almost completely slurred, "what the just jump do."

Mary frowned at Martha. "What?" she asked.

"She talking about me," Jarvis said. "Calling me the leech. That's right, y'all. I'm the leech now. Jarvis is the leech."

"Lord ham mercy Jesus," Mama said and looked up to the heavens. Titus, a man who appeared to be in his mid-fifties, just stood there, staring at my crazy siblings as if they were escaped lunatics, wondering through his terrified eyes, how in the world did he get mixed up in this?

"Why don't we go inside and talk?" I suggested, mainly for Titus's sake.

"Fuck you!" Mary yelled at me.

"Fuck you!" Joseph yelled too, backing her up.

"Fuck all y'all," Jarvis said. "I ain't no leech. But no-o-o. Jarvis the leech now. Everybody can live off of everybody else, that's fine, that's all right, but let Jarvis try it and oh boy, he's a leech. Somethin' wrong with him. But you shat up, Jarvis. Kick they ass, but shat up, J."

"Josephine," Mama said, interrupting psychobaby, "I want you and the judge to meet Titus, my fiancé. Titus, this is my daughter Josephine. The reporter. The one I told you graduated from college."

"Don't nobody care about her graduatin' from no college," Mary said.

Ben and I shook Titus's hand. He smiled, apparently glad to know that somebody might have some sense in the family. "We gonna work this out," I said. "I don't want you and Mama to worry."

"Ah, check you out," Joseph said. "The big-time daughter gonna work it out. You hear this shit, Mary?"

"Hear what?"

"Josie. She telling Titus that she got this, that she gonna work this out."

"Oh, really now?" Mary said and walked up to me. "What you gonna work out?"

I looked at Ben. He just stood there, his arms folded, staring at Mary. "Get out of my face," I said to Mary.

Joseph laughed. "Get out her face, Mary."

"Who you think you are?" Mary asked. "I'll get in yo face if I wanna get in yo face."

She moved closer as she talked. I backed up.

"You're barking up the wrong tree," I said.

"Uh-oh," Joseph said. "She calling you a dog, Mare."

"Don't go," Martha said, trying to play peacemaker but just barely able to stand up, "to just let dog there."

"So I'm a dog now?" Jarvis asked.

"Not you, fool," Joseph said.

"You calling me a dog?" Mary asked me. By now she was completely in my face.

Mama quickly grabbed me by the arm. "Let's go in the house, baby girl," she said as she began hurrying me toward the front door. "Judge, you and Titus come on too!" I looked back at Ben. He and Titus surprisingly obliged.

"Yeah, you better go in the house!" Mary yelled after me. "Before I drop-kick yo ass!"

We ended up in the small kitchen, sitting at the kitchen table.

"What's wrong with them, Mama?"

"They crazy," Mama said, lighting her cigarette. "Damn loony tunes!"

Titus shook his head. "I ain't never seen nothing like 'em," he said. "But why Joseph so angry? He didn't used to be like this."

"That's what you think. When was the last time you was home? That boy somethin' else. Bebe used to could calm him down, but then they started havin' all them kids and now he just loony as they come. And Jarvis? Jesus. That boy is an embarrassment. He ask a question and then answer it himself. Then he starts cussing people out in the third person!"

"Just because you and Titus plan to be married?" Ben asked.

"Them kids of mine don't care nothing about us getting married. It's this goddamn house. They think they own it. And you can't talk to 'em. Don't even try. 'This my daddy's house,' that's all they got to say. Their daddy's dead. Been dead. This my house. But you can't tell them that. My kids somethin' else, Judge."

The "kids" came into the house. Titus shuttered. Mama sighed. I sat erect. And Ben laughed. Yes, he laughed! We looked at him surprised, especially I, but he couldn't help it. This horror show was so ridiculous to him that it was hilarious.

Joseph came up to the kitchen table. "Okay, what's the deal?" he asked.

"What you talkin' about, boy?" Mama asked him, frowning.

"He talkin' about Titus," Mary, who had settled in the living room along with Martha and Jarvis, said. "He talkin' about understandin' where we comin' from."

"Y'all better leave me alone with that nonsense, that's what y'all better do."

"But this our daddy's house, Mama," Joseph said. "We ain't gonna sit back and let some crack head take over our daddy house!"

Titus's mouth gaped open. "Crack head? Who a crack head?"

"Don't pay them no mind, baby," Mama said.

"But I ain't no crack head, Irene."

"You on somethin'," Joseph said, "if you think you gonna take over this."

"But I ain't never done no drugs in my life."

"They know that," Mama said. "They just tryin' to push yo buttons, Tie. Don't worry about it."

"But they tellin' lies on me."

"I said don't worry about it!" Mama said firmly, and then smiled.

"I betcha he is a crack head," Mary said. "And I betcha he get his drugs from boyfriend over there."

Mama spoke up this time. She didn't bother defending Titus, but Ben was another matter. "Josie's boyfriend ain't no drug dealer, Mary, and you know it. He's a judge in a court."

Mary laughed. "Is that what they told you? Hear that, Jarvis?"

Jarvis, who was too busy mumbling to himself to hear anything, looked up. "What?" he asked. "What you talkin' about?"

"Big man 'sposed to be a judge now."

"Yeah, he the big man all right. He the judge all right. But I'm the leech. Jarvis ain't no big man. Jarvis the leech."

"Lord knows," Mama said, looking at psychobaby and shaking her head.

"But be cool, Jarvis," Jarvis said. "Them motherfuckers know not to mess with you. Jive-ass motherfuckers. Better not go to sleep, that's all I got to say."

Titus looked at Mama and shook his head. "There is something wrong with that boy," he said. But what was he thinking? Psychobaby jumped up, Mary jumped up, and Joseph got in his face. He had just given them the ammunition they needed.

"What did you say?" Jarvis asked, hurrying toward the kitchen.

"What you called my brother?" Mary asked, hurrying behind him.

"My brother ain't got no problem, asshole," Joseph said, moving closer to Titus.

The situation was tense as hell, and I could see my brothers jumping on top of Titus and pummeling him, until Ben stood up. Everybody, even Jarvis, stopped all movement when he stood up. He was a big-time drug dealer, in their eyes, and they weren't quite sure what he was capable of. "Titus," Ben said, "have you and Irene had dinner yet?"

Titus, who appeared stricken with fear, looked at Mama. Mama shrugged her shoulders. Then he looked back at Ben. "No, sur," he said, "we ain't have no dinner yet."

"Good," Ben said. "Why don't we go and get something to eat?"

Everybody was puzzled. Especially my siblings, who were looking at each other trying to figure it out. But Mama knew what time it was. She stood up quickly. "Yeah, let's go," she said, "before I beat the shit out of somebody!"

And before my siblings seemed to understand what was really going on, we walked out of the front door, piled into the SUV, and got the hell away from them.

We dined in a small, quiet restaurant near downtown, and we sat as two couples: Mama and Titus on one side, Ben and I on the other. Mama and Titus didn't really want anything to eat, just some beer to drink, and Ben ordered exactly what they wanted. "Beer, beer," he said, pointing to Mama and Titus. But for me, he ordered a full-course meal: a T-bone steak, a potato, and a bowl of broccoli soup. I hadn't eaten much for almost two days so I didn't argue with him. I knew I needed to eat. But when he said orange juice for my drink, I had to step in. "I prefer sherry," I said.

"Orange juice," he repeated to the waiter and the waiter nodded and left. I looked at Ben.

"I drink sherry, not orange juice."

"I know. That's the problem."

"What's the problem?"

He wouldn't answer me.

"Because my siblings have drinking problems doesn't mean I do too, Ben," I said, but he still wouldn't respond.

"What are we gonna do, Josie?" Mama asked me. "I can't take much more of this."

"There's only one answer really," Ben said.

"What?" Titus asked, anxious for a solution.

"Irene, I think you should consider turning your home over to your children, and move on."

I looked at Ben as if he were crazy. "Now wait a minute," I said. He didn't understand what he was saying. It was a shack to him, but it was all my mother had. But he kept talking, without looking at me.

"You won't get a moment's peace as long as you have that home."

"No way, Ben," I said. "Those lazy scoundrels should be the ones moving on, not my mama."

"Where do you live?" he asked Titus. He wasn't thinking about me.

"I got me a house," Titus said. "Just in need of a lot of repairs."

"You plan to marry Irene?"

"Absolutely. If she'll have me."

Mama smiled. "You know I will."

"If I bankroll renovations to your home, will you put your new wife's name on the deed and make your home her home too?"

This was an easy decision for Titus. "Yes, sur," he said. "I'll be glad to do that."

"But what about my daddy's house?" I asked.

"Now here you go with this daddy's house bullshit," Mama said. "I'll keep the house in my name so they won't try to get no second mortgages or nothing like that. But what else can I do, baby? Them children drivin' me slap crazy."

"You can put them out, Mama. And if they won't go you can call the police and have 'em thrown out. Then maybe they'll get jobs and do something with their lives."

"I know what you sayin', baby girl. I know you mean well. But I ain't kickin' my kids out on no street."

"They aren't kids anymore, Mama."

"They my kids. I don't care if they live to be a hundred years old, they gonna still be my kids. And when me and your daddy bought that house it was so those kids of ours would always have a roof over their heads."

I shook my head. "So no matter what, you gonna let them stay there?"

"That's what she's saying, Josephine," Ben said impatiently and looked at me. He understood exactly where she was coming from. He had already concluded that those siblings of mine weren't riding roughshod over that house by accident. Mama was their enabler. And she always would be.

I threw my hands in the air. "Whatever," I said. "Y'all do whatever y'all want."

"It's for the best, Josie," Mama said.

"And what if your relationship with Titus doesn't work out? Like all those other relationships? Then what?"

"It'll work out."

"But if it doesn't?"

"Her name gon' be on the deed," Titus said. "It'll work out."

I shook my head. "This doesn't make no kind of sense," I said. Ben sighed. I was irritating the mess out of him.

"What do you suggest, Josephine?" he asked.

"Kick them out."

"She's not going to do that and you know it. What else you got?"

I closed my eyes. There was nothing else, and I was the last one to realize it.

We dropped Mama and Titus off at Titus's place, which actually looked better than my daddy's house. It was a shack too, but it had some potential. Ben had worked out all of the arrangements as if it were nothing at all. The plan was for them to set a wedding date. Mama would continue living with her children but seeing Titus only at his home or somewhere else. After the wedding, Ben would take care of the renovations and Titus would place my mama's name on the deed as an equal owner. It wasn't the best plan in the world, since I still would have kicked my siblings to the curb first, but in the end, given my siblings, and my mama, it was about the only way to go.

Ben and I had planned to leave Alabama that same day. And we would have. But when we went to the hotel room to grab our luggage and check out, we ended up sitting on the bed beside each other. Ben, who was exhausted, lay back. I started to get up, to make sure I had everything out of the bathroom, but he grabbed me by the arm. Then he pulled me down on top of him.

"What are you doing?"

"Holding you."

"We've got a plane to catch, Ben."

"Maybe we do. Maybe we don't."

"And what does that mean?"

"There's always tomorrow."

"But if we stay over, will we make it back in time for the wedding?"

"Of course we will. It's only an hour-and-a-half flight, Josephine."

"But this is Tuscaloosa, Ben. This ain't no Key West. There's very little to do here. What will we do?"

He looked at me. "You're kidding, right?" he said. And once I thought about what he was saying, I shook my head and laughed.

MY WATERGATE, MY HEADACHE

I wasn't ten minutes back at work when Mel hurried out of his office and yelled for me to come with him. I thought it was more of his bullshit so I continued sifting through my huge stack of mail and told him "in a minute."

"Excuse me," he said, and I turned to look at him. He was standing at the door, his hand on the knob, his face definitely not in the waiting mood. "Not in a minute, Ross. Now."

Something was up. I could tell by the way his thick eyebrows curled and he kept hitting the side of his leg with the newspaper he had rolled up in his hand. He was hot. And he couldn't wait for me to find out why.

I dropped my mail on the desk and followed him. I was dressed in a yellow and brown African-style pantsuit, high heels, and had my braids in a ponytail, but Mel, who appreciated ethnic dress more than most, didn't compliment my appearance the way he usually did. He just rolled up the newspaper tighter and kept pressing the elevator button. I was sleeping with the enemy in his eyes, a hellava tribute to him when you consider that I was supposed to be his protégée, the liberal who would follow in his footsteps, and he wasn't about to be a turncoat too. Everything was black and white with him. You were either a good liberal or a racist; a left-wing activist or a conspirator. It now seemed so ridiculous to me, to be that inflexible, and to think that I was once that way myself suddenly didn't seem possible.

"Where are we going?" I asked him when the elevator doors opened and we stepped inside.

"Dinkle's office," he said without looking at me, and pressed number four.

Lawrence Dinkle was the managing editor of the *Gazette*. His office, located on the fourth floor, was a large, open area filled with books and old newspapers and three different conference tables. Dinkle was on the phone when we first arrived so his secretary ushered us to one of those tables.

Mel pulled out a chair for me and then sat down too. I smiled and told him thank you, but he didn't say anything in response.

Dinkle finished his conversation quickly and hurried to the conference table. He was a big, burly man, with a small head and wide body, and long, grayish blond hair. "That was my son-in-law," he said as he sat down. "What a jerk. He wants to know why I dislike him. 'You got a year?' I said to him. Idiot." And then he looked at me. "And hello to you, Miss Josephine."

"Hey, Larry, what's up?"

"You, as always. The vacation girl. Key West. How was it?"

I couldn't stand Dinkle's phony-behind repartee. And I hated that he knew anything about my vacation. "It was okay," I said.

"Good. Good." Dinkle said this and glanced at Mel. "Sanchez is next."

Mel didn't even smile. His broken-heart routine was beginning to get on my nerves. "So, Larry," I said, "what's this big meeting about?"

"We've got an exclusive, Miss Ross, that's what it's about."

"An exclusive?"

"Yes." Then he hesitated.

"Are you going to tell me more, Larry?" I asked.

He glanced at Mel before proceeding. "A woman came forward last week." He said this as if that said it all. I looked at Mel to make sure I hadn't missed anything. Mel, of course, was too busy sulking.

Dinkle continued. "She clerked for Judge Braddock twelve years ago."

Judge Braddock? What does Ben have to do with this? "Okay."

"To make a long story short, and I'm sorry to tell you this, but she says Braddock sexually harassed her while she worked for him."

I could feel an ice-cold chill slowly creep up my spine when he said those words. *Braddock sexually harassed her. Braddock sexually harassed her.* "Braddock sexually harassed her?" I asked.

"That's what she said. And she told a very compelling tale too. But, of course, Ben Braddock is a well-respected jurist in this community and we couldn't just take her word for it. The implications of what she's saying, Jesus, it would be the Florida version of Clarence Thomas-Anita Hill. So, being the good journalists we are, we decided to sit on the story until we could get some corroboration."

My heart sank. When it rained, it poured. "Another woman?" I asked.

"Yes. She came forward yesterday. She, too, worked for Braddock some years ago and her story and the first woman's story are eerily similar. A check of employment records confirms that both women worked for Braddock at different times and both, just as they claimed, quit suddenly after having worked less than three months in the first case, just one month in the second."

I sat stunned. Ben sexually harassing somebody? It wasn't possible. I knew it had to be a mistake. I also knew instinctively that this so-called "exclusive" had liberal Dumpster diving written all over it, a gold mine for the *Gazette,* just the kind of trash they were digging for. "Who are these women?" I asked Dinkle.

"That's what we need to find out. We want to be fair to Braddock. Our publisher, who's a very close friend of his, made that perfectly clear. Just because the women came forward is not enough."

"And what do you mean they came forward? Did they just wander in from the street out of some incredible civic duty or did we wander out there and drag them in?"

"What do you think?" Mel asked bitterly. "Braddock's no great man, Josie Ross, face it, all right?"

"They came to us, Josie," Dinkle said. "After, of course, we made it clear that we were interested in any information on Benjamin Braddock. It's no secret that the *Gazette* doesn't support Braddock's nomination, we think he's bad for the court, and we'd like nothing better than to see that nomination derailed, of course we would, but when we go public it will be with irrefutable evidence."

My heart was pounding. I couldn't deal with this right now. "What does all of this have to do with me?" I asked. Mel sighed. I rolled my eyes at his vindictive behind.

"I want you to personally check out both stories," Dinkle said.

No he didn't say that. He knew I had been in Key West, not alone, but with the very man he just asked me to rat on. "Me?" I asked, my face so shocked that it made Mel's frown.

"Find out what kind of women we're dealing with here. What's the motive? Do they know each other? Is this some kind of scam to get Braddock? That's what I want from you. And yes, you, Josie. I chose you because you're his friend. You'll go in biased. If these women can convince you, then I figure we've got a story here."

"And if they don't convince me?" I asked this and folded my arms. I knew even then Dinkle was blowing smoke. Those women weren't about to convince me of anything but their own twisted grudge against Ben, and Dinkle knew it.

"If they aren't convincing to you, then we move on. But you've got to give a compelling reason for us to move on. None of that *I just don't like them* rhetoric. And, Josie, this story must remain under wraps, not even the judge himself is to hear a word of it, until the investigation is complete. Understand?"

They didn't know what they were asking, and they didn't care. They just wanted the story. "Understood," I said.

"Good. Wonderful. I knew we could count on you. I told Sanchez we could. You've always been a team player. And an ambitious young lady. That's what I like about you. And you're an equal opportunity destroyer." He said this and laughed. "You don't let anybody get away with anything, especially those rigid conservatives like Braddock. So we'll look forward to your report, Josie. Have a nice day."

You're good, we love you, but get lost, in other words. Since it sounded like a good idea to me too, I rose quickly. But Dinkle touched my hand and looked his bloodshot blue eyes into my bewildered hazel ones. "This is your Watergate, Josie," he said. "This is your big story. Every good reporter dreams of this kind of break. You're like a general without a war until you get that big story. Who the hell ever heard of Woodward and Bernstein before Watergate? Now it's your turn to make your mark. And I'm giving you the opportunity. But just don't blow it, young lady."

I looked at Dinkle and Mel, knowing that their minds were already made up, and I walked out. I took the stairs, hurrying down as if somebody were chasing me, and then I stopped midway and leaned against the rail, my heart beating so erratically that my stomach churned. I thought it was settled. I thought I had finally found the answer to happiness, and it was love, and it was Ben, but now, in one quiet morning, my comfort zone, my hopes and dreams, were all slipping fast.

They gave me two names: Tonya Wright and Marlene Wingate. Tonya Wright agreed to meet me at Polly's, the café across from the *Gazette*. She was a tall, thin sister with a short, to-the-skull haircut and a pretty, cheerful face. She wore a business suit and carried a briefcase and Gucci bag. When she saw me (I had described myself to her), she hurried to my table and set both her briefcase and bag on the floor. "I don't have much time," she said in a deep, well-practiced voice. "I've got a deposition in an hour."

"You're an attorney?"

She seemed surprised by the question. "Yes. Of course." And then she leaned back. "I thought we were here about Judge Braddock."

"We are."

"They didn't tell you that I clerked for him?"

"Yes," I said. "I just forgot."

She nodded and then smiled a great smile. And as soon as she smiled she reminded me of Desiree. Which meant she was definitely Ben's type. "So," she said, "how can I help you?"

"Would you like something to drink?"

"No, thank you."

She was a to-the-point gal and that was cool too. I wasn't exactly bursting at the seams to hang out with her either. "Why?" I asked her.

"Because it's true."

"You clerked for Braddock ten years ago?"

"Twelve years ago."

"Twelve years ago. And now, all of a sudden, you just had to tell your story. Please excuse me if I find that story hard to believe."

"I don't care how you find it."

"But why did it take you twelve years to come forward?"

"It didn't take me twelve years. It took me two minutes. That was when I decided to speak out. It was the day the governor announced Braddock's nomination to the supreme court."

"And of course you don't feel he's worthy to be on the court?"

"I know he's not."

"All because he wanted to date you twelve years ago?"

"He wanted more than that, Miss Ross."

I was trying like hell to minimize it, but she wasn't going along. My heartbeat quickened because she just wouldn't go along. "Really?" I said.

"Yes."

"What exactly did he want?"

"He wanted to have sex with me. And trust me, he was very descriptive."

I pulled a pack of cigarettes from my bag. The only time I smoked was when I was nervous as hell. This certainly qualified. "Have one?"

"No," she said.

I pulled a cigarette out and lit it. Girlfriend moved around in her seat. I didn't even care. "So you told him no?"

"When I kept telling him no, he began trying me. He'd touch me inappropriately, or make some sly remarks about what I was wearing or how I spent my nights. When that didn't work he got serious. He threatened to fire me. He said if I didn't give him what he wanted I was out on my ass. I wasn't from Florida, Miss Ross. I was from South Carolina. From a very small town in South Carolina. I couldn't lose that internship."

I took a slow drag on my cigarette and looked at her. *What's the angle?* I wondered. A bullshit artist always had an angle. "So you complied?"

She hesitated. "Yes," she said. "I'm not proud of it but I did. I slept with him. One time, he said. Just one time and he would leave me alone. So I did it. My girlfriends thought I was crazy at the time. 'That good-looking man,' they said, 'who wouldn't wanna sleep with him?' Well, I didn't, Miss Ross. He was my boss. He was the man I looked up to back then. I was so positive about life then, and people, I was so hopeful. He robbed me of everything when he forced me to sleep with him."

"Now just a minute here. You didn't say anything about being forced. You said yourself that you complied with his wishes."

"Under duress, I complied," she said. "I had to work. But he didn't care about me. He just wanted to leave an imprint on my life. That's what he called it. He said he knew I was going places and he wanted to leave his imprint. And that's all he wanted too because after that, after his imprint was established, he fired me. He fired me! That was my internship, Miss Ross, which meant I failed it and had to start all over again. Nobody wanted me by then. I was damaged goods. In more ways than one." She looked at me, her eyes wide, distressed. "You can call it whatever you want, Miss Ross, but I call it theft. And wrong. And illegal."

Illegal? *Ben?* "You said you have girlfriends who knew about you and Braddock at the time of the relationship?"

"I wouldn't call it a relationship, but yes. There were a number of them."

"What if I track 'em down?"

"Please do. Please. Look, I have nothing to hide. You think I'm enjoying this? You think I want my name in a newspaper describing my sexual encounter with Benjamin Braddock? How could I want that? This will hurt my career, there's no doubt about it. But he's got to be stopped, Miss Ross. A man who would do to a young girl what he did to me isn't worthy to sit on the highest court in this state. And if you don't believe me, and y'all don't wanna print it, that's fine. That's on you. But at least I told the truth."

I leaned back and looked at my empty notepad. I didn't expect this. I thought I would see it. I could always be counted on to see through the bull. But I couldn't see a damn thing. Just a successful sister deciding to not take it anymore; to open up old wounds; to put herself on the line for what she believed was the right thing to do. My kind of sister. But maybe it was too neat. Maybe it was too real. Ben said I always went for the obvious when the obvious was usually the wrong answer. And maybe he was right. But it was also right that some things were just too obvious to ignore.

Marlene Wingate was sitting at a booth in the front of the restaurant. She was smoking a cigarette when I arrived. She was about my height, a little plump around the middle, with a gorgeous face and long, silky black hair. Unlike Tonya Wright, she was no high-powered lawyer on her way to a deposition, but a waitress on break from her job at the Thunderbird Bar n' Grill. Yet she relayed a hauntingly similar story of harassment by Ben and, ultimately, her acquiescence.

I crossed my legs. Tonya Wright had rendered me numb with confusion. Marlene Wingate could only add to it. "Were you sexually active when you agreed to sleep with the judge?" I asked her so dispassionately it made her smile.

"You mean was I then the way I am now? No. And you're right, I wasn't exactly a virgin either. But I was foolin' around with boys back then, not some big man like Judge Braddock."

"Sex is sex, don't you agree?"

"No, I don't agree. What's wrong with you? You act like I did somethin' wrong. I'm just tellin' you the truth. I was innocent compared to him."

"I see. Everybody was innocent back then."

"I don't think I like your attitude."

"You don't?"

"No. I don't know what everybody else was. I just know what I was. And I was a nineteen-year-old kid who thought it was gonna be neat working for a judge."

"You did your internship with Braddock, right?"

"An internship? You mean like college? Shit nall. I was working on my GED and they had the classes at the junior college, but that was about it. Mr. Braddock was advertising on the job board for somebody to sit with his wife. I went by his office, he took one look at me, and I was hired." She smiled. "It was the easiest interview I ever went on." She puffed her cigarette. "I didn't know shit about sittin' with no sick people, but hey, he seemed to think I had what it took. So I took the job. His wife was a trip, but she was sweet, you know? She just had problems, man, that's all, and nobody didn't seem to understand it."

"I guess he mistreated his wife too. Didn't he?"

"Matter of fact he didn't. He loved her. Treated her like she was his kid. But she just couldn't give it up for him. And guess who he decided on to fill the void?"

My heart skipped a beat. Another neat story. Another nail in Ben's coffin. "You said you turned him down over and over. What made you give in?"

"He threatened to fire me, that's what! And I needed that job, you know? So I gave it up. I mean, who wouldn't? He was extremely good looking and polite, you know, like he knew how to treat a girl. And he was so different than any boy I'd ever met. So I gave it up. He seemed real excited that he was gonna be the first real man I'd had, so I got excited too. He seemed like a good guy, you know? Different. But guess what? After all the whoopee, after I actually enjoyed myself and thought he might care for me, he fired me on the spot. That same night." She blew a big cloud of smoke into the air and stared up at it. "I was on the right track, you know? I was a good kid. Was gonna get my GED, maybe go on to college or a trade school, I hadn't decided. But I was gonna do something with my life." Then she looked at me. "But he taught me well, lady. Real good. He may have been my first real man, but he sure as hell wasn't my last. Now, six kids later, never married, no prospects, look at me. I'm thirty years old and this is the best job I ever had. A goddamn head waitress is my best shot yet."

I was coming out of my numbness and was suddenly conscious of a taste in my mouth, a nasty, bitter, horrible taste. Ben had turned her out, had ruined her life, had taken the budding talents of another up and coming sister and stunted her growth. If it was true, it was devastating. That was why it couldn't be true. "So Braddock is the cause of all your problems?" I asked her.

"Let's put it this way," she said, dousing out her cigarette in the ashtray on the table. "He didn't help."

I leaned back. It felt true, it sounded true, it even looked true, but how could it be true? "Why are you coming forward now?" I asked her. "Because of the nomination?"

She was smiling. I was dying. "When the governor said he was gonna put him on the supreme court I said shit, I use to work for that asshole, but I didn't think nothing else of it. Until one of my friends called and said some investigator was asking about me. He was interviewing everybody who worked for Ben Braddock. What I didn't know at the time was that some other woman had made some allegation and they were trying to find other women who might know something about it too. I didn't know nothing about that. I just knew what happened to me."

"You don't know Tonya Wright?"

"No, I don't."

"Never heard of her?"

"Never."

I sighed. I had to think of something to rile the sister, to get her to break down and admit it wasn't true. "He had sex with you and then fired you, is that your story?"

"That's it."

"He fired you for no other reason?"

"None. He got what he wanted and then kicked me to the curb."

"You said yourself, Miss Wingate, that you didn't know anything about home health care. Perhaps it was your lack of skill, not your relationship with Braddock, that sealed your fate."

"Two minutes after he slept with me he fired me, lady. Maybe it was my lack of skill. Maybe I wasn't skilled enough in bed. And even if you're right, even if he knew my work wasn't worth a damn, why did he sleep with me before he fired me? That don't make him look good either."

Of course she was right. None of it made him look good. No matter what scenario, none of it was looking good. "Which political party are you affiliated with, Marlene?" I asked her.

She smiled at this. "Which one you think? The Democrats. Ain't everybody?"

"How do you feel about Braddock becoming a member of the supreme court?"

"That's what that other guy asked me, that investigator. I don't know. That's not something I think about. But I wouldn't hire him, if that's what you mean."

I looked at her. That was exactly what I meant. Before I fell in love with him I would not have hired him either. But that was the problem. I was in love with him. And this Marlene Wingate, this thirty-year-old, promiscuous waitress, who had to have been turned out by a pro to be so seductive now, could turn out to be his downfall. This once insignificant single black female, welfare-recipient, mother-of-six, never-married walking statistic, could hold the dagger that would spell not only the end of Ben's date with destiny, but my life with him.

If she was some political operative trying to bring a brother down, I couldn't help but admit that she was good. Good, hell, she was better than good.

I left the Thunderbird around seven that evening and drove aimlessly for over an hour. I thought about getting down and dirty too and checking out every word those women spoke to me. And if there was one discrepancy, no matter how minute, I would proclaim them both liars and scrub the story.

But I thought about Key West and Desiree. It took them three hours to pick up steaks and then he spent nearly four hours at her house, even after he knew I was leaving. I thought about Angela and her key to his house (a key I didn't even possess) and how eagerly Ben always checked out her ass. I thought about all those dates with these mysterious friends he was always going out on. There was always an excuse, always an explanation. Deep down I knew something was wrong. But my love for him clouded my judgment and my desire to believe every word he spoke eclipsed my common sense.

That's why this was supposed to be simple. I would listen to the women and pick their tales apart. Then they were supposed to admit their culpability and fess up to their gotcha agendas. But that was before I met the women. That was before I looked into their eyes and saw pain and grief and anger, not political agendas or tear-a-brother-down crusades. They might very well have been after something, but maybe it wasn't just revenge, but that old staple of the American way we call justice.

I ended up in Neptune Beach. Ben wasn't home so I waited on his front porch. I waited until ten P.M., which didn't help at all. But he eventually found his way home. His Seville turned into the drive, with its lights blinding me as they swung past, and our eyes met momentarily. He should have been home hours ago, there was no court in session this time of night, but his behavior only crystalized the truth for me. I was in love with a man who had a lot of qualities, a lot of great, endearing qualities, but faithfulness didn't appear to be one of them.

He took his pretty time getting out of his car, as if he could just sense what was up, and when he did get out he walked slowly toward the porch. He wore a black suit and tie and didn't take his eyes off of me as he walked. He hesitated when he stepped onto the porch, and then he sat down beside me. We were so close that our arms touched.

"Good evening," he said, not jovially, but with that tinge of contempt that was now his trademark.

"Where were you?" I asked and looked at him. He seemed irritated by my directness, and at first I didn't think he would respond. But he did.

"Dinner," he said.

"Dinner? With who, Ben?"

"A friend of mine."

"A woman?"

He paused. "No."

"Then who? Fred? Because that's the only male friend I ever saw you with. All of your friends seem to be women." He did not respond, which I expected. "What time did you go?"

He frowned, which I also expected. "What?"

"What time did you meet this friend for dinner?"

"What business is that of yours, Josephine?"

"How can you say that? Everything about your life is supposed to be my business, especially since we . . ." I couldn't go on. It was a roller-coaster ride being with this man. Up and down. Up and down. Every time I turned around it was something else. I thought our time together in Alabama sealed the deal for us. I was in love with him and he was in love with me. Period. The end. But it didn't seal anything. He was still his mysterious self. And I was still naive, believing fairy tales, embracing the good, and completely overlooking the bad.

"You're right," I finally said. "It's none of my business."

I said this and looked at him. He didn't know what to say. Then something rather remarkable happened. He began to explain himself. "I had dinner with a friend of mine. He and his wife are going through a rough patch and he just wanted somebody to talk with. His name is Mike Davis—"

"You don't have to tell me his name. That ain't my business, remember? We're two free individuals. We can go out with whomever we wanna go out with. Right?" He didn't say anything. I wasn't sure, but it seemed to me that he didn't like my line of reasoning at all. That was why I kept it up. "You wanna have dinner with men, women, or whatever, you can. That's your thing. I wanna have dinner with men, I can. That's my thing."

He leaned back and stretched his long legs all the way out. I was on to something. "What are you trying to say, Josephine?"

"I'm just stating the truth. We're free to do whatever the hell we wanna do and if I wanna accept some man's invitation to dinner, a movie, then I can. That's all I'm saying."

"What man?"

I smiled. His frown was so deeply embedded in his face that it was almost funny. "Any man."

"You wanna be with somebody else, is that what you're trying to tell me?"

I shook my head. "What?" He wouldn't respond. "What are you talking about, Ben?"

"What are *you* talking about?"

"I'm talking about Marlene Wingate and Tonya Wright. That's what!"

I looked at him. His expression at first didn't change. But then his memory kicked in and his entire countenance changed. "Tonya Wright?"

"And Marlene Wingate, yes."

"I don't know a Marlene Wingate."

"But you know Tonya Wright?"

"What is this about?"

"Just answer the question."

"I will not just answer the question. Why are you asking the question?"

I exhaled. *Here we go.* "They're claiming that you sexually harassed them when they worked for you."

He didn't say anything. "Tonya Wright is claiming that?"

"Yes. They both are."

He nodded. "It's not true."

"I need more than that, Ben."

"Excuse me?"

"That's not good enough. I talked to these women. They ain't no jilted lovers or political activists. They're just regular, hardworking sisters who think, based on what you did to them, that you aren't fit to be a supreme court justice. And guess what? Maybe they're right." He looked at me. "Now you're gonna have to tell me more than 'it's not true' to get out of this one."

He paused so long that I almost spoke again, to try and get it through his thick skull that this was some serious shit we were up against. Desiree and Key West paled by comparison to this shit. But then he leaned forward, his elbows resting on his thighs. "Tonya Wright clerked for me a long time ago," he said.

"Did you sleep with her?"

He hesitated. "No."

"She said you did."

"She's lying."

"She said you wanted to leave your imprint on her life." He

glanced at me, and then looked away. "When she wouldn't go along, you started threatening to fire her. So she went along. One time. And you fired her anyway."

"That's not true."

"Why would she lie like that, Ben? What does she have against you?"

"I didn't think she had anything against me."

"Then why would she lie?"

"I can't answer that. But it's a lie."

"What about Marlene Wingate?"

"I told you I don't know her."

"She was this foolish kid you hired to help out your wife."

"I don't know her."

"She said you begged her to have sex with you since your wife couldn't. And after she did you suddenly didn't need her services anymore. Sound familiar?"

"No."

"We checked it out, Ben. She did work for you just like she said. And it lasted for less than a month, just like she said."

"Do you know how many people have worked for me before? You expect me to remember all of them?"

"You remembered Tonya Wright."

He paused. "She was different."

My heart sank. He loved her? Is that what made her different? "What was different about her?" I asked him nervously, my energy drained.

"She had a good head on her shoulders and one of the best analytical minds I'd seen in somebody that young. We had a lot of lively debates. She was a sharp lady."

His flattery of her angered me. "I see. Sharp, was she?"

"Don't use that tone with me. Yes, she was sharp."

"Then if she was so sharp, so together, why did you fire her in less than three months?"

He hesitated. I was sharp too, he just didn't realize it before. He stood up and walked over to the porch rail. He leaned against the rail and turned toward me, his hands in his pockets, his face concerned, nervous, uncharacteristically anxious. "She wanted a relationship with me."

"She wanted one with you? But you didn't want it?"

"That's right."

"She was smart?"

"Yes."

"I saw her today and she's attractive now, so I'm assuming she was attractive then."

"Very."

"And she was young?"

"Yes."

"And available?"

"As far as I knew."

"Then why wouldn't you want a relationship with her? She had the total package, the way you're telling it. Why wouldn't you hook up with her?"

"Let me see. Oh yeah, I was married." He said this and frowned at me.

"So you fired her because she kept coming on to *you,* because she kept harassing *you?* Is that what you're telling me?"

"That's exactly what I'm telling you."

"Prove it."

He looked at me. His facial expression went from contempt to disbelief to undeniable anger. "You prove it!" he yelled, pointing his finger at me. And then he walked away from me, went inside his home, and slammed the door behind him.

It was a bad night. I tossed and turned, walked the floor, got into bed, and tossed and turned some more. Follow the facts, Josephine. Not the fiction. Not the emotions. Not what you hope should be the answer, but what is the answer. And Ben was wrong. Sometimes the answer was obvious. Sometimes that person you think so highly of, who could do no wrong, who you just know has your back, doesn't. Two women. Two very different women. Neither knows the other. Their stories checked out. Those friends of Tonya Wright all confirmed it too. She worked for him. He kept harassing her. But she was tough. She held in there. But then he threatened to fire her. She could have fought it then. She could have gone to the chief judge and filed an official complaint. She was a law student. She knew her way around. Why didn't she do something? Then there would be no story, no debate, no sleepless nights over a man I never would have known, because he wouldn't have been the judge he is today and his

views wouldn't have been included in our black professional class series because his views wouldn't have meant jack to the *Gazette*.

But she didn't do anything. She swept it under a rug. Sleeping
with him was her misjudgment. Sleeping with him to get him off her
back got her in cahoots with him. Firing her then was a piece of
cake. Her decision to sleep with him sealed the deal. She couldn't
complain after that. It would be like the prostitute who got raped.
All the evidence was there, and it was compelling, but who in hell
would believe her?

Mel wasn't surprised. He sat behind his desk and stared at me. I
tried to justify my reasoning, insisting that the women told compelling stories but, in the end, I did not find them credible. From
Mel's expression it was obvious that my face was betraying the truth.
I should have been telling him the truth, that those women were very
credible and didn't appear to have an ax to grind whatsoever, but I
couldn't do that to Ben.

"Are you listening to yourself?" he finally said. "What you're
telling me is that their stories are credible, but you just don't believe
them. Is that what you're saying?"

"I don't think there's a story here."

He smiled. "You don't?"

"No."

"I never thought I'd see this day, JR."

I rolled my eyes. *Here we go.*

"What kind of power does this guy have over you? He's an arrogant, obnoxious, right-wing bastard. He's old enough to be your father. He's gonna emasculate the lower classes once he gets the power
to do so. But you protect him. You. Of all people. And you protect
him against two black women, two victims, whose only crime is that
they refused to remain silent. You used to keep me going, you know
that? When I wanted to quit the business because nobody gives a
damn anymore, they're all just a bunch of hairdos sitting around on
those cable news shows calling themselves journalists. But then I'd
read one of your stories, one of your biased, judgmental-as-hell stories, and realized immediately that it's still worth the fight. If JR can
keep the faith, so can I. But what happened?"

Loneliness happened. And it wasn't okay anymore. Love hap-
pened. And I liked the feeling. Happiness happened. And it was full

and complete and I needed it. Life happened, Mel. I wanted to live. I
wanted to know what all the fuss was about. That's what happened!
But I didn't say anything. Mel was heartbroken. I had let him
down. He wouldn't understand. "Write the story, JR," he said to me.
"And I don't want any sugarcoat either."

"Larry said we wouldn't print it if I didn't give my okay."

"Larry gave you the okay, but he gave me the final word. And my
word is final. We're going with the story. And you're writing it. And
you're dotting every I and crossing every T. Now if your boyfriend is
worth losing your job over, then fine, get lost, but we're going with
the story."

It was certain now. Mel was exacting his revenge. Just the innu-
endo would be enough to derail the nomination. Mel knew it and I
knew it too. And in the end, that's all he wanted. A derailment. An
immediate halt to that out-of-date train called conservatism and that
out-of-date train conductor named Ben.

We stood at the window in his chamber. The sun was shining
through and his perfectly chiseled face was almost unexpressive. My
concern rose as I laid out the case against him. He listened carefully,
but more as a judge would to a defendant than a man about to be
raked over the coals. "They're going with the story whether I write it
or not."

"Then write it."

"But if you just give me something to look into, to investigate,
maybe I can slow this down."

"Just do your job, Josephine."

"How can you act like this? Don't you understand what's going
on here?"

"Of course I understand. Two women have made allegations
against me. It's your job to write the story. That's what's going on."

"The story that you so nonchalantly suggest I write can destroy
you, Ben. Don't you get it?"

"What do you want me to say? I didn't do it. It's untrue. It's a
pack of lies. What more can I say?"

"You can stand on top of this courthouse and shout out your innocence! You can call a press conference this very hour and declare
that you're being steamrolled by a couple of attention-seeking, agenda-
driven females! You can fight back, Ben, that's what you can do!"

"I can fight back?"

"Yes!"

"They destroy me, so I destroy them. Is that how the game is played? Is that what you mean by fighting back?"

I sighed. "Yes."

"I see. So you don't practice what you preach after all."

"This is different."

"Like hell it is! You've devoted your career to stamping out racism and sexism wherever they may happen to appear. But because I'm involved now, you're just going to forget about all of that? You're going to put these victims on trial too?"

"But you said they're lying."

"Yes, Josephine, they are. They know it and I know it. But I'm not compromising my principals because somebody chooses to tell lies on me, and I would hope you wouldn't compromise yours either. Not for me. Not for anybody!"

His insolence was angering me more than the allegations themselves. How could he be so smug? How could he treat this monumental problem as if it were some everyday thing? "Two women have said that you harassed them for dates, coerced them into having sex with you, and then fired them when your need was satisfied, and all you can say is 'it's not true'?"

He paused. "Yes," he said.

"That's it?"

"Yes."

I couldn't believe my ears. Didn't he understand what position he was putting me in? I was willing to fight for a man who wasn't willing to fight for himself. I was willing to overlook facts, to bring on the fiction, if it meant sparing him. All for him. And he didn't give a damn. "You know what?" I said when I could hold back no longer. "You're going to get exactly what you deserve because you're being nothing but an arrogant asshole!"

He smiled. He actually smiled! "That's me," he said. I shook my head and left. If he didn't care that his neat little world was about to come crashing down, why the hell should I?

THE FIRST LINE OF MY OBITUARY

TWO WOMEN ALLEGE MISCONDUCT BY BRADDOCK, the headline read. By ten it had circulated across the state as a wire service pickup. By noon it led two of the three local newscasts. And Dinkle was right. It was by far my biggest story. Ben was shown leaving the courthouse, flanked by reporters urging him to comment on that big story of mine. I sat at my desk and looked up at the television set in the newsroom. Ben would not say a word, not even "no comment," and the expression on his face was decidedly less optimistic than it was when he made the decision to go with the flow.

"Josie?" someone said and I turned to find Kay Denshaw, a photographer, standing at my desk. I looked behind her to see that Helen and Cathy were watching, waiting for some response from me. Not again, I thought. As if I didn't have enough to deal with, they probably sent Kay over in some damn dare. "Get Josie's advice," I'd bet they told her. "She's our love expert, after all." And I'm sure they laughed at that one.

"What's up, Kay?"

"How you doing?"

"Good."

"I liked your story. And congratulations for making the lead. But I'm sure you're used to that by now."

"What's up?"

She sat down in the chair in front of my desk. "I need your advice."

"Why?"

She laughed. "That's a good one. But really I do. You remember Phil, don't you? He's the guy—"

"Who used to play for the Jaguars, yeah, I remember him."

"We're really tight, you know? And we're supposed to be getting married."

"But?"

"This girl's been telling me about him. She says he slept with her a few weeks ago."

"You believe her?"

She couldn't respond right away. She had to think about this. "Yeah," she said. "And I know what you're going to say. I know a village will be missing an idiot if I give that cheating dog another chance, I know that, but it's not that simple."

"It never is."

"This is my future, Josie, you know? I love the guy."

"Then stay with him. And love him."

She didn't expect that line. She even turned and looked at Helen. Then she looked at me. "But he cheated on me."

"Nobody's perfect." I glanced at Helen. She unfolded her arms.

"They aren't?" Kay asked, shocked as hell.

"No. Confront him about it and if he's forgiving, then forgive him and go on with your life. It's not worth losing everything over. Is it?"

"I guess not."

"Life without love is cold as ice, girl. And all those pictures you take with that camera of yours, not one of those pictures can kiss you and hold you in that midnight hour!" I said this and stood up, grabbing my shoulder bag. Kay looked at me as if she didn't understand a word I had just spoken.

"What midnight hour?" she asked me. But I was already heading for the exit door.

I drove around Jacksonville as if I were a woman of leisure with nothing better to do. The traffic was sparse so I was able to stay under the speed limit without worrying about some impatient jerk trying to force me off the road the way I usually did those who wanted to sightsee and drive too. I kept seeing the look on Ben's face as he left the courthouse, seemingly shocked that the press would hound him like this. It was no big deal to him. Just a pack of lies as he saw them. The truth always won out, he believed. And normally it did. But with a press hungry for blood, and with a girlfriend like me who seemed more than willing to supply the meat, truth was often beside the point.

I ended up at Ben's house. Although his car was in the drive, I couldn't get any response to my doorbell rings and knocks. I started to sit on his porch and then I thought the better of it. I walked around back instead.

And that was when I saw him. He was on his patio, in a lawn chair recliner, a half-filled glass of wine in one hand, a cigarette in the other, wearing a pair of shorts, sandals, and a light blue shirt unbuttoned to the navel. The sound of jazz music could be heard from the house, coming out of speakers hidden from sight. He looked as if he was through dealing. I started to turn around. It was a good bet I wasn't the one he wanted to see right about now. But since I felt like hell too, that guilt getting the best of me all day, I decided I had nothing left to lose.

I walked up to his recliner. He did not look my way. His eyes were fixated on the Atlantic Ocean that surrounded his backyard, the sound of gushing waves ramming against the shoreline and that jazz music of his seemingly too dramatic for peace. But it was peaceful there, but lonely too, and so damn depressing.

When it was apparent that he wasn't about to so much as acknowledge my presence, I sat on the edge of his recliner, near his feet. I stared at the ocean too, and couldn't help but feel the weight of my decision not only on my life, but his as well, and my heart ached. "I'm sorry," I said.

He said nothing.

"I wasn't trying to hurt you, Ben. I was doing my job."

"I know," he said. I turned and looked at him. He was so distraught that just looking at him depressed me. "There's nothing to apologize for."

"You still can fight it, Ben. You still can refuse to let other people define who you are."

"I had a meeting this morning, after the story broke. The chief judge called me into his office and suggested, suggested, mind you, that I resign."

"What? Based on what? Those women didn't present any evidence. It's just their word against yours. I wrote that in my article."

"He suggested that I resign or face being hauled before the Judicial Conduct Board and publicly embarrassed. Too late, I told him."

"Are you gonna do it?"

"And I refused to resign."

I nodded and our eyes met. I had never seen him so hurt. I moved up on the recliner until I was sitting beside him. He took his arm and wrapped it around me, and his touch calmed me down.

"You're shivering," he said.

"I can't believe I wrote it. I just can't believe I did it."

"Oh, Josephine," he said and pulled me up on his lap. I leaned into his body, his bare chest warm against me. "Stop second-guessing yourself. If you didn't write it, somebody else would. Those hounds at the *Gazette* would see to that. You gave me fair warning."

"But I should have told them no. I wouldn't do it to you. But Mel kind of threatened to fire me if I didn't write the story, and you wouldn't . . ."

"I wouldn't what?"

"You wouldn't back me up, Ben. It's like you just gave up. How can I put myself on the line for somebody who gives up?"

"You couldn't. You did the right thing."

"But what about you?"

He tried to smile, revealing too many wrinkles. "I told you not to worry about me."

"What are you going to do?"

"What I've been doing, Josephine. Live. Work."

"Have you heard from the governor's office?"

He paused. "No."

"Not a word?"

"Not a one."

I leaned up and looked at him. "I'm so sorry, Ben."

This time he managed a real smile, his mustache lifting up and his bright brown eyes wide and hopeful. But it was painful too. "You ever had a dream job, Josephine?"

"Not yet."

"Well, to sit on the highest court in this state, to make decisions that could have such far-reaching implications, that would have been mine."

"It still could be yours."

"Don't do that."

"Do what?"

"Kid yourself. Don't you ever do that."

I sighed. "But how can I help you, Ben? I don't know how to help you."

He looked at me, and then pulled me to him and held me tightly. "Just say you believe me."

"I do."

"Say it."

"I believe you." I looked into his eyes. "I believe you."

And I did. With all my heart I did.

We fell asleep on the patio, clutched in each other's arms, the rhythm of the ocean and the turmoil of the day draining the life out of both of us. We could have slept right there, all night, and would have, except my cell phone began ringing. It was Scotty.

"What's up, Boo?" I asked him.

There was an immediate hesitation in his voice. "What you doing?"

"Chillin' with Ben."

"Ben? Even after what you wrote about him?"

"Something like that. What's up?" I hadn't heard from Scotty in days, which wasn't that unusual, but I expected some comments from my best friend on the biggest story of my life.

"You think you can break away from your boyfriend long enough to come over?"

"Why? What's going on?" When he wouldn't say, and asked again if I could come over, I knew then that something was seriously wrong. "I'm leaving now," I said to him and flipped closed the cell.

Ben could feel me sliding off of his lap, and his eyes suddenly opened. He smiled when he saw me. "Hey," he said.

"Hey," I said and began putting my cell phone back in my bag.

"You're going somewhere?"

"Yeah. Scotty just called. He doesn't sound too good."

"What's wrong with him?"

"I don't know. He just wants me to come over."

Ben nodded. He seemed disappointed. "Are you coming back?"

"It's pretty late as it is."

He shook his head. "Right."

I had never seen him so frail. "I'll walk you to your car," he said and stood up. And as soon as he stood and looked into my eyes, tears began to well up in his. It was so astonishing to see him in such a state that it scared me.

"Oh, Ben!" I said and hurried to his side. I fell into his arms and he pulled me so tight to him that I could hardly breathe. When I tried to release, he wouldn't let me. I looked at him.

"Everything's gonna be all right," I said.

"Doesn't look very good. Does it?"

"But you're innocent. That's all that matters."

He nodded. "Yeah."

"Truth will win out. You said so yourself."

He smiled and ran his hand across my braids. "Do you always listen to everything I say?"

"Always."

"Then listen to this: I love you." He placed his hand on my chin and kissed me lightly. I hugged him again but released before he could tighten his grip.

"I love you too, kid," I said, "but I gots to go."

"Right," he said, that disappointment returning as quickly as it had left. "Scotty needs you."

I looked at him when he said this. I was needed, that was for sure, but it wasn't clear if Scotty was the one who needed me the most. "Look, if you aren't doing anything why don't you ride with me?"

"Ride with you?"

"Why not?"

"You sure?"

"Now why wouldn't I be sure, Benjamin? Of course I'm sure. Come on."

"Okay. Yeah, I think I will. Just give me a minute to change and I'll be at your service."

"And, Ben?"

He turned. "Yes?"

"No suit and tie, okay? It's ten o' clock at night. Nobody gives a fuck."

He laughed. He needed that. "Yes, ma'am," he said and hurried into his house.

I waited in my Mustang for nearly fifteen minutes before he came out of his front door. He wasn't in a suit and tie, thank God, but he had on a pair of dress pants, a dress shirt, dress shoes, and a bowler. As soon as he plopped down in my front seat I knew what time it was.

"Kill the hat, brother," I said to him.

"What's wrong with it?"

"Kill the hat, brother."

"I'm almost fifty years old, Josephine. This is how I dress."

"I see. So you're almost fifty and you gotta look every bit your age, is that how it goes?"

"No."

"Good. Then kill the hat."

He smiled. "I'm not myself these days," he said, removing the hat, "or I would have told you to kiss my ass, you know that, don't you?"

I laughed. "I know it," I said, determined to enjoy this newfound power of mine while it lasted.

Scotty lived in a modest three-bedroom home in Turtle Creek. It amazed me how a flamboyant man like him, whose flash and excess were notorious, could fit so snugly amongst the housewives and schoolteachers of suburbia. But he did it. His house, third from the corner on SkyLaden Lane, was a simple brick home with a mani-cured lawn and rose garden on the side. Nothing about his home, in fact, drew attention to it. It wasn't the biggest or the cutest or the best designed of even the two houses that sided his, let alone the other homes on the block.

My Mustang's loud, high-revved engine ground to a halt on his empty drive, his Miata no doubt inside his two-car garage, a garage almost as big as the house, and Ben and I stepped out. We walked swiftly across his sidewalk and up on his porch. Two rings of the doorbell didn't yield a response. So I used my key and we walked on in.

The house was dark when we opened the door, and I quickly flicked on the light on the side wall. Scotty was a neat freak and his house always, and I mean always, demonstrated it. That was why, when I saw as little a dishevelment as one of the sofa pillows on the floor as if it had been thrown there, I knew then that something ter-rible had happened. I panicked. "Scotty?" I yelled. "Scotty?"

"He doesn't appear to be at home," Ben said.

"Something's happened to him," I said, hurrying toward the hall.

"How do you figure that? Josephine?"

But I couldn't answer. Not until I saw Scotty. So I ran down the hall, calling his name, over and over, each call more desperate than the one before, until I pushed open the door of his bedroom and stumbled inside.

He was coming out of the bathroom with a washcloth covering the left side of his face, his long hair hanging wildly along his back like a mop on top of his head, his face calm but annoyed. As soon as I saw him, I hurried to him. "Scotty!" I yelled. "Are you all right?"

"I was fine before you came in here with all that noise," he said as he walked to the edge of his bed and sat down. "Scared me half to death!"

"What happened?"

He shook his head. "What didn't happen, girl?"

"It was Bruce, wasn't it?"

Ben came into the bedroom by knocking lightly on the door as he entered. I expected Scotty to be surprised to see him with me, but he wasn't. "Hello, Judge Braddock," he said. "Welcome to my nightmare."

"Let me see it," Ben said. Scotty at first hesitated; then he removed the cloth from the side of his face. His yellowish skin was so badly bruised and swollen that it was turning purple.

"How bad is it?" Scotty asked.

"Pretty bad," Ben said, his voice calm, his demeanor showing no surprise whatsoever.

"Do you think I need a paramedic, Judge?" Scotty asked this with a weak smile on his face.

"Do you think you need one?"

"No, sir, I do not, but I'm sure Miss Dupree here thinks so. But I'm glad to know that you agree with my assessment."

"He didn't agree with anything," I said.

"Who did that to you, Scott?" Ben asked.

"Bruce," I said. "Wasn't it?"

He sighed. "Yes, Miss Thang, it was Bruce, and before you say I told you so I already know you told me so."

"You should have called the cops when he stole your credit card. But you wouldn't. Now look at what he's done."

Ben walked farther into the room and sat down in the chair by the door. Scotty placed the cloth back over his face and ran his hand through his hair.

"Where is he now? Did he beat you up and just leave?"

"He didn't beat me up, okay? His face in a lot worse shape than mine, trust me."

"So tell me what happened."

"Will you at least sit down first?"

I sat down on the bed beside Scotty. "Thank you," he said. And then he crossed his legs. He was wearing a pair of shorts and a tank top and it was obvious by the gingerly way he moved his body that more than his face had been bruised. "I saw him two days ago at this party I was attending in Mayport. We spoke, talked for a few minutes, and that was it. At least I thought so anyway. Then he showed up at the gallery yesterday. I told him then that I didn't mix my business with pleasure and he couldn't be showing up on my job like that. But he wouldn't leave until I agreed to have dinner with him."

"Dinner? That thief? He has some nerve!"

"Well, apparently I have some nerve too because I had dinner with him."

"Scotty, no."

"Josephine?" Ben said. I looked at him. "Let him finish."

"Thank you, Benjamin, because this witch here can be a handful when she wants to be."

"Just finish," I said to him.

"Anyway," he said, giving me what he referred to as his "evil eye," "we went to the Cut, you know, and it's always crowded so I didn't think there could be no harm."

"The man stole your credit card, charged up two thousand dollars, and you have dinner with him?"

"Yes, Josie, okay? I ain't no she-woman like you. I need me some companionship sometimes. Bruce ain't perfect but hey, who is? So yes, I had dinner with him. We even went to a movie too. And then we spent today together. Everything was fine until he asked to borrow my car. He had this to do and that to do and he didn't see why I was being so mean to him and oh, he pitched a fit. But I wasn't tryin' to hear his tall tales today, I wasn't thinking about it. So he jumps an attitude. And I jumped one back. Then that sucker had the nerve to push me out of his way, as if he was gonna get my car whether I liked it or not. So I pushed him back. And the rest, as they say, is written all over our faces."

"Did either of you contact the authorities?" Ben asked and Scotty and I looked at him at the same time. He was leaned back in the chair, his long legs stretched completely out and his hands interlaced and resting against the back of his head. I smiled, because he seemed so at home in Scotty's room, and that was one of the reasons why I loved him so much. He was always himself, no matter where he was, and he didn't expect those around him to conform to some preconceived image either.

"I didn't call the cops, no," Scotty said. "And I'm certain he didn't."

"But why didn't you, Scotty?" I asked. "He comes to your house, gets mad at you for refusing to give him *your* car, and then he jumps on you? Why didn't you call?"

"I'm not calling the cops, Josie, all right? I am not going to be responsible for another black male going to prison. No, thank you very much."

"So why did you call me? What can I do?"

Scotty took the cloth and repositioned it on his cheek. "I want you to give me a lift," he said.

"A lift?"

"A ride, Josephine," Ben said.

"A ride, Scotty? Where's your car?" Scotty looked at me. "Oh my God," I said. "He took it?"

"I didn't even know he had the keys. He knocked me over the chair and when I got back up he was running out of the door. So I told him he better run and I locked the door, to make sure he didn't try to come back in. I didn't realize he had my car until I heard it crank up. By the time I got to the garage, boyfriend had booked."

I shook my head. "And you still won't call the police?"

"I'm not calling no cops, J! You can forget that."

I threw my hands in the air and looked at Ben. Ben was as calm as a cucumber. "Where does he live?" he asked Scotty.

"In Springfield. He's renting him a room over on Liberty Street."

"Okay," Ben said, standing up. "Let's do this."

Scotty looked up at Ben and smiled. "Thanks, man." Then he looked at me. "Are you coming or would you rather stay here with your righteous indignation?"

"Go to hell," I said and walked out of the room. Scotty laughed out loud. "How can you stand her?" he asked Ben. I slowed down, to hear Ben's response. But he didn't say a word.

Ben took my car keys from me and drove to Springfield. From Harts Road to Dunn Avenue to 95 South to the MLK Parkway. From there he took the Liberty Street exit and Scotty and I were both surprised by how well he knew his way around the hood.

Bruce lived in the 400 block of a one-hundred-year-old street loaded with one-hundred-year-old once beautiful but now dilapidated and all but abandoned two-story rent houses. And his place of residence was no exception. It was a green-and-white-frame structure so old and neglected that it appeared to lean to one side. A small group of men were sitting around on the stoop drinking beer and listening to loud rap music, and they were the kind of crowd that often put chills up my spine. The Sopranos didn't have anything on these brothers. You could tell they didn't play. You could tell they'd seen murder up close and personal, and even may have been the culprit— the kind of brothers who would just as soon shoot you than deal with you. And this was where Scotty's boyfriend lived? I shook my head.

All eyes turned to my Mustang when we drove up. Even Ben, who'd seen enough murderers in his day too, who even may have recognized one or two of them, appeared apprehensive. It was after eleven o'clock at night, we were in Springfield of all places, and the up-to-no-good gang was our welcoming committee.

Although Scotty's Miata was nowhere to be seen, Scotty got out in a hurry. I started to get out too, but Ben touched me on my arm. "You stay here," he said, and got out instead.

Scotty was already at the stoop by the time Ben walked up to it. Although Ben dressed like a nerd, he certainly didn't look like one, and all the guys on the porch seemed to understand it too. They glanced at Scotty, but they looked at Ben, and although Scotty was talking his head off, asking for information on Bruce's whereabouts, it wasn't until Ben started talking that they bothered to turn that loud-ass music down.

I couldn't hear anything clearly, and I couldn't stand not hearing, so I got out of the car and hurried to the stoop too.

"But he was here earlier?" Ben was asking one of them when I arrived by his side. He gave me a quick glance, but it felt more like a glancing blow, all because I didn't sit in the car as he had commanded. But he was learning me, I think. He was slowly understanding that commands rarely worked on me.

"He came by, yeah," the youngest of the group, who looked to be nineteen or so, said.

"What was he driving?" I asked, and Ben and Scotty both looked at me. The dude looked at me too, but he wouldn't answer my question.

"What was he driving?" Ben asked him.

"Some little fancy sports car."

"Silver and blue?"

"Yeah. He said it was his car. But we knew better than that. That faggot ain't owned no car a day in his life." He said this and looked at Scotty. Scotty looked at Ben.

"Did he say where he was going when he left?" Ben asked.

"Like I said, no. He just left."

Ben stood erect, as if he'd reached a dead end. I whispered in his ear, since all questions apparently had to come through him or the gang wasn't going to answer, "Ask him if he knows where Bruce likes to hang out." At first Ben looked at me, annoyed, but then he asked the question.

"At gay bars, shit, man, how the hell should I know?" His partners laughed and gave each other five.

"Other than gay bars," Ben said, "have you seen him around anywhere?"

"He be at the Cut a lot," another dude on the porch said and they all looked at him. "I be there a lot too, that's all. Damn."

"Okay," Ben said. "Thanks." He then reached on the porch and shook the nineteen-year-old's hand. "Thanks a lot."

Then he grabbed me by the arm and we began hurrying back to the car, with Scotty following suit.

"And, Judge?" the kid asked and we turned around. "You gonna remember my cousin though, right?"

"I will be fair to your cousin if he comes before me, yes."

"Thanks, Judge," the kid said. Ben told him that he was welcome, and with no desire to hang around a moment longer, we left.

*   *   *

We had to tell Ben how to get to the Cut nightclub from where we were. Liberty to East First Street, East First to A. Phillip Randolph, and then park on the side of the road, not in the back, if he could find a spot.

But we didn't have to park. Scotty's little Mazda Miata was awaiting us, parked on the side of the road too, under a street lamp, and all I could do was think about how much nerve that damn Bruce had.

Ben turned his body completely around to Scotty. "You have an extra set of keys?"

"Yeah."

"Go get your car, Scotty, and go on home. Don't try to confront this Bruce tonight. Lock your garage, lock your house. If your friend comes to your home again, phone the police."

Scotty nodded.

"He's not gonna do it," I said.

"He'd better do it," Ben said. "And if you don't, Scotty, then you're on your own. Josephine will not be coming out here, in places like Springfield or up to this nightclub, because you're in love with a thug. Understand me?"

Scotty nodded once more. "Yeah, I do. And thanks again, man. I'm through with Bruce, trust me."

Ben said okay, Scotty kissed me good night, and he got out of my car. We stayed and watched as he cranked up his car and left, waving as he went.

"I hope this taught him a lesson," I said.

"Don't count on it," Ben said, cranking up too. "He's desperate. And in love. And that's always a lethal combination."

Back at work and Mel was in too good a mood. He walked past my desk twice, staring at me like the oddball he was, and then Larry Dinkle came down and they called me into Mel's office.

"Sit down, JR," Mel said and Dinkle smiled at me.

"How have you been, Miss Josephine?"

"Good, Larry, how about yourself?"

"Wonderful."

"So, what's happened?"

"Oh my," Dinkle said. "You're far too young to be so pessimistic."

"Nothing's happened?"

Dinkle sighed. "Yes, Josie, something's happened."

My hands clenched the arms of the chair. "What?"

Dinkle hesitated. "Another woman has come forward," he said. That sinking feeling returned. "Another woman? What do you mean?" I knew full well what he meant. But the idea terrified me.

"Her name is Jameela French," he said, handing me a folder. "Go check her out. She's in Baker County."

"Baker County?"

"She said she can see you this afternoon."

"Wait a minute, Larry. What's going on here?"

"Another woman claims to have been sexually harassed by Braddock," Dinkle said.

"Are we supposed to just drop everything and check out every crank allegation now?"

"This ain't no crank allegation," Mel said bitterly.

"How the hell do you know? She reads my article on Tonya Wright and Marlene Wingate; now she wants a piece of the publicity too. Now she wants to derail Braddock. And we just let her? Whosoever will, let them come. The lynching of Benjamin Braddock is now in session. Is this what we're about now?"

"That's not what we're doing here at all, Josie," Dinkle said.

"Isn't it? What would you call it?"

"It's our job to—"

"Lynch Braddock."

Mel sighed. I didn't give a damn.

"It's our job," Dinkle went on, "to check into every credible lead."

"But what makes this one credible? The fact that this Jameela French opened her mouth and said 'yeah, me too, he did it to me too'?"

"This one is credible because Jameela French is credible."

I looked at Dinkle. What the hell was that supposed to mean?

"Jameela French is a family court judge in Baker County. A *conservative* family court judge in Baker County, Josie. She's no joke."

I leaned back. A conservative judge was accusing another conservative judge of sexual harassment? So much for the tear-down-the-conservative angle. So much for the politics of it. And a family court judge at that? *Family* court judge? I sat mute in my chair. If ever there was a how-to book written on how to put the last nail in a brother's coffin, this woman, this woman number three, may very well have written it.

RUMORS OF MY DEATH WEREN'T ALL THAT EXAGGERATED

She walked in swiftly, carrying a brown paper bag and a thermal mug, and she was no sex goddess with wild tales and an easy smile, but a middle-aged, gray-haired sister in a business suit.

"Sorry to keep you waiting, I do indeed apologize," she said as she hurried behind her desk. We were in her office within the Baker County Courthouse, a Gothic-looking brick building located in Macclenny, Florida, a small town about twenty minutes from Jacksonville. Her secretary had seated me in her office nearly thirty minutes ago, an office half the size of Ben's but loaded with family photographs (a husband, two grown sons, grandkids) and numerous judicial awards on her wall. But her delay was crippling. Just before she came in I was about ready to give up and deal with this tomorrow. I wasn't sure if my heart could take it anyway. But she came in.

"You're the reporter from the *Gazette*," she said as if she had to remind me, and then she extended her stubby hand across her desk.

I had to stand to shake it, so I did, and her grip was firm and certain, and she looked at me in such a curious way that I almost felt as if she could sense my agony. "Sit back down," she ordered. I guess ordering people around was what judges did because Ben had it down to a science too. So I sat back down.

She sat down too and offered me half of her ham and cheese sandwich, which I quickly refused, and then she spent the next few minutes eating her lunch, drinking her coffee, and talking about Ben. She

mainly talked about her job as his researcher, until she said something in such a cavalier manner that I almost missed it. "I was in love
with him," she said, and continued talking.

But I stopped her. "You were in love with him?"

"Why, yes."

"You and he were lovers?"

She smiled. "Yes, Miss Ross. I wasn't always a gray-haired
grandma."

"But I mean, he knew?"

She looked around as if she had missed something, and then she
looked at me. "I would call it knowledge, yes."

"So you slept with him willingly?"

"Yes. Oh yes. Initially he didn't have to harass me at all. I was
more than willing." She smiled. I couldn't even try.

"You knew he was married?"

"No. He told me he was divorced. But when I found out the truth,
and especially when I learned that his wife was ill, I ended the affair.
But that's when the trouble started."

"The harassment?"

"Right. When I wouldn't continue having sex with him, he made
my life a living hell. He even threatened to fire me. He harassed me
to such a degree that I became physically ill. So I quit a job I loved.
But I had no choice."

"Why didn't you go to his boss, or even the EEOC?"

"Because I felt culpable. I was his mistress. Why would anyone
believe me?"

I looked at her. She was a shrewd woman if she was anything.
"That wasn't the only reason, was it?"

She hesitated, and then proceeded cautiously. "No, it wasn't. I always had lofty goals for myself, Miss Ross. This judgeship is a ful-
fillment of that, so you're right. I also didn't want to blemish my
career."

"Why are you coming forward now?"

She leaned back, now eager to talk. "That's easy," she said. "He
has no business anywhere near the highest court in this state. The
idea that a man like him would be nominated to become our next
justice nauseates me, Miss Ross. There was no way I could remain
silent now."

So there it was. A new twist. She was his lover. And it wasn't a onetime thing either. And he was a married man. "Do you still love him?"

"A part of me always will. But right is right, Miss Ross. Isn't it?"

She said this and looked at me, her face warm but concerned. It used to be, I wanted to tell her. "Yes," I told her instead.

Scotty met me at the Jacksonville Landing and we found a small table overlooking the Saint Johns River. The breeze from the river was blowing back my hair, and I spent nearly half an hour saying nothing, just watching the sailboats slowly drift by while the jet skis would lift up, drop down, and then zoom by. When I finally explained the Jameela French problem to Scotty, he leaned back in his chair. "She's a judge?" he asked.

"Yes. A family court judge."

"Damn. What she got against Ben?"

"Nothing, Scotty. I don't see where she has anything against him. That's the point."

"Damn."

"I know."

"Well, what's her politics? Is it this right-wing, left-wing thing?"

"No. She's a conservative too. She's no conservative activist, but her rulings from the bench have been very conservative, she's a registered Republican, I even saw her voter's registration card, Scotty. I even talked to some of her colleagues. There's no political angle here. She probably wouldn't mind Ben's ascension to the supreme court philosophically."

"Then why is she lying on him?" I closed my eyes. Then Scotty added: "*If* she's lying on him."

"You know Ben, Scotty. He wouldn't treat women like that, I know he wouldn't."

"Maybe he's changed, Josie. Maybe he just used to be an asshole. Hell, we don't know him like that."

"I believe Ben."

"What has he said about it?"

I hesitated. "I haven't spoken to him yet."

"Look, girl, I like Ben too, you know I do. But I mean, she's a fellow judge, Josie. A judge! And a conservative too? With grandchildren? Come on, sweetie, let's get real here. She ain't gonna put herself out there like that unless it's true."

"I know. And I know it's crazy to think that all of these women would conspire to lie on Ben, I know this, Scotty. But Ben wouldn't treat women the way they're suggesting."

"But again, she's a judge, Josie. Why would she lie?"

I didn't know. And that was the problem. I told Ben that I believed him. And in a way I did. But Judge French raised the stakes. She was a fellow jurist like Scotty said. And unlike the others, she didn't just claim that Ben harassed her. She claimed that she and Ben were lovers once. I leaned back and sighed. I didn't know what to do. I couldn't keep running to Ben every time somebody spoke ill of him. Besides, he wasn't about to fight back now, if this woman was once his lover.

I went to Fred. He was still in his office and I walked in hurriedly. When I told him the new news, he looked at me and nodded. "She's lying," he said.

"Did you investigate her?"

"When your Tonya Wright story broke I had my man check out every woman who's worked under Benjamin. That included Jameela French."

"What did you find on her?"

He paused.

"Well?"

"Nothing. Not yet anyway."

"Then how do you know she's lying, Fred?"

"Because I know Benjamin. He doesn't harass women, Josie. Never has and never will. Have you looked at the guy lately? He doesn't need to harass women for dates, let's make that perfectly clear here."

"But why would this conservative judge lie on him? It doesn't make sense. And you yourself said there was nothing in her background to suggest a problem. Why would she just lie like this?"

"I don't know her. But I know Benjamin. Your problem, Josie, is that you never had faith in anybody but yourself. But loving Benjamin Braddock isn't going to be as easy as proving or disproving a rumor. You've got to believe in him despite the rumors."

I shook my head. "I can't do that."

"You can't believe in him? That's all he wants."

"I follow facts, Fred, not fiction, and I can never turn a blind eye to the truth."

"So you'll believe these women over Benjamin?"

"It's not that simple."

"It's just that simple, Josie."

"I was always taught to follow the evidence. That's all. And if it ain't turning up the way I want it to turn up, then I can't act as if I don't understand that something's wrong. Something is wrong here, Fred."

"But it can't be true. That's the problem. That's what's wrong."

The intercom on his desk buzzed. "Excuse me, Mr. Caldwell, but Judge Braddock is here."

Fred and I looked at each other and sighed at the same time. Neither one of us was ready for Ben. I walked over by the big bay window. Fred sat behind his desk. "Send him in, Jan," he said to his secretary and then he turned to me. "Let me handle this," he said.

I agreed easily, because I wanted no part of it, but I knew, in the end, something had to give. I could overlook Marlene Wingate's tales and even Tonya Wright's. But Jameela French was somebody's grandmother, for crying out loud. A conservative woman whom even Fred's hounds couldn't tarnish. Now she, too, was supposed to be a part of some grand conspiracy to get Ben? I closed my eyes and held my head back. Too much. Too much. Too damn much!

Ben walked in and my eyes opened. And I could tell by his hesitancy that he knew, just by my presence alone, that we had a problem. But he managed a smile anyway. "Hello, Josephine, this is a nice surprise."

"Hey," I said and folded my arms. I tried to smile too but the obvious agony on my face wouldn't let it through. Even after he spoke to Fred and walked up to me, giving me a big bear hug, I still couldn't handle any phony show of lightheartedness. This situation was too serious for games. We had a problem here.

Ben may have suspected it when he first walked in, but when he released me and saw that I wasn't playing along, he knew it was true. His entire countenance changed. "What is it now?" he asked so wretchedly that I could feel his anguish. And I couldn't speak.

He turned to Fred. "Well?"

Fred looked at his friend and shook his head. "Another woman, Benjamin, has accused you of sexual harassment."

He just stood there, staring at the two people he most depended on in this world, and neither one of us seemed hopeful. Then he unbuttoned his suit coat, walked over to the chair in front of Fred's desk, and sat down. He glanced at Fred. Then he looked at me. "Who?" he asked.

"You've got to fight it," I said. "If it's not true you've got to stand up and fight."

He frowned. "Who is it, Josephine?"

I hesitated. The last person it needed to be. "Judge French," I said.

He leaned back. *"Jameela?"*

I nodded. "Yes."

His face grew somber, almost unnaturally gloomy.

"She said she had an affair with you," I said. "Is it true?"

He didn't answer. I don't think he could.

"She said she discontinued the affair when she found out you were married. But you still wanted her. You harassed her so badly that she became physically ill. And her story checked out, Ben. The *Gazette* obtained hospital records that clearly indicate she was hospitalized because of what the doctor at the time called 'job-related stress.' Her hospitalization occurred at the exact same time as her alleged problems with you. Is she telling the truth, Ben?"

He looked up at me, his face so devastated that he didn't look well. "I did not have an affair with her," he said, the words trembling from his lips.

"So she's lying too?"

He paused. "Yes."

"Bullshit."

Fred turned around and looked at me, but I wasn't thinking about him. I had met Jameela French. She was no flimflam gal, that was for damn sure. "Yeah, I said it," I said to Fred. "It's bullshit." Then I looked at Ben. "When I said her name you nearly jumped out of your skin. What's up with that? You can't tell me she was just another delusional female in love with you too."

"That's exactly what I'm telling you."

"And I'm telling you it's a lie! I don't believe you. I'm not saying you harassed her but it's for damn sure that something happened. Now tell me what's going on, Ben. I need to know what's happening here."

"Nothing's happening here," he said, his voice calm but his demeanor becoming increasingly combative. "I didn't have an affair with that woman. Period."

"You never loved her?"

He looked up, his anger rising. "I did not have an affair with her, Josephine, and I will not discuss it any further."

"You were in love with her, weren't you?"

As soon as the words dripped from my lips, Ben stood to his feet and began a fast dash for the exit. Then Fred stood quickly. "Ben, wait!" he yelled. Ben waited, near the exit, and turned around.

Fred looked at me. I knew what that look meant. "Have a nice day, Josie," he said.

It was like that. Just like that. Ben was his friend and to hell with me and my facts. Believe the mirage. Believe Ben.

I walked up to the chair, grabbed my shoulder bag from the floor, and walked toward the door. Ben grabbed me by the arm just as I was about to pass him. Our eyes met. We were both exhausted.

"I'll call you later," he said.

I looked into his eyes, his bright brown, gorgeous eyes. I loved him so much that I would believe a lie if only he would tell me something. But he wasn't telling anything. It was up to me. I knew right then and there that if the truth was going to come out, I would have to force it out.

He called me later and invited me to dinner. He made it sound like a peace offering, but I needed more. I needed him to come clean with me and tell me what was going on. So I accepted his invitation. If it was up to me, and I was going to make sure that it was, the truth was coming out tonight.

I dressed up for the occasion, in a tight green evening dress, heels, matching clutch. When he arrived at my door and we walked toward his car, I could feel his eyes all over me. And I was grateful. I needed him relaxed. I needed him comfortable enough that he would be willing to put it on the line and tell it like it is.

We went to the Lighthouse jazz club and took a seat at his regular back booth. Some dude in a white cap was playing the piano and singing too, and it didn't take much for Ben to groove along with him. I sat back and chilled. After the music, I decided. After the music I would bring it up. But the music went on too long, all the way through dinner, and it wasn't until I told Ben that it was getting late and we'd better get going that he looked away from that piano player and paid attention to me. "You're ready?" he asked.

"Yeah," I said, relieved, and grabbed my clutch. Ben wasn't thrilled about leaving already but he knew that I wasn't with that jazz set at all. So he helped me up and we walked slowly out of the club. Even then Ben kept his eyes on the piano man. "Get Your Kicks on Route 66," he was singing, and Ben was nodding, as we left.

Once we were inside the Seville, Ben said he wanted to go to his place. But I told him to take me home. He lived practically around the corner. That wasn't far enough of a drive to hold the kind of conversation I needed to hold with him. And his house wasn't a good idea either, because, once inside, talking was usually the last thing on his mind. A long, slow drive to my place was the best way. Enough time to talk. Enough time to let it all hang out.

But he wasn't interested in taking me home. Not yet anyway. "We'll just swing by my house," he said again.

"I'm ready to go home, Ben," I said again.

"Come on, Josephine. It won't take that long."

"What won't take that long?"

He sighed. "You know what."

"I'm not up for that tonight."

"We haven't done it in a long time, honey. It's been a while."

I shook my head. I didn't want to go there, but he left me no damn choice. "How can you think about sex at a time like this?" I asked him.

He turned his body toward me. Now he was agitated too. "At a time like what?"

"This. Jameela French, Ben!"

"Oh, I get it now. I'm supposed to stop living my life because some woman makes an allegation?"

"Tell me about the relationship."

"What relationship, Josephine? What are you talking about?"

"Tell me about you and Jameela French."

His look was so exasperated that I thought he was on the verge of exploding. "I'm not telling you anything!" he yelled. "You wanna know all the lurid details of this soap opera nonsense, then ask the source. Ask Jameela. She's your buddy now. She's this tower of truth you and your idealism have been waiting for. So ask her. Because I've said all I plan to say about it. You understand where I'm coming from, Josephine? You understand me, goddammit!"

I looked around, at the parking lot filled with cars and the people moving in and out of the club as if they were having the time of their lives. They were with the ones they love, the music was good, all was at peace with the world. "Just take me home," I said to Ben, and he did, with fire under his tires.

I forced it out. At least I attempted to. It was two days later. I had persuaded Mel and Dinkle to keep the story under wraps a few more days so that I could check out some source material. Then I phoned Jameela. At first she said no, that she could not bear a confrontation with Ben Braddock, not at this late date. But within the hour she phoned me back and agreed to come. "Just to see if he's man enough to deny it to my face," she said.

And then I phoned Ben. All I told him was that we needed to talk. He seemed anxious to talk too. He hadn't heard from me since our night at the club and I refused to return his calls. This was make-or-break time for us. The up and down had to stop once and for all. He either harassed Jameela French or he didn't. He was either the man I knew him as or some monster I didn't know at all. It was underhanded and sneaky and not ordinarily my style by a mile. But these weren't ordinary times. I had to know the truth. And Ben was right, he wasn't telling me a damn thing. He was no help *at all*. So I invited Judge French over at seven and Judge Braddock at eight. Hell yeah, I did it. I was thinking about spending the rest of my life with Benjamin Braddock. I wasn't going to be wondering about this for the rest of my life or, even worse, wake up one day to find that the man I'd committed my life to was guilty as sin. I couldn't live with that. I knew I couldn't. So the stage was set.

Jameela wore a red business suit and sat on my sofa nervously. She said this was one of the hardest things she ever had to do. I told her this ranked up there for me too, and we both enjoyed a glass of nerve-calming sherry together.

Ben was late, ringing my bell at eight-fourteen. I was in my African garb, a gray and black pantsuit, and I walked to the door slowly but confidently, knowing that fireworks, one way or another, were about to begin. But when I opened that door and saw Ben, my heart dropped. He was smiling greatly (quite a feat for a stern man like him) and was bearing a dozen red roses. "For you, my love," he said and handed them to me. He was dressed casually for a change, in a pair of khaki pants and a brown pullover shirt, and Timberlands. And before I could even invite him in he stepped across the threshold and pulled me to him. "I know I've been a bastard," he said. "And you have every right to leave me. But I wish you'd reconsider. Please. I don't know what I'll do without you."

My life always ran in reverse. When I needed him to be prince charming, he was a bastard. When I needed him to be a bastard, he was unbelievably charming. "Oh, Ben," I said, "don't say that."

"It's true. You want the truth, that's the truth. I don't know what my life would be without you, Josie. See? I called you Josie. I'm coming around."

I smiled. And he hugged me. He kissed me so long and passionately, his sex so full against me, that even I forgot that we had a spectator. I pulled away from him. "Ben, there's something I've got to tell you."

He was still pulling on me, kissing me on my neck, my chest. "What, honey?"

"There's someone here to see you."

He stopped kissing me and looked at me. Then he looked beyond me. When his eyes met hers he quickly released me. "Jameela?" he asked, so confounded that it scared me.

"Hello, Judge Braddock," Jameela said and I looked at her. She was standing now, her arms to her side, her resolve as strong as mine was weak. This was her moment. And she wasn't letting my passion disturb it either.

Ben was dumbstruck. He gazed at her in a state of unbelief, but then he stared at me. "Josephine?" he asked.

"I need the truth to come out, Ben."

"The truth?"

"That's the only way we can have a future."

"You call this truth?"

"Tell me, in front of her, that you didn't do it. Tell me that you could never do the things she claims. Just tell me, Ben, and I'll believe you."

He looked up, at the ceiling, and then he looked down at me. I could tell he had a zillion things he wanted to tell me, and all probably unfavorable, but he didn't say a word. He just folded his arms and stared at me.

But Jameela French had a lot to say. "We had an affair," she said. "Didn't we, Ben? We were lovers. I was your chief assistant and you were my lover. It started out beautifully. I loved you, oh, how I loved you. And you said you loved me and you didn't know what you would do without me, all the same fairy tales you're telling this young lady tonight. You told it to me once. And I believed you too. What you failed to mention, however, was that you were married. We talked an awful lot but somehow that never came up. And your wife was ill too? How could you expect me to continue a relationship with you? How could you think that I would stoop that low? So I ended it, and I foolishly thought that was the end of it. But you wouldn't take no for an answer. You badgered me. You called me at home. You called my mother's house. You followed me around town. Everywhere I went, I saw you. And even after I quit that job you continued to hound me. But I wanted to be a judge someday. How could I admit to having an affair with a married man and expect my dream to come true? And you knew it. You knew my vulnerability. Those other women were just plain naive, and you played on their naivete. But you played on my ambition. And it worked. I should have turned you in then. Maybe the other victims would never have met you if I would have turned you in. But I was weak, and wanted more out of life. And you knew it."

She wasn't crying, but she sounded as if she was heartbroken and angry and determined to finally exact her revenge. She refused to be silent a moment longer.

I looked at Ben. He wasn't looking at Jameela, as I had suspected, but was staring at me. His eyes were soft and sad, as if he saw through me, and had X-rayed every inch of me, and he finally could see just how diseased and wretched I really was. And it was clear as day that he didn't care if I believed him or not. It was over. We were done. I did what he had predicted I would do and even his mother, who barely knew me, predicted too. I broke his heart.

He never said a word to Jameela French. He didn't even look in her direction. He stared at me longer, to make sure that I understood that there would be no second chance, and then he turned and walked out of my life.

Jameela left too, after telling me how bad he made her feel, how his refusal to so much as acknowledge that she once meant something to him, hurt her to her core. But I was too hurt myself to comfort her.

By the end of the week the writing was on the wall. I was at work when the announcement came.

"He's gonna do it!" Helen yelled and everybody in the newsroom gathered around the TV. I stayed at my desk. My hands were trembling as I tried to type. My heart was pounding so deeply that I thought each beat could be heard.

Governor Gibson walked up to the podium and made it official. "My administration and I are determined to fight sex harassment wherever it rears its ugly head," he said. "I, therefore, have no choice but to rescind the nomination of Benjamin Braddock to sit on the state supreme court."

The office, led by Mel and Helen, cheered. The *Gazette,* they said, singlehandedly brought that conservative hotshot down. The circuit court was next, they said. He should resign his current post there too.   ·

My stomach was knotted up all day. The mood was festive in the office, but I wasn't with it. Even when they were congratulating me. Me. The mouth of the South. The slash-and-burn queen who slashed and burned the only man she ever loved. Pardon me if I didn't jump for joy. Excuse my manners if I didn't dance on the side of the road. I wanted to die, not dance. I wanted to know beyond a doubt that I had done the right thing, not rejoice because another brother had been knocked down.

Later that day Mel called me into his office. He was so full of himself and his victory that I could hardly stomach him.

"What is it, Mel? I've got a lot to do."

"I know you're depressed—"

"I'm not depressed. Now what is it?"

"Okay, okay. Don't bite my head off. I have some good news for a change."

I looked at him. What was his game this time?

"Dinkle has approved my decision," he said.

"What decision?"

"I'm making you the *Gazette*'s newest assistant city editor. Effective immediately."

I hesitated. A dream job to be sure. "You're what?"

"You've arrived, Josie Ross, that's what. You've been promoted."

"I've been promoted?"

"Yes!" He stood up. "You've earned it."

I stood up too. "I guess you can say that."

"I know I can say it. Look, JR, Braddock's actions, not your stories, caused his downfall today, and you should be smart enough to understand that."

"What if it's not true?"

"Here we go."

"What if those women lied?"

"All three of them?"

"Yes."

"Jameela French too?"

I hesitated. It was implausible, but nothing was ever impossible. "Yes."

"No, Josie Ross. Hell no! Don't ever get to where facts fade into fiction, because when that happens, we all might as well go home. You followed the facts. Those stories checked out. That's a fact. Those women are credible. That's a fact. Ben Braddock would have set back civil rights fifty years or more. That's a fact too, kid. You followed the facts. Now you're vindicated. You did the right thing."

I wanted to believe him. I wanted to embrace every word he uttered. I was just following the facts. I was just doing my job. Ben chose to remain silent. He chose not to defend himself. And his silence could only mean guilt. But I was the one feeling guilty. I was the one feeling as if I had taken a knife and plowed it through his heart, and then had the nerve to get angry when he chose to feel the hurt from the stab wound, rather than stab back.

And that was the end of my three-month affair with Benjamin Braddock. Now it's two weeks later and I'm trying to go on with my life. I'm at the Stargate restaurant, a small bistro in Mayport, waiting for some blind date Scotty has set up for me. I needed to forget Ben, he said, and dating would be the shot in the arm I needed. So I threw on yet another one of my tight dresses and a pair of high heels and now I'm sitting in a back booth waiting.

A precondition of this particular blind date was that Scotty would show up too. He didn't have to stay if all went well, but if it didn't and the dude was not somebody I wanted to bother with, then he and his blind date selection could hit the road. Scotty acquiesced to my wishes so quickly that I wondered if I was missing something.

And I was. I'm realizing it now as Scotty enters Stargate, not with some hunk of a mystery man, but with Mel Sanchez, my boss. There was a third of a sherry left in my glass when they first walked into the restaurant, but by the time they make their way up to my table, not a drop is left.

"Hey, girl," Scotty says and sits at my booth. Mel, easily nervous too, sits beside him.

"Hello," he says.

I smile at them both, kick Scotty under the table, and try my best not to show my obvious displeasure. I don't play this shit. He's my boss and that's the way it's going to stay. But Mel and Scotty don't seem to think it makes any difference at all as they laugh and talk about everything from the Jaguars to the Gators, hamming it up big time as if their great repartee is supposed to relax me too. But all it succeeds in doing is heightening my impatience.

"I don't mean to be a party pooper," I tell them, "but I really think I'm going to just go home and get some rest. It's been a long day."

Mel gives Scotty such an odd look that I have to look at Scotty too. "You did tell her, right?" Mel asks him.

"Tell me what?"

"You said she said okay."

"I know, I know."

"Well, did she or didn't she, Scotty?"

"What are y'all talking about?"

"Scotty?"

"Look, Mel—"

"Don't look, Mel, me. Did you or did you not tell her?"

"I didn't quite get around to mentioning you by name. . . ."

"Oh, *man!*"

"What are y'all talking about?"

"I'm sorry about this, JR," Mel says. "He came to me with the idea. He said he talked to you about it. But it's obvious he didn't tell you a damn thing."

I look at Scotty. "No, he didn't."

Mel throws his napkin on the table and stands up. "You don't have to leave," he says. "I'll leave. I didn't think you'd go for this, I don't know what I was thinking either."

He looks so pathetic that I decide to cave. "We can still have dinner, Mel."

"Thanks, but no, I've got a lot to do at the office anyway. This was all Scotty's grand scheme, believe that."

"I was only trying to be helpful," Scotty says. "Damn."

"You were only trying to meddle in my business, Scotty," I say. "Pure and simple."

"And mine," Mel says, "which ain't necessary." Then he looks at me. "See you later, JR."

"Okay, Mel." And he leaves. And I kick the mess out of Scotty again.

"Ouch, woman!"

"Me and my boss? Are you insane?"

"It was a date for your horny ass. And he likes you. He even promoted you."

"Yeah," I said. "I rise up, Ben gets knocked down. That's some trade-off."

"It wasn't meant to be no trade-off and you know it."

"Do I?"

"Yes. Shit happens, Josie. I'm sorry but it does. But look on the bright side. At least he got to keep his judgeship."

"Which he'll probably lose next election."

"That's life, Josie, all right? Ain't nothing you or me can do about that. You didn't dredge up those women. You just reported on what they had to say. So you need to get over it, girl. I mean it."

He's right. There's a lot I need to get over.

"Will you at least take off your crown of thorns for one night and have dinner with me? We're already here."

I hesitate. Not because I want to say no, but because I want Scotty with his mismatchmaking schemes to sweat a little. "Okay," I finally say, and Scotty smiles.

We eat dinner slowly and talk about Scotty's new romance (Albert— an unemployed truck driver). He's nothing like Bruce, Scotty declares, but he does have his drawbacks too.

"Drawbacks? What drawbacks?"

Scotty doesn't answer right away. A terrible sign. "He was in prison before."

"In prison? For what?"

"It's his temper. Sometimes he just can't control it."

"Oh, Scotty!"

"But he's getting it together. He's taking anger-management classes at the Salvation Army."

"Scot-ty! You can't be serious! Why was he in prison? And don't tell me because of his temper. What did the brother do?"

Scotty sighs. "It was self-defense."

"He murdered somebody?"

"No! But he tried to."

"Oh my God, Scotty. Why do you keep putting yourself through this crap?"

He looks at his glass of wine. And there's a long hesitation. "I'll be forty-one in three weeks."

"I know that."

"And that witch called Loneliness is too bitchy for me."

I understand where he's coming from, I do. But damn. "A murderer, Scotty?"

"He didn't murder anybody."

"An attempted murderer then. He was just lucky the victim didn't die. That don't somehow elevate him. He's still shady."

"Maybe he is, Josie. But maybe he isn't. And I live my life hoping that he isn't. I don't like living like this but I don't see any alternatives out there for me. I'm not like you. People don't have to be perfect for me to love them. They don't have to be these great purveyors of all of your idealistic bullcrap, because I don't care if they don't have a brain in their head, just as long as they be with me and spend time with me and enjoy my company as much as I enjoy theirs."

I drop my dinner fork and lean back. "I don't expect perfection either, Scotty. Just honesty and integrity. I don't play you, you don't play me. That's not too much to ask!"

"Sure it's not. And that's why you're having dinner with me instead of some dream man you can easily get if you drop your guard a little and allow him in."

"Go to hell."

"I think I'm already there."

I look at Scotty. We're both loaded with all of this advice on love when neither one of us has a clue. "Let's just go," I say to him, and he agrees.

He waits for me to take the lead and then we head for the exit doors. This was supposed to be a cheer-up-Josie night for me but it's anything but. And to think I'll have to face Mel at work, who already's been getting on my last nerve as it is. What was Scotty thinking? Me and Mel?

My thought process stops cold, however, when I push open the exit door just as Ben is pulling it. I stop so suddenly that Scotty rams into the back of me, pushing me out and into Ben's arms. To my surprise he breaks my fall by catching me. Or is it just a reflex reaction?

He helps me stand erect, his big hands warm on my arms, his smell, still sweet and strong, relaxing me. "Thank you," I say. "Sorry about that."

Scotty makes his way outside too and Ben nods in his direction. "Hello, Scott."

"What's up?"

I can feel Ben's hand holding mine, and I expect him to let it go at any moment. But he doesn't. And we just stand there, unable to find words to say. But as soon as I look into his bright brown eyes, eyes that once emitted a powerful stare but now can only manage an almost grief-stricken gaze, he releases my hand.

"How you been?" I ask him.

"Okay," he says. "And you?"

"Good."

He nods. "Well, I don't mean to keep you folks from your business. . . ."

"You aren't keeping us from anything, Ben," Scotty says, surprised that he would even think so.

"Yeah, whatever," he says in a peculiar tone and then attempts to push open a door that you must pull to enter. He crashes into the glass, looks back at us and smiles an oddly sheepish smile, and then pulls the door open and hurries inside the restaurant.

Scotty and I both stand dumbstruck. Scotty even shakes his head. "The man is pitiful, girl."

"I've never seen him like this."

"Damn." Then Scotty looks at me. And I know what he's thinking because I'm thinking it too. But I can't.

"Why not?"

"Those women weren't lying, Scotty. All facts lead to the same conclusion: those women were telling the truth."

"But what if he's changed, Josie? What if he was like that once, but he turned his life around?"

"I ain't even trying to hear that, Scotty. That's the kind of bullshit you like to tell yourself. But I ain't having it, okay? Ain't that much changing in this world. Your wife is ill, needs you completely, and you're out banging your employee and then running her down because she won't keep seeing you? No way. I can't trust anybody like that. He did it to his first wife, what makes me think he ain't gonna do it to me? And what about Tonya Wright? She was his protégée, his prized student. And he fires her? Why? Nall, man, I don't want to hear it. Ain't that much changing in this world."

Scotty exhales and throws his arm around my waist. He understands. "Come on," he says and we walk, arm in arm, across the parking lot.

I lean against Scotty's car and fight the tears. Scotty leans against the car too. "Sometimes love doesn't work out," he says.

"Sometimes?"

He nods. "Most times. You're right. But it's still worth the plunge, Josie. Don't ever think that it isn't."

"I don't know about that. I've never been more off balance and out of sorts in my life than I've been since love paid me a visit."

"And you've never known such happiness either, have you?"

"Now?"

"Not now. But when it was working between you and Ben."

"Oh yes. When it was working it was great. But it usually didn't work."

"It usually don't, Josie. But when it does . . ."

"Bump it," I say, standing erect, certain now that no tears are coming tonight. "That's too long a shot for me. It's like living the exception rather than the rule. Most times you're going to be on a roller-coaster ride. But sometimes, you'll land. No, thanks. I ain't gettin' on the shit."

"So you've tried it one time, didn't like it, and that's it for Josie?"

"Damn straight. Once is a-fucking-'nuff. I want my life back."

"Your boring life?"

"That's right! My boring life. A life I was enormously happy with. I just didn't know it at the time."

"Why don't you go with me this weekend? It could really cheer you up."

"Go with you? Go with you where?"

"To Fort Myers, Josie. Remember? The art dealers convention? The one I attend every year? I told you about it two weeks ago, girl."

It's the last thing on my mind, going with Scotty to some boring convention, but I say I'll think about it just to get him off my back. Seeing Ben excited and depressed me at the same time. And just like that I'm thrown off balance. Those emotions again. Those roller-coaster rides again. I throw my hands in the air and without so much as a good-bye to Scotty, head for my Mustang. *Who needs this?* Scotty's calling my name but I don't even turn around. All I want to do is get away, get out, leave the scene, book, whatever the hell else it's called. I'm thrown by the littlest thing, like just seeing Ben again, and I can't live my life this way. Scotty's cussing me out, calling me everything but a child of God for just walking away like this, but I don't care. *I'm stopping the ride right here and right now and getting the hell off. He can keep on turning and hollering and believing all the fairy tales he wishes. But as for me? I am so out of here.*

WILD-GOOSE CHASE

Story after story and I'm running on autopilot. Cathy's bitching because I didn't give her the big baby kidnapping assignment even though she was the first reporter on the scene, but it's too big a story for her limited experience so I sent Eddie Harris instead. Coop's complaining because his story on the drug bust of a Jaguars player didn't make the front page, just the sports page, and I'm telling him that an athlete getting busted is no big deal anymore and he's telling me that I don't know what the hell I'm talking about. And Mel's sitting back and letting me handle it all and I'm about ready to tell him a thing or two but I can't, because a woman's waiting in my office and she's been waiting for nearly an hour as it is and I'm this close to telling Mel to take this so-called promotion and shove it but I've got to see what this woman wants first.

I exhale. "I'm sorry to keep you waiting," I tell her, "but it's been one of those days."

"Quite all right," she says and crosses her legs. She's one of those big, bosomy sisters, with an arrogant air about her even though she may be the sweetest person in the world. Her name turns out to be Katherine Marveaux and she was, until recently, a senior executive with the Ambri Corporation. Before I became assistant editor, I was working the Ambri case. The CEO publicly accused the city council president of misappropriating funds when she worked for Ambri back in the eighties, an allegation she denies, and this Katherine

Marveaux's here to tell me that the councilwoman is telling the truth.

"I was there," she says, "when it was all set up. It's a lie. A total fabrication. They're just trying to dissuade her from running against the mayor, who, as you know, used to be on their board of directors. They're just trying to bleed off some of her popularity."

As she talks I'm only half listening because I'm also trying to decide which reporter can handle the story. It's not a juicy one yet, but it could be, and the right reporter can make all the difference. Helen can handle it, but she wouldn't want it, and Cathy would want it, but she can't handle it, so I split the baby and settle on Andrea. Her writing is sometimes sloppy and she has been known to leave chunks of relevant information out of some of her stories, but with some guidance she can make it work. I'm, in fact, just about ready to tell my visitor to hold on a minute while I call in the reporter who will handle the story, when that visitor of mine says the damndest thing.

"I was shocked when you didn't get in touch with me," she says, and I'm immediately shocked myself.

"Why would I have gotten in touch with you?" I ask her.

"You were questioning everybody who worked for Councilwoman Hughes. I was certain you would check out the flip side too."

"What flip side?"

"Those who know the accuser. Shouldn't you talk to those people too? I mean, Ambri accused the councilwoman, not the other way around. They're the ones who should be investigated. And I don't mean you should talk to the people who Ambri recommends you talk to. They're good. They cover their tracks. You aren't going to find anything on them unless you look beyond the surface. And I mean well beyond. That's when you're find people like me, the proverbial disgruntled employee. We've got a lot to say and we're not hampered by any loyalty either."

And that's what throws me. They cover their tracks, she said. Talk to the people who know the accusers, she said. And I realize it as soon as she says it. That's what I didn't do, that's what Fred didn't do. We checked out Ben's background thoroughly, questioning everybody who worked for him. But what about the people who know his accusers? We were so focused on surface matters. Jameela French, on paper, checked out. And so did Tonya Wright. But it was all too neat. We should have caught it. They cover their tracks. They always cover their tracks. On paper Jameela French was this wonderful, conservative judge, a member of numerous conservative organizations, a grandmotherly figure with all the right words on paper. What more could there be? But what was behind the paper? What about the people who knew her, not the list of colleagues she recommended I speak with? Suddenly it's making sense to me. Ben stumbling around and running into glass doors, his entire world devastated on the strength of a damn paper tiger? We should have caught it. I was so busy watching the magician that the trick was pulled in plain view, right before my very eyes, but I was watching the wrong thing. I was watching Jameela French. Not the rabbits in her hat. And everybody has some rabbits somewhere. Everybody's got a trick or two up their sleeves. I think about Ben and the pain on his face when I invited that woman to my home, a woman I had just met, but all she had to do was tell her story and present her papers. I'm perfect, those papers said. She didn't have to prove a thing. She just had to show up. But Ben, the man I purported to love, had to do the impossible. He had to prove his innocence. Her word, I ate up. His wasn't enough. What in heaven's name was I thinking? What in heaven's name have I done?

I call Andrea into my office, tell her to get Katherine Marveaux's statement and take it from there, and then I hurry out of the *Gazette* building, jump into my Mustang, and drive like a bat out of hell to Baker County. Maybe everything will check out on Jameela French, maybe it won't. But I owe it to Ben to see, to at least take a closer look at the right things this time. I'm doing ninety in a fifty-five mile-an-hour zone, flying instead of driving, zooming in and out of lanes as if Interstate 10 were the Talladega Speedway, and just like that I'm on the roller-coaster ride I swore I'd never get on again. I'm thrown by events once more. But this time I don't have a choice.

Lynette Harris is Judge French's secretary. She's the one I want to see. But first I've got to check the docket. Wayne, the Baker County Courthouse security guard, is glad to see me when I walk in. He remembers me from my visits with Jameela and congratulates me again on my articles. He also doesn't hesitate to tell me that Judge French is in court right now, and it's a messy custody case that could take a while, and I thank him and hurry upstairs.

Lynette is behind her desk doing what she does best: running her mouth on the phone. When she sees me she waves me in, takes another two minutes telling her friend to let the dude spend up his money on her if he wants. "Then tell him to take a hike," she says. "But not before. You the fool if you don't take full advantage of his behind and then you drop him like a wet dog." And then she says her good-byes and hangs up.

"Hey, girl," she says. "I ain't seen you in a good lil' while."

"How you doing, Lynette?" I ask and help myself to a sit-down. She's around my age, but acts younger, with that teenage enthusiasm and bluntness. I like her. But right now, I need to use her.

"I'm doing good," she says. "But I'll be doing better when five o'clock rolls around."

"I hear that."

"I'm afraid you may have made a blank trip, though."

"Why you say that?"

"She's in court."

"Oh, is she?"

"Yeah, 'fraid so. They may not even break for lunch."

"Damn. That's tough. And all I needed was a little background information from her."

Lynette leans back. Her natural nosiness peaks her interest. "What kind of background information?"

"The *Gazette*'s doing a story on successful women and I thought Judge French would make a good candidate for one of the articles."

"Oh, she'll love that. But you already got enough information on her. Don't you?"

"I thought so. But you know how bosses are. They're never satisfied. They want a little dirt. Which doesn't make any sense to me. I mean, how can you want to praise these great women but at the same time ditch the dirt on them?"

"Tell me about it."

"But the bosses still want the dirt. They don't care. They want dirt. So I came by thinking that maybe Jameela can just give me something. I don't know."

"You ain't too good a reporter if you think Judge French is gonna gossip on herself. You ain't gettin' no dirt from her. She's an angel, if you listen to her."

"What about you?"

"Me? Hey, I'm an angel too."

I smile. "No, I mean, would you agree that she is?"

"Nobody's an angel, Josie, at least nobody I know. She's cool. She ain't perfect, but she's cool."

"You ever have any problems with her?"

"Not really. She get on my nerve sometimes with her complainin' about how slow I type, but other than that she's aw'ight."

"You ever hear her mention any trouble she may have had with anybody else?"

"You mean besides Judge Braddock?"

I nod my head. "Yes," I say, sadly, "besides Judge Braddock."

She thinks about it. Then she shakes her head. "Not really, no."

"Nobody?"

"Sorry."

"Don't be. My boss is gonna be ticked but hey, I'll just have to keep digging."

"Well . . ." she says, and my heartbeat begins to accelerate.

"Well what, Lynette?"

"There was this one girl. Judge French had to fire her."

"Really? Who was she?" I say this and take out my writing pad.

"Chick name Nancy Block. She was her secretary before I got the job. I replaced her, in fact. But from what I heard, this Nancy Block had it in for Judge French. She hated her. She even threatened to file a complaint with the Judicial Conduct Board. But she didn't go through with it."

"Why was she fired? And why did she hate Jameela so much?"

"Judge didn't like her politics, is what I heard."

My hope begins to dash. Is that all? "I see. She was a little too liberal for the judge, huh?"

"Too liberal?" Lynette says. "Hell nall. Too conservative."

I look at Lynette. Did she say what I thought she said? "What did you say?"

"Nancy Block wasn't no liberal. She was too conservative for Judge French's taste. Nancy, from what they told me, didn't believe in abortions and thought that women should be submissive to their husbands, stuff like that, and she and the judge argued about it all the time. Until the judge had enough of her."

I shake my head. I'm so excited I can hardly keep my seat. "You're confusing me now, Lynette. Why would a conservative judge like Jameela French have a problem with a conservative secretary?"

"That's what you wrote in that paper. Called Judge conservative, over and over. I wondered why."

"What you mean?"

"Ain't nothing conservative about Judge French, girl. Nothin'. You should see some of the papers she have me typing, where she's giving advice to all of these wacko organizations. I think she's on their payroll the way she's always writing to them."

"What kind of organizations?"

"The Women's this and the Women's that, I can't remember those names. But you know the ones. They always be talking about how women should have the same rights as men and should be paid the same and all."

"Do you have copies of any of these letters?"

"Me? No way. Judge don't play that. I type 'em while she be standing right beside me. That's why she's always complaining that I type too slow. If she wasn't standing over me like some dark shadow that wouldn't be a problem, you know? But she stands right here and waits for me to finish."

"But her court decisions are conservative. Or at least moderate. She's no flaming liberal on the bench by any means."

"Oh, she play the game now. This Macclenny. This ain't Jacksonville. These country-ass folks round here ain't havin' no liberal nothing on their benches, and you know what I'm talking about. She play the game."

And so she does. Plays it damn well too. She certainly played me.

After some searching that I just know will be interrupted by Jameela suddenly returning from court and squashing the whole thing, Lynette manages to find me an address for Nancy Block: 238 Booker Avenue, right here in Macclenny.

I get directions from Lynette, race to my Mustang, and fly like hell to Booker Avenue. It's a dead-end street across the railroad tracks; 238 is a shack house surrounded by lazy-looking dogs. Reminds me of Tuscaloosa. I blow my horn a couple of times, but no one responds. So I take a chance. I get out of my car and hurry to the front door, the dogs checking me out but then, as I was hoping, ignoring me.

"Yes?" an older black woman in a blue housedress asks as she comes to the door. "May I help you?"

"Hello, ma'am, I'm looking for Nancy. Nancy Block. Is she at home?"

"Nancy? She don't live here."

Panic sets in. I need to see this woman and I need to see her fast. "This is 238 Booker Avenue, isn't it?"

"Yes, it is. But Nancy don't live here. She moved two, three years ago."

"But you know her?"

"I should think so. She my granddaughter."

Some relief anyway. "Do you know where she moved to?"

"She my granddaughter. I should think so."

I wait. No response. "I'm an old friend of hers, we worked together at the courthouse, you see, and I just wanted to say hello to her. Can you give me her address and phone number?"

"She ain't got no phone. But her address is—"

"Just a minute," I say and hurriedly pull out my writing pad. "Okay."

"Fourteen four-twelve Northwest Sixty-forth Street."

"How can I get to it?"

"How?"

"I mean, could you give me some directions?"

"She in Miami."

Tell me she didn't say Miami. "Miami?"

"Yes. She moved from Macclenny two, three years ago."

"And relocated to Miami?"

"That's right."

"And she doesn't have a phone?"

"That's right."

"What do you do when you want to get in touch with her? Is there a neighbor or other relative or friend that you can call?"

"Ain't no kin of mine in no Miami except Nancy. I don't even know why she there. All them Cubans down there, and Haitians. What she doing there? And she ain't got no phone and I don't know none of her friends. She calls me from a phone booth every once in a while and I writes her when I can get somebody to dictate a letter for me. My eyesight ain't what it used to be."

I smile weakly at the old woman. This is just great. But nobody said retracing steps was easy. Besides, this should have been looked into long ago. "Where does she work in Miami? Do you know?"

"Why you need to know all that?"

"Because I can maybe call her at work, and we can talk."

"She don't have no job right now. At least she told me she didn't."

"What about a boyfriend?"

"She don't be telling me nothing about her boyfriends and all of that. And I don't wanna know nothing about it."

"Okay. But can you give me some idea where this Sixty-forth Street is located in Miami?" I say this and flip the page. I'd never been to Miami a day in my life. But it looks like I'm going now.

"She told me she lives near some kind of center and a lot of liquor stores."

"But what part of town?"

"What part? Liberty City all I know," she says.

"I don't believe I'm doing this," Scotty says as we fly up Interstate 75 in his Miata, his top down and my braids floating on the wind. I recruited Scotty because he once lived in Miami and knows the place like the back of his hand, although I'm not so sure if it was a great idea to let him drive.

"Don't kill us, Scotty."

"Don't talk to me. You couldn't go with me to the art dealers convention in Fort Myers, oh no, that's too boring for you. But as soon as you want me to go somewhere, you expect me to just drop everything and run. Don't talk to me."

"Okay, I won't. Just slow down."

"This wild-goose chase. That's all this is. A wild-goose chase. What if she ain't got nothing to say, Josie?"

"Then we'll come back home. But I owe it to Ben to see."

"And if it's true, what's the end game?" He says this and look at me.

I lean back. "I apologize to Ben."

"And if he don't wanna hear it?"

"Then he won't, Scotty, I can't do anything about that."

Scotty shakes his head. "I hope you know what you're doing is all I got to say," he says.

Because of his inability to drive any way but fast, we arrive in Miami a full hour sooner than is normally the case. Miami, Florida. A big, sprawling metropolis where mansions and ghettos abound.

It's like a maze to me, where streets are one way and then dead-end and then flip over into an entirely different part of town, but I'm glad I recruited Scotty because he knows his way around. Sixty-forth Street is in the hood, in Liberty City just like Nancy's grandma said, and Nancy's place is above a pool hall whose front is a building-length mural of Martin Luther King.

She's not home. We ask around, from the old ladies hurrying by with their plastic shopping bags, to the old men playing cards in front of the pool hall, to the young men on the street corners, trying to hustle Rap CDs and T-shirts. We find out more than we will ever need to know about Nancy Block, but we also find out that she works at a liquor store on Seventy-first.

And that's where we find her. At Topaz Liquors. She's behind the cash register watching *All My Children* on television in between serving her customers. She fit the description given to us by her neighbors: In her late thirties, dark skinned, thin as a rail.

"Nancy Block?" I ask as I walk up to her. Scotty walks slower, behind me, more defensive because he knows the area.

"Depends on who wants to know," she says.

"My name is Josie Ross. I'm a reporter with the *Jacksonville Gazette.*"

"The *Jacksonville Gazette?*" She looks at Scotty and then back at me. "What's this about?"

"We're doing a story on Judge Jameela French, and we heard you once worked for her."

"Again, what's this about?"

Get to the point, Josie, in other words. "She fired you. I wanna know why."

A customer sets a pint of whiskey on the countertop. She rings the order. "We didn't get along," she says.

"And?"

"Ain't no *and*. Me and the bitch just didn't click. That's it."

I look at Scotty. She's got to give me more than this. We didn't come all this way for *this*. "What kind of person was she to work for?"

The customer pays and leaves. Nancy Block sighs and folds her arms. "Look, I don't know what this is about and I ain't got nothin' to say, okay? You wastin' your time here."

"I heard she fired you because of your beliefs. That's illegal, you know."

"What's illegal? What you talkin' about?"

Now Scotty sighs. "You're a conservative, right?"

"A what?"

Scotty looks at me. "Wild-goose chase, girl," he says.

"I was told that Judge French hated your politics," I say to her. "Your pro-life stance? Your belief in traditional values?"

I may as well be talking Greek because sister girl ain't feeling it.

"First of all," she says, "I was fired because me and Judge French didn't get along. Period. My politics wasn't none of her business. Besides, I didn't have no politics, okay? Now whoever told you that I did, they didn't know what they were talking about. Just runnin' off at the mouth, like you're doing now."

I shake my head. That damn Lynette and her grapevine. I could kill her! I look at Nancy. "I'm sorry to disturb you," I say.

"That's it?" Scotty asks.

"She doesn't know anything."

"She might. You haven't asked her."

"She said it's not true. She wasn't fired because of her politics."

"Look, lady," Scotty says to Nancy, "was there anybody else? Did Judge French get rid of anybody while you worked for her?"

"She got rid of a lot of people. I worked for her for six years."

"Does anybody stand out?"

"Not really."

"Think hard, Nancy, please," I say. "Did anybody have any arguments with the judge or differences of opinion with her?"

"Hell yeah."

"Anybody in particular, Nancy?"

She immediately smiles. "There was somebody."

Scotty and I look at each other. "Who?" I ask her.

"She gave Judge French hell. She was a trip. If Judge said it was white, she declared it was black. She was cool."

"What was her name?"

"Karla. Karla Davenport. She clerked for the judge."

"And Judge French fired her?"

"She quit before she got the chance. Judge was going to fire her, but Karla was too smart to just sit back and let somebody get rid of her."

I pull out my writing pad, praying that this isn't more wrong information. "What did they argue about?"

"Everything. Now Karla, she was the conservative."

I look up. "Are you sure?"

"Hell yeah. She was conservative and a black girl too, can you imagine that? But she was."

"What do you mean by conservative?" Scotty asks her, rightfully suspicious.

"Some blacks in Macclenny were gonna sue this bar because the owners made the whites sit on one side of the bar and the blacks had to sit on the other side. Karla didn't see anything wrong with that. If the blacks didn't like it, they shouldn't go there, that's how she saw it. But Judge French, man, she cussed Karla out. She talked about how she fought her entire life against discrimination and racial bigotry and she wasn't gonna let some Aunt Jemima Negro like Karla turn back the hands of time; oh, she told the girl about herself."

I smile and look at Scotty. "Perfect," he says.

"Do you know if Karla Davenport is still in Macclenny?"

"I doubt it. She was from Georgia. She probably went back there."

My smile fades. "Where in Georgia?"

"Atlanta."

"You're certain?"

"Yeah, I'm certain. Me and Karla was tight back in the day. And when she quit she told me she was going back to Atlanta. Going home."

"You wouldn't happen to have an address or phone number for her. Would you?"

She shook her head. "When I left Macclenny I wasn't keepin' up with all that stuff."

I look at Scotty. He throws his hands in the air. "Forget it, girl. I am not about to drive to no Atlanta too. Not today. You can forget that."

I look at Nancy. My mind is in overdrive. *Go*, it says, and then *no, call first.* Good idea. *Call directory assistance for the Atlanta area, pray she has a phone in her name, and call first.* "Can I use your phone?"

"There's a booth out back," she says.

I hurry to the booth. Scotty follows me. And within the hour Scotty's in his Miata driving back to Jacksonville, and I'm on a plane heading for Atlanta.

She agreed to meet me that same day, at the Buckhead Café on Peachtree Street. My flight, from Miami to Atlanta, takes a little over an hour and I take a cab to the restaurant. I'm early. Nearly two hours early. But I eat and relax and try to get my notes together. The good news is that she seemed anxious to talk. The bad news is that she will talk only if I never reveal her name. Mel hates anonymous sources, especially on a story he'll probably have to be convinced to run, but I agreed to her terms anyway.

I call Mel, tell him only that I'm following up on a juicy story that I'll fill him in on later, but he wants details. When I won't bite, he settles. "Please tell me that this juicy story somehow connects to something at least relevant to the *Gazette*, Josie, please tell me that much." I tell him that he can say that and before he can ask for further clarification, Karla Davenport walks in.

"Gotta go, Mel," I say and hang up.

She's wearing a brown pantsuit, just as she said she would, and sits near the back wall, as planned. I go back to my table, grab my drink and papers, and walk over to where she's sitting. She's younger than I imagined, she can't be any more than twenty-five, and she's nervous as hell. I smile. "Hey," I say.

"Hey."

"Mind if I join you?"

She looks at me, and then around me, and then reluctantly nods.

"Relax," I say as I'm sitting down. "Nobody's following me or filming us or anything like that."

"I know. I'm just . . . What did you say your name was?"

"Josie. Josie Ross."

"And my name will not be used?"

"Not ever."

"Who told you about me?"

"Would you like something to drink?"

"No. Who gave you my name?"

"Nancy Block."

She nods. This gives her a little relief. "What do you want to know?"

"Why did Jameela French fire you?"

"She didn't."

"But you quit before she could. Why?"

She sighs. "She didn't like the way I viewed things. She felt that she and her law clerk should be on the same page. We weren't."

"Politically?"

"Right."

"You were too conservative for her?"

"Yes."

"So what are you? One of those fringe dwellers? One of those far-right-wing ideologues?"

"No, I'm not. I have some conservative views, but I consider myself pretty moderate. But she didn't want a moderate. She wanted a left-wing zealot like herself."

"A zealot? Judge French?"

"Yes. Absolutely."

"But . . . her opinions aren't liberal."

"A lot of them are. If you look closely."

"Okay, so you decided to quit because you and she just couldn't agree. Is that it?"

"Yes. After I found out about SOS she acted as if I had the goods on her. I wasn't thinking about that woman, honestly, but she just didn't believe it."

"SOS?"

"Yes." And then she frowns. "That's why you're here. Isn't it?"

"Yes, of course," I say, trying like hell not to show my ignorance. "But why don't you explain the whole deal to me again, just explain it to me, because I'm not sure if I understand it. And also tell me your role in all of this."

"I found out about it, that's my role. I didn't mean to, but Judge was out sick one day and I was like in charge of the office. So I took a little liberty and made her office my own, for a day. So I was looking around in her office, maybe even snooping, I don't know, but I ran across this disk. It was in one of her locked desk drawers, where she keeps a lot of her personal stuff, but she had, mistakenly, I'm sure, left the keys. We weren't getting along particularly well anyway, so I decided to check it out. Why not? I didn't owe her anything. It was a disk filled with all of this old e-mail. And every letter was from somebody using the name SOS. SOS One, or SOS Two, SOS Three, and so on. And they were all talking about how this nomination of this person has been withdrawn, or this other person lost by a landslide, and on and on. And they would say how SOS strikes again, or SOS does it again. Naturally I'm extremely curious by now. So I revisit this desk drawer. And there's more disks. And I find out quite a bit about SOS. That next day, I come to work and she's waiting for me. And she knows. She knows that I'd been reviewing her disks."

"Somebody told her?"

"The computer told her. They were Word documents. . . ."

"Right. At the end of the File menu it lists the last programs that were run."

"It didn't even occur to me."

"Did you make copies of the disks?"

"They were all write-protected. I couldn't. And her printer wasn't working. At least I couldn't figure out how to get it to work."

"Damn."

"She was astounded to see that disks she rarely ran at all were dominating the menu. So who but me, she decided, even would have bothered? She wanted to know all I knew, but I wasn't telling her a darn thing, and she said okay. But she did not hesitate to remind me that SOS is a powerful organization, and if I ever wanted to practice law or even work as a maid somewhere, I had better be discreet. That's all she said. I asked her to explain herself but she wouldn't. 'That's all, Miss Davenport,' she said. So I knew what time it was. And I quit."

"But tell me about this SOS. What is it?"

"It stands for Sisters of the Struggle."

"Sisters of the Struggle?"

"Yes. They're women from all around the country but they work in cells, by state."

"You mean there's a Florida group and a Georgia group, and so on?"

"Right. Judge French heads the Florida group."

"Do you know any of the other members?"

"Almost all of the names that I saw I never heard of."

"Was Tonya Wright one of those names?"

"I don't think so."

"Damn."

"But she could be a member, and probably is."

I look up. "Why do you say that?"

"She and Judge French. They're friends. She visited the judge a few times when I worked there and she and I would talk. She was an attorney and she would give me some pointers, you know, because I was still a law clerk then. She and Judge always tried to act as if their relationship was purely professional, but they seemed chummy to me."

"But you didn't see her name as one of the members?"

"No, but that doesn't mean much. I saw only a few names."

"What about Marlene Wingate? You remember that name?"

"No. I never heard of her."

"To be honest with you," I say to her, "I've never heard of SOS."

"You aren't supposed to have heard of it. From what I could gather, they don't have meetings, or even a whole lot of phone calls. They usually communicate through e-mail."

"Why e-mail?" I ask her.

"I don't know."

"It sounds so clandestine."

"They make it their business to stay out of the spotlight. So many women's groups are pigeonholed because of that very reason. Too much publicity. But they're more issue-driven activists than publicity hounds."

"And what are their issues?"

"They are a group of women who work tirelessly to slow down what they call the 'right-wing agenda' in government, the judiciary, and education. There may be other areas too, but those were the ones I ran across."

"How do they slow it down?"

"Propaganda."

"But how?"

"They're slick, Miss Ross—"

"Josie, please."

"They're real slick. They don't do that wide-open stuff. They hit hard and run, cover their bases, they don't leave anything, and I mean anything, to chance."

"And according to those e-mails they've had some successes?"

"Oh yes. Plenty. And the targets apparently never knew what hit them. From important school board appointments to federal judge-ships, they don't play around. They seem to pick their enemy based on what they perceive as the level of threat this person poses, and then they strike. And hard."

I lean back and I'm scared and excited. "Did they have anything to do with Braddock's derailment?"

She shakes her head. "Braddock?"

"Yeah. The judge Governor Gibson recently nominated to be on Florida's Supreme Court. You haven't heard about that?"

"No, I haven't. Since I left Florida I don't keep up with Florida news. But that name—"

"Braddock?"

"Yeah. Donald or . . ."

"Benjamin Braddock?"

Her youthful face lights up. "Yeah. Him. He's on the list."

The list? I lean forward. "What list?"

"One of those SOS e-mails contained a list for Judge French. A list of their next targets. That's not what they called them. They called them their next projects, but it was obvious what they meant. I wrote down the names."

"And Benjamin Braddock was on that list?"

"Yes. Along with twelve, no, eleven other judges. They had a list of judges, school board officials, and political appointees."

"May I see the list?"

She's not ready to go that far. But I lean forward. I've got to see that list. "Karla, this is vital. All I need are the names, that's all."

She hesitates again. And then she produces a sheet of paper from her pocketbook, a small, crinkled, handwritten sheet of paper that carries more value to me right now than a million bucks. I contain myself long enough to very politely receive the paper from her hand, and then I write down each name so fast that my fingers begin to cramp. But she's right. Ben's name is near the top. When I see his name, I feel as if a heavy load were being lifted from me.

"But you can't mention my name," Karla enjoins me as I hand her back the list. "I'm just starting out good. With a corporate firm who hates publicity of any kind. You can't, in any way, tie me to this. I hope you use it. And I hope you somehow manage to do to her what she and her group do to others, but I can't be a party to it."

"Karla, trust me," I say to her, "you've done more than enough. You'll never know what this means to me. Thank you. Thank you so much."

*   *   *

But my roller-coaster ride isn't over yet. I fly back to Jacksonville and arrive at JIA at eight-thirty that night. I catch a cab to the *Gazette* and hurry to the computer in my office. Only a skeletal crew is still at the newsroom and I'm thankful that Mel's nowhere to be seen. I quickly click to the Internet and go to FloridaNews.com. I search information on every judge on the list, except, of course, Ben. Articles turn up left and right on each one of them. I don't find anything negative on three of the judges, and one judge died of natural causes, but the remaining seven judges have two very glaring similarities: all are known for their conservative views and each one was forced to withdraw his name from a possible judgeship, or lost an election for a judgeship, or was asked to resign his current judgeship after allegations surfaced accusing each one of them of some form of sexual misconduct. I lean back and exhale. There it is. In black and white. Ben was telling the truth.

But I know Mel and Dinkle and everybody else who works for this paper. They're going to want more. And I want more too, before I go to Ben.

So the next day I'm at it again. I search through my desk, rifling through it, until I turn up the Jameela French file. Six organizations are listed, all conservative, all she is supposedly a member of in good standing. I search the phone book and find phone numbers for all six organizations. Five of the six answer the phone. One refuses to give out any information on membership, but the other four admit that Jameela French is on their rolls but she is not active in any way. One group, the very conservative, anti-abortion Life First Association, even admits that she has yet to attend her first meeting, although she has been a card-carrying member for well over nine years.

And for me, this seals the deal. Jameela French, on paper, was flawless. But behind the paper, behind the facade of conservative consciousness, she was as phony as the teary-eyed speech she gave to Ben. A con is only as good as the willingness of its participants. And I, with my fanatical liberalism, was more than willing to believe Jameela French over Ben, because her papers were too orderly and therefore caught me off guard, and because her life itself was the bait. And Mel, sitting behind his desk, his legs propped up, his beliefs certain, is a willing conspirator too. In the name of justice, in the name of civil rights, we alone decided that we could destroy whomever the hell we wished, and it doesn't touch us, because the ends justify the means, when the means don't justify anything, and we know they don't, but we do it anyway.

I have my story, the story that should have been written when the allegations first came to light, but I can't deal with Mel or Dinkle or anybody else right now. Not now. Ben has a right to know first. We all colluded somehow in destroying him, but there will be no collusion when I go before him, not to rationalize what I've done, but to tell it like it really is for a change, to slash and burn my own ass, and try for once in my life to get it right.

QUE SERA SERA

I am in the parking lot of the Duval County Judicial Complex, waiting beside Ben's car. It's after five so I know he'll be here soon. But I can't keep still, walking and fidgeting and mumbling to myself. In my head I'm rehearsing my speech, over and over, and I still don't know if I can pull it off. Why should he even listen to me? He said I was going to break his heart, and I did, case closed. What's there to talk about? I consider walking away. Just write the story and deal with this shit tomorrow. *Que sera sera.* What will be, will be.

But then I see him. He's heading my way. I feel doomed. I feel as if I don't stand a chance. I try to stand erect, but my balance is shot, so I lean, trying to look casual, trying not to show the nerves of clay bubbling inside me. And he looks so gorgeous, why does he always look so gorgeous? He's wearing a dark gray suit, perfectly tailored to every muscle on his body, and he has a cigarette between his fingers. He moves fast and sure, confident despite his setbacks, until he sees me. When he sees me, his movement becomes lumbering, almost hesitant. I stand erect again and can only hope that everything's in place: my hair, my African kitenge suit, my smile. But he doesn't return my smile. I don't know if he can.

"Ben, hi!" I say with an overexaggerated enthusiasm.

"Hello," he says with no enthusiasm at all. He continues to look guardedly at me, sizing me up, wondering just what am I up to now. But he doesn't say a word, causing us to stand there like strangers beside his car.

"So, how you been?" I ask him.

He folds his arms. The hurt is still there. "What is it, Josephine?"

"I need to talk to you."

"Talk."

"Not here. Could we go somewhere?"

He looks at me, at my clothes and then my face. "I don't think that's necessary. Now what is it?"

"I promise I won't take up that much of your time."

"I know you won't because whatever you have to say you can say it here."

"*Ben,*" I say, and the urgency in my voice compels him to hear me. Even his tone softens.

"What?" he says.

"We need to talk. You don't even have to drive me. I'll follow in my car. But I think it's something you really ought to hear."

He still hesitates, still stares at me, but then, seemingly against his every instinct, he agrees to go along. He doesn't say anything, but he begins moving toward his driver's-side door.

"Where're we going?" I ask him.

"I'm going home," he says. "You may follow if you wish."

I follow him. I follow him as if my car were chained to his. Through downtown, across the Matthews Bridge, down the unbearably long Atlantic Boulevard stretch, to Portland Road. Destiny's Child is singing "I'm a Survivor" on my car stereo and I'm pumped up, ready to make my case. But when his Seville pulls into the driveway of his home and I park my Mustang beside it, that nervous queasiness comes over me again and I'm forgetting every word of the speech I had so carefully laid out.

He stands beside his car, waiting for me to get out of mine. I walk toward him slowly and I can see on his face that his irritation has turned into marked curiosity. And his look alone lifts my hopes again. *I can do this,* I tell myself. *He'll understand.*

He doesn't understand. I can see it all over his face. We're in the kitchen. He's preparing his dinner and I'm seated at the counter watching him. He's seasoning skinless chicken strips and boiling water for his pasta. Then he sips from his glass of wine and looks at me. "Why?" he asks.

I started out slowly, telling him only that I believed him, without presenting my evidence of his innocence, but that may not have been the best strategy to employ.

"I believe you, Ben."

"You believed me before. Remember? Right at this house on my patio out there, you said no matter what you would believe me. Then some woman shows up and you suddenly believe her. Now you believe me again? After all that's happened? Credibility isn't lining up favorably here."

"But this time is different, Ben."

"What's different about it, Josephine? My story hasn't changed. It was all a pack of lies then, it's still a pack of lies now."

"But I found out some things."

He smiles and nods his head. "That figures. My word is never good enough for you."

"That's not what's going on here."

"Yes, it is. That's exactly what's going on here. Don't fool yourself."

"Will you just hear me out? Please?"

He sips more wine and stares at me. "What have you found out?" he asks.

I brace myself. This is it. Sink or swim time. "Jameela French is a member of an organization called SOS."

He says nothing, just stares at me.

"SOS stands for Sisters of the Struggle. It's a liberal women's group." I say this and look at him to gauge his reaction. There is no reaction. "Did you hear me, Ben? I said Jameela French is a member of an extremist, left-wing women's group. Aren't you surprised by that?"

He shakes his head. "No."

"No? How can you say that? Jameela French presented herself as this bastion of conservatism."

"Not to me she didn't."

"You mean to tell me you knew she wasn't conservative?"

"Yes."

"But . . . why didn't you tell me that, Ben?"

"You never asked."

"What are you saying? I begged you to tell me about your relationship with her."

"Stop playing games with yourself, Josephine. All you cared about was whether or not I had sex with that woman or if I had harassed her for sex. I told you no on both concerns, you didn't believe me, there was nothing further to talk about."

My heart is pounding. Was I that far gone? Was I so arrogant and short-sighted that I didn't even try to get beyond the obvious? I look at Ben, and our eyes meet. He looks away from me.

"What does this SOS group have to do with me?" he asks, with only a quick glance in my direction.

I can barely speak, but I continue to anyway. "The goal of SOS is to make sure that conservative voices are not heard in the political arena. Voices like yours. You get nominated for a high post, they de-rail that nomination. And they're good. Oh, man."

"And Jameela's a member?"

"Yes. And I think Tonya Wright too, although I'm not certain of that yet. Did you know that Tonya Wright and Jameela French were friends?"

"No," he says.

"They apparently were. And with the backing of SOS they con-spired to bring you down."

He sighs. "What about that Marlene Wingate? She's a member too?"

"I haven't been able to tie her to any of it. I figure she's just some-body who jumped on the bandwagon, that's all. The *Gazette* was looking for trash and she volunteered her supply."

He smiles weakly, derisively. "It's a strange feeling."

"What?"

"To be hated by so many people when you didn't even know you were disliked." He says this and looks at me. He once had confidence in Tonya Wright and Jameela French. Believed they were sisters with possibilities. But they broke his heart too.

"Where did this information come from?" he aks me. "I know Jameela didn't volunteer it."

"I have a source. A confidential source."

"How do you know this source is on the level?"

"I know."

He shakes his head. "You amaze me," he says. "A stranger can tell you anything and you believe it. But me, oh boy."

"I should have believed you, Ben."

"Yeah, you should have. But you couldn't, could you? I don't think it's in your makeup. Unless the proof is irrefutable and in black and white, you'll never believe anything a man tells you. A man is supposed to be a lying, cheating dog. You're predisposed to think that way. That's how you operate."

"But they lied on you. And used me to help their cause. But it'll all come to light. I guarantee you that."

"Don't do it for me, Josephine. Do it for journalism or for right and wrong or for your own satisfaction. But don't do it for me."

"I wish I never doubted you."

"Yeah, me too," he says and sips more wine.

"But you didn't give me anything to hold on to, Ben. I begged you to, but you wouldn't."

He looks at me. "You're blaming me?"

"No. Of course not. But you knew Jameela French and Tonya Wright. You could have told me more."

"I told you they were lying!" he yells bitterly, angrily. "What more do people want from me?"

The disappointment in his eyes is unbearable. Fred said he couldn't take another heartbreak, and he may have been right. But as quickly as Ben riled up, he has just as quickly calmed back down.

"It doesn't make much difference anyway," he says.

"But it does make a difference, how can you say that? It's not right what happened to you."

"I've submitted my resignation, Josephine."

My heart drops. "Ben, no!"

"I've been a judge for almost nineteen years. That's a long damn time. Long enough anyway."

"But you can't give up like this. You can't let them win."

"Stop telling me what I can't do."

"But why? We can turn public opinion around, Ben. We can prove that you were telling the truth all along and those women were up to something, that they did have an agenda."

"No."

"But you've got to fight."

"I've lost my moral authority, Josephine, don't you understand that? I'm done. I've had it up to here with these goddamn liberals who seek to destroy me just because I disagree with them. I'm tired of explaining myself and dignifying their nonsense and excusing their behavior!"

"But that's why you've got to fight. You can expose this thing, Ben. We can expose it."

He looks at me, not as if he's understanding what I'm saying, but as if he wants me to clearly understand what he's saying. "I'm done, Josephine. Understand me well. I am done."

His eyes aren't exhibiting anger, as I had assumed they would, but bitterness, hard, cold bitterness, and it's entrenched, like a comfortable, almost placid defeat. He's not taking it anymore. No more heartbreaks. No more disappointments. No more roller-coaster rides for him.

I take my notepad, the one loaded with all of this remarkable information about SOS and his accusers, and place it in my bag. My fear of what this all means is so intense that I can hardly keep myself from shaking. I look at Ben.

"What about us?" I ask him.

The look he gives me causes me to shutter.

"Us?"

I swallow hard. "Yes."

"There is no *us*, Josephine. *Us* became no more when you allowed Jameela French to tell you, the woman who was supposed to love me, who I was. You knew me . . ." He says this so bitterly that he chokes up and has to calm himself back down before he can continue. "You know me, Josephine. You knew I wasn't capable of what those women were claiming. But I couldn't prove my innocence. My proof was nothing more than my word. And thereafter your first impression of me kicked in. I was this conservative asshole after all, you knew it all along, and too much suspicion surrounded me as it was. But in the end there was no proof on their side either. That's why it initially didn't bother me. Truth always wins out. It was their word against mine. But my word, for you, wasn't good enough. That hurts, you know? I was beginning to think that I could count on you, that you were different. You'd stick by me. Nobody else did, but you would. But I was wrong, as usual."

My heart can barely take it. I feel sick to my stomach, and exhausted, my body almost lifeless with anguish. I realize clearly now how badly I hurt him. I *hurt* him. And it's a devastating thought.

"You once wanted to know why I learned to cook," he continues, as if I can bear more. "I said necessity, and that was true. I thought I would spend the rest of my life caring for my ill wife, and I was pre-

pared to spend the rest of my life doing so. But she died unfortunately, and it was painful. She didn't deserve the life she got. But I re-
covered and tried to move on, I even started dating. And falling in
love. And getting used over and over again. All I wanted was companionship. That's all. But that's not what I got. But in your idealistic world, it's the woman who gets used and abused. Never the man.
A man has no heart to break, you see? Well, this man does. And he's
not getting used again. There's an old saying: if you find a willing
horse, ride it. And every woman I've ever known has done just that.
But this horse isn't willing anymore."

He pauses and stares at me, through me, dissecting every inch of
me once more, killing me again and again with his eyes. "So don't
talk to me about *us*," he says. "There is no *us*. Thanks to you." The
dagger is in, and I'm bleeding to death, but he decides to twist it ever
so slightly. "And by the way," he adds, "congratulations on your
promotion."

It's like drowning. The water's filling my lungs and consuming
me, and I'm kicking and kicking and pushing against the tide. But it's
too much water. That's how I feel, as I head for his front door.
There's too much water. I jumped in, and I thought I was swimming,
but I wasn't swimming at all. I wasn't showing my independence
when I didn't believe Ben. I wasn't this great victorious woman because I didn't let some man dupe me. That's not swimming. That's
sinking. I was sinking with the baggage that contained all of my fears
and all of my preconceived notions, baggage that had weighed me
down. Now it was drowning me. I didn't know it then. But I know it
now. Now, when I'm trying to come up for air, and I can't even see
the top. There's too much damn water.

Larry Dinkle and Mel Sanchez listen to everything I have to say.
They don't interrupt, they don't even allow their true feelings to surface. When I'm done, they look at each other. And Mel laughs. "I'm
very familiar with the vast right-wing conspiracy," he says. "But a
left-wing one? You've got to be kidding!"

"Has Jameela French admitted that she belongs to SOS?" Dinkle
asks.

"She denies any involvement in the group. But she's definitely involved. I've also investigated her so-called conservative ties in the
community. Although she's a member of conservative organizations

on paper, it's all window dressing to keep the hounds off. She doesn't even attend any meetings of these conservative groups, nor is she active in any way. She's just a name on a roll."

"And because of that you now believe everything she said is untrue?"

"I know it is, Larry. She heads the Florida chapter of SOS. She's one of the founding members in fact. It's my theory that she knew Ben was going places and she was determined to have something on him. So she works for him for a few months and quits, does that little hospital scene, mentions it to a few other members of the group, and holds on to her knowledge until the right time arrives. That's how SOS works. They know how to pick their moments. When Governor Gibson nominated Ben to the supreme court, that was the right time. And she came forward. Same thing with Tonya Wright. They picked their time."

"Wait a minute," Mel says, leaning forward. "This is some far-fetched plot you're expecting us to believe, JR. Nobody's that clever."

"Oh, yes, they are, Mel. That's why conspiracies work. Most people refuse to believe they even exist. SOS depends on that disbelief. They cover their tracks in every way. They're the ones who derailed Judge Midland's nomination to the federal bench last year, and Joe Issel's the year before. They've had many successes. I could go on and on."

Dinkle's taking my information seriously. He leans back and takes it all in. Mel, on the other hand, is his usual skeptical self. But Dinkle is the one who counts. "Braddock submitted his resignation. You know that?"

"Yes," I say, regretfully. "Our stories ruined his career."

"Who the hell cares about his career?" Mel says. "He's the enemy, JR, how many times do I have to tell you that?"

Dinkle agrees. "In the end," he says, "Mel's right. Printing this information will only help Braddock and his conservative headhunters and undermine an organization who just might have figured it out."

I almost did a double take. "Figured what out?"

"How to beat the right wingers at their own game. This is wonderful if it's true, Josie. SOS is not a bad thing. They're the good guys. Exposing them will be crazy."

"But they lied, Larry! They lied on Ben Braddock."

"Ah, come on. Braddock's yesterday's news. Who cares about him?"

"Everybody should care, when it's a question of somebody's rights. An injustice has been perpetrated here and we participated in the con."

Dinkle shakes his head. "We didn't participate in anything. Ben Braddock was a bad choice, I'm sorry, but he was. Governor Gibson was totally out of line for even considering him in the first place. It's too bad if Braddock's reputation got a little messy in the process—"

"A *little* messy?"

"Yes. A little messy. But it's a positive thing."

"I see. The Machiavellian approach again. Is that it?"

"That's right. The ends do justify the means sometimes, Josie."

"Especially when we're not the ones the means are being justified on."

"What's with you, JR?" Mel asks. "Do you realize what you're asking us to do? Braddock is the problem. Not SOS. The problem has been eliminated. How can that be a bad thing?"

"Because he's a human being, Mel. He has feelings too. What about Ben?"

Dinkle shakes his head again. "It's not about Ben. He's just a casualty of war. It's unfortunate, but it happens."

"And the kind of politics Braddock advocates," Mel says, "how could you care about him or his goddamn feelings?"

I've never felt more disappointed than I do at this very moment. Mel Sanchez was once my hero. The man I looked up to as the champion of civil rights. Now he's more than willing to trample on Ben's because he disagrees with his politics. Nothing else matters. And I was just like him.

Scotty, however, surprises me. He leans against the counter in his art gallery and shakes his head. "I agree with Mel. I'm sorry. But he's right."

By now I'm sleepwalking, unable even to garner the energy to argue. "SOS lied on Ben," I say halfheartedly.

"I know they did," Scotty says. "But it ain't about Ben, that's what Mel's trying to tell you. This bigger than Ben. Think about it, sweetheart. He stands for everything you hate."

"Not everything."

"Come on, girl, you know what I mean. This SOS did him wrong, they did, but he ain't on the supreme court. That's what matters. His right-wing agenda has been stopped. That's what counts. I feel bad for Ben, don't get me wrong, I like him a lot. But this shit bigger than Ben, honey, way bigger."

"So what am I supposed to do? Bury the story?"

"Shove it in the grave, girl. Yes, ma'am. You print that story and yeah, you may exonerate your boyfriend, but damn, Josie. What about the rest of us? I'm a gay man, in case you haven't noticed lately. Ben could get on that supreme court and he and his fellow conservatives could suddenly want to ban my lifestyle and lock me up in prison or something."

"How can you say that about Ben? You know him. You know he wouldn't do anything like that."

"Knowledge is relative these days, girl. You knew him way better than I did. And look what you did to him."

I look at Scotty and shake my head. "You're wrong for that," I say.

"The truth is the truth, girl. So I don't understand why you trippin'. But if it was up to me, I'd bury that story, wash my hands of it, forget about it, and move the hell on."

I shake my head. He's right. He doesn't understand.

NO MORE DRAMA

Mel's waiting at the entrance door to the newsroom. Helen Mc-Coy's there too, and so are Eddie Harris and Coop and Cathy and Andrea and I don't have a chance to check out every face. Mel has the front page of a newspaper in his hand, but it's not the *Gazette*, but our rival, the conservative *Daily News*.

"Good morning," I say to one and all as I walk in. Everybody just looks at me. So I look at Mel. "What's up?" I ask him.

He immediately hurries to the desk nearest us and slams down the *Daily News*. The headline covers half the fold. THEY LIED ON BEN BRADDOCK! it reads, floating across the front page emblazed in red-ink glory. I look at the headline, at the story that was supposed to be my crowning achievement because I had to fight for the right to see those words in print, but I don't feel anything.

"Why did you do it, JR? How *could* you do it?"

"Somebody had to tell the truth, Mel. All I did was tell the truth. And if the *Gazette* wasn't willing to print it, then I knew the *Daily News* would."

"So you stab me in the back, stab all of us, for the sake of some damn story? You take the cake, you know that, lady? You're more ambitious than I thought."

"My ambition hasn't anything to do with it."

"Like hell it doesn't!"

"I went to the *Daily News* because they were willing to print the truth. You weren't. They were."

"So the *Daily News* is the hero now? Spare me, all right? You and I both know about the *Daily News*. You and I both know that it's nothing more than a right-wing piece of shit pretending to be a newspaper!"

"And the *Gazette* is a left-wing piece of shit pretending to be the same! What's the difference?"

Mel shakes his head. "If you don't know that, then I really feel sorry for you."

"Right is right, Mel, I don't care what y'all say. It was the right thing to do!"

Our eyes meet. All our years of struggle. All our loud talk and big ideas. This is what it comes down to. Him against me. And all he can do is shake his head.

"I never thought I'd say these words," he says. "Never in a million years did I think I'd live to see a day like this." He inhales, and then exhales slowly. "You're fired, JR," he says. "I want you to get your belongings and get out of this building immediately." He stares at me longer, as if to see if I got it, if I fully understand what terrible crime I had committed, and if I'm showing any signs of remorse. Seemingly convinced that I'm not, he grabs the front page he had slung on the desk, tosses it in the trash, and walks away from me. The others look too, as if I were some carnival act, but none speak, and soon they leave my side as well. And I stand there. On my own. I have no tears left. I have no more emotion that I can force out. I'm drained.

I load my personal items in a small box and close my office door. The newsroom is bustling, everybody's got something to do, and no one says a word to me as I walk out. Even Helen ignores me. Even she doesn't feel I'm worthy of so much as a snide remark from her. I've committed the greatest sin of all in their book. I told the truth when it wasn't convenient to tell the truth. It didn't aid their agenda or conform to what they decide is right and wrong. Now I'm no longer welcomed in their world. I'm no longer one of them.

Outside is better. I can breathe again. I inhale and walk swiftly down the steps of the *Gazette* building for the very last time. I want to turn back, to look up again at the *Gazette*'s motto, at my warning:

WHERE THE RIGHTS OF CITIZENS DARE TO BE HEARD. But I don't turn around.

I walk to the side of the building, to the parking lot, but as soon as I see my Mustang I freeze. Fear begins to grip me, the kind you feel when you slip and are in the midst of a fall. Where will I land? *How* will I land? I'm twenty-nine years old and starting over. And it's a trembling thought to me.

But there's no other choice. I have to begin again. And my new life will start with my first step, one step at a time. So I walk, slowly at first, and then swiftly, hurrying to my car as if my course were set. Once at my car I open the back door and slide my box of belongings across the seat. I see my nameplate in that box, and my artificial flower, and my little ceramic bear reading a newspaper—the gift my coworkers presented to me when I received my promotion. I pick up the gift and smile. Even Helen congratulated me that day. And that should have been a good day, my crowning achievement too. But it wasn't.

I drop the gift back into the box, step back, and close my car door. But when I turn, Ben is standing there.

"Ben!" I say as if his name were already on the tip of my tongue.

"Hello, Josephine."

I try to compose myself, but I'm only mildly able to. "What brings you to this end of the world?"

"To see you."

"Really?"

"Yes. I read your article this morning. I didn't know you worked for the *Daily News.*"

I smile. "You know I can't do that."

He smiles too. But then he turns serious. "Why did you do it?"

"Don't you mean why didn't I do it a long time ago? I was trying to right a wrong, Ben, that's all."

He stares at me. "Thank you," he says. "I know what a sacrifice it was for you."

"Do you?"

"Yes. Coming out of your office building with a box of your be-longings is usually a good indicator."

I smile. "Well, it's certainly strange, that's for sure. I love the *Ga-zette,* you know? But I'll land on my feet."

"I know you will."

"What about you? How are you?"

He looks down, because it's been hell for him, but then he manages to look back up. "It was strange for me too, at first, but not anymore. I feel good. Free, you know? I'm ready to see what's out there."

"That's good, Ben."

"I'm thinking about giving the Midwest a chance."

"The Midwest? Why?"

He has to consider my question. "I have no idea," he finally says and I can't help but smile.

"You're a trip, you know that?"

"I know. It ain't easy being me."

He's changed. He's sounding more like the person I used to be. Talk about strange. "Well, at least you've got a plan," I say. "That's the important point."

"It is. And a plan is always needful. I guess I know how to move on."

"And how do you move on, Ben?"

He hesitated. "I can show you better than I can tell you."

Now he's really looking at me, and his stare is no longer that *who is this person?* stare, but less circumspect. More certain. He knows who I am now.

"Maybe you can show me after all," I say. "I have a lot to learn."

"That could only mean one thing then."

"And what's that?"

"You've got to tag along with me."

I hear the words, and they're clear, but I'm afraid to believe it's true. "Let me get this straight. You want me, you're asking me, to go with you?"

"Why not? We'll see America together. And it's not as if you have anything to lose because, honey, I don't know if you realize this, but you ain't got no job either."

A broad smile appears as he seems amused by his uncharacteristic show of humor, and I'm not sure what to do. *What does it all mean? More roller-coaster rides?* And that's when I decide not to think about it. Just laugh. *That's all, Josie. Just enjoy the moment and laugh.* And so I do. With all my heart, I do.